EVERLAND

Rebecca Hunt

EVERLAND

Europa
editions

Europa Editions
214 West 29th Street
New York, N.Y. 10001
www.europaeditions.com
info@europaeditions.com

Library of Congress Cataloging in Publication Data is available
ISBN 978-1-609452889

Hunt, Rebecca
Everland

Book design by Emanuele Ragnisco
www.mekkanografici.com

Cover photo © thp73/iStock

Prepress by Grafica Punto Print – Rome

Printed in the USA

For Simon, for ever

EVERLAND

1
April 1913

Running on the beach. Chaotic noises, busy. A call; a male voice shouting in the wind. The sound of something happening in the surf.

It was a dream perhaps, or perhaps a memory leaching out. Such a sweet dream though. 'Ship-O! . . . *Napps* . . . Are you there? Are you all well?'

A glimmer of consciousness brought him back into the overturned dinghy. He remembered Everland as a colour, an immense blackness, where the cycle of time had dilated to a single endless night. But to permit even a fraction of wakefulness was to suffer. The pain was monstrous. Think of God, if at all.

He heard digging. Snow was being shovelled away from the dinghy's buried sides.

'We have him! We have one of them!'

A burst of activity surrounded him as men crawled into the dinghy. His arms were clenched around his head, covering his face, and they talked in low whispers, afraid to touch him.

Someone said tentatively, 'Is he alive?'

'I don't know, I can't tell. Where's the doctor? Hurry, *get Addison.*'

Boots pelted off across the shingle.

'Napps? . . . Millet-Bass? . . . ' Men were searching the beach and yells echoed from every direction. 'Any sign?' they called to each other.

Addison arrived and knelt close. 'Can you hear me?' he

said, leaning down to talk to Dinners directly. 'We're taking you back to the ship. Can you hear me, Dinners?'

Then he asked for assistance from those nearby. 'Be very careful, on my instruction. Very, very careful, this will hurt him. So easy does it. All hands ready?'

In agony, Dinners moaned and ground his teeth as they lifted him on to a stretcher. He was carried to the shoreline and passed over to men on a boat. Oars drove against the ice-crusted waves.

'It's all right, we're here and we've found you now,' Addison said when Dinners looked up at him and started to cry.

The gratitude was overpowering. Dinners cried for the miracle of being found He cried for not being driven out of his collapsing body and made to die alone in the cold. And he cried for Napps and Millet-Bass; for the heartbreak and the pity of what had come before.

2
April 1913

S waying from a hook on the ceiling, the lantern's orange light slowly passed from one side of the cabin to the other. It illuminated the desk, then the sink, then Dinners's bulk beneath the covers, then Dinners's greenish deadened ear. Sitting beside the bed, Addison was thinking of Napps and Millet-Bass, most keenly of Napps. He tried to believe in a divine love which would choose to shield and save.

They were in the Captain's room, as Lawrence himself had insisted before setting off to Everland again with the rescue party. It was the most luxurious cabin on the ship. The bed was built in at one end, the walls decorated with a selection of pictures. A couple of shelves housed Lawrence's slight personal library and his records of dance-hall music and opera. Pinned above the desk was a photograph of Lawrence shaking hands with a man Addison recognized as Joseph Evelyn. It was midafternoon and a number of the crew were finishing lunch in the Officers' Mess.

Unlike the Mess Deck, that cramped dump of a room for sailors, the Officers' Mess had the air of a gentlemen's club. It was spacious and glossily wood-panelled, with an impressive fireplace. Officers didn't pack together on unpadded benches as the sailors did; they weren't jammed around a table which was little more than some planks nailed to a rough frame. The officers sat at a beautifully designed and polished table. Their comfortable chairs were secured to the floor with a metal peg, and could be swivelled in a full circle, allowing the sitter to turn himself either away or towards any of his companions. Although the sailors slept like animals in a clutter of bunks and hammocks, the walls of the Officers' Mess were lined with monogrammed doors which opened into private quarters. Because Lawrence had an amused, slightly bohemian attitude to class division, some men who weren't officers had been granted access to this civilized paradise. These lucky individuals were perhaps favourites of the Captain, or friends of other officers, or were neither but had a talent for blagging.

The mood was pensive. No one spoke much. The majority of the crew were still ashore searching for Napps and Millet-Bass, and those left on board were grimly aware of the probable outcome. Dr Addison was an exceptional physician and Dinners might be able to relay the events if he could be coaxed into health. But the man sent to take Addison some food had returned with a heavy expression, shaking his head: no change in his condition. No, it didn't look good.

'Shall I say what we're all thinking?' said Coppers. He looked around the room. 'Or should we continue to pretend that we're surprised the decision to send Dinners to Everland hasn't worked out. As if it ever made sense to any of us. Send someone with the resilience of a newborn lamb on that kind of expedition, and you expect, what? That it's going to be a success?'

Coppers never knew when to keep his mouth shut. Everyone listening averted their eyes, embarrassed by his tactlessness. This didn't mean they disagreed with him.

A festering stench had warned them of Dinners's state. They'd placed him on Lawrence's bed and stripped off his outer garments, cutting away the dog-fur gloves and finnesko boots. Someone had gagged and then whispered, *smells of rotting meat*. Addison had cautioned the man's lack of discretion with a sharp glance, and the other men kept quiet when they saw what lay inside Dinners's mitts and boots. All toes and fingers

were black and burnt-looking relics. Suppurating wounds
showed where gangrene was poisoning living tissue.

Dinners's feet and hands were bathed and sterilized, then
bandaged as well as could be done immediately. They removed
a torn green sledging flag tied over a hopelessly infected knee
and swabbed out the foul liquid. Once Dinners had rested,
Addison would assess if he could cope with being fully
unclothed and washed, his wounds inspected more thoroughly. Piled under blankets with his filthy long underwear
still on, Dinners was given brandy mixed with hot water and a
cup of sweet tea. He'd slept briefly. On waking, Addison had
spoon-fed him broth, holding Dinners's head and drying him
with a napkin as he choked and retched with each mouthful.

Hours had passed. Addison was nearly dozing when he
heard a sound. Gripped by an involuntary fearful instinct,
Dinners struggled. He was trying to talk.

'It's all right,' Addison said, stroking his hair to comfort
him. 'I'm here with you.'

Dinners would not be comforted. He pulled away from
Addison's hand, his face twisted in misery.

'Shhh,' Addison said. 'I promise you are safe.'

Dinners's eyes were a fascinating blue, almost a chalk-blue.
They lolled up to show the whites and then swam back. 'I
would have gone with him,' he said, his voice little more than
a rasp of air. 'I wanted to. But I couldn't find him.'

3
November 2012

The Antarctic base Aegeus was currently home to an international community of one hundred and fifty people. It was a stark industrial hamlet of featureless buildings with rough roads bulldozed into the snow. Metal and scrap were piled next to sealed storage drums, lengths of pipe, and stacked wooden pallets bound with plastic cable. Forklifts and heavy-duty vehicles stood against corrugated iron barns and yellow shipping containers. Chains with links wide enough to push a fist through lay coiled on chipboard slats. Above the garage doorway was a pair of antlers nailed in the position of drawn cutlasses. Screwed to a wooden post at the end of the runway was a walrus skull wearing a Yankees baseball cap that had been there for as long as anyone who'd ever been to Aegeus could remember. The buildings were either a dirty white or pale silo green, and lined with rows of triple-glazed windows.

The base's interior aesthetic was comfortably, tastelessly neutral. Long corridors in the facilities block led to rooms of blinking machines and small offices with views of Portakabins or the accommodation blocks. A constant ambient temperature allowed for slouching around in jeans and T-shirts, trainers squeaking on the polished linoleum floors. There were ergonomic beech-effect desks, pastel apricot hospital-coloured walls and computer screensavers showing dolphins or twirling cosmos graphics. Lucky little toys and dog-eared photographs and the occasional day planner with cheesy life-affirming quotes decorated the windowsills. Pashminas and college sweatshirts hung over the backs of padded swivel chairs. A pink photocopied poster on the storeroom door advertised an aerobics class.

With its lights out and curtains taped shut against the brilliant evening sunshine, the common room was now dark apart from the whirring glow of a projector screen. Flirtatious or snappish tussles over sofa space were already happening, as they always did, no matter how many extra chairs were stolen from the canteen. People hissed apologies as they picked their way through the crowd towards the honesty bar in the corner for bottles of beer. A massively anticipated weekly event at Aegeus was about to begin. Tonight was film night.

The MGM lion's head appeared to cheers from the audience. Shadow hands appeared on screen to pat the lion or make other roaring animal heads. Some genius flipped up two shadow fingers. As a tribute to Brix, Jess and Decker, the film chosen obviously had to be the old sixties classic *Everland*, which was based on Captain Lawrence's famous book about the *Kismet* expedition. It was the centenary of that Everland voyage, and a prestigious fieldwork trip had been organized. Tomorrow, Decker, Jess and Brix would begin a comprehensive study of the island, becoming the first party in a hundred years to relocate there for two continuous months. Pretty much everyone at Aegeus, regardless of qualification, had competed to be one of those selected.

'Speech, speech.' Everyone took up the call, shoes drumming on the carpet.

Decker was shoved to his feet by the people on the sofa beside him. The stamping increased in volume. 'Yes, all right, take it easy. Bunch of heathens.'

Decker took a swig of beer. 'You may or may not know this is my last expedition,' he said to howls of dissent. 'Yeah, yeah, you love me.' He let affectionate heckling die out. 'But twenty years in the field is enough for anyone. So, uh. I want to say how much of an honour it's been to work with you all. I can't imagine a more fulfilling, more rewarding, more worthwhile way of—' Decker stopped, perhaps a little emotional. 'Raise your glasses. Here's to Everland, here's to Aegeus, here's to you lot, and here's to the next twenty years. Roll the film.'

Thunderous applause. Decker sat down, high-fived by everyone in reach.

The title sequence was of mountainous vistas, accompanied by the celebrated film score. There wasn't a person watching who didn't know the tune, and the common room erupted into song. Then the volume dropped to a tone of menace. The galloping heroism of the brass section and kettle-drums suddenly gave way to Everland's oboe solo, which perfectly embodied vengeful justice and comeuppance. The audience moved their arms in witchy, belly-dancing ways, laughing at each other.

Jess's laugh was the loudest. She was sitting beside the Dutch biologist Andre. They had a close, cliquey friendship, and were even more cliquish than usual this evening. Andre was an exceptional biologist, Jess was an exceptional field assistant, and they'd both been confident about being chosen for the Everland team. They'd have put money on it. Yet Andre hadn't been selected.

'It's a conspiracy,' Jess muttered to Andre. 'Just unbelievable.'

Andre was looking at Kimiko, a Japanese meteorologist who was sitting with the rest of the meteorology crew. 'Right? Conspiracy,' he said when Jess elbowed him.

Dinners was portrayed by an androgynously beautiful man, strangely clean-shaven, who had an almost feminine physique compared to the muscular and enormous Millet-Bass. The hard-faced actor playing Napps was incredible at emotionally turbulent stares. He glared at the horizon during the opening scene until Millet-Bass, a fabulous caveman, walked into shot chewing his pipe.

'An unknown, uncharted island, and you the first to explore there,' handsome Captain Lawrence said as the scene cut to the three men boarding their notorious dinghy, the *Joseph Evelyn*. Surrounded by smiling crew, Lawrence leant over the *Kismet*'s lee rail in his white Aran jumper and black braces. 'What will you call it, Napps?'

'Captain!' Napps clasped his chest. 'In honour of Joseph Evelyn, friend and generous sponsor of this expedition, in whose boat we now proudly venture forth, I name it *Everland*.'

Cheers came from the *Kismet* men as the dinghy rowed away to jaunty seafaring music.

'*Boo!*' The common-room audience were offended by any affection or respect given to that bastard Napps. They knew what to expect and hated him as the film showed a flashback of the ship's cat getting killed on Christmas Day, a crime Napps lied about to Smith, the young sailor. Napps treated him with contempt and then false brotherliness the moment Coppers came into the room. The death of Smith's pet wasn't an accident, and the audience yelled in disgust when another flashback revealed Napps hefting his club down on a screaming baby seal despite the Captain's explicit instructions to harm no pups. The audience were outraged by Napps's brutality to an officer named McValley, who nearly died of scurvy. I wish he *had* died, Napps sneered.

Now no one in the common room was joking around any more. Tissues were being dug from pockets. It didn't matter that this film had been shown every Boxing Day for years and they'd all seen it a thousand times. The following scenes were impossible to watch without crying.

The camera observed Napps's expression transform into Academy Award-winning iciness as Millet-Bass relayed the news about Dinners's worsening condition.

'There is nothing I wouldn't do to return,' Napps muttered to himself. '*Nothing* I can't live with if it gets me home.'

At approximately five square miles, Everland could be walked all the way around in a few hours. Apart from its history, it wasn't a particularly notable place in terms of scientific research, and before the centenary, it had been considered too small to justify the large-scale expenditure of a fieldwork trip. Aerial images showed a pear-shaped island with a cove resembling a bite mark cut into the northern end. Everland's interior was mostly impassable slatelike terrain that sloped up into the seven-hundred-foot-high peak of Antarctica's smallest volcano, which was live, but had no record of ever erupting. The island had two colonies, an Adélie penguin colony in a bay at the southern end, and a fur seal colony at the northern cove where the *Joseph Evelyn* was preserved in situ by the Antarctic Heritage Trust as a site of cultural importance. The Trust was responsible for conserving the legacy of Antarctic exploration for the international community. It cared for huts built by Captain Scott and Shackleton, as well as the *Kismet*'s hut at Cape Athena, which was a larger, more accessible territory seventy miles north of Everland. Most Aegeus expeditions were based at the Cape, and some fieldwork groups had sailed across, staying on Everland for a day or two. They had brought back photographs of themselves doing thumbs-up poses next to the *Joseph Evelyn*, or crouched beside Adélies, and told anecdotes about Everland being a creepy place. Undercutting these tales was an unbearable smugness that they'd got to visit.

'Hard pounding this, gentlemen,' cried Dinners. 'Let's see who will pound longest.'

Everyone knew Napps's next line. A number of thespians in the audience hammed along, raising their hands to a pitiless universe.

'How time tricks us . . . '

'*Tricks us!*' they echoed.

' . . . into seeing who we really are,' Napps said in his single moment of self-reflection. 'And what choices we make.'

Muffled sobs filled the common room. People tried to cry discreetly while, on screen, two figures trudged away into the dark.

Left abandoned under the *Joseph Evelyn*, there was a long, lingering shot of Dinners's wide eyes, and then the legendary narration began. Richard Burton's masterful voice suddenly boomed from the sky to preach about the frailties of men, sieving the just from the unjust in a blistering monologue.

Braum cursed in Danish, banging his chair. '*Come on, Addison. Hurry . . .* '

The camera retreated from the dinghy as Dinners, his arms bent to shield his poor head against the cold, lay alone in the blackness.

And finally there was the sound of voices shouting: 'Ship-O! . . . *Napps* . . . Are you there? Are you all well?'

The audience went crazy, whooping as sailors ran for the sledge and Addison said, 'Dinners, it's all right, we're here and we've found you now.'

Brix sensed Decker was looking at her from across the room, and shot him a jittery smile.

He grinned at her and mouthed, 'You're going to be *fine*.'

4
March 1913

W hat will you call it, Napps?' Lawrence had asked through gritted teeth, as men crowded around him. He wouldn't have chosen to give Napps the honour of christening a dustbin, let alone an island, but tradition dictated that the first man to set foot on virgin land also got to name it. He could hardly change the tradition now.

' . . . *Everland*,' Napps had replied to cheers from the crew.

Napps had insisted that he and his two men leave once the island was within sight. Manoeuvring the *Kismet* through the potentially reef-laden waters was slow and unnecessary, he'd said, when the dinghy could easily row across. Whilst this was all true, Napps's chief motive for departing was that he needed to get away from the Captain before he killed him. Despite days of arguing, both he and Addison had failed to talk Lawrence out of his senseless decision to include Dinners in the Everland team, and Napps was about ready to choke the stupid Captain to death.

Napps had a way of looking directly at Lawrence, but also through him. He retrieved an envelope from his jacket pocket. 'Could you put this with the post, sir?' he said, using the condescendingly polite tone which could be relied on to enrage Lawrence. 'I forgot to do it myself.'

'Is it a written apology to me, your Captain?' Lawrence asked. 'It should be.'

'It's a letter to my wife.'

To Lawrence, the relationship between the First Mate and

the Captain had a clear structure. The Mate was a command-ing presence, yet the Captain was indisputably superior. But Napps had a natural authority which Lawrence neither pos-sessed nor could imitate. And to see how the men instinctively deferred to the Mate kept Lawrence awake at night, pacing his room with envy-induced heartburn.

When he first hired Napps, Lawrence had congratulated himself on being the cleverest man alive. By employing this impressive Mate, he, Lawrence, was free to be an adored Captain who never need sully his days with the management of apishly behaved sailors. He'd leave all that unpleasantness to Napps. Except what he'd actually done was employ someone who was not only exceptional at his own job, but far better at being a Captain than the Captain.

'Shall we clarify a few things?' Lawrence said, snatching the envelope from Napps's hand. 'We're here to advance science for the British flag by exploring uncharted territory across the Antarctic continent and claiming new discoveries of interest. So you'll go to this island with the team that I, *your Captain,* have appointed, while we sail round Cape Athena for a last geologizing excursion. It's not some epic quest, Napps, I'll be back to collect you in a couple of weeks.'

Lawrence's manner had changed as more excitable men packed around them, watching Millet-Bass and then Dinners climb down the rope ladder on to the dinghy.

'Look, you're sure you don't want the *Kismet* to take you closer to shore?'

'Positive, sir,' Napps had replied. And what a mistake that had been.

The *Joseph Evelyn*'s journey to Everland was supposed to have taken about four hours, but Napps, Millet-Bass and Dinners had now been in the dinghy for six hellish days. Napps could hear Millet-Bass slopping around with a bucket behind him, trying to bail. The ten-foot dinghy was wallowing so low each swell caused water to gush across the brim. In the semi-lucid trance of the very ill, Napps pulled at the oars and considered that beyond the terror and almost out-of-body levels of exhaustion, his principal torment was actually thirst.

'Keep on at it,' he croaked to Millet-Bass.

The storm had broken with no warning less than an hour after they had boarded the dinghy. Waves rose into unfathomable masses and the sky blackened. For the next two days, the men buried themselves among the cargo while the boat fell sidelong into deep trenches and veered close to rolling. Ropes snapped and loose supplies volleyed down the length of the boat or disappeared overboard, along with their rifle. The mast shattered off and lanced through the heaving incline of a mountainous wave. Hiding under an oilcloth, the three men clung to each other as Napps shouted encouragements and the dinghy threatened to shred beneath them. He said, 'We'll survive it,' which they obviously wouldn't. They were going to drown or freeze. 'We'll be all right,' he said, guessing they'd probably be dead before dawn.

On the third day he'd weakly lifted his head to discover they were on a flat ocean which stretched away emptily in every direction. The sky was a crystal blue and the wind was so tame it barely wrinkled the surface of the water. Napps snarled his face into an expression of utter repugnance. Preparing the soul for annihilation was difficult work, and all he'd been rewarded with was a miracle. He watched an albatross glide a low nomadic route towards the horizon and wondered if he had the courage to kill himself. He only needed to leap into the sea. Bludgeoning his head against the torn mast stump was another alternative. If he dug out one of the clasp-knives without Millet-Bass stopping him, he could perhaps slash his own throat.

'Shame we lost the gun,' Millet-Bass said hoarsely, looking at the albatross. Apparently they weren't bad to eat, even raw. Also, don't imagine blood isn't a drink.

To have the gun, wished Napps.

He assessed their situation. Fact number one was that Napps didn't believe they had any chance of ever finding either the *Kismet* or the island. They were just too lost. Fact number two was that the mercilessly lucky fluke which had spared him had consequently trapped him into dying a terrible, lingering death. It was something he needed to make peace with, as did Millet-Bass. The scrawny Dinners didn't have this problem. Unlike the two robust men, he'd been ruined by the storm.

When they pulled him from the oilcloth, he lay rattling on the floor like a man succumbing to venom, his legs and arms twisted into distortions.

Batter holes in the dinghy with an oar to sink us, Napps thought when Millet-Bass asked him what their plan was. Or throttle me with your bare hands. But he'd had his chance to kill himself and wasted it. So he could either sit here waiting to die, or he could die whilst striking out towards an island they could never expect to reach. At least the second option gave him something to do. 'Fetch the compass,' he said to Millet-Bass.

They started navigating the *Joseph Evelyn* towards Everland, using Napps's calculations and logistical guesswork. Too ill to row, Dinners was placed on a bed of sacking, where his condition slowly worsened as frostbite set in and his face became a swollen mass of sores. Napps looked at him and privately cursed Lawrence with every vile word.

The quantity of their supplies which had been smashed or washed away by the storm included their drinking water. The only remaining cask was three-quarters empty and tasted strongly of seawater. They took minuscule sips and managed to make it last for another day before it ran out and they began to lose their minds with thirst. Their lips split and they couldn't swallow the wet, briny sledging biscuits. The salt that scorched their skin and crusted on to their clothes seemed to produce an evil capillary action which sucked the moisture from their internal organs. Their tongues swelled into throbbing log-like clubs, but Napps ordered them not to eat the snow, reiterating that the worthlessly tiny amount of water yielded from ingesting ice did nothing apart from poison the body with cold. And although they were all aware of this, each of them secretly took little mouthfuls to relieve their diabolical thirst and then sat in agony.

Dinners continued to deteriorate until on night five, convinced he was dying, he cried for his mother. The other two tried to reassure him and told him he would feel better tomorrow. Chin up, they said, you'll be fine. When Dinners apologized for crying, Millet-Bass's expression was so desolate it was clear he didn't believe what he was saying any more than Napps did.

The impossible notion of reaching Everland alive had presented itself on the morning of day six in the form of a greasy rug of kelp floating on the sea. Despite knowing kelp always grew within proximity to land, neither Millet-Bass nor Napps could tolerate the pain of being hopeful, even as the frequency of the patches increased. Several hours later their oars were clogging in huge mats of kelp, and hope had become like a filthy secret which both men were too ashamed to speak of. Once Millet-Bass spotted a cormorant, a bird species that never went too far from shore, the suspense became a kind of sickness. To believe in salvation was just as gruelling as accepting defeat.

If Napps had imagined the moment he saw land, he'd have pictured himself howling with joy. Instead the shock left him sounding confused. ' . . . We're saved,' he said absently as Millet-Bass hammered his fist against the dinghy in such ferocious delight it seemed he'd punch through the wood.

Everland appeared as a black-and-white-striped molehill in the distance, its profile dominated by the squat peak of its volcano. Snow banks had lined the island's dark terrain with thick vertical bands which ran down from the higher slopes to the beaches. A glacier lay across the volcano's shoulder like a crumpled stole, and filled the waters ringing the shore with splintered ice. What struck Napps, at that moment, was how much the low belt of cloud encircling the island resembled a halo.

'*Keep on at it,*' he said to Millet-Bass as they rowed a path around the loose ice, being doused with spray as the waves crashed against them. A tidal current funnelled the dinghy towards a cove, and Napps leapt into the waist-deep water to guide the *Joseph Evelyn* past the reefs.

In his haste to assist Napps, Millet-Bass practically threw Dinners overboard, where he sat gasping in the water until Millet-Bass splashed across the side and grabbed him. Running through the waves with Dinners in his arms, he headed to the beach. Napps saw him talking to Dinners, crouched in front of him and holding his face. Dinners was nodding, yes I will, and Millet-Bass turned and charged back out to Napps.

Astonished by their weakness, Napps and Millet-Bass pulled the dinghy beyond the tide's reach and overturned it to stop it filling with snow. Millet-Bass propped up one side of the boat with a large rock to keep the inside aired and prevent rot or mildew from setting in. Then they relayed to unload the provisions, wheezing as they hauled crates of canned food and sacks of flour. Boxes of biscuits were dumped in the cove with tins of sugar and tea. Millet-Bass lugged sodden piles of equipment and the bulky tent while Napps struggled to cope with even a few pots. The drawstring ration bag of rocks Dinners kept with him as a charm was found, along with the small sledge flag his wife had made. The leather wallets containing the men's diaries and a few weathered photographs were thrown on top of everything else.

Millet-Bass's chest was heaving. 'There, fur seals,' he said, pointing towards a group of seals thirty yards further along the shore. 'Thought they were extinct.'

Leaning on his knees, Napps glanced at the seals. 'Yes, for several years now.' Then he looked again. 'Ha,' he said, staring at them closely. 'Fur seals. You're right.'

With dusk already greying into evening, they packed a sledge with essentials and went to collect Dinners, who begged for his bag of rocks.

'That was a precious waste of time,' Napps said when Millet-Bass came tramping back with Dinners's bag. 'We have better things to do. How's he going to appreciate his rocks? He's barely conscious, someone's going to have to carry him.'

'Would you rather tow the sledge?' Millet-Bass asked dryly. Napps didn't dignify this with an answer. He lifted the delirious and boyishly light Dinners while invincible Millet-Bass toiled off with the heavy sledge.

Napps decided to locate the campsite in a central position on the long beach. It was fifteen minutes' walk from where they'd unloaded the supplies and offered a wide panorama of the ocean which would allow them to see the approaching ship. After they'd put up the tent and transferred Dinners into his reindeer-hide sleeping bag, Napps explained that one of them had to do a reconnaissance of the area and search for water. He was holding an empty gallon can.

'I'll do it,' Millet-Bass said, reaching for the can.

'You stay here,' Napps answered, striding away.

'Isn't it safer if I join you?' Millet-Bass shouted after him.

'Cook something,' Napps said without looking back. His mood had taken an odd turn. A strangeness was building inside him and he didn't think he could resist it.

The craziness ruptured out once Napps discovered a spillway, one of the many glacial streams which flowed down to the sea. Emitting a weird strangled whine, he knelt to fill the can with water and found he couldn't quite hold the can properly, or stop it dropping from his grip. And he couldn't prevent himself exploding into laughter so violent it didn't have a sound. Safely out of sight and earshot, he held his sides and screeched with it. He put his head on the ground and laughed into the sand. The can of water was kicked empty as he stomped in circles, bellowing *thank you, thank you, thank you* to a nameless, nonexistent providence. Sobbing with laughter, he gradually composed himself, then refilled the can and returned to camp.

That night they feasted. Their gorging was so extreme it was almost torture. Millet-Bass stirred pemmican, the concentrate of protein and fat, with crumbled biscuit and water to create a thick hoosh. Another meal of pemmican was followed by more tea, more cocoa, corned beef and a tin of peaches. Napps took his turn to feed Dinners, whose deadened hands were useless, and Dinners was barely able to swallow what the spoon ferried to him because Napps was impatient.

Dinners didn't say much, but smiled and tried to be cheerful as they rubbed him with blankets and dressed his horrifying feet with boric Vaseline. They shook him awake and gave him brandy, then kneaded his fingers straight and bandaged his hands. Once finished, Millet-Bass and Napps tamped their pipes with tobacco and smoked.

This simple enjoyment, teamed with their ballooned stomachs, transported them into a new plane of cosmic pleasure. They revelled in the glory of dry land and the numb satisfaction of gluttony. Millet-Bass's hat was off and his dark hair was ratted into several horns, his mismatched red beard like the stuffing from a chair that had spent twenty years mouldering in the rain. Using Millet-Bass as a mirror, Napps knew he'd have an equally furry, haggard appearance. No one who loved them would recognize them now. They were unidentifiable beast-men.

5

November 2012

Decker finished confirming weather conditions to Aegeus and crawled out of the tent they'd call home for the next two months. This 'living tent' looked like an orange tepee, with a diameter and height of roughly two metres. In terms of internal floor space, it translated into an area about the size of a children's inflatable paddling pool.

Decker said, 'Toshi again.'

This time Toshi wanted his guitar. All radio conversations to check in with the base ended with a similar request. It was a classic fieldwork joke. Whoever answered the call at Aegeus noted the weather and then immediately started haggling for coveted belongings if they died on the trip.

'Good, give him the guitar,' said Jess. After enduring six months of Decker's tiny playlist, everyone now shivered with hatred when 'Hey Jude' twanged out.

'Shut up, no,' Decker answered. Field assistants, they were always the same in his experience. Fun but mouthy. Jess laughed.

A field assistant wasn't a scientist, and had no scientific qualifications. Their role was to support the team by cooking, maintaining equipment, keeping the camp running smoothly, and generally helping out with whatever needed doing. They tended to be adventurous, practical types, often trained in out-door pursuits, and the blonde tomboyish Jess was a textbook example. She'd worked for three years in the Mountain Rescue, spent two summer seasons as an Alpine guide, and had been on five expeditions with Aegeus. It was good going for someone who was only twenty-nine, although Jess possessed a toughness and self-sufficiency which made her seem older.

The red and white Twin Otter plane was now visible above them as it relayed back to Everland. Even with these perfect conditions, getting the camp established was an epic operation which had already taken more than fifteen hours.

Sitting in what felt like a winged jeep, their first sight of the island had come when Oar pointed out a dirty mist of volcanic steam on the horizon.

Jack the co-pilot's voice blared over the tannoy. 'Say hola to your new home, amigos.'

'Ever-ever Land,' Jess shouted above the engine noise. The nervous excitement had given them all a sort of headache. 'Second to the right, and straight on 'til morning.'

'Let's hope Peter Pan had some pretty hardcore bushcraft skills,' Decker replied as the plane flew over ragged escarpments and cliffs, ice slopes fanning out across the beaches. 'He'd need more than a load of magic buttons.'

Jess put her forehead against the window to look at the glacier passing beneath them. 'Everland does have a history of Lost Boys, though, if you think about it.'

Guess so, they agreed, their ears popping as the plane descended.

Brix's initial reaction to Everland had been disappointment. She'd climbed out of the plane and thought, really? It had none of the remote splendour she'd expected. Instead the Antarctic presented her with a rubble moonscape that had all the charm of a builders' yard. The coarse shingle and claylike sediment of the beach were puddled with water, and the snow lay in semi-thawed porous films of grey ice which disintegrated underfoot. Everything was shades of ash and tar and mud and rust, except the sky, which was the colour of dirty wool. The volcano that comprised seventy per cent of the island was a drab, slagheap-like mound when seen up close. Everland was silent and lifeless, and brutally unimpressive. More than bleak, it was ugly.

Fieldwork missions had a well-established procedure. The first flight brought in the expedition party, plus essential survival gear in case weather blocked the plane's return and they were stranded. In good weather it took two and a half hours to travel to base, and the same back to Everland with more supplies. Once they'd unloaded, the Twin Otter immediately wheeled round to depart, Jack making a sign of the horns hand gesture in the mini-cockpit as the plane took off.

'The peg goes here?' Brix asked at a discreet volume as she and Decker hammered in metal stakes to secure their 'office' tent. This was a generous name for what amounted to a second living tent, furnished with a bare crate for a seat.

'Nearly, not quite.' Decker showed her the correct place and smiled as she bashed it into the ground. 'Good job, chief. You're strong for a skinny chick.'

Brix looked at him sideways, amused. She was a mid-thirties academic with a practical bobbed haircut and a unisex dress code of jeans and jumpers. It was fair to say she'd never thought of herself as a 'chick' before. Being addressed as 'chief' was also a new experience. Brix hadn't just warmed to Decker, but was so grateful for his cheery encouragement that she almost loved him. He understood how out of her depth she felt without her having to say it, offered help without needing to be asked, and did it with such an infectious sunniness that it reassured even the most self-doubting person.

'See, I knew it. I knew you'd be a natural,' Decker said with an approving nod, as if Brix's successful tent-pegging was the work of a prodigy. Then he got to his feet and cranked his aching back. 'Where's Jess?'

Jess was waddling along with the large red first-aid crate. 'What's up?'

'Would you make an old man happy and deal with these pegs for a minute?' After the office tent, they still had the bathroom to construct, which was a small, Boy Scout-style tent with a chemical tank for a toilet hauled inside.

Jess's tone conveyed a certain interest in why Brix couldn't just peg the tent. 'Yes, boss.'

'Boss? Guys, no. I'm not your boss,' Decker said, although he was actually the boss, with overall responsibility for the expedition. 'Don't expect any rank pulling to come from my direction,' he said, leaning right to stretch his back, and then making a face as he leant left. 'I, your beloved leader, pledge that to you, my obedient servants.'

With his chunky build and wafting long hair, Decker had the appearance of a musician from a seventies progressive rock band. He was regarded as something of a hero at Aegeus, a kind of polar Socrates who could be relied upon to have the answer for everything, whether it was advice on crashed hard drives, or Antarctic mite species, or Thai curry recipes.

Jess ditched the first-aid crate at the tent's entrance, where regulation advised it should be stored for easy access. Just remembering the purposes of the various implements inside the crate gave Brix a sickish twinge of anxiety. The medical training had been intensive and graphically advanced as they were taught to deal with various horrors, such as smashed and protruding bones or drama with arteries. Things might break or blacken or burst, they were told, with a slideshow of nightmarish images. Things might freeze and thaw, or, like you can see here, freeze and *rot*, the instructor had said as Brix thrashed weakly in her chair.

The Twin Otter's next trip brought the rest of the food. Each large crate would sustain three people for one week with bland but hearty meals. There were packs of quick-cook spaghetti and tins of tuna with mayonnaise, cereal bars and chocolate. Tubs contained individual sachets of instant coffee, or instant enriched potato powder, or full-fat milk powder. Cans of processed cheese were designed to be forced down with the tough, high-calorie sledging biscuits that hadn't changed much since the *Kismet*'s era. For dinner there were packets of grit which could be rehydrated into beef stroganoff, chicken korma, or lamb and pilaf rice. Jess had brought a hoard of condiments and stolen a small plastic box of sausages and bacon from the industrial fridges at Aegeus. This would be the only fresh produce they'd eat, so she'd buried it in the snow to freeze until an occasion was deemed spectacular enough to deserve it.

Brix was admiring the mountain of crates in a purposefully conspicuous way, hoping the nearby Jess might notice and then comment. Because she found Jess-types intimidating and normally avoided them, it was therefore crucial to Brix that she became friends with Jess quickly, as a method of self-defence. The major obstacle to her plan was the absolute lack of chemistry between them. But this, she'd decided, was a defeatist attitude. Of course they had things in common. They were both women, for example. They were both human. That was two things right there. Deploying her most winning smile, Brix lifted an arm towards the food pile and said, 'I cannot believe we'll get through this in two months.'

Well, here it was, thought Jess. More proof that Brix's selection for the Everland team was an inexplicable mistake. Nothing about the past fifteen hours had done anything to dispel the impression she'd formed about Brix whilst at Aegeus, which was of a person with all the charisma of a chicken bone. And now Brix was, what. Declaring herself amazed at the food crates. No one who knew anything about fieldwork would be amazed at the food crates. It was like a builder being amazed at a brick. Her answer came after a longish pause. 'Not been on so many fieldwork trips, hm?'

The camp was taking shape. In order to prevent a vortex of

wind dumping down great drifts of snow which would need to be dug out later, the living tent, the toilet tent, the office tent and the sledges were laid out in an expansive, well-spaced line to allow the wind to pass through cleanly. They'd just finished setting up as the plane returned for the final time with the quad bikes and more delicate scientific gear.

Big Norwegian Oar, hilariously secretive Oar, climbed out and said, 'This had better be everything. I've been in that seat so long my whole body's locked.'

'I feel your pain, man, my back is wrecked,' Decker replied in middle-aged sympathy.

Brix was hefting their bags of clothes into the tent. It wasn't many clothes, considering. Aside from the thick quilted freezer suits, they'd also got a couple of fleece jackets each, around six thermal tops and bottoms, and a scant ten changes of thermal socks. Aware it would be their last proper wash for months, they'd all spent an extravagantly lengthy time in the shower that morning.

'Watch, can't move my head,' Oar said to Decker, and then turned his head effortlessly and began to windmill his arms.

'You're such a big baby, Oar,' Brix said as she walked over to them.

'*Stor babyen*,' Oar corrected, never missing a chance to remind Brix that her mother was also Norwegian. 'Embrace the mother tongue!'

'Don't listen to him,' Jack told Brix. 'He's too selfish. I ask to have a go at steering, he says no. I ask to try on his glasses, the answer's no. Everything's a constant no. But he did tell me about his girlfriend.'

Brix and Jess stared at him with open-mouthed anticipation and Jack grinned.

'Nah, not really,' he said. 'I've been wedged next to him in that little plane for, like, a hundred hours and he won't even tell me his middle name.'

'It's driving him crazy.' Oar had a soundless laugh. His shoulders bobbed.

Having appeared infinite right up until the moment it finished, their transfer was suddenly complete. Oar celebrated by offering everyone a stick of chewing gum. It was a poignant moment for the Everland party. Chewing Oar's slightly old-looking gum was the last rite before the dawn of a great solitary era.

As well as surveying the island, the fieldwork team were here to identify key oceanic areas surrounding the island and designate them for protection. Known as 'foraging hotspots', these fertile hunting zones were essential for all Antarctic life, starting with krill and the microscopic things they fed on, and then intersecting up through every size and weight of beast to end with the tonnage of whales. The resulting data maps would inform scientific papers for the Commission for Conservation of Antarctic Marine Living Resources, an international body which oversaw the conduct of fisheries in polar waters. Since seals' and penguins' offspring bound them to the island during the breeding months, they were ideal for research into 'foraging hotspots'.

'Yeah, and we've all seen the film *Alive*,' Jack said unoriginally. 'So, you know. Severe consequences if you're the least popular.'

'Give me one good reason to ever come back and collect you,' Oar said.

The unspoken code of goodbyes was that they were goofy in order to disguise the enormity of the situation. But when the jokes came from Oar his naturally blank voice made them sound like harsh bargaining exercises.

'Okay then,' said Oar, when no one responded to his chilling attempt at comedy. He shook hands with each of the fieldwork party in turn. 'I'm sure you'll have a happier experience than Napps and his team.'

'Not much of a vote of confidence there, friend,' said Decker.

'No, don't go yet. Stay for dinner,' Jess said, to stop the dreaded send-off. 'Bag of nuts and raisins? There's enough for everyone if you hate nuts and raisins.'

'Ah, I wish, but we've got plans,' said the deadpan Oar.

'*It's time to put on make-up!*' Jack sang, doing the Muppet dance at the nose of the plane. '*It's time to light the lights!*'

'Keep in touch,' were Oar's last words from the cockpit.

'Isn't going to be a problem,' Decker said, as the phone still rang, even in earth's last wilderness. Calls to Aegeus on the VHF radio were scheduled daily, and the base would initiate a rescue mission if twenty-four hours elapsed with no contact. They also had a laptop and satellite phone, which they'd charge with solar-powered generators. It was all very reassuring, to a point.

Jack made a peace sign at the window as the plane gathered speed and lifted. And then they were a population of three.

6
March 1913

What was this thing behind his shoulder? Napps reached into his long-sleeved woollen vest. He'd forgotten about the pair of socks he'd been drying there. Pushing them into a less obstructive position down his sleeve gave his left arm an impressive strongman bicep as he assembled the primus stove for breakfast.

It was their first morning on Everland. The ruinous after-effects of the dinghy voyage meant Napps couldn't work fast or accurately, so he dropped things. Because his aching stiffness prevented him moving in any decisive way, it took him for ever to pick things up. Not that he minded. Every grinding joint and squealing muscle was just another happy souvenir from the stony beach of dry land. He would have enjoyed lying across broken bricks, loved it, he didn't care as long as it was solid. Even the hideous smell didn't trouble him. Their odour had reactivated in the tent's warmth, and the reek of unwashed bodies pickling through filthy clothing was intense. But they were alive, so Napps relished it.

Their green, pyramid-shaped tent accommodated three grown men so long as none of them wanted to move around much. The tent was the length of a man lying on his back, the height of an upright man in its peaked centre, and every inch of space unused by sleeping bags was crammed with equipment. A small gap opened on the groundsheet once Napps sat up and crossed his legs tightly. He poured the very minimum of oil into the primus and started to worry. The need to make their fuel supply last, or increase it with seal blubber, was at the top of his list. Absolutely number one on the list, he decided, although he wondered if it could really be called a list when everything was equally urgent. Napps had a neat strategy for these situations. He exchanged what should be done first with what could be done now. And that was to loudly jangle a spoon inside an aluminium mug right next to Millet-Bass's ear.

His big hairy head lifted into sight. 'Rude.'

They got the water heating and the promise of sugared tea was enough to generate movement from the opposite side of the tent. Most of Dinners's face emerged from his sleeping bag, the sores on his nose and cheeks already blackened. 'Did you ever see a lamb being born?' he said inexplicably.

Napps didn't bother to reply. One of the many rank ironies of preparing food was that the chef's hands were far cleaner at the end of cooking than they were at the start, as some of the dirt was rubbed off on to the meal. There was nothing to be done about it and they were long past caring, which was fortunate because Napps's hands looked like he'd spent years in a dungeon. But it was his habit to wipe the blade of his clasp-knife on his woollen leggings before he started chopping biscuits to thicken the hoosh. It was a nod to the memory of hygiene, an acknowledgement that it did exist.

Once the tea boiled, Millet-Bass filled their sledging mugs and put the pan of hoosh on the stove. ' . . . Lambs?' he said to Dinners.

'The farmer has to rub them to bring them round when they're born,' Dinners said, his shiny grey fingers so swollen that he struggled to grip the mug as it was passed to him. 'And that's what I knew this tea would do for me. I can feel myself coming back to life.'

How lucky, because Napps was the closest thing they had to a doctor.

'And I'm the closest thing you've got to a nurse,' Millet-

Bass said chillingly, as Napps served their metal pannikin trays of hoosh.

Dinners gave him a weak smile and tried to eat. Did he have any sensation in his fingers? Some, perhaps. He couldn't really tell. If Napps noticed that Dinners's spoon moved at awkward and feeble angles, or that Dinners had almost lowered his head into the pannikin to bite at the falling food, he made no attempt to help. Ignoring Napps's conspiratorial look, it was Millet-Bass who stopped his own meal and fed grateful Dinners.

Breakfast was the least exhausting part of the day. It was the time least likely to kill you. You were rested and warm inside a sleeping bag, all surviving parts of your body still presently alive, and you were, in the meagre amounts meted out by a place like Antarctica, comfortable. As a result, the end of the meal was approached with reluctance. But the weary business of dressing needed to be tackled. The size of their tent meant they had to take turns to get dressed, and Napps took the first shift, out of his bag and already petrifying to stone. He kicked his way down the fleece-lined trousers and punched his feet into the socks. The lower layers of clothing were never removed and no one had properly washed or been fully naked in many months. Since all water had to be melted from ice using the ship's precious coal supply, bathing was a long-forgotten luxury. Occasional glimpses of skin during changes were a teasing reminder of the body hidden beneath and prompted the thought, what would it look like? And then the next thought: do you really want to know?

No, Dinners did not want to know. Frightened enough by the sight of his hands, he shut his eyes and refused to look at his feet when they removed the bandages to treat him.

'We can't all hide from your ravaged feet, Dinners,' Millet-Bass said as Napps grunted over his finneskos. This final tribulation of ramming on the stiffly frozen animal-skin boots was the worst. 'Think how I feel, I've actually got to touch them.'

The day was bright, with a rinsed, blue clarity. A nearby group of skua gulls paid no attention to Napps when he hauled himself from the tent. He limped a quick perimeter and then went to examine the low, uneven cliff-bank which edged the beach behind their camp. An overhanging section in the rock face had accumulated such a dense build-up of snow the drift had compacted solid. Since they'd need to hunt, they could hollow a larder for storing meat out of it. Pleased with his discovery, Napps hobbled to the shoreline and stared out at the sea.

The slushy film of ice on the ocean's surface would steadily thicken into a sheet several feet deep as winter pressed in. Over the next few weeks, the ocean would be transformed into a vast ice plain which enclosed the coast for months, stretching from Everland to Cape Athena. And near the Cape, somewhere to the north, the *Kismet* would be on its way to rescue them.

Inside the tent, Millet-Bass was swivelling into his boots.

'Hurry up,' Napps demanded.

'*How?*' Millet-Bass shot back.

'I've seen where we can make an ice locker,' Napps said.

'Should I get dressed?' Dinners asked. It was an idiotic suggestion.

'No, stay in your bag,' Napps said.

When Dinners protested he was given the sewing kit and told to mend a pair of Millet-Bass's horrendous trousers. His bleated questions about how he might conceivably operate the needle went unanswered, and another inspection minutes later revealed Dinners had angrily flung the trousers into a corner and was asleep.

When Millet-Bass had finally got his finneskos on, he gave them a salute and tramped off with the axe. It wasn't decent to talk of worries or let pessimism infiltrate the mood of the group. But once he was standing alone at the snowdrift, he allowed himself to vent some of those fears against the ice. He voiced them manually with his strength and professional aggression towards the job, his arms hurting in a satisfying way.

'To strive, to seek, to find—' he said as he swung the axe, smashing out a shower of ice chips and splinters, '—and not to yield.'

Decker was on his side of the tent, very purposefully turned away from Brix and Jess. It was how every day would start. Decker stared at the inner lining while they washed, and then they turned for him. This was the extent of privacy afforded in the tent. One redeeming feature was that they only had a cup of melted snow-water and a flannel each, so the process of bathing didn't involve much undressing and was over in a couple of minutes. But even marginal nudity in such close quarters was enough to bring out a certain prudishness in Brix.

Unlike Brix, Jess had zero self-consciousness. She'd stripped to her bra and leggings without hesitation, exposing a tattoo of co-ordinates on her left shoulder.

'Washing's a complete waste of time anyway,' Decker said, questioning what a damp flannel could realistically achieve when pitched against the same ripening clothes they'd be wearing every day.

'Yeah, but you think hairbrushes are a waste of time,' Jess said, as if she and Decker had lived together for years. 'Which is why you comb your hair with a pencil.'

He drank his coffee. 'A maverick like me finds a pencil does the job just fine.'

'I've also seen you clean your teeth with a match,' Jess said, shuffling round to let him start.

His sleeping bag was separated from theirs by two low wooden boxes. The pots box at the head of the tent was filled with a jumble of enamel plates and mugs. The VHF radio was stationed on top. It was the size of a shoebox and resembled a military field phone, with switches and a large dial on the front, and a telephone receiver plugged in via a curly black cable. The personal effects box at the foot of the tent contained some books and DVDs and a few comforts, such as Jess's collection of Tabasco sauce bottles. The primus stove occupied the space between the two boxes, secured in place by two thin metal safety rails which screwed to the box sides. Even with the rails, the stove wouldn't be hard to knock over, so they moved carefully. Dodging a flying wall of boiling water wouldn't be fun. Neither would be trying to extinguish a burning sleeping bag while still inside it.

'Oh, and P.S., Brix?' Decker said as he zipped up his fleece. 'I mostly clean my teeth with a toothbrush, like ninety-nine times out of a hundred.' He shot Brix an encouraging wink and she smiled at her knees. Jess noticed this exchange as she served out bowls of porridge.

Jess wasn't as easy to befriend as Brix had hoped. Instead of being daunted, however, she'd resolved to treat the challenge as a fun project. 'Your tattoo,' she said. 'It's the coordinates of the North and South poles.'

'Right. Got it when I was eighteen,' Jess said with minimal interest. 'It was a mission statement to myself that I would get to either the Arctic or the Antarctic, which is what I've wanted to do since I was five years old.'

'So why get it written on your skin?' Decker asked. 'Couldn't you have just remembered what you wanted to do in your head?'

'I was eighteen, *dad*,' Jess answered. 'I wanted a *tattoo*.'

Once they'd finished breakfast, Brix tuned the radio to find Aegeus over the airwaves. Decker mimed for her to hang up when Tom's voice blasted into the tent. Tom had a particularly high-speed enthusiasm for life which was hard not to hate when bombarded with it first thing in the morning.

'Hombres! Everland!' Tom shouted down the phone. 'If you even knew how much I love fur seals!'

'Everyone loves fur seals,' Jess said to Decker.

He was typing on the laptop, a pen in his mouth. 'You know they were practically wiped out, don't you?'

'I'm a field assistant,' Jess said. 'So nope. I don't know.'

'They were decimated.' He shut the computer, removing the pen to make a note on one of the Everland maps. 'Hunted for their pelts so voraciously that they were presumed extinct by the start of the nineteenth century. It's called a population bottleneck. There must have been a small pocket of fur seals hidden away somewhere which were able to regenerate into the healthy numbers we have today.' He shrugged at Jess. 'Sort of a happy story.'

'More of a happy ending,' Jess said, putting sachets of chilli con carne into a pan of water to rehydrate for that evening. 'Not so much the story. The story's pretty horrific.'

'Well, considering how many species have been bottle-necked into terminal decline it doesn't get much happier. It's an ending sound-tracked by the Jackson Five,' Decker said, watching Brix try unsuccessfully to get off the phone.

Her looping repetitions of, 'Goodbye, Tom. Okay, I'd better go. So goodbye, Tom,' finally ended when Decker reached over and turned off the radio.

Such directness was alien to Brix. 'Won't he think something's wrong?'

'Little tip,' Decker said. 'Aegeus only know what you tell them. Whatever you say, they believe it. So you tell them the battery ran out? Done, case closed.'

The daily routine of assembling several hundred kilograms of equipment on to a sledge before leaving the camp, and then dismantling the load when back at the camp, felt reasonably Sisyphean. Every morning the primus stove, the medical box, the pots box, two boxes of food, cans of fuel, and their three sleeping bags were dragged out and strapped on to the wooden sledge, the emergency pup tent lashed across the top. And every evening the same cumbersome things were unstrapped and dragged to their original positions. It was a procedure designed to ensure that necessities were to hand in the event of a crisis. It was also a monumental bore.

Everland presented them with an oppressively low-clouded day the colour of diesel fumes. The wind carried a sawdust-fine snow which immediately worked its way down Brix's collar and made her eyes stream as it blew into her face.

'There's no way this is all going to fit,' she said, blinking and squinting while she tried to find room on her quad bike for a small bag of extra clothing among the masses of rescue gear. The bikes were compact, powerful four-wheel vehicles, with wide black leather saddles, oversized tyres, and sturdy racks at the front and rear for luggage.

Jess rearranged the gear to accommodate the bag, accomplishing in ten seconds what Brix had failed to achieve in ten minutes. 'Seems sort of crazy to me,' she said.

Despite knowing she wouldn't like the answer, the same malignant itch which compelled Brix to scratch at a rash also compelled her to ask, 'What does?'

'Well, Everland's not the kind of place I'd send a rookie,' Jess said as she walked off. 'But whatever. That's cool. I guess Aegeus know what they're doing.'

'Field assistants are supposed to assist, Jess,' Decker warned.

Jess directed her embarrassment into the unnecessary task of unpacking and repacking her rucksack. Her bag was the largest and heaviest. It contained their lunch and flasks of tea, and some first-aid things, such as painkillers, antiseptic gel, and a number of electrolyte sachets to mix with water and drink. Jess also kept her medical kit in the bag. It was a small yellow plastic box which she'd had since her time as an Alpine guide, her name scrawled artlessly across the lid in black marker pen.

Decker was examining the harnesses which fastened each rider to their quad. 'Minus ten.' He made an amused noise, stamping the blood back into his feet. 'Oof, with the wind-chill it's more like minus fifteen,' he said and turned his attention to the thick ropes which tethered the quads together.

If one bike fell into a crevasse, the next would act as an anchor until a rescue strategy could be implemented. The ropes were strong enough to withstand weights several times heavier than a quad, and were trusted implicitly by everyone right up until the moment they were actually used. At the sight of a colleague plunging through the floor, even the most rational person understood they'd just witnessed a fatal yet undeniably stunt-like tragedy. Yet no one was more astonished to find the rope hadn't snapped than the guy buckled to a quad inside a chasm, as Decker knew. He'd celebrated his fortieth birthday this way.

He remembered some fool screaming, 'Sing a song, Decker!' as the bike's creaking revolutions gave him a slow, vomitous tour of the abyss. He'd risked a look down, seen his hat fall, and gathered that there was nothing below him but an interesting death.

Stay calm! The situation was under control, they'd shouted from above.

'I'm forty, don't let me die,' he'd said, crying with an emotional purity which felt so unlike anything he'd ever experienced before, it nearly distracted him.

'That's it, keep singing!' was the reply. '*Na na na na, hey Jude . . .* '

If Decker had ever cared that his previous attempts to rouse them into a Beatles sing-along had all failed, that concern was lost to him now. They'd never understand, as he did here, twisting above oblivion, how beautiful the world really was.

Statistically, he'd had a one in however million chance of being born. He'd survived infanthood and childhood and a good chunk of adulthood. And what he should have done, he realized, was everything he ever wanted. He should have loved more, risked more, travelled more, said yes more. And now he'd die in a crevasse.

'Here's a birthday you won't forget,' someone had said to him once he was rescued. 'Yes, lovely birthday,' he'd answered in a trembling voice.

'*Decker*,' Jess said. 'This is paranoia. We've done the safety checks, we're ready.'

'You think I'm being paranoid about the threat of a blizzard?' Unwilling to trust anything, Decker was completing a fourth or fifth inspection of the quad ropes. 'Then I have a list for you, Jess, which will illustrate that seemingly implausible things are absolutely possible and happen all the time. Listen and learn.' He stood up. 'For instance, spider farms—'

'Yeah, hello? What do you think I was doing with the Mountain Rescue?' Jess said, her hands raised. 'Organizing picnics? I might know a little bit about blizzards, Decker.'

'Spider farms,' Decker said, undeterred. 'Spider farms don't work but have genuinely been tried.' Also real, he said, was a Children's python. Locust forecasting was a real job.

'Someone gets up in the morning, eats a bowl of cereal, and then goes to the office to *forecast locusts*,' he finished with emphasis.

'I can't believe any of those,' Jess said.

'Yet all are true.'

'A Children's python?' Brix said.

'Not what you expect,' Decker replied. 'Much as we might like the idea of someone trying to appoint a snake for kids, no. The name comes from the scientist John George Children.'

He wondered if they understood what he was saying. Their two blank faces suggested the answer was no. 'The point I'm making here,' he continued, 'is that the ground suddenly caving in beneath you can happen, believe me. It doesn't have to be your birthday. And blizzards can definitely happen.'

Brix thought about whether any job could be creepier than spider farming until Decker eventually completed his inspections and said, 'Okay, let's hustle.'

8
April 1913

It was well after midnight when the search party finally returned. Addison was on deck to greet them, and Lawrence remained there to talk with him while the rest of the group disappeared down below to speak among themselves.

Despite fears that Napps and his men were dead, the small hope that they'd survived to reach Everland was enough to haunt everyone aboard. From the moment the storm abated, the *Kismet* had been trying to get to the island. The first delay was the storm damage to the ship, which had forced them to go to the nearer Cape Athena, where repairs had taken a month. Once they were ready to leave the Cape, the second delay came in the form of an abrupt and unseasonably low temperature drop which trapped the *Kismet* in sea ice for several more days. These setbacks, combined with the fear of winter's approach, had left the men dispirited. They'd begun to talk of ill luck, worrying that there was a doom-tinged poetry to the situation which should be heeded.

The tall, dignified Addison had aged significantly in the last few weeks. He'd lost weight and developed anxious frown lines. At forty-four, Lawrence was only two years younger than Addison, but the doctor looked a decade older, and somehow vulnerable compared to the big, handsome Captain.

'Any news?' Addison asked.

'None.' Lawrence rubbed a hand over his face. 'We can't find them.'

The search party men had been divided into three teams, with Lawrence leading his group to the cove and dinghy site. They'd waded across land floes which collapsed under their feet and struggled against a viciously cold wind in order to grub around in the blackness and find nothing. Find nothing at all. Because it wasn't only Napps and Millet-Bass who were missing, Lawrence explained. The camp was empty. Their supplies were also missing.

'How can everything be gone?' Addison said.

'I think the question is where has it gone. Or rather, where has it been taken.'

Addison looked at him. 'I don't understand.'

Don't you, thought Lawrence, because he certainly had a theory.

Addison possibly guessed more than he cared to admit. 'But I'm sure we should refrain from making any hasty conclusions.'

'I doubt we're going to like the conclusion, Adds, hasty or not.'

'Yes,' Addison said softly, 'I'm aware of that.'

Are you? thought Lawrence. Are you aware of what I'm actually saying?

Addison had mediated between the Captain and the Mate for three years. The nature of their volatile relationship meant Addison's door would fling open on an almost daily basis as either Napps or Lawrence burst into his cabin to rant about the latest offence. Whenever Lawrence went to him, the doctor would remain sympathetically neutral, let the anger burn itself out, and then offer calm advice. Addison could never be baited into making even the mildest derogatory comment. Lawrence would describe Napps's behaviour in vitriolic detail, expecting Addison to overturn his desk with shared fury, and instead he'd be asked if he wanted a glass of water. Perhaps, if the Captain was tired of pacing back and forth, he'd like to sit down? Lawrence wondered resentfully if the counsel was equally impartial when Napps raged off to find Addison. The two men were annoyingly close. Their friendship might be enough to make the doctor resist understanding the ugly inferences of that bare camp and its lone inhabitant.

'And how is Dinners?' Lawrence asked.

'We've bathed and re-clothed him,' Addison said. 'He's asleep now. I checked his pockets for a diary, as I know he had one. Millet-Bass also kept a journal, and Napps regularly wrote to his wife. I'd hoped we'd discover a record to help explain the situation. But no, unfortunately not.'

At the mention of Napps, Lawrence had sought to confirm the location of an item in his jacket pocket. 'That doesn't answer my question, Adds,' he said, something rustling against his fingers. He smoothed the pocket flat. 'I asked you how Dinners was.'

'He's a very ill man.'

'How long will it take for him to recover?'

'I feel it's best not to speculate too much on—'

'Don't dance around it,' Lawrence said hotly.

'I'm afraid his condition is serious,' was Addison's only comment.

'Christ. You can't even give me an approximate recovery time, can you?' Lawrence's voice had suddenly lost all power. He shut his eyes, aware that the intensity of his reaction was surprising the doctor. 'Addison, if you knew what you were saying to me.'

Addison had the tact not to articulate what they were both thinking. From the morning of the selection onwards, Addison had persistently registered his concern about Dinners's inclusion in the Everland party. Dinners was unsuitable and his lack of experience was a real worry, he'd argued in his unaggressive yet politely relentless way. It was unwise to send him, he'd warned Lawrence, even as the Captain chucked around insults and barked that Dinners wasn't a child, or a little toy teddy, but a fully grown *man* with a *wife* and *young daughter*. And who's the Captain here, Lawrence had pompously demanded. Who tells a Captain what to do?

Addison heard the faint sound of laughter coming from beneath them in the Officers' Mess. 'I suggest—'

'Don't,' Lawrence interrupted, in case Addison planned to draw his attention to this colossal mistake. Addison wouldn't, he was too considerate, but Lawrence still felt it was safer to pre-empt the conversation and ban it.

'Another search,' Addison said. 'That's what I wanted to suggest. I believe we should organize a final search tomorrow.'

'Late April already,' Lawrence answered. 'It's close to beating us. We can't risk much more of a delay.'

They were behind schedule and the possibility of being frozen in ice until spring was becoming a serious danger. Although one extra day might not make a difference, the distinction between today's relative stability and tomorrow's jeopardy was growing thin. They were approaching the very end of plucky assumptions.

'We'll see if we can hold out, though, won't we?' Addison said, expecting this battle to be difficult.

'Wishful thinking is fast becoming wilful ignorance, Adds,' Lawrence said, staring forlornly at the sea, 'as I think we're both now realizing.'

9

March 1913

Did Millet-Bass have children? Ha, not that he knew of. Napps suppressed his natural reaction.

Their period on the dinghy had ignited a fierce union, but it wasn't friendship as much as dependence. The two men were essentially strangers, and the differences between them were becoming uncomfortably obvious as they started down the beach to sort through the supplies unloaded at the cove.

'So there's a chance you may have children?'

'There's a chance I may be a grandfather, all considered.'

An extraordinary response. This man was a rare moon, never before seen in Napps's galaxy.

And what about him? Well, Napps was married with two daughters. Married for over twenty years! He and Rosie were practically children themselves when they met, so. Anyway. It was a very sweet story.

Millet-Bass hoped his smile looked approving. His romantic priorities had been more or less the exact opposite.

The ship's crew separated into distinct tribes, and the first, crudest divisions were decided by rank. Scientists, officers and navvies automatically gravitated towards their own kind, and these clusters then divided again into smaller splinter groups as personalities sought reflection and tried to create a version of family. It was a system which meant you could learn more about a man's character than anyone else on earth knew, or exist in complete indifference to him. It was possible to forge monumental relationships with some and spend three years as a hairy object blocking the view to others. Napps, the omnipresent yet distant figure of First Mate, saw more than most, and even then the majority of the men remained anonymous beyond their duties.

The officer family Napps had drafted into enjoyed a studious type of fun. They argued about politics and cracked intellectually dry jokes. It was here that Napps and Addison, two reserved and emotionally aloof men, discovered a soulmate in each other. The sailor Castle was another great friend of Napps's, which was one of the more unexpected alliances on board the *Kismet*. Uptight Napps and rowdy Castle had managed to form a close bond despite the total absence of common ground. Nobody knew how it worked. It was a friendship which didn't make sense to them or anyone.

The lawless band Millet-Bass was initiated into always seemed to be having a good time. They'd famously invented a wild game which Napps had played once or twice. Some crazy rules he couldn't remember, everybody hysterical and being thrown to the floor. An interest in environmental topics had meant Napps very occasionally mixed with Dinners's placid scientific tribe. It was enough for Napps to form an unforgiving opinion of him. There was something odd about the runtish Dinners; he'd never been at sea before the *Kismet* voyage, which was bizarre, and didn't act as though he had any sailing knowledge whatsoever. It would perhaps explain why Lawrence appeared to shield Dinners from the rougher tasks aboard. He didn't seem to do his share of night watches, for example, or ever get sent up to the crow's nest. He was basically a pet, Napps had decided, a useless misfit.

In the *Kismet*'s social Venn diagram, the three men had occupied almost entirely distinct spheres, and would have been perfectly happy to let the situation remain unchanged. But then the Captain made his proposal. He wanted volunteers to explore an uncharted island while the ship detoured north to Cape Athena. Claiming new territory would be a matter of pride for the *Kismet*, obviously, and the island would be of great scientific interest. You can imagine what a triumph it would be for Britain, Lawrence had said, for us to return with a significant new discovery, either geographical or ecological. The potential benefits of these trophies are immense, not simply for this expedition but with regard to securing sponsorship for future ones.

'So who's interested?' he'd said, as every hand in the room shot up.

As First Mate, Napps was the natural choice to lead the island team. He was also the worst person to negotiate with, as Lawrence discovered for the millionth time as the two men went to the Captain's room to fight over the merits of each volunteer.

'Oh, we all had stakes on who'd be chosen,' Millet-Bass said as he and Napps walked to the cove, still too battered to muster anything more energetic than an achingly slow trudge. 'Coppers owes me some jug he inherited from his uncle.'

'What are you going to do with the jug?' Napps asked.

'Fill it with the money Matthews owes me. That donkey also bet it would be him here instead of me.'

Millet-Bass's arrogance was amusing. 'Did you have bets on anyone apart from yourself?' Napps said.

'There was an interesting point when most people suddenly put a wager on Dinners.' Whatever reaction Millet-Bass seemed to be anticipating was making it hard for him to keep a straight face. 'Even Dinners placed a bet. Quite a substantial one if what I heard was true.'

'*Giuseppe*,' Napps said furiously.

Lawrence and Napps had agreed on Millet-Bass being a member of the island party. He was strong, capable, and his talents as a sailor were unanimously admired, but Dinners proved to be a point of intense controversy. Since what possible reason was there for choosing an amateur like Dinners over a veteran when the ship was full of them and many had years of Antarctic experience? Napps concluded that he'd rather take Smith's stupid cat. Slamming a hand down on the table, Lawrence was moved to remind Napps that Dinners was a *brilliant* scientist, and therefore this resistance to taking him to a location where his skills could be used was absurd. Look, we need expertise, not illiterate force, Lawrence said, still hammering the table. A couple of sailors stoning birds and grubbing up random slabs of granite won't exactly enlighten us. Evidence of Dinners's commitment to science was there in the numerous books he kept on marine and mammal life, the soft bladderlike creatures he trawled with nets and dissected, the hundreds of watercolour diagrams he'd already produced. And it was precisely this kind of expertise which made him so vital to the island party, Lawrence shouted. Because what do you know about geology, Napps, beyond recognizing a rock when it's flung at you? And what do you really know about biology, beyond what you can and cannot eat?

If there was a knock at the door they didn't notice it, and the young steward Giuseppe had sidled in just as Napps made it unbelievably clear how little he cared about what bladder things Dinners trawled up. Captain, *with respect*, your man Dinners doesn't look like he'd survive the night with a window open, let alone two weeks on a remote Antarctic island. Giuseppe was spotted as he tried to creep from the room, and the language provoked by his trespass made him cower and shake his head, promising on his mother's soul that he hadn't heard anything.

Except what the lying little turd had actually done was repeat the lot, line for line, to everyone on the ship, including Dinners.

'Well, the good news is you were wrong about the window,' Millet-Bass said. 'In that dinghy he did six days without a roof.'

'He nearly died and he still might,' Napps answered. 'The bad news is I was absolutely correct to doubt his abilities. Dinners has put us in a tight spot indeed.'

'We pulled him through, didn't we?' Millet-Bass said.

'I don't need to tell you about the burden a sick man puts upon a team.'

The ill made excessive demands on resources and energy. They needed to be fed, which took extra oil, and they needed to be nursed, which took extra time. They shackled the healthy to their feeble limitations and put everyone in danger. Both Millet-Bass and Napps knew the workload of three could just about be managed between two well men. And they both knew the workload of three was doubled with one man incapacitated.

'The weak aren't buoyed by the strong, the weak sink them,' Napps said.

Millet-Bass stared ahead and didn't comment. The sunshine seemed to lend colours a starched precision. Looking inland, Everland's volcano was a perfect matte black, above which the sky was a perfect white.

As their conversation recovered from a period of uneasy silence, it returned to the fascinating subject of Millet-Bass. Napps was learning there were many ways to live a life, and none of Millet-Bass's ways had ever occurred to him.

There were those summers Millet-Bass had spent digging up roads or laying bricks or milling flour before sailing off with that ship. At one point, for no real reason, he'd constructed himself a den in the woods and experimented with living in nature, which he'd found very easy. He'd spent a few months snaring rabbits, swimming naked, and guddling fish, whatever that entailed, something to do with groping around barehanded in streams. There were periods when he'd worked as a game beater or a carpenter or at a distillery, or been involved in some eel-poaching racket. And in between these exploits, from the age of fourteen onwards, he'd headed out to sea.

Napps tried to remain neutral as he listened to all this. He didn't think a man should run around in the woods with no clothes on, he thought a man should accept responsibility. Secretly, he felt glad of his scorn for Millet-Bass's anarchic past. It stopped him analysing a different feeling underneath the scorn, which was perhaps jealousy. The only job he'd ever had was in the Navy, where he'd unadventurously plodded his way through the ranks. It seemed very bland now. So Napps hinted at a recklessness of his own, saying enough to imply that he was embarrassed about an impressive history with women which far surpassed anything Millet-Bass could ever imagine.

When Millet-Bass mentioned that Napps had told him he'd met his prospective wife at fifteen, Napps was too busy inspecting their supplies to answer.

The cove was littered with large, salt-sculpted chunks of ice from the neighbouring glacier, the sand frozen into the messy ruts of yesterday's footprints.

'The sum total of our possessions,' Napps said. 'Everything we have in the world.' He turned to see if Millet-Bass was in an equally philosophical mood.

'I used to be able to carry three of these,' was all Millet-Bass said. He tried to lift one of the thirty-pound boxes and made some unhealthy sounds, dropping the box.

Millet-Bass's weak display only confirmed Napps's decision. Shifting all the supplies to the camp would involve grunting through fifteen or sixteen trips with a fully loaded sledge, and Napps doubted he even had the strength to rip an envelope in half. 'The cove is sheltered enough for the supplies to remain where they are,' he said. 'They'll be fine here until the ship arrives.'

Millet-Bass said nothing, just looked at him.

'It's been two days,' Napps said, a little testily. 'Allow them some time.'

Many of the crates were damaged. Napps and Millet-Bass sniffed the punctured cans and squeezed the swollen ones distrustfully. Some jars were cracked and they wondered about sieving out the glass fragments. They thought saturated powdered goods could potentially still be edible after drying, a theory they tested with a bite of wet flour and then disagreed on. What could be saved was organized into a loose pile. Napps took a pencil and notebook from his pocket to write an inventory.

They had Bovril sledging rations and nut food, pemmican, Huntley & Palmers Antarctic biscuits and some butter. There was also a selection of tinned meats and fruits, jams and fish. Cans of kidney soup, nobody's first choice, were listed with lukewarm gratitude. Giblet soup followed, which wasn't exactly worse but certainly wasn't better. Cans of Moir's lunch tongue and cans of pineapple in syrup were received with more enthusiasm. Tea leaves, Cerebos salt and packets of Trumilk were found. Sugar and Fry's Pure Concentrated Cocoa caused the sweet-toothed Napps to rap his notebook with a fist. Millet-Bass whistled in relief at the discovery of several pouches of tobacco. There was also a decent stash of candles, additional Alpine ropes and tackle, and another sack of clothing. Napps discovered a compass, which he shook and studied. He frowned at the few viable boxes of matches. There wasn't much paraffin either. Napps grimly counted which oilcans weren't leaking.

In one of their typically hostile discussions, Lawrence and Napps had collided over the amount of food necessary for the trip. To Napps the quantity was entirely justified, but Lawrence had seen the boxes being piled on deck for the *Joseph Evelyn* and yelled, 'Where's your head, Napps?' Napps had won the argument by being the man happy to carry the debate on through the night. It was also significantly preferable for him to be the one proved wrong, as he had explained to the idiot Captain. Because if he was wrong then they could always return surplus food to the hold, but if Lawrence was wrong it meant they'd starve.

Napps muttered absently to himself as he calculated the inventory into units of days and meals, units of fuel and men. Millet-Bass heard him mumbling that he wanted to start rationing in order to save a month's worth of supplies.

'Wait, hold on,' Millet-Bass said. 'How long do you plan on us staying here?'

'I don't want to have to explain it again to Dinners,' Napps said. 'We'll discuss it at the tent.'

Watching Napps snap shut the notebook to put it in his pocket, Millet-Bass considered for the first time that there might be a rift between them over what they proposed to do next.

10
November 2012

W hy Everland?' The member of the selection board looked over his spectacles at Brix, his pen ready. 'Why this field-trip?'

Enthusiasm, curiosity, ambition. It was nothing the board hadn't heard countless times before. Everybody who'd been interviewed would have said the same thing in the same passionate way. So Brix told them about her trilobite fossil.

This marine animal had once ruled the earth. For nearly three hundred million years, these flattened helmets with legs had mowed across the ocean bed, feeding on small organisms or detritus. Trilobites looked suitably basic and warlike for a creature that had emerged from the beginning of life, in an age so ancient they'd already died out before dinosaurs existed. The first trilobites belonged to a different planet, without trees or grass, or fur or feathers, when the various permutations of eyes and organs were in their very earliest, craziest stages. Which made it all the more incredible to Brix that she could just own one of these things. She'd been fifteen years old when an aunt gave her a trilobite fossil as a birthday present and changed the way Brix saw the world. Something had clicked in her head. For half a billion years, animal life had been evolving, from crawling, slithering, modifying, and then running, flying, diversifying. And this history wasn't lost, as an apple-sized fossil demonstrated. That's what had amazed the teenage Brix. All of existence could be traced back, from the start until now. It was still there, but as rock and bone, as layers of soil, or clay, or resin, or preserved in tundra ice and peat.

'The same trilobite sits on my desk at home as a paper-weight,' Brix had said.

Someone on the board laughed. 'Extremely profound for a paperweight.'

Brix's answering laugh was self-conscious. The trilobite speech which had seemed so captivating in her head revealed itself to be peculiar, perhaps even a little dorkish. 'It reminds me why I became a scientist,' she said in a serious tone, to emphasize that she was in fact a studious person, not a kook. 'Once I understood that everything connects, I knew I wanted to be involved in the process of discovery.'

Wish granted. Here Brix was, on yet another overcast morning, clouds draped across the volcano like a rotting woollen rug. The sky was sludge-coloured and ominous, as always. They'd never once seen the sun, even for a second.

Decker, Jess and Brix had driven the quads to a bay at the southern end of the island to begin monitoring the estimated four thousand Adélies which located here each summer. Although the colony was still eight hundred metres away, they'd travel the last distance on foot, pulling equipment on sledges to prevent the quads' engine noise from disturbing the birds.

The last week had taught Brix several interesting yet largely unpleasant facts. By far the quickest thing she'd learnt was what it meant to be cold. It wasn't discomfort, or shivering, or any of the things she'd experienced before: being truly cold meant being unable to think for the pain, and feeling sick with the pain, and remaining shaky for hours afterwards. That field-work was physically relentless was another lesson Brix had learnt with every single muscle in her body. If they weren't dragging equipment on or off sledges, they were fighting against headwinds, or trying to read maps in the sleet, or trying to return to the tent, or waking up to start the battle all over again. Their camp was on the eastern side of the island, and they'd been to the western coast, where the beach was a thin stretch of black rubble and deader than the moon. They'd hiked across the lower slopes of the volcano, where nothing lived except a purple moss which resembled burnt rice. They'd tried to drive north to the *Joseph Evelyn* cove and had been beaten back by such heavy snowfall they couldn't see three metres in front of them.

Decker was the best thing about Everland, in Brix's opinion. He was also Brix's protector from the worst thing about Everland: Jess.

Her plans to befriend Jess had been absurdly naïve. From the start, Jess had made no effort to hide the fact that she not only preferred Decker to Brix, but appeared to actively dislike Brix, which she showed by having an opinion about whatever Brix did. It seemed Brix was too slow at dressing, or eating, or walking, or digging out the supplies. Brix sometimes got her revenge by talking very scientifically to Decker, which was the one conversation Jess couldn't monopolize. Brix would start an impenetrable discussion about phytoplankton, the microscopic aquatic organisms. Or she'd mention the Southern Annular Mode, the wind belt that circled Antarctica. More often, she would invent reasons to spend time alone in the work tent. She'd say she was going to write her notes. What she'd really do was sit there on her own and feel unbelievably lonely.

Brix's sledge was no heavier than Decker's or Jess's, but it had become her habit to lag a few steps behind them. She examined the chunks of stranded ice which littered the shoreline. The pieces ranged in size from bars of soap to half-ton lumps, all sculpted into futuristic shapes by the wind, and arranged by the tide in such an orderly row that the display seemed curated rather than organic.

'Man, it's a constant inquisition with you,' Decker said to Jess, because she deemed no topic too sensitive. She would prise any subject apart with a barrage of questions, such as why Decker and his wife Viv had no children and how they felt about that.

It was no big surprise to learn that Viv was charmingly eccentric. She favoured cardigan coats, giant jewellery, and a karmic slant to life. They lived in a farmhouse in Somerset, and were the kind of people who brewed their own alcohol to drink in riotous celebrations with similar people. They had driftwood sculptures in the garden and curios from their extensive travels covering the shelves. It was all very loose and joyful and free. And as for children, Decker and Viv had come to accept it wouldn't happen. They'd been through their share of heartbreak about it, he said. 'But we're okay. And that's how it goes. This'll be my last fieldwork trip, though.'

Jess shot him a canny, incredulous smile.

'No, really. I'm serious,' Decker said. 'It's not fair on Viv, I'm never home. And expeditions are a young man's game. I probably should have retired a while ago.'

Ahead of them, the winding coastline rounded into a small-ish, sheltered bay, which sloped up from the sea to the base of twenty-metre-high cliffs. The breeding season's first arrivals were visible at the far end. About a hundred Adélies were grouped together in a black mass, with occasional white flashes of chest feathers as individual birds toddled out of the surf.

After years of analysing data in a sterile laboratory, it was more than just an uplifting sight for Brix. That she was here on an expedition herself, seeing a wild colony, released a surge of happy energy which made her want to dance on the spot, or let out a victorious whoop. Instead she rewarded herself with a discreet fist pump and walked faster, almost bouncing.

An audience of curious penguins watched while they unpacked the tools and rolls of fencing. The stumpy, knee-height Adélies had white rings circling each eye and were as conspicuously immaculate as brand-new trainers.

'Okay, let's get this party started,' Decker said as he looked at the sky, felt the threat of snow in the air, and then looked worriedly at Brix. He looked at confident, unfazed Jess and could have hugged her.

The Adélies would be monitored with an automated system. A low wire mesh fence separated a large section of the beach from the ocean, leaving a two-metre-wide gateway for the penguins to filter through. The birds had to cross this gateway whenever they went to forage at sea and then returned to the colony, shuffling over a pallet-sized platform on the floor which logged their weight. Everything about the breeding season was defined by weight. Life and death were measured in grams. It took between twenty and thirty kilograms of food to transform an eighty-six-gram hatchling into an independent bird. For its five-to-six-kilogram parents, this meant providing ever larger catches as the chick grew, until they were finally hauling back up to a fifth of their bodyweight in krill; which was also the amount of bodyweight the adults would lose by the end of the summer, as they exhausted themselves running to and from the ocean on their pink rubbery feet. Electronic readers buried alongside the platform would identify microchipped birds as they went past, recording the duration and frequency of their trips. Since lengthy trips and poor catches indicated that food was scarce, the data wouldn't only provide information on the Adélies' health but the health of their environment as well.

It took four gruelling hours to get the automated system established and dig in the electronic readers. Although neither Jess nor Brix had any experience with this equipment, Jess only needed a job to be explained once before she grasped it and was then amazing at it. Unlike Brix, whose contribution was not just weak but virtually worthless. The mood became tense as freezing mist rolled in from the sea and drenched everything. Dew saturated their red Gore-Tex suits, water dripping from faces and plastered strings of hair. Hands became paralysed, causing the sufferer to swear and drop whatever they were holding. When sleet started to drum across the beach, the cold became internalized as an encompassing, unsolvable misery.

Decker alone was able to remain patient with Brix. He was saintly when Brix couldn't work out where to position a fence post, which meant he had to show her, and then show her how to hammer it in. Her inability to nail the fencing to the posts correctly meant Decker had to come back and redo it. Since Brix also kept letting parts of her face freeze, Decker twice had to pull her to one side and revive a whitened patch of skin. It became difficult to tell who'd win in the competition to hate Brix most between Jess and Brix herself.

Jess observed from under the brim of her sodden hood as Brix failed to manage some other job and Decker jogged over and talked to her. They were only thirty metres away, yet the waterfall roar of the pelting sleet masked their voices. The ground jumped with millions of beads of ice, steadily filling the hole Jess and Decker had been gouging out of the cast-iron sand for the weighing platform. Jess watched Decker put an encouraging arm around Brix's shoulders as she shook her head in frustration. *Good, you cry*, Jess thought, staring at Brix. *Cry and waste more time, that's just perfect.*

Decker made a scooping gesture to tell Jess to keep digging.

Yeah, great, thought Jess, shovelling angrily with her spade. I'll finish my work, and then her work, and any work you haven't done since her bullshit means you're constantly interrupted. And, then, once I've done everything else, I'll make you both dinner. Because this team is composed of one useless tourist, one biologist, and one *slave.*

Decker relieved Brix of her fence-nailing duty and sent her

off into the colony with an armload of nest-marker poles. The nests built closest to each of the individually numbered and randomly placed marker poles would be monitored to provide a cross-section of information on the year's breeding success. The chicks raised in these nests would have their progress measured as they either survived to fledge or perished.

'Why is she here, Decker?' Jess said when he returned.

'You could try giving her a break,' Decker said. 'She's an excellent scientist.'

Jess was about to respond with a different, less enthusiastic summary of Brix when Decker cut in. 'You all right there, chief?' he shouted to Brix.

Brix's mood had actually taken a dramatic upturn. She'd discovered an empty can of pineapple lying partially crushed among the rocks. Picking it up, she examined the red lettering and quaint illustration mottled with a century's worth of corrosion. Marks on the rim showed where it had been cut open to bend up the rusted lid.

Napps, Millet-Bass and Dinners had been reduced to sepia portraits, with their centre-partings and utterly joyless expressions. These photographs were stamped through a hundred biographies until the repetition erased any emotional content and their faces became nothing more than the emblems of a tragedy. The three men were almost mythical creatures, so dead it was hard to believe that they'd ever been real. Which made evidence that they'd truly been here, walking this same beach and seeing this same view, as remarkable to find as a trilobite fossil. But the past was a different world. It remained unknowable and evasive, even when you were holding solid proof of it in your hand.

11
April 1913

Y ou sly bastard,' Lawrence murmured to the doctor sitting beside him. 'Don't think I don't know exactly
what you're doing.'

To the uninitiated, Addison remained peacefully oblivious
to either this insult or any of the raised voices quarrelling in the
Officers' Mess. His attention was focused on the remains of his
cold meal. He wasn't averse to confrontation, but understood
that authority in an argument relied on timing and composure.
Addison was a strategist. He would wait until the ideal
moment arrived, then shut off the dispute's airways with a fatal
pincer-grip of clarity.

Lawrence's proposal to launch a final search for Napps and
Millet-Bass before starting homeward had been met with deep
resistance. Morale still hadn't recovered from the storm.

The *Kismet* was a traditional, three-masted sailing vessel with
a heavily reinforced frame designed to withstand the timber-
shattering pressure of the ice. Messy-looking piles of tarpaulin-
covered boxes, coal sacks and fuel cases loosely divided the
deck lengthways down the middle to leave a narrow gangway
at each side. Buckets, oilcans, timber and tools were wedged in
wherever there was room, just as those tragic animals had once
been. For a brief time, eight terrified sheep had lived in a pen
on the deck, before they were strung from the masts, their
skinned and frozen bodies clattering together. Below deck, a
warren of passages ran between the infirmary, the galley
kitchen, the Mess rooms, the hold, the laboratories and the

engine rooms. There wasn't an inch of idle space anywhere. No one was ever more than four steps from someone else. The ship was a home, a village, a centre of scientific research, and an abattoir. She was a kingdom unto herself, with a figurehead of a bare-breasted angel decorating her prow. And although she was beautiful to look at, she was less enchanting to sail.

The *Kismet* had been used for whaling in the Labrador Sea and was nearly thirteen years old when Lawrence purchased her. She was starting to show her age. Water seeped through the deck and rained on to the bunks, or choked the engines. The flat-bottomed hull which worked so well to resist the ice was hellishly unsteady in open waters. She rolled and lurched at wild angles, smashing people against the walls. The *Kismet* was already in a ramshackle condition when the storm hit her.

In the almost month-long repairs at Cape Athena, men had crawled to pack gushing leaks near the propeller shaft with tar and cement, while others worked endless shifts at the pumps. The five-ton rudder had been torn from its truck and needed to be hauled out with chains and laid on the ice to mend. The problem of chronically waterlogged engines took long, oil-blackened days in the engine room to solve. Each new dilemma had weakened the collective buffer of optimism. Once thick sea ice trapped the ship at the Cape, the men's concerns for the Everland team had been replaced by concerns for themselves. Their hearts held an uncompromising will to be safe and the sacrifices it urged were ungallant to say the least.

The sailor Matthews was talking with Smith, a blond sailor of twenty-three who worshipped Napps. There was a vulnerability to Smith, a sort of silliness and cluelessness, which not only provoked but almost invited the more bullying crew members to target him. And it was these same qualities which had proved to be Smith's salvation. Although Napps had plenty of bullying tendencies of his own, he also abided by a perverse type of code. Certain people, such as the idiotic Smith, were so crushable their persecution insulted him. Which meant Smith-baiting was a dangerous sport, as the furious Mate was prone to suddenly appear from nowhere to menace Smith's tormentors. And now his defender was gone, Smith's eyes darted around nervously.

'If we leave, though,' Smith said. 'What if they're alive?'

'If they're alive we'd have found them,' Matthews answered.

For the fiftieth time, Castle said, 'We cannot rule out hope.'

'Spoken like a true friend,' Coppers said. He turned to laugh dismissively with the men near him.

Castle's nose resembled something used to jam open a door. He had crazy red hair which stuck up in tufts, and a charisma which belied his small size. Although his relationship with Napps somehow disqualified his views, he was still persuasive as he talked about the First Mate's abilities. No one could deny that Napps was frighteningly capable. Under his supervision the crew ran effortlessly. He was known for his belief in discipline and his famously blunt assessment of work. If the work was good you'd be told how to improve it, and if the work was bad there wasn't time to catch your breath. Although Napps's professional reputation was faultless, judgements on his character were far less consistent. It depended on who you spoke to. It depended on what kind of a bruising Napps had just given their best efforts.

Castle's speech was received with a polite lack of interest from everyone except Smith, who clapped enthusiastically. A slow, facetious applause came from McValley.

'Careful,' Lawrence said to him. 'We're aware of your opinions on Napps.'

McValley wasn't aggressive exactly, but the men were wary around him. He could be venomous. As the ship's Second Mate, he was third in rank behind the Captain and Napps. He was also sensationally good-looking. His facial expressions always seemed very consciously arranged to accentuate his handsomeness, such as now, with this smile.

'I'm sorry, sir,' McValley said with poorly acted remorse. 'I will admit there may not have been a lot of love between myself and the Mate.'

The audience raised their eyebrows at this colossal understatement.

Smith overheard Coppers saying quietly, 'Hah, practical Napps. Lethally practical with the cat, wasn't he?'

'That isn't decent,' Smith said. 'Napps is a good man.'

Coppers looked at Smith pityingly. 'Honestly, if they were alive we'd have found them,' he said to the room, specifically to Lawrence.

In trying to stay professionally neutral, Lawrence's nod was designed to confirm he appreciated Coppers's point whilst also showing he didn't necessarily agree. It wasn't that he disagreed, but he wanted to project a certain image of himself.

'Captain, let it be documented that I unreservedly offer my services to the next search party,' Smith said with uncharacteristic determination. He was visibly willing Lawrence to immortalize the statement in his journal.

You little *idiot*, Lawrence thought as he offered the same neutral nod. When it comes to you, Smith, let it be documented you wouldn't want me anywhere near my damned journal.

The expedition funding was reliant in part on the book Lawrence was contracted to write about it afterwards. He dutifully spent an hour before bed recording the day's news. It wasn't only the larger traumas and triumphs of Antarctic exploration, but also the minor domestic events. He wrote about their festive meals and birthday celebrations and their games of football on the ice. Everything about their rituals as a community and dynamic as a group was preserved. Just chatty details, he'd say when asked about his diary. Chatty bits to show the reality of life aboard. What he didn't say was that the journal also chatted pretty heavily on the subject of his personal opinions. Certain things were slanderously discussed, certain men. His journal frequently got used to harbour a grudge or channel eruptions of spite. Not that anyone would ever know. The editing would smooth it out later, and he'd insert extracts from other men's diaries to create a balanced depiction. Except he wondered about the notion of keeping his book objective now it seemed they'd taken this enormous emotional detour.

Lawrence felt the Everland calamity as an acidic fire in his stomach. It burnt penny-sized holes throughout the day, which made it impossible to concentrate, and attracted swarms of flesh-eating thoughts throughout the night, which made it impossible to sleep. So now Lawrence lay in the dark with his eyes open until morning. He tried to plan his way out of a labyrinth full of monsters named debt and defeat and ineptitude and failure. And because Dinners's condition was an issue which required supreme caution if he was to navigate it safely, Lawrence had already begun drafting those chapters in his head.

Now Addison spoke. 'We all want to go home,' he said. 'But can we leave without being sure that Napps and Millet-Bass can't be saved? That's the predicament.'

'We *are* sure,' McValley said.

Addison said, 'We think we're sure. It's entirely different.'

Addison was using the level, parental tone of voice Lawrence had come to hate. He regarded it as an act of ethical hooliganism over his right to perfectly normal character flaws. The doctor was forever defying his rank by exerting a strange influence over Lawrence which forced him to be a better man.

Lawrence tried to keep the resentment out of his voice. 'Another search will be dangerous.'

'My belief is that we must not permit ourselves to assume

they're dead because it suits us,' Addison replied, looking intently at the Captain.

McValley listened to this and imagined a happy scenario where he beat Addison to death. He had a baby at home in England, a daughter, and he was being forced to risk his life for a pair of corpses. If he was going to risk it for anyone, McValley thought his wife and baby deserved priority since they were actually alive to appreciate the sacrifice.

'We didn't find Napps and Millet-Bass the first two times,' said Coppers, thumping back against his chair in protest. 'Why should we the third time? What are we searching for?'

'For anything, Coppers,' Lawrence said quickly, since the doctor's morality pincer was crushing his throat. 'Any trace or evidence. If we can't leave with the men, then we'll leave knowing we did everything in our power to help them. It's the honourable course of action. I expect we're all persuaded by that.'

Lawrence chose to interpret the men's silence as agreement.

'The final search will be launched tomorrow,' he said.

McValley responded with one of his wonderfully insulting smiles.

12

March 1913

With no wind-chill it was pleasant enough for Napps and Millet-Bass to shift the primus from the tent and cook their lunch outside. It would be dark within the next couple of hours, and hundreds of bird and seal calls echoed across the island as the mid-afternoon sun set in a flame-red sky.

Millet-Bass put blankets on the snow for himself and Napps to sit on, in front of the tent entrance so that Dinners could join the conversation. He sat huddled in his sleeping bag inside the tent.

'See you've been busy,' Millet-Bass said to Dinners.

Dinners had emptied his little collection of rocks out on to the groundsheet and lined them up for inspection. His ration bag was as personal to him as another journal. He'd stockpiled Antarctic specimens, including diorite quartz and kenyte lava, and he'd also brought a number of rocks with sentimental value from home. Among the opal, jet and pyrite, amethyst was his favourite. These purple crystals had been a present from Elizabeth, before they were married. His February birthday meant amethyst was his birthstone, she'd said, and Dinners had admired her for trying to romanticize his interest in geology. He'd thought the whole birthstone thing was nonsense, but when their daughter Madeline was born on a February morning two years later, the amethysts came to symbolize his wife, his baby, and his life at home. He took them with him everywhere, along with a photograph of Elizabeth.

Dinners's face went a deep mortified red. He scraped the stones into the bag and stammered to Millet-Bass that he'd given himself various jobs. He said he wanted to make a contribution, even if it was only very slight. For example, he'd reached from the tent to place some wet socks on the snow to dry in the sun, which took him a long time due to his awful hands. He'd also peered out at the beach to observe any seals and birds for scientific purposes. It was one of the more troublesome jobs.

'But you had a job,' Napps said. 'You were to sleep and recover. Your contribution, as you put it, would have been to do the job I assigned to you.'

Lying on his stomach, with his head at the open entrance, Dinners could see a long stretch of shoreline. He'd scanned the ocean for any sign of the *Kismet,* and been distracted by the wildlife. The abundance of creatures still on Everland so late in the season was testament to the numbers which would amass here during the breeding months.

'The island will heave from shore to shore,' Dinners said, reciting the list of bird species he'd spotted. 'Gulls, skuas, terns—'

Napps's uninterested expression was purposefully hurtful.

'A range of petrels,' Dinners finished meekly. 'And for a while I thought I was being watched by some large animal in the shadows over there.' He pointed to a collection of large rocks several yards from the camp. Because that was the problem, Dinners told Millet-Bass. The mammals were tricky to identify if you couldn't leave the tent. They tended to remain further away and the light was so jarring and deceptive. 'I probably spent a couple of hours trying to work out what the animal was. It was only when the sun repositioned and changed the shadows that I realized I'd been unable to recognize a boulder.'

Millet-Bass smiled. 'You're a quirky one.'

'I wish I could say I've learnt my lesson!' Dinners said, pleased to be amusing him. 'I can still see it, but it's over there now.' He pointed to another clutter of rocks and described a body crouched on its heels. It had a horned head or something.

Napps exhaled. It was the sound of mildly inconvenienced resignation.

'I'd prefer it if the invisible bodies hiding around the place were female,' Millet-Bass said. He'd be delighted just to imagine they might be here, he added cheerfully, even if he didn't have mad enough eyes to see them for himself.

'I'll try my hardest to see womanly visions on your behalf,' Dinners said, so grateful for the kindness Millet-Bass showed him, he almost didn't mind that Napps was sneering.

'Great,' Millet-Bass said. 'And I wonder if you could knock off the chat about horned heads.'

'What I'm wondering, Dinners, is why a scientist would entertain himself with daydreams,' Napps said, making Dinners's face redden again. 'I'd rather hoped you'd be above such childish games.'

Millet-Bass stopped smiling. 'The meal's ready,' he said abruptly.

Millet-Bass didn't like this cruelty to Dinners. Dinners had been categorized as a sort of genderless fluffy creature in Millet-Bass's mind, and should consequently be treated with the same thoughtful politeness he extended to his sisters. It didn't matter that the four Millet-Bass sisters were every bit as tough as their brother, and therefore a thousand times more robust than Dinners. If Napps tried talking to one of the sisters as he did to Dinners he'd have his throat grabbed and his knees kicked from under him.

Once given his pannikin of hoosh, Dinners worked hard not to make any mistakes while he ate. If his incapacitated hands blundered with the spoon, or he let the dish slope to drip food, it was noticed. Every error was logged and begrudged. But when Millet-Bass asked if he needed assistance, Dinners shook his head.

'No, thank you. My hands are much better today,' he lied, glancing at Napps. 'I'm enjoying my meal.'

'Best enjoy it,' Napps said between mouthfuls. 'Rationing starts tomorrow.'

'Yes, about the rationing,' Millet-Bass said. 'How long are you expecting us to stay here?'

'Not a minute longer than we have to.'

'I agree with you,' Millet-Bass said. 'So why ration?'

Napps reacted to stupidity by speaking in an offensively patient manner. 'Let's be reasonable,' he said slowly. 'We do not know how long we will be here.'

'Well, we can decide that, can't we?' Millet-Bass said.

It took a moment for Napps to understand what Millet-Bass was suggesting. He suffered the first twinges of indigestion. 'You want to get back in the dinghy?'

'You want to stay on the island?' replied Millet-Bass.

'No, but I will stay until the ship comes to rescue us.'

'How can you be sure it will? They might presume us drowned.'

Napps hadn't considered that Millet-Bass might have a different opinion. This wasn't only due to arrogance but to habit. There'd been nothing to debate or speculate about during the hurricane-pounded *Joseph Evelyn* days. He'd forgotten that men like Millet-Bass could be stubborn free-thinkers.

'Which is why I propose we rescue ourselves,' Millet-Bass continued. 'We can't rely on the *Kismet* to come looking for us when it's doubtful that anyone believes we survived the storm. But we know the ship was going to dock for a while at Cape Athena, and I suggest we intercept them. We'll wait a few days for Dinners to recover, and then sail for the Cape.'

'Really. You believe Dinners to be strong enough to withstand a journey of that kind in a few days,' Napps said. 'Millet-Bass, have you looked at him?'

And have you looked at yourself, Napps demanded next. Neither Millet-Bass nor Napps was in a much better state. They were thin, drained, and not far from physical collapse. But no matter! Napps raised his fists in sarcastic enthusiasm. Because what's stopping us? He pretended to reflect on it.

'Can't think of a single reason,' Napps said. 'So, yes, let's rescue ourselves. We'll load the dinghy with supplies we can't lift, and row with strength we don't have, and Dinners will be dead within hours, and you and I will die in the night.'

'Then we'll wait longer—' Millet-Bass said.

'Has it genuinely not occurred to you that exposure is our worst threat?'

'I've been at sea since I was fourteen. I don't know if you'd call it geographical, but you develop an instinct about places,' Millet-Bass said. 'And I'm telling you, I sense it here. Everland is bad luck. We should go as soon as we can.'

Napps's mouth twisted. Millet-Bass believed this rot because he was a typical sailor. In his entire career as a naval officer, Napps had never met a sailor who wasn't full of phobias and superstitions. They all feared harmless things and saw signs everywhere and behaved in illogical ways to appease whatever ridiculous fish or cloud was judged to have mystic powers. The reality was that open water would kill them faster than any supposedly haunted island ever could.

Millet-Bass spoke to Dinners directly. 'What do you make of it?'

Although Dinners wanted to make Millet-Bass happy, he was mortally afraid of being back out at sea. 'I don't know . . . '

Napps's loud snort of derision chastened Millet-Bass, as it was intended to do. Napps had a family and reputation to consider. He had a career as prospective Captain to nurture. He exercised logic and moderation while Millet-Bass lived an irresponsible life and could afford to be daring. It was no surprise to Napps that Millet-Bass had come up with an outrageously heroic plan which he was then forced to disqualify. Assuming they did somehow miraculously survive the crossing, there was no guarantee the *Kismet* would be at the Cape. And if the ship did come to find them, arriving at a deserted Everland would only confirm all suspicions that they were dead. Even viewed through the mindset of rabid optimism, Napps couldn't believe the crew would fathom where they'd gone and route back to Athena. If they left Everland, he reasoned that they would probably end up stranded at the Cape, living alone in that infernal hut until the *Kismet*'s planned return next spring.

The hut was a rectangular wooden shack, large enough to house the *Kismet*'s crew of thirty-five men, which Millet-Bass and a few other sailors had built during the expedition's first summer. There were a galley kitchen and large stove, a larder stocked with a year's worth of supplies, and a year's worth of fuel. On the bookcase was a decent yet bizarrely eclectic collection of reading material. Napps would never agree to Millet-Bass's mad proposal, but there was still a tiny part of him attracted by its promise of glory. He pictured Lawrence's expression when the *Joseph Evelyn* dramatically appeared at the Cape. He foresaw the gratifying astonishment of every crew member as they listened to his story. *So we rescued ourselves*, Napps would conclude with devastating humility. Although he wasn't really tempted to try it, the fact that the utterly foreseen millstone of Dinners made the option impossible was just one more reason for Napps to resent him.

'Look, indulging in the realms of fantasy for a moment,' Napps said to them, 'and imagining the *Kismet* doesn't rescue us, I made sure the *Joseph Evelyn* was overstocked with supplies. We can therefore ration to preserve a month's worth of food. As a very last resort, we would remain on Everland until the sea ice forms and then march across the frozen bay and winter at the Cape.' Napps shrugged at the simplicity of his reserve plan, explaining that even a month's worth of rations was unnecessarily generous, since the bay march could be done in a couple of weeks. 'However, it's a purely theoretical safeguard,' he finished. 'The *Kismet* will arrive any day now.'

'So we wait and hope, or we go and hope,' Millet-Bass said. 'Excuse my ignorance, but it seems to me that your way relies on luck just as much as mine does.'

T he homemade card was taped to a bundled-up towel which contained a present inside. Andre shrugged and said, 'No wrapping paper,' as Jess unfolded the towel and saw he was giving her his Metallica T-shirt. It had been the morning of the Everland departure and he'd caught Jess in Aegeus's big peach-coloured lobby as she went out to load her bag of clothes on to the Twin Otter. On the front of the card was a drawing of a hand with its middle finger raised.

'Because screw you! You're leaving me for two months,' Andre explained. 'People will think we've broken up.'

This was a long-running joke, invented after Scottish David had remarked that they were like a married couple, the way they were always together. Jess and Andre both made horrified noises at the idea of their relationship being anything but platonic. 'Don't be weird, David,' Andre had said. 'Yeah, David, gross,' Jess said, her face heating up as it always did whenever anyone suggested that non-platonic feelings could possibly exist between her and the burly, shaven-headed Andre.

'Didn't see you at breakfast,' Jess said to him, more accusingly than she'd meant to. She had wanted her leaving to produce a more obvious display of sorrow from Andre. Ideally a hint about suppressed attraction.

'Yeah.' Andre's accent became more pronounced as he lowered the volume of his voice. 'Something sort of happened.'

With huge effort, Jess managed to smile. She knew what he was going to say. In preparation for the gruelling day-long transfer to Everland, she'd gone to bed as soon as last night's screening of *Everland* was over. She had left Andre talking at the bar.

'Kimiko, man. The Japanese chick? Turns out she can speak a bit of Dutch. Then, uh.' Andre rubbed his stubbly head. 'I'm really sorry. I meant to get up earlier.'

Kimiko. Of course. Andre obviously liked her, although he always denied it. In an act of incredible self-delusion, Jess had chosen to believe him despite the poorly disguised interest in where Kimiko was, in what Kimiko was doing, in whether Kimiko would be there at the meal, the film, the party, the meeting.

Jess's great talent was for appearing indifferent when upset. It was a skill she'd honed over a lifetime of practice. The problem, as far as she could deduce, was that she was too boyish for girls and for boys. So she cast herself into the role of a thick-skinned, hardworking loudmouth. Since friendships with women seemed to elude her, Jess hung out with the guys as one of the guys. She was your buddy, not your girlfriend. She was never anyone's girlfriend, but Jess made the best of her beer-drinking buddy status. Yet it hurt her deeply when people like *Kimiko* didn't have to try at all for the things Jess wanted so much and couldn't ever get in the end. In the same way that people like *Brix* were just given the rewards Jess had to work for years to achieve.

Wearing her Metallica T-shirt, Jess stirred a pan of beef stroganoff and thought about how wonderful Everland would be if Andre was here, and about how useless Brix was. It mystified her that Brix had got through the selection process, considering the competitiveness of the other candidates. What could Brix do, exactly, apart from discuss microbes and egg incubation periods? Because she certainly couldn't refuel a quad, or stop frostbite from covering her face, or get through a day without crying, or pack a sledge, or fasten a harness, or recharge the laptop. Or do anything worth anything.

'And that's what got me,' Brix said to Decker, who was riveted by every word she said, as usual. 'Although the hair was dirty, it was completely unchanged.'

Their conversation had drifted round to visiting an exhibition of Egyptian mummies at the British Museum. A few had been unwrapped to display blurry forearm tattoos, desiccated child-sized feet, and frayed leather faces. Among this wealth of morbidity, Brix hadn't been able to stop staring at the hair. It was so brown and normal-looking. If you washed it, if there was some way of doing that, and then brushed it, it would be restored.

'Frayed leather faces.' Decker rubbed his hands together, disgusted. 'Thanks!'

'I mean *perfectly* restored,' Brix said. 'The rest of the mummy was disintegrated enough to be comfortably non-human. But then you looked at the hair and all you could think about was your own mortality.'

'Sounds like a fun day,' Jess said in the driest possible voice. It was the first thing she'd said in over half an hour.

'And how old were those mummies?' Brix said, avoiding eye contact with her. 'Thousands of years. So think about Dinners if they hadn't saved him. After spending a hundred years in the dinghy, he'd have appeared much the same.'

'In better shape than this pineapple can at any rate,' Decker said. The ancient tin found by Brix was now used as a container for their toothbrushes and penknives. Decker had been fascinated by the can, he and Brix jabbering on about how it blew their minds. Out of sheer belligerent spite, Jess said the can had bad vibes and she didn't want it in the tent. When Brix and Decker couldn't care less about vibes, she said it was unhygienic. When Decker said that hygiene in the tent wasn't a battle they were likely to win, she'd argued that dirty socks couldn't give you tetanus. But the tin stayed, balanced on the pots box.

'Everyone loves Dinners,' Brix said, peeling the Band-Aid from a finger to examine the blackened nail she'd hit while hammering in the fencing posts. It would probably come off. 'He's the one everybody imagines as a younger brother. Yikes.'

'Or as a man-version of Bambi,' Decker said. 'And who doesn't love Bambi? Here, let me see.'

The following scene repulsed Jess as she watched him study Brix's nail attentively, and then put on a new plaster. The discussion, however, was interesting.

'In Napps's situation, though,' Jess said with new enthusiasm. 'Could you honestly say that it wouldn't cross your mind?'

They were on the same island, in a similar three-person population. It was a delicate subject with massive gaffe potential. Jess saw Brix raise her eyebrows.

Whatever. Jess wasn't bothered. 'Seriously, you wouldn't consider it?'

'No, I absolutely wouldn't have done it,' Decker said.

'Even if I did, I hope I wouldn't have gone through with it,' Brix said.

'Deck, that's a pretty decisive stance,' Jess said, ignoring Brix. 'Realistic?'

'Yep, I know myself and I wouldn't have.'

Brix was left as a spectator now that Jess had roused from her melancholy silence to dictate the conversation, sparring with Decker over an unwinnable debate.

Jess maintained that you couldn't judge what you were capable of and Decker categorically thought you could. Why pretend otherwise, he said. He wasn't going to go from being one type of guy to being this other completely different type of guy. Jess insisted that there was no way to be certain without being driven to those limits. So could you surprise yourself? Maybe, and that's the thing. Maybe you could.

'No,' Decker countered. 'As I said before, I know myself. It doesn't depend on the context. I'm not suddenly going to make some wildly uncharacteristic decision.'

'My argument is that you haven't been in a bad enough situation to know for definite,' Jess said. 'And you've got to admit that Napps and Millet-Bass were on the island in exceptional circumstances.'

'Sure,' Decker said. 'But I still don't believe it means they can be absolved of responsibility, specifically Napps. He led the expedition, and I think what he did to Dinners tells you a lot about what kind of man he was.'

And evidence of what a bully Napps had been wasn't exactly hard to find. They only had to watch the *Everland* film or read Lawrence's book, or any of the hundreds of other books. He clearly didn't deserve much in the way of sympathy.

'Well, considering how wrong it all went,' Jess said, 'he certainly received his due punishment. In karmic terms, it was meted out to him several times over.'

'No kidding,' Brix said, the brief pause allowing her to get a word in. 'If what goes around comes around, for Napps it came swinging back like the biggest, baddest bastard.'

Even Jess couldn't disagree with this. 'His whole life reduced to one action,' she said. 'Imagine if he could have known how he'd be demonized.'

'Ah,' Decker said. 'That's the peril of being a world-famous explorer. It writes your epitaph. Doesn't matter what else you do or have ever done, the expedition will come to define you. You'll be lionized if it's successful, condemned if it's not.'

'Well, whichever way you dice it, Napps was catastrophically unlucky,' Brix said, making a millimetre space between her finger and thumb. 'He was this close to getting away with it.'

14
April 1913

We don't have long, so let's do the very best we can for Napps and Millet-Bass, Lawrence had told the men assembled on the moonlit beach. It was too cold for the search party to stay on Everland for more than a couple of hours. The minus thirty temperatures meant breath vapour immediately crusted into solid ice on their balaclavas. It felt like their teeth were being screwed out at the root.

While Lawrence's group marched west and Addison's group went east along the beach, Coppers and McValley's team set off towards the cove at the northern end of the island. The men privately cursed Addison. They imagined him receiving a thump to the stomach or a smack on the mouth. Lawrence was envisaged chained in the hold and flogged. It seemed the only purpose of this useless task was to remind every man of his paralysing vulnerability when off the ship and make him cramp with desperation to be back on it. At that moment, they'd never loved anything more in their lives than the leaking old *Kismet*.

'I'd rather sail in a bin, I'd feel safer,' Castle had said that morning at breakfast. The faces around the table in the Officers' Mess were shades of green. The *Kismet*'s tendency to roll in choppy weather could reduce even the hardiest sailor to a seasick mess, and the wind had blown savagely all night. Feeling delicate, the men stared at their bowls and thought the porridge had an oily sheen, toadish. Today the lamps hanging from the ceiling seemed to cast out a repellent orange light.

Even milky tea was as offensive as a cup of petrol. The men drank water in queasily tiny sips and tried to ignore Castle.

Castle's alliance with Napps meant he was now treated with extreme wariness, as if his unpopularity was contagious. Too much fraternization with Castle and they might also start blurting out oppositional statements whenever the Mate's chronic failings were discussed, or spring to Napps's defence with a seemingly mad wish to antagonize the more frightening personalities. And fine, if Castle wanted to act like a gutsy little cockerel kicking its spurs at a pack of angry dogs every time Napps was discussed, then let him. But it was the opposite of what they wanted.

'This wreck will fail us so fast you won't even know you're about to drown until you wake up bobbing by the ceiling,' Castle said, ostensibly to Smith, yet mostly to the audience he knew were only pretending not to listen. 'One day we'll be sitting down to dinner and the floor will just burst in half.'

'That's an awful thing to say,' Smith said.

'No need for thanks,' Castle answered to noises of stifled amusement from around the table. 'You'll be recording this conversation in your diary tonight and the main mast will suddenly crush your bunk.'

The atmosphere lost its chill. It was so easy to forget to dislike Castle.

That the men hadn't slept well or eaten anything at breakfast left them less resistant to the brutal temperatures as they searched. The cove was encircled by a barricade of hundred-foot-high cliffs, its beach strewn with large free-standing stones and sprawling granite outcrops which projected from the ground. Coppers and his team disappeared from sight into the sandy enclosures behind the rocks as they searched, their voices echoing. Giant human silhouettes rose up and stalked across the cliff face as the men passed by with their burning torches.

'We've already looked over there,' Coppers said when he

saw McValley set off alone to the far end of the cove. 'We're about to leave.'

'Who's Second Mate? You?' McValley said.

Coppers was emboldened by his suffering. 'Five minutes, McValley,' he said, swallowing compulsively in reaction to the sensation that his throat was being glazed with ice. He was unable to stop himself visualizing his intestines as a frozen coil of rope.

'Yes, yes,' McValley replied with his typical disregard as he walked away.

The glacier was hidden in the dark somewhere to the left of him, slowly churning itself into the ocean. McValley could hear the gunshot cracks of ice breaking as he dug the toe of his boot into snow which had built against seams in the rock, patting his boot at the drift to spread it and see if there was anything underneath.

Noticing a five-foot-high crescent-shaped fissure in the cliff-side, he went to grope an arm around inside. It was only when he was shoulder-deep in the fissure, his head pressed against the stone wall to maximize his reach, that he thought of the possible outcomes. He was probing the blackness with a grasping hand, expecting what? Perhaps to feel something yield stiffly once his fingers met it. To have his hand close on a face. To brush over eternally open ice-silvered eyes that didn't flinch when they were touched. McValley yanked back his arm, pebbles grinding under him as he scrabbled clear.

'Four minutes,' Coppers said distantly. 'I'm serious, McValley.'

'Yes, I know,' McValley replied, standing very upright. He smiled in an insinuating way. It was an act of self-conscious assuredness for anyone who might be watching. He repeatedly checked the area behind him to be sure no one was. Isn't it funny, his expression said, that I'm even bothering.

Further along trapped snow had amassed in the windshield

of a boulder ridge. Ice scattered as McValley chopped at it with his heel, exposing a darker inorganic texture. Kneeling to investigate an object frozen into the ground, he prised at the loose edges and then methodically levered it out.

McValley grunted his way off his knees with the bag. The leather was rimed and bonded to seal the bag into a flattened pouch. It didn't contain much, just a few sledging biscuits and other miscellaneous bits of food. He prodded through it and found a weathered photograph of a young woman iced to the bottom. Carefully peeling free the photograph, he squinted at the woman. Then he flipped the photograph to peer at a hand-written quote on the reverse.

'We're about to launch the dinghies,' Coppers shouted.

'I said yes! I said yes all right!' McValley called. The flour-fine sleet blew past his legs in vaporous patterns. A granular dusting collected on the photograph.

'You've got thirty seconds, McValley, or I'm coming to fetch you.'

McValley knew the quote. *Hard pounding this, gentlemen. Let's see who can pound longest.* Dinners habitually recited these words from the Duke of Wellington whenever he started to lose a game of cards, which was every single time he played. And McValley thought he recognized the woman as Elizabeth Dinners.

'How could they leave you, Dinners,' McValley said. Then he stopped himself. He was talking to a photograph. He made another insinuating smile to disguise his embarrassment, a per-formance only he benefited from, as no one else was around.

Coppers shouted again from the opposite side of the cove, where he was waiting with all the other men, ready to leave Everland.

'Then goodbye, Napps, wherever you are,' McValley said to the empty cove. 'You may have fooled some, but you never fooled me.'

15

November 2012

D ecker was talking on the radio phone to Dutch Andre, notifying Aegeus of their intention to visit the *Joseph Evelyn* as part of the next day's schedule. He had a technique of repeating questions as he answered them so his audience could follow the conversation.

'How's Jess doing? Yes, she's amazing. Yes, Brix is amazing.' Decker grinned at Brix. 'And how am I doing? Well, hm. Not bad.'

He laughed at whatever Andre said. 'You ask if I'm okay, and I'd say okay is the wrong word. A better word would be mangled.'

Brix stopped smiling. 'You know what?' she said. 'I think I left my journal in the work tent.'

Both Decker and Jess now joked about their collection of bruises and sprains. Muscles never got the chance to fully recover before equipment had to be loaded or unloaded again, or some other exhausting duty had to be done. And despite trying her best, Brix's inexperience meant she didn't have that shorthand knowledge which got jobs completed swiftly, with minimum fuss. She needed guidance, but it wasn't always convenient to hang around teaching her when there were a million things to do. So while her colleagues ended each day shattered, Brix remained embarrassingly preserved. She was very conscious of being the least trashed. Although Decker was too kind to ever mention it, she was also aware that her share of the workload still had to be done, and it was he who did it.

Jess had been motioning for Decker to give her the phone the instant she realized it was Andre at the other end. She practically snatched the receiver from him.

'Ha-ha!' Jess said, oblivious to anything except Andre. 'Aha-ha!'

'Where are you going?' Decker said, confused by Brix's sudden tenseness. When she didn't answer he threw a filthy sock at her leg. 'Hey, what's wrong?'

Brix was already crawling out of the tent. 'Nothing, I'll be back in a second,' she said with the emphatic merriness of the secretly upset. Then Decker understood.

'Film night?' Jess screeched into the phone. 'No! I can't believe I'm missing it. Have you got any plans?'

'Brix, I didn't mean—' Decker glanced quickly at Jess to check she wasn't listening. 'We're a small team with a lot to do. That's all I meant. The "mangled" comment wasn't about you.'

'I'll only be a minute,' Brix said, not looking at him. 'My journal's in the work tent and I should probably get it.' It wasn't a convincing lie. The diary was in the right-hand pocket of her fleece, which was balled up beside her sleeping bag among the other clothes.

'Oh, Kimiko, huh? Sounds nice. Cosy,' Jess said with a strange laugh.

Sitting on the crate in the work tent, Brix shut her eyes and pressed her cold fingers against them. It was as refreshing as if she'd applied slices of chilled cucumber. 'You're useless,' she said to herself, which was also kind of refreshing. It was cathartic to feel so shamelessly miserable. Whether or not Decker admitted it, Brix worried she was a burden. Taking a long, wallowing mud bath in despair, she thought about her ineptitude. She was a needy, revolting baby of a woman who couldn't even return with the stupid diary she'd allegedly gone to fetch, as she hadn't put on the stupid fleece. Because self-pity isn't interesting for long, Brix gradually bored herself into the state of empty-brained gormlessness that comes after a torrential outburst.

She'd been in the tent for quarter of an hour when a voice outside said, 'Knock, knock.' Decker's face appeared in the doorway. 'Found the journal?'

Brix wiped her eyes with a sleeve and sat up straighter. 'Yes, found it.'

Decker looked at her empty hands. 'Cool.'

At first Brix decided she'd make it easy on them both by acting as though the past fifteen minutes hadn't happened. Then she decided this was a wasted opportunity to talk openly with Decker. There was also a residual trace of self-pity. 'I don't blame you if you're sick of me.'

'Brix.' He leant his head to one side in the way of the sorrowfully misunderstood. 'I'm not sick of you. Not for a moment.'

'Jess is, and she's got a lot less of a reason to be annoyed than you have.'

'Jess is a hard-ass,' Decker said. 'Don't let her get to you, chief.'

'Hard-ass' was an overly forgiving description of Jess's attitude in Brix's opinion. 'Would it be simpler to explain the situation to her?' She'd considered telling Jess the whole story, out of spite as much as anything. Just to see Jess's reaction.

'Truthfully?' Decker made a reluctant noise. 'No. Don't say a word about it.' He crossed his arms tightly, his hands clamped in his armpits, and breathed out in a low whistle. 'Well, I'm guessing you're as cold as I am. So should we stay here and die of hypothermia, or do you want to come back with me?'

Ideally there'd have been a third option which allowed Brix to stay alive and remain in the work tent indefinitely. Since there wasn't, she gave her eyes another wipe and followed him out.

Everland was as silent and barren as usual the next morning.

Snow fell thickly, its sound-dampening quality similar to high altitude pressure in the inner ear.

The *Joseph Evelyn*'s transformation from dinghy to carcass was still in its very infant stages. It would be the work of centuries to strip the frame to its skeleton and wear it into collapse. Protected by the Antarctic Heritage Trust, the boat would remain on Everland as one of the world's most famous but least seen cultural artefacts. One edge of the upturned *Joseph Evelyn* was partially elevated by a large rock to create an opening wide enough for someone to squeeze through. Brix remembered Captain Lawrence's book. Along with maps and photographs, Lawrence had included some illustrations from his journal. One was of Dinners being rescued from the dinghy by lots of identically posed men. It wasn't a great sketch, as Lawrence could only draw people standing upright, side-on. Yet now Brix was here in the same place, she could visualize those sailors shouting for Napps, their boots pounding in the dark.

'Strange atmosphere, isn't there,' she said pointlessly to Jess. 'Evocative.'

If Jess heard, she didn't respond. She crouched to peer into the empty dinghy.

The cove was just beyond the dinghy, a distance of perhaps forty metres. Like the ruins of a fortress wall, the cliffs were notched and crumbled, arching round to meet the ocean. The beach was cut into sections by mounds of rock, some car-sized, some three-metre-tall hillocks, all studded with limpets. Huge columnar stones, tall as the cliffs, had been isolated from the headland by millennia of erosion. Now standing alone, they resembled battered monuments. The columns stationed closest to the tide were ringed with trenches of seawater, rags of black seaweed drifting beneath the surface. Fur seals colonized this beach every year, although there were none to be seen. The cove's melancholy beauty was compounded by its history of missing and abandoned men. With enough time, the emotional impact of any tragedy becomes fossilized. The wrongness or sadness can still be appreciated, but it can no longer be felt. However, being at the cove undid that remove. The men's pain became too easy for Brix to imagine, which meant it became too real to disregard.

She'd given herself the job of documenting their first venture to the *Joseph Evelyn*. Since the bear-paw mittens she wore over her woollen gloves were useless for fiddly tasks, Brix took off the mittens and stuffed them in a coat pocket. Unzipping her bag with hands that were already numb, she removed the camera and checked the battery was charged. She thought she heard something fall to the ground as she yanked the mittens from her pocket, which was crammed with the normal junk, from tissues and glucose energy sweets to ChapStick and a spare camera battery. Brix was searching to see if she'd dropped anything when Decker called across.

'What do you guys make of the rope?'

Although the dinghy was too far from the sea's reach to need securing, a frayed rope ran from the boat's gunwale to a nearby stone embankment, where it was tied to one of the rocks. Decker had clambered up the embankment and was perched on the top, examining the knots.

'Does the placement of this rope make sense to you?' he asked.

'Maybe it's a guide?' Jess answered.

'To where?' he said, climbing down again. 'Why guide yourself to a dead-end?'

'Has something been left there?' Brix said. 'Perhaps for safekeeping?'

Decker's head was visible as he scouted around behind the embankment. 'Nope. Nada.'

The natural metabolism of time was suspended in Antarctica. There were stories about the eerie spectre of domestic life found in expedition huts after decades of vacancy. The galley would be discovered stocked with immaculately preserved food, a batch of pristine yet historic scones cooling for ever on a rack by the stove. In the riotous scramble of the ship's arrival an officer's reading had been interrupted and his book was open on the table beside the salt cellar and a bread roll with one bite missing. Cutlery lay haphazardly around unfinished meals, and coats hung in the porch above a messy line of boots. Jumpers with holes darned in mismatched wool lay crumpled on the bunks. There was no dust and no decay. The process of deterioration was on such an infinitely low heat that the butter still held knife marks.

In these places the past didn't linger but invaded with a clap of immediacy. The thirty-two-thousand-year-old Chauvet cave paintings in France, and Brix's Egyptian mummies, possessed a similar type of magic. All those remote, long-extinct people who never seemed as real or vivid or loud materialized to cause a tremor of recognition. It was uncanny, and drew something shivering and electric out of modern minds. As with every shock to apathy, it briefly allowed your own death to come close enough to speak in your ear.

Decker stood beside Jess as Brix balanced her camera on a rucksack and set the self-timer to take a photograph of them in front of the *Joseph Evelyn*.

'Part fungus, part plant, with a life cycle so slow it's immortal by our standards.' Decker gestured towards the lichen on a stone near the dinghy. Big as a monster pumpkin, the stone had a large orange doily of lichen crusted over the top. 'Virtually unchanged from when Napps saw it,' he said.

'Really?' Jess said.

'Yup. With around a millimetre of growth each century, this lichen is thousands of years old.'

Decker went on to explain that, if you thought about it, their lives were little more than a flash of light in comparison.

Look at us against the lichen's permanence, he'd said, and we are what? Bang, gone in the same minute we arrived.

'That's sort of depressing,' Jess said.

'Yeah, you bet it is.'

Brix ran to get into the shot. The timer was blinking red when Decker suddenly ruined the photograph by bending to pick something up which was lying half buried in the snow.

When Brix saw the set of quad keys in his hand, she experienced a pressure drop of shame through her chest. Decker's kindly expression somehow made her feel worse.

'Doubt I need to elaborate on what a bad idea it is to lose your keys,' he said, almost as a jokey aside, as if this wasn't Brix's mistake but a screwball fluke they'd laugh about later. Then he pretended to reflect. 'Tell you what. New rules. From now on we'll keep your keys in Jess's bag, with Jess's keys. Good plan, uh?'

Despite hating the plan, and prepared to store the keys in her mouth if it meant she didn't have to give them to Jess, Brix grudgingly accepted.

With a withering smile, Jess paused what she was doing to receive Brix's keys. She'd swept clear a patch of snow at the dinghy's entrance, and had been wedging pebbles in the sand to form a discreet letter J.

'Vandalism!' Decker said.

'Oh, chill out. They're tiny,' Jess answered, starting to make the next initial.

J B D: it was a piece of graffiti to commemorate the three of them, who like Napps and his men would be the only things here to vanish perfectly.

S itting outside on an oilcan, Dinners posed one bandaged hand behind his awful haircut. 'How do I look?'

Napps stared at him in the manner of someone tasked to assess fire damage on an already worthless property.

'Improved,' Millet-Bass said. 'Best-looking man on the island.'

Everland had grown increasingly silent as the remaining animals continued to migrate for winter. With each passing day the shriek and cackle of the gulls and the seals' dull barks became more infrequent, muted and dispersed. The sun had diminished with the sound. Dawn now came at around nine o'clock and dusk fell by mid-afternoon. For the short period in between, a horizontal light flared across Everland which caused crazily elongated shadows and burnished everything in golden, almost unbearably nostalgic colours.

Dinners let out a screech as Millet-Bass lifted him off the oilcan and sat him on a blanket.

Napps was not a talented barber. He'd said, fetch the puppy, and Dinners had been carried from the tent so Napps could scissor haphazard chunks from his filthy hair. Now it was Millet-Bass's turn to have his wild head-nest refashioned. He nervously balanced himself on the oilcan.

'It's not a haircut if you remove the hair with the skin attached,' Millet-Bass said.

'I'd talk less,' Napps said, hacking at Millet-Bass's odd red beard.

'It's technically a scalping. None of the skin,' Millet-Bass said. Then he released a grunt of surprise. 'Ha, we've got a visitor.'

Napps and Dinners turned to see a new iceberg in the bay.

While the smaller bergs rode past Everland in a few days, the larger ones were more permanent occupants. It was an unavoidable element of human nature that the men had bestowed the resident lumps with various individual qualities.

'There, you see it? Coming up next to the Little Sisters,' Millet-Bass said about three bergs clustered together. 'To the left of Mr. Popular.'

Christened by Napps, Mr. Popular's battered appearance reminded him of a sailor with a prodigious talent for causing fights. Even the Sunday service ended with chairs flung across the room when Mr. Popular was in the congregation.

'Eighty foot high?' Dinners said, guessing at the size of the berg. 'Ninety?'

'Possibly more.' Millet-Bass shut an eye and tried to estimate. 'A hundred foot, maybe? Certainly the biggest yet to take a detour and pay us a call. Not such a pretty guest, either.'

Facing the island from a central point, the berg had eroded into an unusual shape. It tapered down at the front, resembling an overturned pyramid with its point lopped off, and was horned with two distinctive turrets.

'What shall we call it?' Dinners said, admiring the horns. This practice of naming a berg was a shamanistic ritual masquerading as inconsequential fun. The men didn't admit to it. They shrugged as if it was meaningless to them. But every berg had to be named or something terrible would happen. It had to be done immediately.

'I once knew a bull which looked like that,' Millet-Bass said. 'It belonged to a friend's father. Thanked him for filling its trough one day by trampling his arm into fifty pieces. He tried to chain it to a post but it bashed through into the farmyard, the post clattering behind. He threw a metal bucket at it. Might have thrown a fried egg for the good it did him.'

'Very dramatic,' Napps said aridly, to crush Millet-Bass's story. He sensed it would to link into some type of superstitious sailor's nonsense if he let it continue.

'And the bull got even friendlier when it smelt cows,' Millet-Bass said. 'It would scream and gore holes in the barn walls. My friend told me the reason his father didn't shoot the bull was because it sired enormous calves. But I heard he'd had a go once, blasted a chunk out of its leg, and the bull just swerved round and came at him like a meteor.'

'So we'll call it the Angry Bull?' Dinners asked.

'I didn't trust that bull, and I don't trust this berg. It's a bad omen,' Millet-Bass said with the irrationality Napps had entirely predicted.

'Absurd.' The way Napps exhaled showed how severely his patience was being tested. 'The island isn't alive, Millet-Bass. It doesn't have a macabre charisma.'

'Taurus,' Millet-Bass said to Dinners. 'The bull was called Taurus.'

'That's an ideal name for the berg,' Dinners said. His patchily shorn head turned to look from one man to the other, hoping for signs of agreement. He was also hoping for a different conversation which wasn't about bad omens.

'And it isn't any more stable than the original Taurus,' Millet-Bass told Napps. 'It's moving towards the supply cove.'

Napps dismissed the idea, saying that such a large berg would be beached in the shallower waters surrounding the island before it got anywhere near the cove.

Their dispute was interrupted by Dinners crying, 'There, there, there!'

The landscape was hallucinating itself. Fata Morgana had replicated the scenery as a ghost surface mirroring the ocean. Each iceberg was roofed by a phantom image which rose and slurred into immense hourglass forms. An inverted twin reared from Taurus and grew huge above its brother, straining against the tethers of the horns. These carnivals were fleeting, and with the abruptness of lightning or splitting glass or a gas explosion everything unearthly was gone. The existent world was left with a post-party drabness. After the spectral distortion, the reality seemed leaden.

'At least I know you both saw it,' Dinners said. 'You definitely did, not just me.'

Of course they'd seen it, weren't they right here beside him?

Dinners nodded embarrassedly and said he was stupid. No, not stupid, what he meant was impressionable. 'Everland plays tricks on me. That's why I asked.'

'Tricks,' Napps said, wanting a better explanation.

'Ah, don't worry about it,' Millet-Bass said quickly.

The hint was completely lost on Dinners. 'Well, the stones want to become animals whenever I'm alone. And the shadows waste my time with funny pranks. It makes me wary and so careful not to fall for these tricks that I can occasionally take against the wrong thing.' He had an example which would amuse them. 'Like yesterday!' He covered his eyes in a performance of comic shame. 'I refused to believe in Millet-Bass. It was the tent flapping, I was absolutely sure. But what language the tent used!'

'Then keep quiet and don't make me repeat it,' said Millet-Bass, giving Dinners a sociable yet forceful nudge before he could say anything else.

Napps didn't respond. He watched the fading tide marks, and then watched the waves roll in across the shore to darken them again.

17

November 2012

We definitely couldn't hear it from this distance before,' Decker said. He glanced sideways at Brix. Something was obviously bothering her.

'Um hm. Louder,' Brix said in the same noncommittal tone she'd been using for the past hour.

As the penguin colony grew, so did their noise. The increase in volume was noticeable as they trekked back into the Adélies' southern bay, hunched against the minus-eight winds. Brix didn't know how to tell Decker what she'd realized, pretty much from the moment they'd left the camp. In a crazy way, she kept hoping she was mistaken, as if the situation might magically resolve itself if she regretted it forcefully enough. That this had never once happened to her in her entire life didn't stop her from trying to believe it still might.

Around a thousand Adélies had now arrived in the bay, and their lively presence made Everland seem like less of a desolate hole, as did the brighter-skied periods. That morning had seen the sun emerge for the first time. Although it was nothing more than a pale beach ball glowing through the smog-thick clouds, the appearance of any sunlight, however weak, automatically reduced the landscape's bleakness by at least a third. What had previously been as visually unappealing as a scrapyard became almost attractive. The three humans, however, had become far uglier. They were wrinkled and unwashed, with ratted hair and mottled faces. Fingers and toes were always an inflamed shade of red, and throbbed with their own hot pulse at night.

'Sucks to be him,' Jess said about a nearby Adélie which was standing guard in the wrong direction, unaware that another penguin was looting rocks from his nest.

'That guy? His problems are only going to get worse,' Decker said while he began to unpack the microchipping equipment from his bag. 'This whole season is a monumental headache for him.'

Just say it, thought Brix as she watched Decker. Just tell him, don't wait for him to find out, she said to herself, and then continued to observe silently.

'Because if he's lucky,' Decker continued, 'he and his mate will hatch two chicks, one of which will die, as they can't feed them both. He'll routinely travel up to two hundred and fifty kilometres out to sea to gather krill for the remaining chick, but since the vessel for his genes is essentially a fluffy snack, he'll probably return to find it's been eaten. Even if his chick survives long enough to fledge, there's an eighty per cent chance it won't make it beyond two years of age. And they breed at three, earliest.'

Jeez. Jess made a face. Her previous field-trips had involved climatology, tectonic shift and glaciology. They were very sterile, non-bloody subjects, and she was learning the grisly realities of a biological research trip. Such as for example gulls pecking chicks to death, which Decker informed her she could expect to witness daily.

'Oh, trust me, you get used to it,' he said, passing the chipping gun to Brix. Jess made no effort to disguise how obvious it was to her that Brix had never operated a chipping gun. This fact was underlined when Decker handed Brix a box of microchips. Instead of loading a chip, or doing anything useful, or even pretending the equipment was familiar, she just stood there cluelessly.

The gun was a small plastic device, of the same type used by veterinarians to microchip domestic pets. Once a chip was slotted into the shaft of the thick hypodermic needle which attached to the nozzle, it could be injected into a bird's abdomen by squeezing a trigger. Although being grabbed and stabbed wasn't especially nice for the Adélie, the procedure was over in seconds and the microchipped bird was then identified whenever it waddled through the automated gateway. The aim was to get fifty birds chipped during this session, which wouldn't overly disturb the colony.

So here it came. The moment of awfulness. Decker was rooting through the bag with a new desperation and Brix had the urge to offset the pain of his imminent discovery by biting into her tongue, or bending her thumb the wrong way. Whether imagined or not, it seemed to her that dread had a particular taste. Something chemical, like hairspray. This taste only got more potent as Decker upturned the bag, emptying its contents out on to the snow, and then sat back on his heels.

'Ah, shit.' He thumped the palm of one hand against his forehead. '*Shit.*'

If Jess had looked at Brix, she'd have seen her slack, bloodless expression. But she was peering over Decker's shoulder into the bag, trying to spot the problem.

Jess nudged him with a boot. 'Deck?'

'Seems I've forgotten—Sorry, I haven't brought enough microchips.'

His performance was so convincing it was as if he really believed it. Snow had drifted up around the quads overnight, and since Decker couldn't say that it was far quicker if he and Jess dug out the bikes alone, he'd asked Brix to fetch some microchips from the work tent. There was a box of chips in the rucksack already, he'd said, so could she bung in another couple of boxes? But in her determination to be useful, Brix had decided to do more. As Jess was busy, Brix had adopted the role of field assistant and loaded the sledge herself. She'd bagged spare clothing and hauled across their sleeping bags, then carried the primus stove and the medical case. It had felt so good to be a valuable person, except she'd left the microchips in the tent. And by doing that, she'd hijacked the purpose of the entire day.

Hearing Decker say, 'My fault, my fault,' and pound his head again, forced Jess to turn and contemplate the ocean with hard eyes. The situation was too insulting to comment on.

Brix said, 'Maybe we could use the tags we've got, then—'

He nodded as if she were reading his mind. 'And then do the rest later, exactly. Yes, good plan.'

'So, okay,' Jess said icily. 'Great. Shall we start chipping?'

'Yes. Just, uh.' Decker cleared his throat. There was an unspoken code that 'taking a reconnaissance' meant wanting to be alone, and he put it into operation. 'What I'm thinking is that I'd better take a quick recce of the site first,' he said, striding away at a speed which wasn't aggressive, yet was purposeful enough to deter any efforts to stop him.

The southern bay's transformation from penguin village to penguin metropolis was fully under way. As the Adélie numbers swelled, their circular pebble nests began to fill the beach, all built just beyond reach of the snapping beaks of their neighbours. The increasing density of the population also had another effect, as the penguins' krill-rich diet resulted in pinkish excrement which stank of ammonia and stained everything pink, including the birds themselves. Most Adélies now had a dirty bib marking their white chests, and leg feathers like a little pair of pink shorts.

Decker wasn't exactly angry with Brix as he marched between the nest-marker poles, weaving around the penguins hunched over their eggs. He didn't blame her necessarily, but he'd needed a minute to rage aloud at the weight of his responsibilities. There was no part of the day which didn't require a maximum investment of energy from him, starting from the second he woke up and lasting until the second he shoved himself back into his sleeping bag at night. They were a three-person team, and although Jess was an obvious asset, despite Brix's best efforts she wasn't making anywhere near enough of a contribution. The truth was that everything went at the pace of the least skilled person, which meant every job Brix did took twice the time and twice the labour, as Decker had to first explain it to her and then check she'd done it correctly. And he was beginning to suspect he'd made a massive mistake.

Because Antarctica was so unforgiving to the human body, it wasn't possible to attain Decker's level of fieldwork expertise without it having a physical impact. His knees and back had taken an absolute hammering in the twenty years he'd been leading expeditions. He'd torn muscles, fractured bones, knackered ligaments, snapped the tendon in a finger. There was his famous drop into a crevasse. And the ghosts of these old injuries now returned to ache in a non-specific yet troublesome way. So Decker had decided Everland would be his last trip. He was fifty-four, he was tired, and he was done with roughing it in tents for months on end. But here was the difficulty. Leaving this part of his life behind was not as easy to accept as he'd thought. It caused a whole mess of emotions related to his pride and identity. Which perhaps explained why he'd ignored how this expedition differed from his other expeditions of the past five years, and had agreed to it anyway.

What am I doing, Decker asked himself. All those trips had been based in familiar territory, such as Cape Athena, and had involved groups of eight or more. Why did I do this, he said to the horizon. I could be at home.

Without Decker, Brix and Jess were reduced to prickly silence. Because Jess's mute hatred was worse than her scorn, and any conversation was better than none, Brix eventually said, 'I've been having the weirdest dream. It happens like this every time. A sound wakes me, and I think it's someone shouting outside. Except I'm not awake, because then I open my eyes and there's this other thing in the tent. I'm not sure what, something big, but I—'

'Dream-talk is the dullest thing in the world.'

'You're in it,' Brix said. 'Decker is, too.'

'And do you, in this dream, remember to pack the microchips?' Jess gave her a sarcastic look. 'You can't really think I believe it's Decker who forgot them.'

'Jess . . .' Brix stared down at the chipping gun. 'There's got to be an easier way for us to spend two months together.'

'An easier way?' Instead of addressing Brix, Jess directed her speech to an invisible jury somewhere out to sea. 'Well, there's the difference between us. Do you have any idea how hard I've worked for this opportunity? This is the culmination of years of effort for me. So I'd say I've earned my place. And Decker's been leading expeditions for years, so that's his place earned. Which brings me to my question. How come you're here, Brix? What did you ever do to earn it?'

Brix was not only regretting the conversation, but the entire day. If I choked to death on a stone, she thought, that would be less painful than having this discussion. Or if a freak wave rose out of nowhere and drowned me. It was too late to back out, though. Regardless of Decker's advice, she began to tell Jess about her marriage.

She'd spent a whole year making inexplicable decisions as Joe's affair continued despite the wall-shaking arguments and teary pledges and constant grinding loneliness. They'd battled through another degrading eleven months before Brix realized that of Joe's two relationships, it was hers which was finished. So then she'd done a whole lot more crying, and a fair amount of ranting and drinking, and said enough to worry her friends, one of whom was Angie, the superhuman friend.

Brix had first met Angie at university, where they'd been a pair of science geeks with nose rings and badly dyed hair. Angie had since transformed into a sleekly groomed powerhouse, becoming a director at Aegeus. She chaired the committee on field expedition selections, including the Everland centenary. Her relationship with Brix obviously wasn't something she'd publicized, and the two women appeared to be no more than polite acquaintances whilst at the base. Angie was better at maintaining this pretence than Brix was, because Doctor Angela Pennell was brilliant at everything.

It was Angie who helped Brix pack and then unpack into the new south London flat she'd helped her to find and then decorate. It was Angie who staged one-woman coups on Brix's resistance to do anything, and took Brix to the pub or the cinema, or to a restaurant, or just came over to hang out. And it was Angie who listened to the repetitive, emotionally exhaustive monologues in bars and cafés and late-night phone calls and marathon weeping sessions at kitchen tables. She listened through long walks and coastal daytrips and the entire duration of several weekend mini-breaks and finally in a tapas restaurant in Barcelona, on a wasted summery afternoon, where she said to Brix, 'Okay, stop. Here's what we're going to do.'

'She got you selected.' Jess smiled unpleasantly. 'Which means that he knows all about it,' she said, watching Decker walk back towards them.

'Yes,' Brix said. Except Decker didn't just know. He'd played an integral part.

18
March 1913

The man had said, 'Want this?' Napps couldn't have been more than six years old as he stood on the jetty, watching fishermen unload the teeming crab baskets. The baskets were ancient-looking things, with furred ropes and some natty contraption which locked the crabs inside. He could see them through the bars, flat brown shapes swarming over each other with their claws raised. He could hear shells clatter when the baskets were lifted. The man had tugged out a magnificently sized crab, its articulated legs roving at surprised angles in the air, and offered it to the boy. 'As a treat, you want this?' Yes he did. 'Give it to your mother to deal with, she'll love it.' Perhaps not so much, but Napps knew he'd be able to talk his mother round. She'd only have to look at the crab to be convinced it should live with them for ever. Then the fisherman killed the crab by forcing a screwdriver into its mouth. Napps had silently reached out to accept the clammy body which was handed to him, holding it in his arms like a dead baby.

He'd vowed then, at six, that he would murder anyone who hurt an animal in front of him again. He would protect all animals.

Napps had then gone on to break his own vow thousands of times. He'd hurt scores of animals himself. By joining the Navy he'd chosen a career which meant brutality was an unavoidable part of life. Worse still, his revulsion for harming creatures had never diminished. If anything it got more extreme with age. The same boy was there shrieking his horror whenever Napps's job required him to go against his fierce love of animals, which it did constantly, in hideous ways, such as with the pony Nelson.

Death was integral to the success of Antarctic expeditions. The dogs and ponies were tools, with every one of them starting as an engine and ending as fuel. The dogs were cannibalized by other dogs, held down by the men to have their hearts pierced with a long blade before being dismembered into sinewy chunks and fed to the pack. The ponies were fed to both man and dog, shot and stored as meat after they'd been worn into devastation over one epic outward trek. And so it was with Nelson, the pony who made low welcoming rumbles whenever he saw Napps. Small friendly Nelson who'd willingly sloughed alongside Napps for months.

Because the pony had to be shot, and because he was unable to bear the idea of anyone else doing it, and because he believed Nelson deserved the real, heartbroken sorrow which only he, Napps, would feel at his slaughter, Napps dealt with it himself. He'd led his stumbling, emaciated pony a long way from the group in order to give the task some privacy and also to hide the fact he was about to burst into the wrenching sobs of a child. He'd put his hand on Nelson's shaggy cheek, the pony's ears twitching at his voice while he told him he was a good pony, one of the greats, and that he would be missed. He was a heroic little pony, Napps reassured him, barely able to speak, who should be very proud of his contribution to the team. And then, with a gunshot, Nelson was nothing at all. The men had cut him and buried the pieces to freeze as they did with every ruined pony. They'd stripped him like a bed.

So when Millet-Bass reasoned, 'Look, taking the fur seals won't matter. We'll be hastening their decline, nothing more than that,' these two seminally affecting deaths shimmered into view. The crab and the pony hovered beside Napps while he said weakly, 'They might be able to regenerate if we left them.'

'Napps, these are *living ghosts*,' Millet-Bass said. 'What's left, a handful? Nowhere near enough for them to recover.'

He could practically feel the wet crab in his arms again. 'I suppose an argument could always be made in favour of hope.'

They'd walked to the northern end of the island and Millet-Bass spotted the Everland fur seals first. He'd pointed to the dark blimps clustered together near the cove and said, 'There! Twenty at a guess?' The sight of twenty edible objects caused him to rhapsodize on the subject of meat. It didn't concern Millet-Bass that fur seals had been hunted so insatiably they were presumed extinct, or that these were clearly miraculous seals. What concerned him was his own annihilation. Thumping the handle of his ice axe on his palm, he talked of blubber and iron-rich organs, and the steaks he could almost taste, and his new idea of mixing brains into the hoosh.

Napps listened without reaction. He was exceptionally good at hiding his secret. Although the prospect of butchering seals made him ill to his soul, his face remained placid. He might have even appeared keen. It was an expression honed over years of leading men into peaceful seal colonies. To Napps, no matter how essential the need for meat, hunting always carried a sense of profound loss. So the idea of hammering out the last few surviving fur seals on earth seemed like an act of unspeakable evil. He'd be forcing a screwdriver into the mouth of a whole species with his own hands.

Napps continued to remain placid-faced as Millet-Bass told him his argument in favour of hope was a ton of horse manure. You couldn't live on baseless sentimentality, he said, and you also couldn't inflict damage on something which had already been destroyed. He'd also got a theory of his own. Hope was fine, it spoke of faith; faith was nice, it spoke of justice; yet we all learn, don't we, Napps. We learn that not everything true is fair.

'And you've never had a problem with killing seals before,' Millet-Bass said, his smile suggesting that Napps's enjoyment of shattering animal heads was an open secret they'd long indulged.

During the expedition's first summer, a group of men had been sent ashore to restock the *Kismet*'s supplies. Under Lawrence's command and Napps's guidance, they had been instructed to take bulls if possible, lone cows if not, certainly no cows with dependent young, certainly no pups. But with weeks of pent-up energy to use and only minutes to apply it, the mood had become hedonistic. The sound of bludgeoned flesh and screams rang into the dense blue mist. No one was thinking of the instructions, they were thinking of sport, and if McValley realized the cow he went to strike was shielding a pup, it hadn't stopped him. While McValley hauled her corpse off to dump with the catch, Napps had seen the baby seal struggling after its mother. Since the depravity of using his club on a pup was overridden by the greater cruelty of leaving it, what he did next he did out of compassion. A scurrilous laugh had come from behind him. '*Well, well, well,*' McValley said, returning before Napps could complete the dispatch.

The sensible thing would have been to clarify the situation immediately. What Napps should have done was vehemently brand the offence on to its rightful owner. Except he'd been too saddened by the pup to think clearly, and to explain the situation later seemed pointless and, as time went on, increasingly petty. It felt demeaning to even try and justify his actions. Of course, if Napps had known then just how vengeful Second Mate McValley was, how gleefully opportunistic with any weapon against him, he'd have reconsidered. Better yet, Napps thought, he'd have left McValley to die of his fucking scurvy when he had the chance. What happened instead was that rumours of the pup and its unlawful death circulated around the ship until even the Captain was aware of it. 'Killed a pup, did you, Napps?' Lawrence said in the artificially languid tone he used to stop himself spewing out rage. 'I specifically order that pups be avoided, yet you beat one to mince. Tell me, what am I to make of that?'

At this point, in the middle of one of their mini-wars, Napps hadn't cared what Lawrence made of it. Lawrence's jealous insecurities about the First Mate had reared up again, so if he wanted to use the pup as ballast to his mad notion that Napps would willingly debase himself in order to undermine the Captain, then let him. It was for these stubborn reasons that Napps never refuted the claims against him.

'We'll take one seal,' Napps said to Millet-Bass, who was thinking of liver and fried heart and hot strips of blubber. 'Is that clear? One seal will provide more than enough meat to last us the few days until the *Kismet* arrives.'

The fur seals had brown otter-like faces, with long moustaches of whiskers and tiny drooping earflaps. Unaccustomed to people, they watched Napps approach a female at the edge of the group. She was young, about three years old, and had probably been born on this beach. Napps was swamped by the same familiar heartache as he looked down at her, knowing that to kill her was to destroy something perfect. Although the seal couldn't understand him, he hoped the tone of his voice expressed kindness so she wouldn't be afraid. I'll do it quickly, he promised her, like he promised every animal. Swear to God, you won't feel it, I'll make it painless. And he did, using his axe to deliver a mercifully efficient blow.

Alarmed noises from the other seals became a louder chorus of frightened barks. Napps turned to see they'd broken into a lumbering gallop, followed by Millet-Bass. Despite Napps's instructions, the semi-tame seals had proved to be too much of a temptation for him, and the body of a second dead seal lay on the snow.

'*Enough,*' Napps called. 'That's an order.'

Millet-Bass either didn't hear or chose to act like he hadn't. The mysterious light contorted his outline and he appeared to run up into the sky on a translucent glass band suspended above the ground.

'I said enough,' Napps shouted furiously at him. 'I said one seal was plenty.'

Millet-Bass threw his axe in frustration, vigorously disagreeing that one or even two seals were anywhere near enough. It made no sense that Napps would sabotage their chance to eat fresh kidneys for every meal.

'What's gained by letting the seals go?' Millet-Bass demanded. 'So they can die out of their own accord? Your pity would be better spent on us, your men.'

Napps answered that Millet-Bass should stop whinging. They had now two seals to flense, double what he'd sanctioned, and sullenly watching while Napps tried to deal with a carcass on his own was not a helpful attitude, and frankly Napps expected better.

Millet-Bass hissed a few criticisms under his breath about *Napps's* attitude and *Napps's* sullenness and *frankly* Napps couldn't peel an egg, so *frankly* the idea of him flensing was hilarious. It was so satisfying, Millet-Bass forgot that he hated Everland and thought again of his excellent recipe for mixing brains into the hoosh.

The strenuous business of disassembling a carcass was the work of two men or more. First the seal's skin needed to be sliced and removed with its inconceivably thick mat of blubber attached. Slabs of flesh were carved from each animal and buried there on the beach to freeze. Heaps of entrails steamed alongside two yielding livers. The snow was covered with bloodied footprints and slushy quagmires of blood, and trailing hose lines of blood, and the thin crosshatched streaks drawn as they wiped their blood-sodden gloves. What bothered Millet-Bass wasn't the stomach-turning gore but their lack of the proper flensing knives with robust handles. These slender clasp-knives were useless and their hands kept threatening to skid down on to the blade. You needed something to hold on to, Millet-Bass complained, not this smooth little thing which was so ripe for accident they might as well just sever a couple of fingers now and get it over with. In tedious detail he told Napps exactly how he planned to bind the handle of his knife to give it more grip, Napps's reply being, 'See?'

'See?' he repeated, because he hadn't been listening to Millet-Bass. He'd said it in answer to his own internal conversation about how much brighter life would be the second this loathsome job was finished. Now it was, he was immensely cheerful. 'See?' he said, gesturing at Taurus, their pet iceberg, which had drifted noticeably closer to the island. 'Our mascot is bringing us luck already.'

L isten up. Fur seal interaction is not the cute gig you
think it is,' Decker said to Brix and Jess. Behind them,
slumped around the *Joseph Evelyn* cove like an airport
lounge full of passengers waiting for a delayed flight, were
approximately two hundred fur seals. These were the newest
arrivals to Everland's annual breeding festival. The cove was
perfect for the seals, as the large reefs which barricaded the
shore formed sheltered nursery pools for pups, and the vari-
ously sized rocks covering the beach provided ideal platforms
for basking. Seals sat propped up on their front flippers, their
heads raised to the sky in a manner of curious haughtiness.

'You wouldn't believe how fast they run, and that's without
anything resembling a proper leg,' Decker said. 'Their acceler-
ation rate is mind-blowing. One minute they're lolled harm-
lessly on the beach, the next you're swerving in front of a four-
hundred-pound hooligan with your thigh slashed open.'

He was hoping for more of a reaction than Brix's attentive
nod and Jess's terse, 'Um hm.' It seemed to Decker that he
wasn't only leading the expedition, but was also in charge of
generating all conversation. If Brix and Jess hadn't liked each
other before, they had been at least civil, and then some kind
of social permafrost had descended for reasons he didn't
understand. He couldn't even read their expressions because
they were wearing large, ski-mask-type sunglasses.

The temperature had risen to minus one degree and the sun
now was a constant glaring presence. It made the tent glow a

nuclear orange throughout the night, and reflected from the snow throughout the day, which made working without sunglasses impossible. Their faces had become a patchwork of different shades, with brown cheeks, pale hat-screened foreheads, and whitely goggled eyes above noses the colour of jerky.

Jess held her hand out to Brix. 'Keys,' she said abruptly.

Decker's rule was the experiment in tyranny Brix had predicted it would be. If she absentmindedly pocketed her quad keys, Jess reacted as though she had desecrated a grave. Requesting the keys from Jess meant watching Jess huff through the same indignant performance, slowly searching her bag and then slowly passing the over the keys, like Brix was robbing her at knifepoint. They both knew the whole obnoxious process was Jess's way of punishing Brix for the Everland selection.

Jess hadn't said anything about it to Decker for selfish reasons. She wasn't going to isolate the only friend she had here by embarrassing Decker and making it awkward between them. Interestingly, Brix didn't appear to have mentioned it to Decker either, which Jess thought was a weird, self-defeating move. If Brix had gone whinging to Decker, he'd have surely become even more repulsively protective of her than he already was. Although Jess wondered if she was wrong about this. Because perhaps Decker wasn't entirely immune to frustration. He hadn't sounded wildly upbeat when he spoke to Aegeus that morning. Brix had gone to the toilet tent, the only thing she seemed capable of doing by herself, when Toshi answered the call.

'Well, I'm not sure I'd say things are fantastic,' Decker had said to Toshi. 'I mean, yes, we're getting the work done, but it's hard going.'

Using classic eavesdropping tactics, Jess became very busy rehydrating sachets of pilaf rice so as not to break the spell.

'There is no "why", Toshi. The work's tough, the weather's been bad, there's a lot of—no one's to blame is what I'm trying to say. Some of us just require a bit longer to settle in.' Decker laughed at Toshi's reply. 'Who? Shut up, I'm not telling you who. No, not me, you dick. No—' he'd glanced furtively at Jess. 'Not her either.' His voice became businesslike. 'I'm sure it'll be easier now the weather's improved.'

Over decades of Antarctic research, the technology had advanced beyond recognition. The evolution of the equipment used on fieldwork was rapid and transformative. In a constant race for sensitivity and precision, the apparatus shrank each year to become more ingenious. What had been a box turned into a button and then a microchip the size of a grain of rice, as the new breed of minuscule self-powering devices wiped out their clumsy predecessors. Modern machines decoded an increasingly complex wealth of data about hunting regions and dive range and a hundred other things. The changes were revolutionary, but not everything had changed. However sophisticated the technology became, it still involved dealing with wild animals. And some of those animals, such as an adult male seal, had the muscle and weight to make any middle-aged scientist think hard about what medical supplies he had access to.

'Never trust a fur seal, even when it's sedated,' Decker said, crackling with nervous adrenaline as he studied the seals. 'The head snaps round like a pressurized hose and pulps your foot.' He wagged a finger at them. 'And the pups aren't any safer. Yes, they look fluffy, yes, they look sweet. Let me tell you about a colleague who thought the same. His thumb was torn off.'

Preparation for siring the next fur seal generation started in early November. The bulls arrived on Everland first, followed a few days later by the cows. The mating season then occurred during two violent weeks in December, once pups conceived the year before were born and the cows briefly became fertile again. During those few vital days, war and gore and birth and creation turned the beaches into a red mire of chaos. Blood drenched the sand as bulls lacerated their competitors and battles for supremacy thundered down the shores.

And to be successful was itself devastating. For a bull to remain king he had to guard his harem from scores of challengers. It was a task which demanded such Herculean fury and vigilance he couldn't rest, and so weakened; couldn't eat, and so gradually starved. Since the heavily pregnant females were only a few days away from giving birth, this summer's carnage was about to begin.

The cows were dwarfed by three bulls dozing at the edge of the group. Unlike the sleekly pretty females, the males were ragged and massive. They were lion-sized and couch-like, with thick brown ruffs which looked similar to matted old towelling. Instead of neat flippers, they lolloped about on huge leathery rudders.

'So I'm going to aim for him there,' Decker said about the nearest two-and-a-half-metre bull. 'That thirty-stone piece of cake there.'

Jess looked warily at the syringe Decker was taping to the end of a pole. 'Won't that thing just break off when you stab him,' she said.

Decker's tenseness didn't allow him to answer. He drew a measure of Valium derivative into a syringe and flicked at the needle, thinking of blood loss and bite marks with the diameter of a dinner plate. Thinking of his creaking knees and reduced agility. Thinking about how much easier this used to be even two years ago.

Bulls came into sexual maturity at seven years of age, but they only began mating at around ten, when they were tough enough to survive the punishment. It took a decade to be worthy of competing in this arena, and the honour quickly killed them. Although the cows lived to twenty, the bulls were dead by fourteen.

'Hi buddy!' The bull jogged up on its flippers as Decker skirted round, holding the pole like a bayonet. 'Take it easy, buddy! Nobody's going to hurt you.'

Exactly how much the bull was going to fail to cooperate became clear when it let out a low corrugated roar and pumped to its full height.

'Not going to hurt you! Stay where you are,' Decker said, and jabbed in the needle. He sprinted off along the beach with the seal pursuing him. Within seconds the bull had slowed to a halt. It rocked unsteadily and then fell down in sedation.

'Quick, Brix. Hurry,' Decker said.

They had about fifteen minutes before the bull revived. While Jess helped Decker with the microchip, Brix was attaching a plastic tag of identification to the rear flipper with a cattle-tagging applicator. It was a staple-gun type of machine which operated in the same way as an ear-piercing gun, a prong on the lower jaw punching through the skin to rivet the two sides of the tag together.

'*Quicker*, Brix. Want your arm ripped off? Because that's what's going to happen if he wakes up and finds you driving a spike into his tail.'

Brix had become mesmerized by the flipper. It felt like a wetsuit, she thought. Heavy like a side of pork belly. She was aware of Jess watching her as she fastened the tag, anticipating a hilarious response. Pathetic squeamishness, maybe, or hand-flapping screechy pleas for assistance. Whatever Jess had expected, Brix didn't give it to her. She'd drafted her first ever wild seal into service and was too elated to care.

Seal-wrangling the smaller yet equally aggressive cows required either Jess or Brix to snare the tail in a dog-catcher-style hoop on a stick and keep the cow steady until Decker fastened immobilizing wooden stocks around her neck. Each cow made scouring burp noises of protest as she received her microchip and had a satellite tag glued to the fur between her shoulders, where it would stay until it moulted off in March. The tag resembled a miniature walkie-talkie, and used a satellite-based navigation system to track where the cow went to feed.

The pup she'd soon deliver would take four months to rear, and since the pups couldn't survive without their mothers, it meant the cows were tied to the island. Unlike the males, who frequently disappeared, the females guaranteed a solid, reliable body of data.

'Why are you wrenching out her teeth?' Jess asked.

Decker had applied some local anaesthetic to the seal's gums and was using pliers to remove a small tooth from behind one of her lower canines. His explanation was mostly drowned out by the seal's now screamingly loud fury. 'One *tooth*,' they heard him say. 'Single *extraction*.'

'It's to record her age,' Brix said, ignored.

'So why didn't you take teeth from the bull seal?' Jess asked Decker.

'Don't need to.' Decker wiped the freed tooth on his trousers and let it rattle into a Kilner jar. 'You'll see why in about a month,' he said, and then saw that Jess wasn't listening.

Being upset didn't make Jess soften, it made her harder. Both her hands were in fists, and her eyes were fixed with an angry intensity on something beyond Decker at the edge of the beach. 'We've got to help,' she said with her jaw clenched.

The seal had injuries consistent with an orca attack. Its side was split to show tissue and a white waxy rind of blubber, with deeper wounds revealing a mass of tubes. The giant petrels surrounding the seal temporarily withdrew in loping, hopping steps as the seal thrashed its head. These were vulturous birds whose large beaks could strip a carcass, or gash rents through thick hide. They danced back when the seal lunged, and then regrouped to tear dangling red scraps from the open places, eating it alive.

'How many expeditions have you done, Jess? Five?' Decker said. 'So you know what helping the seal means. What it is we can realistically offer.'

'I wouldn't ask if I could do it myself,' Jess said. No one was less likely to delegate or refuse a job on the basis of its unpleasantness than she was. It didn't matter whether it involved dismantling oil-blackened engines, shifting drums of fuel, clearing snowdrifts from Aegeus's runway, or scrubbing out the industrial freezers. She would dig or carry or build or clean for as long as it took to get the work done, but she wasn't able to do this. Something in her just couldn't. She had the will to end an animal's suffering. What she didn't have, and had never had, was the ability to actually do it.

'Jess, it isn't fair to intervene,' Decker said, because the petrels' behaviour was part of the cycle of existence. However uncomfortable, however sad, it needed to be tolerated. 'Right, Brix?' he said, his tone urging her to agree. 'We shouldn't intervene?'

'I'm not sure, I think maybe we should.' It occurred to Brix that leaving the seal to its torturous death wasn't about any reverence for nature as much as convenience. Whilst mercy could be granted in one minute of ugliness, the guilt of denying that relief seemed likely to last through tonight, and the next day, and the next, probably for weeks, possibly for months. 'I think we should,' she said again.

'Decker, I'm asking,' Jess said. 'Please. We can't leave it.'

Yes, we can, thought Decker. Or rather he thought, *I* can, since it was he who'd have to do it. He knew from experience that he'd feel sickened for hours afterwards, and there was still a whole afternoon of exhaustion ahead of him.

'I'm sorry,' he said. 'I'm sorry, I genuinely am, but no. Jess, turn away. We're not getting involved.'

The momentum of having made the decision propelled Brix into finding what she gauged to be a large enough rock. And then, before she could think, she'd started to walk. She was actually doing it. 'Don't watch this,' she said to Jess, crunching across the snow towards the seal.

Τ he search party men had reboarded the ship and were
trooping down the narrow stairs. Among the hot bread
and coffee smells which billowed from the galley was a
less pleasant smell. Someone nudged Coppers in the ribs.
'Kidney soup!'

Coppers puckered his lips, sickened.

The *Kismet* had departed from Cardiff on a rainy October
morning in 1910 with the sponsorship of around eighty com-
panies, in exchange for a promotional photograph of their
products being enjoyed in Antarctica. Since Coppers despised
kidney soup, it was naturally he who'd been forced into posing
with it. He'd sat on a branded box, holding an open can with a
spoonful of the kidney poison raised to his mouth. The instant
the pictures were taken he'd jumped up. 'Only time you'll ever
find me grinning over that *filth*,' he'd ranted, the can somehow
kicked empty despite instructions not to waste it.

'But that's the joke!' Smith had said. 'Don't you get it? You
hate kidney soup, yes, but to the countless people who will see
the image you *love* kidney soup. What you actually feel is overruled by what the majority believes you feel, so you'll be seen
as the kidney soup-loving man for the rest of time. Isn't it
funny?'

No. And it was even less funny now, after months of stupid
kidney soup jibes. In the Officers' Mess, Castle made a loud,
rattling sigh at his empty mug. He was sitting beside Smith at
a purposefully deserted end of the table. The men weren't

bothered about Smith, but advertised their coolness towards Castle with subtle yet deliberate physical snubs. Shoulders were angled, lofty non-seeing sweeps of the gaze to avoid eye contact. The sense of division on the *Kismet* had hardened as winter set in around them. It was difficult to claim fence-sitting opinions on the First Mate without being taken as a member of the leprous pro-Napps party. Smith could mope for Napps without fear of recrimination, since he was viewed as a boyish oddity. Similarly, Addison was a doctor so could behave how he wanted. But for everyone else, remaining safe meant treating Napps, and anyone who defended Napps, with suspicion and doubt. As a sailor under Napps's command, Millet-Bass attracted a different type of scrutiny. Because he was no genius, was he? Poor simple Millet-Bass, in many ways wasn't he a lot like the ponies and dogs? You just told him what to do and he did it, without the mental capacity to evaluate a decision as either right or wrong.

If Castle noticed that his loyalty to Napps was making it increasingly risky to be associated with him, he didn't appear to care. It was a problem for many of the crew, as they were bored of pretending not to like his company.

Castle said, 'Who do I have to fight around here to get another brandy?'

'You've had your quota, that's all you'll get,' said Jennet, the ship's cook.

'Good! I didn't enjoy the first one,' Castle said, and then kissed the gold crucifix hung on a chain round his neck. 'Except I felt it was my duty to raise a glass in tribute to my grandmother, bless her soul. Today would have been her birthday.'

The cook on any ship had to be vigilant about guarding the supplies, and Jennet wasn't a man to test. Every packet and tin was protected, down to the last dried lentil. In Jennet's definition of crime there was no moral distinction between stealing a sugar cube or the ship's entire hoard of frozen mutton. Food was food, the food was his, and the loss of anything, however small, was thuggishly avenged. The thief would be grabbed in a scalp-hold and sent splintering through one of the chairs before he could even begin to apologize.

Jennet unfolded his massive arms. 'Then why didn't you toast her with the drink you just finished?' Deceased Castles always sprang out of nowhere whenever alcohol appeared. And here was another, some dead old woman leaping from the grave to rob Jennet's precious stockroom.

'I forgot the date,' Castle said. 'But then her spirit came to remind me.' The crucifix was pressed to his lips again in thanks.

This practice of his, kissing the crucifix and deferring to it for protection, had started ironically, as had his practice of signing the cross over his head. Recently, however, Castle found himself sleeping with the cross in his hand at night, because these dangerous days had triggered a hunger for reassurance in whatever form.

Even the most cynical among the men had started to believe in rituals, charms and symbols. The divine significance of weather was suddenly both accepted and trusted. Wind was a sign, sleet and types of cloud cover were signs, thunder was obviously a sign. Animals were the mouthpiece of a newly talkative God whose voice was now heard daily in the scores of fish and birds he used to communicate.

The hostility towards Castle was postponed in order to mutter congratulations to him as Jennet stumped off to fetch more grandmother-toasting brandy.

Lawrence drained his mug. 'And if we needed another reason to celebrate, we're homeward bound tomorrow.'

McValley held a hand over his coughing, slapping his chest.

Lawrence nodded at McValley. 'Uplifting news, isn't it?'

'Beautif—' McValley choked out a word. 'Beautiful.'

'What did Addison make of the bag?' Smith asked.

McValley recovered. 'What is there to make of an empty bag? I told him where I'd found it, told him about the photograph. He identified the woman as Dinners's wife, Elizabeth, just as I had.'

'I don't care what you found,' Coppers said, tired enough of everything to speak bluntly. 'I don't care if it was the severed head of Elizabeth herself as long as it means we can go home.'

'Ah, how sympathetic you sound.' McValley snorted. 'How very like Napps.'

'Yes, let's keep it civil,' Lawrence said as Coppers was heckled. The vanished party were always smouldering beneath any conversation, and it took only the slightest mention for debate to flare up again. The subject turned to Napps and his famous capacity for rage.

Remember Napps's rage when someone was late for breakfast or untidy for the Sunday service? Or his rage when an order was met with a cheeky remark?

Matthews, the source of that particular anecdote, said rapidly to Lawrence: 'Cheeky, sir, but, swear on my life, innocent.'

'He instructed you to go bail out the engine rooms and you replied by telling him to go break his neck.'

'I told him to break *my* neck,' Matthews said.

'Mm,' Lawrence said, not believing a word of it.

'You're smiling, sir. Does it mean I'm forgiven?'

'Mm,' Lawrence said again. 'No.'

The stories had a noticeable tendency for underlying resentments to accidentally, or perhaps artfully, slip in. Lawrence acted as though he disapproved. Since it was improper for him to visibly relish the men's criticisms of Napps, he declared himself appalled. He was careful to make sure his proclamations were firm enough to be acknowledged, but never so accusatory that they actually succeeded in discouraging the men.

The conversation had switched to McValley's case of scurvy.

He'd become unwell during an expedition around the Ross Barrier that had been one long nightmare for everyone involved. From being a mostly forgotten episode, the explosion of speculation triggered by Everland meant McValley's scurvy was now treated as an issue which deserved incredible attention.

'Oh, be decent,' Castle objected, causing Smith to whisper nervously to him.

The problematic Ross Barrier trip was notorious for two reasons. The first was that Napps and McValley had realized they hated each other more than anything else in existence. McValley was a man who actively tended grudges and sought revenge in small malicious ways, which was exactly the type of man Napps delighted in bullying. The second reason was the crisis which struck towards the end of the expedition.

Birch grinned with resentment. He and Matthews were the unlucky sailors who'd been in the Ross Barrier sledging team with McValley and Napps. 'Well, you all know my opinion on the matter,' he said to boisterous noises of agreement.

Castle raised his voice above them. 'If you could only hear yourselves.'

McValley's health had deteriorated in the expedition's final weeks. He'd struggled on with painfully swollen joints even as he started to pass blood and faint. When he became too ill to haul they'd let him totter along beside the sledge. When he became too ill to walk they'd towed him on the sledge, his teeth grinding in agony. And one morning Napps had decided upon a hazardous plan, announcing that he and Matthews would cover the last forty miles alone to get help, while Birch remained behind with McValley.

'Oh, trust me, he'd made up his mind,' Birch said, recounting the heartless speed in which Napps had overruled his pleas for them to stay together.

The truth was that a solid argument could have been made

for either option. Although continuing with McValley on the sledge was desperate work for three weakened men, dividing the group and their meagre resources meant gambling on clear weather and a swift return. For Birch it meant becoming as incapacitated as his scurvy patient, with no way of leaving the camp or being found if Napps and Matthews failed to reach the hut and alert a rescue party. That the outcome was successful and Napps went with Addison's team to save McValley was enough to dispel most of the controversies. The matter would have lain dormant if it wasn't for the interesting new details which had begun to surface in Everland's aftermath.

For example, although Matthews couldn't remember the precise wording, he'd definitely remember the moment for the rest of his life. They'd been marching to get help when Napps had suddenly turned to him and said it would have been better for the team if McValley had died.

Died. Men shook their heads in disgust and said they were shocked, but not surprised. It was as they'd privately expected. Call it instinct, call it whatever you like. They'd always understood there was this ugly ruthlessness to Napps.

Castle angrily shook his arm free from Smith's insistent, sleeve-tugging placations. 'You understand him?' he shouted, his face arranged in vicious disbelief. 'From your descriptions I don't even fucking recognize him.'

'*Castle!*' Lawrence barked at him to moderate his tone. It was exactly as McValley and a few other men had advised him. Castle was growing disrespectful.

'I apologize, sir,' Castle said with no detectable contrition. 'But do these accounts of Napps sound anything like the man you remember? Because they don't to me, none of them.'

'I find it fascinating that you should know so much more than Matthews does about the journey, when, unlike him, you weren't there,' Coppers sneered.

'Which is my point. That's my point exactly, as Napps *was*

there,' Castle said, imploring the Captain. 'Yet it's his side of the story which is so absent in all this.'

'I see you've been talking to Addison,' Lawrence said sourly.

Lawrence's responsibility to truthfulness in his book was a topic Addison felt infuriatingly concerned about. He was concerned that Lawrence was being unfairly influenced by the men's stories. He was concerned that Lawrence didn't appreciate the power he wielded over another man's reputation. Close to throwing something at the wall, Lawrence had asked Addison whether he'd ever even once bothered to consider that the men's impressions of Napps were equally valid. Maybe even more so, since Addison's friendship with the Mate could be read as disqualifying the validity of his opinion. Judgement on an individual's character wasn't the exclusive right of those most sympathetic to him, Lawrence concluded, pretty sure this point had just won him the argument and unable to hide his delight. And listen, if anyone was guilty of trying to prejudice anything, it was Addison himself.

'Because when it comes to Napps,' Lawrence had crowed, 'how can everything I hear be wrong? What you forget is that my responsibility is to represent us all, Addison. *Us all*, not only the men you champion.'

Addison had a particular way of looking at a face which saw beyond the expression, however resolute the smile or deep the frown. It was a skill honed over years of dealing with coy patients. It also crushed a Captain's sense of delicious self-righteousness to dust.

He'd said to Lawrence, '. . . What aren't you telling me?'

The Mess had fallen quiet as the men became aware that McValley was about make a sensational disclosure. He kept his voice low, his head bowed in theatrical humility while he said that, under the circumstances, he felt obliged to reveal certain unpleasant facts he'd previously withheld. Such as the chilling way Napps used to enquire about his health. Such as the way, every evening in the tent, the frail McValley was forced to endure Napps silently loathing him for his illness. 'The night before he made the decision to leave with Matthews, he just sat there staring at me.'

'Staring at you?'

McValley nodded at Lawrence. 'Didn't blink, didn't speak.' He shut his eyes, revisiting traumatic memories. 'I could tell Napps wanted me to do something infinitely more decisive than stay at the depot. I thought I could still get through, but he wanted the gallant gesture . . . A request for five minutes alone with the stash of opium tablets, say.'

Castle slammed both fists on the table. 'You lying bastard.'

'Ask Matthews and Birch,' McValley replied. 'Ask them yourself.'

'Lying *bastard*.'

McValley smiled dangerously. 'Now, now. That's twice you've called me a liar.'

21
March 1913

Dinners was improving. He now did general domestic chores in the tent and some of the cooking. He'd even started to make short hobbling trips along the beach to search for geological specimens.

'Quartz feldspar, an igneous rock created from lava,' he said to Millet-Bass, showing his latest discoveries. 'That one's pegmatite, another magma rock . . . '

Three o'clock in the afternoon and the sun was already dying. Each dawn was later than the one before, and each evening came earlier. What daylight there was amounted to an ashy twilit interim which kept getting shorter and colder and darker as the hours of night expanded.

'How are the polar stumps?' Napps asked.

Dinners hated this nickname for his frostbitten feet. 'I can't quite stand to look at them, but I can certainly stand to stand on them,' he said cheerfully, careful to always emphasize constant progress. If he ever hinted that his feet caused him pain or any sort of discomfort, Napps's expression became coolly analytical. It implied he was evaluating Dinners's worth, perhaps in comparison to things such as a piece of wet paper, or a used match, or a fishbone. He said Dinners looked tired.

Sleep was a topic Dinners avoided talking about. Napps told him to rest, so he rested. If they checked on him, he was obediently in his sleeping bag as instructed. But he was always awake behind his shut eyes. He never slept when the others weren't with him, and had found it was safer not to sleep much at all.

Dinners's solution to the quandary of neither answering Napps nor lying to him was to point at the mascot iceberg. Taurus was in motion, as Millet-Bass had attested. With his superstitious dislike of the berg, only Millet-Bass really invested this with any meaning. Napps failed to see how its movement was of the slightest importance.

'Taurus has been especially active for the past couple of days,' Dinners said. 'I've been monitoring it closely, since there's not much else left to watch.'

The continuing winter migration had left the shoreline as mute and desolate as the cindery sky. There was the rare sighting of a petrel overhead or the brief outline of a seal in the waves, but it merely accentuated Everland's emptiness. So when Dinners told them that actually, despite the lack of animals, there was still plenty left to admire on the beach, Millet-Bass expressed rude surprise. He'd just spent hours plodding around the island, dismayed by everything.

'No, no, it's a fascinating place.' Dinners levered himself up from the large rock he'd been perched on. A rough circular crust of orange lichen grew on the top of the stone. 'I've spent a long while considering this,' he said.

Napps studied the crust for maybe a second before he believed he'd got the gist of what it could offer. 'Yes.'

'Approximately one millimetre of growth each century,' Dinners said, stroking the lichen with a puffy, bluish finger. 'It'll be thousands of years old.'

Napps didn't stoop to pretend he wasn't impressed.

Dinners noticed. With the overly indifferent voice of someone trying hard not to appear thrilled, he said, 'If anyone ever comes here in the future it will be virtually unchanged. When you measure our lifespan against something as permanent as lichen, we're barely even here.'

Morbid, thought Millet-Bass.

'We're gone in the same minute we arrived,' Dinners added.

Millet-Bass said he didn't want to hear any more about the orange doily.

Napps laughed. 'I wouldn't have expected you to be so sensitive.'

Millet-Bass prided himself on embracing whatever horrors could be trawled into a conversation. Necromancy, blood-letting, body-snatching, cannibalism. Anything, he was fine with it all. 'I suppose Everland must have brought a queasy side out of me,' he said defensively.

'The times are changing and we with them,' Dinners surmised.

'What's that?' Napps said, because the phrase was vaguely familiar.

'It's the Latin motto embroidered on my sledge flag,' Dinners replied, before repeating his motto at a slower, more resonant pace to let them appreciate its significance. 'The times. *Are changing*—'

Millet-Bass began talking about the seal catch. 'How many weeks of meat did we strip off them, Napps? Couple of months' worth?'

Dinners listened with a down-turned smile of regret. Being ill, and his resultant inability to contribute, was a raw, seeping embarrassment he tended every single minute of the day. And this shame had transformed him into a species of shrimp. He dithered around on a frantic, miniature scale as he searched for ways to be useful. Millet-Bass's stupid hat, a green woollen cap he'd altered with disastrous homemade earflaps, was dismantled and carefully remade in a new practical form. Socks were darned with tiny elfish stitches. A missing shirt button was replaced with a replica disc cut from a biscuit box. Dinners's persistent shrimplike efforts even saw him pit himself against the unwinnable battle of the dirt-layered groundsheet, scraping it clean with his spoon. He wafted his jumper until his arms ached to fumigate the tent. And then Napps and Millet-Bass would trudge in, slush raining from their coats. They'd muddy the scraped places with grit. They'd pull on the socks or the shirt without seeing the new button or neat stitches. The freshened air was immediately polluted with the rancid odour of seal blood dried into rancid clothes which were worn on rancid bodies. Whatever Dinners did amounted to tidying a collapsing burrow of sand. But he did it anyway because he was desperate to be seen as valuable, especially by Napps.

It wasn't only a puppyish craving for approval. Dinners knew of the damning comments Napps had made about him to the Captain. Giuseppe had wasted no time in telling everyone what he'd heard, which mortified Dinners so thoroughly he'd put that tragic wager on himself to save face. And Dinners wanted Napps to atone. He wanted Napps to repair his wrong judgement and think better of him. But the issue of atonement didn't only apply to Napps.

The morning before the island selection saw Dinners skulk into Lawrence's cabin. Listen, the Captain had said with a weary dignity, we don't know what the island is like. I can't vouch for your safety. He said, Dinners? Please be reasonable. I'd feel so much easier about it if you had some experience. Pressing the bridge of his nose, his eyes closed, he'd said, look, didn't we both make promises? Before we left you swore to me that you would cause no trouble. And yet here we are. I've kept my promise, and you're being colossally troubling.

'Why this fucking place?' Lawrence had then exclaimed during the negotiations. 'Why must you develop a fanatic interest *now* and why must it be *this*? Because I can guarantee you one thing, Napps will have a lot more to say about it than I do.'

Except Dinners hadn't cared about Napps's opinion. He'd spent his life being seen as irrelevant, and this was his opportunity to alter the course of his destiny. He would become the kind of courageous, purposeful man he'd always envied. Yes, the times were definitely changing, and Dinners had been determined to change with them.

Standing in front of Napps and Millet-Bass, Dinners's shrimp-mind scurried to design seal meat recipes which might please them.

'Seal rissoles,' Millet-Bass said to Dinners, a dish impossible for him to make.

'I'll try my best.'

'Galantine of seal.'

Dinners didn't have the first idea how to even start this. 'I've sorted through and repacked the medical supplies,' he said as a hopeful substitute.

Napps rewarded him with a pitiless smile.

'Good,' Millet-Bass said, wishing Dinners would realize when to keep quiet.

The same smile had appeared earlier as Napps and Millet-Bass walked back from the seal kill. Idly speculating on how fortunate Dinners was to have survived the dinghy escapade, Millet-Bass was interrupted by a particularly acidic response from Napps that in the natural cycle of things, Dinners would have died.

'Ah, he's getting better,' Millet-Bass said, still preoccupied with their meat bounty. 'Well, I say better. He's getting a bit madder, though, isn't he? Have you heard what he says to himself when he thinks we're out of earshot?'

And that was when Napps's bitter smile had sprung up to trap him. 'I think you should probably tell me, don't you?'

Dinners sat stooped and cross-legged, heating up a pan of water for cocoa. The process of cooking anything, even a drink, emptied the brain. All that remained were compulsive throbbing images of food. For Dinners, that image was of an egg.

'*Eggs!* I long for eggs,' he told Napps.

Millet-Bass wasn't in the mood to talk. He sat on his side of the tent, his heart festering with resentment over Cape Athena. Napps's decision to stay on the reviled Everland caused terrible pain to Millet-Bass's sense of loyalty to rank. Although Millet-Bass thought Napps was wrong, he was still the First Mate, which therefore meant he had to be obeyed. So Millet-Bass wrote in his journal, which was the nearest substitute for going alone into a room and slamming the door. Already using a huge amount of exclamation marks, he poured his bile into a letter to Grace.

Grace had first appeared in his life five years ago, mortifying a twenty-six-year-old and mostly naked Millet-Bass in his own family home. Back at his parents' Yorkshire farm after returning from some voyage or other, he'd celebrated by giving himself a world-ending hangover. He'd woken the next day to a sickeningly bright afternoon. Barefoot and reeking of beer, wearing nothing but an ancient pair of pyjama bottoms, he'd gone directly to the kitchen and stood at the sink, chugging down glasses of water. He only became aware of the brown-haired girl sitting at the table behind him when she laughed. 'And what do you want?' he'd rasped, half asleep, in a tone which invited her to leave the house immediately.

'Nothing. I'm Grace, I'm just waiting for Libby.'

That made sense. Millet-Bass's youngest sister, Libby, was always bringing her tedious friends over to the house for screechy gossiping sessions.

Grace watched Libby's giant, wild-looking brother drink another two pints of water. 'Do you usually wear more clothes on a Sunday?'

It was now that Millet-Bass turned to assess her properly, ready to tell her exactly how little he valued her opinion. But then he couldn't say anything. She was around twenty years old, and something about her made him impossibly shy. His sagging pyjama bottoms were suddenly an issue of burning concern and humiliation. 'I didn't expect to be surprised in the kitchen.'

'Likewise,' she'd said with a smile.

'I *dream* of cracking eggs straight into my mouth,' Dinners was saying to Napps. 'But I have discovered that sucking a pebble eases hunger cramps.'

Dinners may as well have said he ate faeces. As an experiment Napps allowed approximately ten per cent of his opinion about this man to show in his expression. Then he retracted it. Even that tiny amount felt like it twisted his face psychotically.

'Although I suppose there are worse things to dream about,' Dinners said.

'Forget the eggs and pebbles,' Napps said. Because what concerned him was these nightmares Dinners had been having. He wanted to talk about that.

Dinners shot a wounded glance at Millet-Bass. 'Oh, it isn't important.'

'It's possible Millet-Bass alluded to something,' Napps said.

Millet-Bass's eyes flicked up at mention of his name, guiltily registered the topic of conversation, and then he carried on writing in his journal.

'Well, I suppose there's one dream in particular,' Dinners said. 'I suppose you could call it a dream . . . ' He'd become very flustered. 'There's a game I play although I don't want to, I'm not sure. No, I'll call it a dream.'

And if Napps only knew how foolish he felt telling him about it! But Dinners always had the same dream. He woke to the sound of what he thought was Napps shouting from outside the tent. Except he hadn't awoken, because then he'd open his eyes and see this thing crouched beside him. Something big, horrible. Except that it was still part of the dream, because then the shock would really jolt him awake. And he'd sit up to find Napps and Millet-Bass asleep beside him.

Dinners? Can you hear me, Dinners?'
Addison sat forward in his chair, two fingers searching Dinners's neck for a pulse. He found the despairingly faint beat and slumped back. Good God, he didn't know how much more either of them could bear. Dinners must surely be at the point where he wished for the end. When Addison talked to Dinners of his family, *they'll be thinking of you*, and talked of his home, *because you'll be back there soon*, his words caught in his throat for this man so far away from anyone who loved him, and the heartache became almost impossible to withstand.

After Dinners's first, frantic hours of assessment in Lawrence's quarters, he'd been moved to the infirmary, where his health had steadily declined. Neither he nor Addison ever left. Addison slept there on a small camp bed and took his meals there. He sat there, tending his patient, or he waited there beside him until he could next be of use. It was a vigil which grew lonelier as Dinners grew sicker and the instinct to withdraw from such suffering made visitors dwindle. When anyone did come, they stood at the bedside and looked helplessly from Dinners to Addison before retreating.

Lawrence was the exception. His visits only increased as Dinners ailed, his mood swinging between sympathetic and demanding, often in the same sentence. You have to make him better, he'd order Addison. I have to know you will. He appeared in the infirmary with these demands several times a day until his concern became oppressive and Addison led him from the room.

'Don't conspire to hide details from me, I'm extremely invested in his recovery,' Lawrence said when Addison tactfully asked him to reduce his visits.

'You need to trust that I'm doing all I can,' Addison replied.

'Then you need to do more,' he shot back hotly. 'Isn't he worse? Jesus Christ, he seems it. Why is he worse? The stakes are higher than you understand. Don't look at me like I'm mad, Addison, you don't know everything about everything.'

'I know that of the two of us, I am the trained practitioner.'

Despite striding off, furiously damning the doctor and his useless infirmary to hell, Lawrence had of course returned. His face peered round the door later that afternoon as Addison was writing in his journal. The now excessively friendly Captain drifted about recounting anecdotes as a form of apology. For example, oh, it made him laugh! He really must find a way of working it into the book! One of the men had told him the most incredible story. Lawrence picked up a scalpel, tested the blade and put it down. He flipped through a medical dictionary, then inspected a pair of surgical scissors, snipping at the air. So once, while helping the carpenter, Millet-Bass's chisel had slipped to gash his thigh. Heard this tale already, Adds? So anyway, Millet-Bass had simply dropped his blood-drenched trousers. I mean right there on deck, I mean just dropped them. He'd called for a needle and sewed the cut together himself. Yes, and he even made jokes as he did it! Honestly, the man could remember him laughing. Unbelievable!

Lawrence turned to bask in the doctor's amazement. It wasn't the gratifying sight he'd wanted. Addison was smiling, but the smile was disdainful.

'Unbelievable, I agree. Because what I remember is Millet-

Bass in the infirmary, shaking and pouring with sweat, while I sutured the leg,' Addison said. 'And it wasn't a cut as much as a hole deep enough to put three fingers in. A thick steel chisel leaves a very nasty mark, especially when struck with the power of a man like Millet-Bass.'

Lawrence raised his eyes to the heavens, wanting to reverse time to the second before he'd tried to lighten the mood with an innocent yarn and therefore spare himself the vexation of hearing Addison say, 'He didn't seem to find it funny at all. Although I suppose it's possible that Millet-Bass cracked a few jokes while he had his head in a bucket, throwing up. I may have missed them. The acoustics aren't good.'

Lawrence threw the scissors into the sink and punched shut a cupboard door.

'However,' Addison said, still smiling in the same terrible way, 'another possibility is that the story is largely incorrect, as other stories might be. *Many* other stories, Lawrence. And you should be mindful of this before you commit any to print.'

There wasn't a subject on earth which the doctor couldn't reroute back to Lawrence's bloody book-responsibilities and bloody Napps. Addison began to speak again and the Captain interrupted stiffly, 'Don't. No need.'

'Thank you for coming by,' Addison said.

'Here's the bag,' the Captain said as he left.

After digging through it himself, Lawrence had passed over the knapsack discovered on Everland. It contained nothing more conclusive than a few broken sledging biscuits. The photograph of a young woman with dark hair was almost certainly Elizabeth. The quote on the back was scrawled in Dinners's handwriting.

Although Dinners didn't respond to the water Addison offered him and didn't respond to food, the photograph caused a reaction.

'Is this Elizabeth?' Addison asked, showing Dinners the

photograph. 'I know you always carried a picture of her with you.'

With great effort, Dinners opened his eyes again.

'Why wasn't your bag with you?' Addison placed the photograph on the bed and clasped Dinners's bandaged hands in his own. 'Why would you leave it in the cove?'

He broke off abruptly as Dinners tried to speak.

'You want to see the photograph again?'

Dinners managed a nod: yes.

Addison held it close and Dinners fought through each weighty, hazy blink to focus on the image of his wife.

'And where's your diary, Dinners? I know you kept one. So did all the men.'

His breath ground from his chest as he remembered the diary. Yes.

'Dinners, can you recall what happened on Everland?'

He looked at Addison. *Yes.*

'Then what is it?' Addison squeezed Dinners's hands and leant closer towards him, searching his face for an answer. 'What is it, Dinners? People believe the worst, and I would too if I had less faith in Napps. You have to tell me what happened.'

Dinners's eyes rolled up, lapsing in and out. His chest jerked, his mouth bubbling.

Disgusted with himself, Addison stopped.

'Forgive me,' he said. 'You're tired.'

Yes. Yes.

Waiting alone in the tent, Dinners alternated between clapping out a rhythm on his knees and staring fixedly at the entrance. One candle burned inside a small tin, and he'd put it on his lap as a sort of substitute friend. He was beginning to panic. It seemed to him that Millet-Bass and Napps should have returned by now.

The sun didn't rise into the sky any more. A thin sliver as red as molten iron appeared on the seaward horizon after a long dark morning, and was then gone by mid-afternoon. Half an hour ago, the light already starting to diffuse through progressively filthier shades of grey, Napps had noticed a densely clouded darkness above the ocean. The early stars were smothered out as the blizzard tightened in around Everland.

Dinners's voice had been a thin, anxious bleat. 'Do we have long?'

'Just—' Napps lifted a hand to stop Dinners. Just don't ask me anything. Just do me a favour and keep your mouth shut.

With brutal clarity, Napps saw what an error he'd made in allowing himself to rely on faith. He'd been so convinced that the *Kismet* would arrive quickly, so arrogantly sure that their stay on Everland would be over in days, that Napps had chosen to prioritize their well-being over the long-term safety of their supplies. With Dinners rendered useless by the *Joseph Evelyn* ordeal, and he and Millet-Bass still weakened, Napps was unwilling to have them drag around crates and risk any further injury. Which meant that instead of rigorously securing the boxes, he'd temporarily piled them in the cove and made a little list. Instead of transferring the seal meat to the ice locker he'd let it stay unmarked and buried on the beach. Except he'd prioritized the wrong things, and it was therefore crucial that he didn't speak until he'd got possession of himself. Because at this moment, if Dinners forced him to answer a question, he would react very badly.

'No,' Millet-Bass had said to Dinners. 'An hour at best.'

On the scale of Napps's anguish the one thing which ranked higher than Dinners's confusion was Millet-Bass's insight. Millet-Bass knew how cataclysmic the situation was. Lose the oil to heat water from snow and health wouldn't stop you from dying of thirst. Lose the food and your strength was good for nothing.

Whenever the flame sputtered, Dinners shielded the candle with his hands and spoke to it. Don't go out, he'd say, coaxing the flame in the tone of someone soothing a shy animal. Please, please. Dinners's ongoing separation from the other two, plus the building fury of the storm, plus the suggestive brown shadows, had conspired to make it extremely difficult for him to avoid intense and aggressively frightening thoughts. He'd become certain that a malicious presence was in the tent with him, and was compelled to make endless checks. If he closed his eyes, noises outside the tent became words. If he opened his eyes, he saw peripheral movements which he wasn't brave enough to look at directly.

The twists of fine snow which smoked across their boots had become a rushing current as Millet-Bass and Napps reached the cove. The two horns of Taurus were blackly outlined above the cliffs and the wind was skimming pieces of debris along the beach. Cracked slates of ice hissed across the snow or spun out of the carbon light and flew. A blade of ice the size of a roof tile caught Napps on the leg, sending him down with the crate he held. He stood up and floundered on.

For each box he stacked beside the cove's sheltered rear wall, Millet-Bass had carried three. In frustration at his slowness, Napps redoubled his efforts and found it made him light-headed. The ache of hail against his face was now a painless sensation, and this worried him. That his feet weren't just numb but felt seemingly dead in his boots was another worry, as was the fact his hands weren't working properly.

'We've got to go,' Napps said. The sky had turned the colour of mussel shells and would soon be the colour of soot.

'Then we'll be leaving the job half done,' Millet-Bass said as he lashed the supplies together to anchor them from the blizzard.

Napps knew his mouth was moving sloppily, but couldn't hear if this affected his speech because his frozen ears were ringing with a low, glasslike note. 'Haven't a choice,' he said to Millet-Bass.

Dinners's relief when they finally did lurch back into the tent made him talk exceptionally fast. *Thank God you're here*, he jabbered as Napps and Millet-Bass argued over him, tersely contradicting each other with predictions about the severity of the blizzard.

Grits of ice sprinkled from creases in their clothing as they squeezed their feet to thaw them and kneaded bloodless hands. They smelt, Dinners thought, of wet stone. And he thought they looked like enchanted statues. He noticed the cadaverous way they radiated cold. He registered the fossil-coloured skin, the rusted automaton movements, and he smiled craftily. If they glanced at him, it was important they understood that it was the smile of a vigilant man who saw everything, and knew everything, but chose not to verbalize it.

Napps was still too cold to snatch enough breath to form more than chopped sentences. 'Storm'll be finished by morn-ing,' he wheezed out.

'I'd describe that as improbable,' Millet-Bass said. 'Another word is naïve.'

Trying to be positive, Dinners said not every day could be good. There were other days.

'What days?' Millet-Bass snapped. 'It's just an endless single day growing darker by the hour. Talk to me tomorrow if you can make the distinction, and tell me then about this apparent wealth of time.'

I need to get more sleep,' Decker said. 'Or a stronger coffee. Or a younger body.'

'Wow, what you need is more suncream,' Jess said, looking at his pink face.

'Jess, is this actually mayonnaise?' Decker said as she handed him the bottle. 'I can't have used it more than an hour ago.'

Thousands of Adélies had now gathered in the southern bay, and gridlocked highways of penguin traffic wound along the beach. The temperature had increased to two degrees, which made the birds pant with open beaks, and caused a film of mossy-coloured lichen to bloom across the cliff slopes. Compact dunes of winter snow had begun to dissolve, rivulets of water snaking down the beach towards the sea. The ice stranded along the tideline made tiny, crackling noises as it melted, which amassed into a pure, effervescent sound that was as refreshing to hear as a glass of carbonated water is to drink. Decker, Brix and Jess had started to unzip their coats when marching and pull off their fur-lined hoods. It was too warm for the mittens they wore over their gloves, or the four pairs of socks and triple-layered thermals.

They were at the colony to monitor the nests built next to the marker poles. Eggs were being laid and brooded in shifts by the parent birds beneath a psychedelic sky. The effect of ice crystals high in the atmosphere had created a trippy visual display. Everland's sun was joined by a mini-galaxy of five other angelic suns and their multi-coloured haloes.

Brix's ability to walk fast was hindered by her interest in the sky. That she was moving at a speed which any of the world's oldest people could easily surpass was something she might have devoted more attention to correcting if it hadn't conflicted with her desire to concentrate fully on the rainbow micro-suns.

'Here's an idea,' Decker said, looking back towards Brix. 'How about we try not to delay the work for longer than is necessary.'

Jess glanced at him. This was an entertaining new pastime. Decker would occasionally let slip grumbling asides when Brix was out of earshot, and for Jess it was like being privy to an excellent secret. She and Decker were in a club, the immense satisfaction of which was only partly marred by Brix, who'd risen in Jess's estimation since she'd dealt with the injured seal. No one could have been more stunned at Brix's actions than Jess was, and her harsh feelings towards Brix had reluctantly moderated as result. Not much, yet enough to make it less hilarious to find fault with every tiny thing Brix did. She'd noticed, however, that Decker didn't necessarily share her sympathy.

'Emotional. A few teary episodes. She's finding it hard, I think,' Decker had told Aegeus that morning, once Brix had left the tent to pack her quad. The psychological vibe to the conversation made Jess suspect he was talking to Canadian Sam. 'Honestly?' Decker breathed in. 'I'm a bit worried, yeah.'

Now Jess watched Decker take off his hat and wipe his forehead with it. 'You think I'm being impatient,' he said. 'Ack, I don't mean to be.'

'Hey, I'm not saying anything.' Jess raised her hands. But she observed that for a boss who'd said he wasn't a boss, he was certainly starting to act quite boss-like.

'Well, I'm under a fair amount of pressure here,' he said. 'We're only the second group of people to stay on Everland, and the first group didn't exactly recommend it.'

He was just so tired, that was the problem. Or rather, it was part of the problem. The main difficulty could be traced to appetite. For most of his career, Decker's hunger for the gratification of fieldwork had verged on insatiable. He returned shattered from one trip, and within a couple of weeks he was freshly ravenous for Antarctica all over again. The laboriousness, isolation and physical discomfort of an expedition were enticing when viewed with this mind-set. But without his old hunger, Decker saw the backache, sleep loss, hardship and danger through far less adventuresome eyes. If homesickness was induced by a hormonal reaction, then he thought that hormone was the opposite of adrenaline. It slowed a person down and made him less alert. The result was a sluggish passivity, a creeping awareness of your own limitations. He was, he realized, in a very weird mood today.

'Sorry,' Brix said when she caught up with them.

'No big deal,' Decker said, although his tone suggested it was some kind of an issue. 'I wouldn't even have to hurry you if there were more of us in the team. But that would ruin the symbolism, I guess.'

Brix was pleased to see the confusion on Jess's face. It seemed that neither of them knew what he was talking about.

'This centenary expedition is symbolic rather than practical,' Decker said in a way which indicated their bafflement was charming yet curiously naïve. 'I mean, yes, of course the job is important, but it's also a device to raise Aegeus's profile, and the profile of Antarctic research in general. Funding bases, funding expeditions, running long-term projects. It's not cheap. It can also be hard to get people excited about. Polar exploration isn't full of sailing ships and legendary escapades any more. These days the pioneers are scientists, working with very technical equipment on a cellular level. Which is far less romantic. So connecting modern Antarctic discovery to that past heroic age imparts a resonance everyone can understand. And although I get that, I've got to be honest. Beyond replicating Napps's venture, there's no real reason why the Everland centenary should be restricted to a three-person group. It'd be a lot easier if we had four people out here, or five even, or six.'

Jess's scorn for the notion of work being easy made more sense to Brix now. Over the past few days, she'd commended herself on her improving fieldwork capabilities. The daily routines were no longer as mystifying. If there was a tent to dig out, she'd do it, along with refuelling the bikes, hooking up the solar-powered generator, packing the sledge, or tagging whatever animal came within grabbing distance. Brix ranked her efforts as going from bad to medium bad, to a medium average, and was aiming to reach a middling good before they left Everland. So she didn't want to hear Decker talk about easiness. It was actually a little insulting.

'Do you need me to get Aegeus on the phone, Deck?' Jess's voice had a coldly humorous edge as she repeated what Decker had said to Sam that morning. 'Because maybe I'm a bit worried . . . you're finding it hard, I think.'

Decker said briskly, 'Ha, yes, very funny.'

He only became more melancholy when Jess discovered a dead Adélie among the rocks. Its head joggled loosely when she prodded it with the toe of her boot. Decker removed his glove and stroked the feathers, feeling that the body beneath was still warm with a living heat. It occurred to him that he was reacting as though the situation was far more poignant than it really was.

'You're present, and then you're nothing at all,' Decker said to himself.

What he'd done, he understood, in touching the bird, was to touch a faultline between the existence of life and its absence. And by doing that, something inconceivably powerful about the brevity of life, particularly his life, had triggered a depth charge in his head. The finiteness of his own life was now exceptionally real to him. It was like hearing his heart-beat.

'Unfortunate that it died before you could get to it and stove its head in, Brix.'

'You make it sound as though that's my hobby,' Brix answered Jess.

When Decker thought of Viv, he saw them both in the kitchen, drinking wine on the evening before he went to Aegeus. Her curly hair had been crazier than usual because they'd spent the windy afternoon out with the dogs, walking for hours to try and make the day last longer. They repeated the same things to each other whenever he left. Make sure you come home, Viv would say. Perhaps, Decker would answer, straight-faced. Then he'd laugh and promise she never needed to worry about that. He'd always come home.

'Maybe it should be your hobby, Brix,' Jess said. 'It's the one thing you seem to be any good at.'

'And I'd do it again, if I needed to,' Brix said with an unusual authority.

'Yeah, well, being serious for a minute . . . ' Jess's words faded into embarrassment. In trying again, she sounded as though she was reading the words from a board. 'The business with the seal. I suppose I didn't thank you for dealing with that. I appreciated it.'

Undecided about how to interpret this suspiciously affable Jess, Brix kept her voice neutral. 'Glad I could help,' she said, ready for the inevitable abuse.

'Thank you, though,' Jess said, with such sincerity that Brix allowed herself to respond with a very small smile.

Decker stood up and stared off in the opposite direction for a moment. 'Want to hear my prediction? We're in for a blizzard later.'

All the signs were there, he told them stiffly. The temperature rise was ominous. He said the snowflakes were too wet and fat. This warm pap was indicative of blizzard snow.

Jess started down the beach. 'Decker, I remember the days when you were fun.'

'What days?' He took off his sunglasses, rubbing his eyes. 'It's just an endless single day, and if anything it's getting whiter.'

'Think of it as a continual fresh start,' Jess shouted.

'I'm sick of your fresh start,' he called after her. 'It's too *bright*.'

L istening to the storm crash outside, Dinners lay in his sleeping bag and estimated that it was around dawn. Which meant he had a few hours in which to play his favourite game before anyone else woke. Shutting his eyes, he transported himself to his family.

He could never imagine himself as having a solid body. Instead he was a sentient mist, hovering past the gold-framed watercolours and antique vases and stone fireplace. He went up the stairs and drifted along, picturing the carpet. In his mind the windows were open and it was a summer morning for all eternity. His ritual was to visit his daughter first, materializing from an exaggerated angle near the ceiling to look down on her cot.

Hello, Madeline, he said, seeing the six-month-old baby he'd kissed goodbye, although she would be nearly four now. The weight of his remembered baby varied dramatically each time he picked her up. It was so long since he'd held her that pieces of Antarctic equipment had been substituted. He wafted around, rocking a child who weighed as much as an oilcan in his arms, or an ice axe, or a drawstring bag of rocks. Then he went to his own bedroom, and without any movement, or any real thought of any kind, he was just in the bed beside Elizabeth.

'I'm sorry,' he said to her. 'I did it because I thought you'd be proud of me.'

Sometimes, if he didn't ruin it by forcing the memory,

Elizabeth would reply in her own sweet voice. Mostly, because he tried too hard to summon her from his memory, she'd reply in his voice. Or he'd have her reply telepathically. She'd say she loved him.

I want to come home, Dinners said. *I made a mistake—*

He stopped, interrupted by a low-frequency noise. A blubbery rubber thunder was vibrating from inside the ground, causing stacked pots to overbalance and clang across the floor, and he sat up, yelling in fright.

Napps and Millet-Bass bolted upright. The island was shaking beneath them.

'What the fuck is this?' Millet-Bass cried, hit by a sliding volley of boots.

T here was a blizzard, yes. Nothing too bad, though,' Brix
told Aegeus, talking on the radio phone to Canadian
Sam. Decker was finishing his porridge while Jess wrestled on her boots. None of them had bothered with a flannel
wash that morning, or the morning before.

The migrainous orange of the sunlit tent lining had been
muted by the overnight drifts of blizzard snow. They'd awoken
inside an unusually dark tent.

'Say again?' Brix said to Canadian Sam, because Jess was
speaking loudly, wanting Decker to check behind him for her
fleece jacket.

'I said I hope you're all right, Brix,' Sam repeated. 'You
know, managing.'

'Of course I am.' Brix tried to laugh brightly. 'Did you think
that I wasn't?'

Sam was using the very sympathetic tone which automatically inspired dread in the listener. 'Well, that's what I wanted
to check.'

Brix watched Decker pull on yesterday's socks, and thought
about the occasions she'd been at the work tent during Aegeus
conversations.

'I want you to understand that you can call me up whenever, Brix,' Sam said.

'Would that be something you've heard needs to be done?'
Brix said, phrasing her question oddly to keep the subject matter private from listening ears.

Sam hummed a note, considering the appropriate response. Jess shoved herself out of the tent while Brix waited for an answer. The immediate cursing and anguished ranting which issued from Jess nearly drowned out Sam's reply. 'Maybe,' Sam said to Brix. 'I might have heard you are having a bit of a tough time, yes.'

Brix and Decker emerged from the tent to find Jess staring, disgusted.

The storm had obliterated all signs of habitation. The dirty, slushy paths they'd tramped around the site had been restored into pristine white anonymity, as had the tyre tracks which led off around the island. The sledges were upholstered into snow-padded tablets, and the quads were half buried. Snow had walled up against the tents to leave abandoned-looking peaks. Their camp appeared as deserted as the *Joseph Evelyn,* apart from a mobile sprawl of litter.

Nothing was ever left behind to pollute a fieldwork site once an expedition finished. Every physical remnant of their stay would be returned to Aegeus, and Jess had hoarded their garbage with the care of an archivist. She'd save every scrap of waste from their weeks of meals, pouncing on strips of foil and shreds of paper. Empty packets had been folded and meticulously stowed, along with tissues and cans and cellophane wrappers. And now her work was flung across Everland to choke wildlife and taint an unspoiled place with plastic. Scattered packaging wheeled in the breeze like luridly coloured autumn leaves, bearing the brand names Nestlé, Cadbury's and Heinz. These food-caked bits of trash would need to be trapped and bagged before they could begin digging out the tents and shovelling free the sledges. Then the quads would have to be revved from ditches of snow. And there was still the whole laborious routine of packing to leave camp to be done after that. The blizzard had delayed them by at least three hours.

It was past noon by the time they were organized to drive

to the cove and tag more seals. But the energy expended was already more than a day's worth of work and the mood was fractious. As usual, Decker had the most to do. He inspected the tents for damage and checked to make sure none of the equipment was lost or broken. Moving quickly, he examined the bikes and flung stuff into his bag.

'Ready?' Decker looked from Jess to Brix. 'Yes? You've got everything?'

Jess regarded him sternly, insulted that he'd even asked her. She was a hundred per cent prepared, for ever.

Brix's conversation with Sam had left her feeling uneasy. They never usually set off without Brix asking Decker something, or checking something with him, mostly for assurance. It now seemed unwise. She said she was ready.

As they neared the cove they saw gulls had amassed in huge flocks. Seal pups were all born within days of each other. It was an evolutionary device which improved their chances of survival, since there was safety in numbers for the weak and edible. Gulls were squabbling over grizzled red banners of afterbirth, their white heads stained with blood. The snow was also bloodied from the bulls' fighting. But the thunderous, neck-gouging battles had been suspended. The seals were agitated, and many were gathered at the tideline.

'What's up with them?' Jess said as they dismounted the quads. In the same breath, she said, 'Keys,' to Brix.

Brix chucked the keys over to Jess and said, 'Good catch.'

The quad keys rule had become like a game which they played, yet both found increasingly dumb. Jess exchanged a wry smile with her. 'Good throw.'

Decker began hunting through the loaded sledge. Although Brix stood observing the seals, she couldn't identify the reason for their restlessness. Her eyes were drawn to a narrow alley-sized gap between the cliff edge and a large stone embankment at the far end of the cove.

Everland's coastline was riddled with channels and hidden bays, only a small percentage of which they'd had the chance to explore. The cove was on the eastern side of the island's tapering point. Brix assumed the gap would lead through to a beach on the western side, where the glacier was situated. The sand leading through the alley was churned into a mess of ridges.

'Can you see that?' Brix said.

Decker kept searching through the gear.

'They're seal tracks,' Brix said to the back of Decker's head. The speed at which he'd started to work, practically throwing items on to the ground in his haste, implied that unpleasant news was imminent.

Decker stopped. He let out a harsh laugh of exasperation. 'Perfect. No seal tags.'

Managing scientific apparatus wasn't the job of the field assistant. First-aid was, food was, all the survival stuff was, all the drudgery. This couldn't be blamed on Jess. She glanced at Brix, whose expression was that of someone unsure how to react.

'Well, it's my stupid fault,' Decker said. 'It's good for me to be reminded that I'm responsible for everything. Otherwise I might forget and start expecting other people to anticipate what equipment is required for the day and then pack it. Which is never going to happen, clearly.' He tapped his head. 'Lesson learned, guys.'

Brix's doubt over whether the forgotten tags were entirely her fault was overruled by Decker's apparent certainty and the shrivelling heat of guilt. She thought again of Sam's inferences that she wasn't coping, but remembered Sam's voice as meaner, and more accusing, and vaguely evil.

'How about we all stop acting like the world's going to end?' Jess said, taking a flask of coffee from her bag. 'Yes, returning to the camp to get the equipment is boring, but it's still way more fun than the time I found a dead man in a ravine while part of the Mountain Rescue. He'd burst into pieces. So bit of perspective here.'

Brix wasn't able to accept the aluminium mug of coffee Jess offered to her. She needed a moment to hate herself in private. 'I think I might investigate those seal tracks,' she said, and broke into a trotting, almost jogging pace.

Jess cocked her head at Decker. Much as she gloated over Brix's mistakes, she couldn't recall Decker mentioning the tags to Brix at the camp. And, anyway, this was Brix they were talking about. Hardly the most proactive person. You had to spell it out if you wanted it done.

'Hey, look, if you say the tag thing is Brix's fault, then okay,' Jess said. 'I'm not going to tell you you're wrong. But did you need to be such an asshole about it?'

The barely detectable smell of decay which mixed with the salt breeze intensified as Brix approached the alley. One deterrent to proceeding any farther was that she'd be out of sight if she kept walking. Another deterrent was what she strongly suspected she'd find on the other side. Powerful motivation to continue onwards came in the form of being unable to bear the idea of returning to Jess and Decker.

Decker allowed himself to be labelled an asshole. It was interesting, Jess thought, that the facial expression for shame was virtually identical to the one for nasty-tasting food, with the same unhappily pursed mouth, the same creased forehead, the same look of internal debate.

'Doesn't mean I don't enjoy the irony, though,' she said. 'And you've got to admit it's kind of ironic, Deck, that you're getting tetchy with Brix, being as she's only here because of you and Doctor Angela Pennell.'

'Mm.' Decker's smile was unreadable. 'So you know about that.'

A favour for a favour was how Angie had put it. So he'd

argued hard to convince the Everland selection panel to offer Brix a place on the understanding that the influential Angie would then return the favour by putting in a good word for him. Getting him on the board of directors for a scientific institute, say. A professorship somewhere notable. What a mystery the whole thing was to him now. Those untrustworthy emotions stirred up by his retirement from fieldwork. It had seemed so crucial that he be this big hero who conquered Everland. And if Angie wanted him to take Brix, then sure, he was too busy stoking his ego to worry about the implications of an inexperienced team, or the difficulty it might cause, or, most crucially, whether he really desired to go on the expedition at all.

The smell hit Brix as she emerged on to a small, enclosed beach. Around fifty male fur seal corpses were rotting through the various stages of decomposition. On a few bulls, the hide had torn to show the bald bonnet of a skull. Others were in a state of undress, their skin draped like washing over the bones. Older skeletons had been polished clean of flesh and lay scattered among the ruins of their neighbours in disconnected piles. Sanded hairless by grits of ice, some bodies were as glossy as saddle leather. Corpses were bloated rigid to split, or had split and deflated into atrophied casings. One bull's physical integrity was intact but for the hollowed eye sockets. Another bull had been raided for its innards, leaving its abdomen as gapingly open and empty as a purse.

At the edge of the beach was a cave, its entrance almost as perfectly arched as a train tunnel. Just within the cave, listlessly staring out at Brix, four dying bulls were panting in a shallow pool. The water eddied in slow circles, foam curling to rift against the seals and spiral into new patterns.

Brix felt it before she heard it. The tremor shuddered up through her feet.

27
March 1913

The primus capsized with a metallic slam. It bashed across the groundsheet to meet loose plates and cutlery. The tent was filled with the sounds of miscellaneous collisions above the deeper tectonic rumble of stone.

'I don't . . . ?' Napps was baffled into silence. '*Grab it,*' he said to Dinners as the can of water listed to one side.

Dinners wrapped the can in a crushing hug. There would be punishing nights ahead of them if the water can toppled over to soak their clothes and sleeping bags. They'd be forced to wear wet things and lie in wet things, to morbidly stiffen and ache, when generating the warmth to keep body parts alive was already enough of a problem.

There was a chorus of astonished laughter as the quakes dissipated. Napps sat on his heels listening. 'Good,' he said, and then hesitated. 'So, good, that appears to be done with. How are we? Are we fine?'

Millet-Bass pulled a boot out from under him and tossed it somewhere. Reeling off joyful obscenities, he drove a cluttered mass of plates and pans into the corner. The situation seemed to have taken on a life-affirming charm for him.

Dinners's timid voice spoiled the fun. 'Could the volcano have caused much damage, do you think?' he asked. 'A landslide, perhaps. Should we be worried for the supplies?'

The two other men went quiet. It seemed the dark had grown blacker and more hostile. They were suddenly highly aware of the cold. Dinners saw Napps's silhouetted head turn to look at him. Millet-Bass's profile turned a second later.

Dinners said, 'On top of any damage done by the storm, the—'

'No point worrying tonight,' Napps said, although now they were all worried. 'Let's not speculate whilst we aren't in the position to act.'

Whilst Millet-Bass buried himself into his bag, and Napps lay down, pretending to heed his own advice, Dinners did neither. He sat with his arms clasped around his knees.

'Staying awake won't achieve anything,' Napps said. 'To my knowledge, wishful thinking has never influenced an outcome.'

'That's a lesson I wish I'd learnt earlier,' Dinners said.

Napps stared at him intently. 'I don't follow.'

He said it didn't matter.

Black smoke poured from the volcano. Snow fell from the cliffs with a voluptuous bang. The ground was jumping beneath them, fractures spreading along the cliff face. Rows of pebbles quivered along the shingle and halted, going on again with the next tremor. Brix's steps were flung into an irregular line as she ran to Decker and Jess.

'Brix, stop. Stay there,' Decker shouted when an explosion from further down the beach caused material to spill out in a thunderous flood of rubble.

Brix dropped into a crouch, shaken off balance by a final heavy vibration. The scene was so undercut with fear she observed it with strangely impersonal interest. The authentic, full-bodied terror was replaced by a sense of idiot surprise. Brix watched herself watching the sand crack in jagged geological webs. She watched herself pawing to remain upright as she was thrown on to her side. Getting up, she went sprinting towards Jess and Decker.

Are you all right?' Decker asked, his face wild-eyed. He held Brix by the shoulders. 'Are you hurt?'

When she nodded that she was fine, he let her go and Brix leant on her knees. The adrenaline was incredible and produced a state of hyper-awareness. She was unnaturally conscious of the texture of her gloves, the process of swallowing. Her hand seemed to leave slow-motion trails as she moved it towards her face. She felt that the blood in her head had drained away somewhere.

'Animals can be sensitive to atmospheric changes,' Brix said in a voice she didn't recognize as her own. 'It's possible the seals' earlier restlessness was connected to—'

'Okay, let's sit down before we fall down,' Jess said. She half lowered, half pushed Brix on to the snow. Getting a bar of chocolate out of her pocket, she unwrapped it and handed a piece to Brix. 'That's it, you remember how to eat.'

This is what Jess's friendship must be like, Brix thought. Forceful, jovially pragmatic. 'Thank you.'

'I wouldn't be doing my job if I let you faint from shock and crack your skull open,' Jess said. Looking sideways at Brix, her expression could almost be mistaken for kindness. 'Besides, I need you around in case we see another wounded animal.'

'Well, that was eventful,' Decker said.

'Is it live?' Jess asked as the volcanic smoke tapered out into a white sky. 'Is it going to go off?'

'Don't think so,' he answered. 'Although it's active, there's no record of it ever erupting.'

Although the spokes of its term were among the slowest on earth, the volcano had a life cycle the same as anything which exists or has ever done. It was destined to rise and perish, to rot like fruit under the infinite lens of millennia, and in an inconceivable future to be gone.

'Just the occasional snore,' Decker said.

'Snore,' Jess said. 'Whoa.'

Brix said shakily, 'Wait until you hear what I've found.'

T hat was rather explicit,' Napps said.
'Knew you'd like it,' Millet-Bass said without looking up. In order to solve the problem of his hand skidding down on to the blade of his clasp-knife, he was trussing the handle with a thick bandage of string.

Unlike Napps and Dinners, who could only remember parts of a few hymns, Millet-Bass had a seemingly unlimited catalogue of sailors' songs. They all centred on a range of themes so narrowly specific, inappropriate and sinfully easy to visualize it made Dinners's face boil red with embarrassment. Not that Dinners really minded. Singing at least stopped them talking, and the only thing they ever talked about was the storm. Feverishly discussing the storm from every conceivable angle was their main recreation. And whatever the angle, whatever the premise, the end result for Dinners was always skull-crushing despair.

The blizzard had now continued through four days and nights. In trying to make the supplies they had with them last, the men's meals had dwindled into spoonfuls of pemmican and quarter-cups of water. Although the tent was designed to withstand one-hundred-knot winds, it shook and wrenched at the guy ropes. The walls strained concave, the whole flimsy-feeling structure threatening to lift airborne and vanish into the dark with a snap of fabric.

Millet-Bass put a rag into the candle tray to soak up the melted wax, then transferred the rag to his thickly bound knife handle and rubbed the wax in with his thumb. 'Strange, isn't it?' he said as he worked. 'The air's almost clean in here.'

Dinners understood that Millet-Bass was referring to their curious lack of odour and pressed his nose into the friendly dirtiness of his top. The reek of their long-unwashed bodies had waned to a point where it was barely noticeable. Napps and Millet-Bass said it was a blessing, and had devised various theories to explain its odd disappearance, but Dinners thought their smell had been comforting and unmistakably human, and he secretly mourned its absence.

'What are you thinking of now?' Dinners said swiftly, filling the lull in conversation before Napps could mention the storm. He liked to ask this question despite the predictably monotonous replies. Dinners would always volunteer that he was thinking of Elizabeth, Napps always answered that he was thinking of Rosie, and Millet-Bass always lied.

'No one. Swords,' Millet-Bass would say, thinking of Grace. Or he'd say, 'Pig farming.' He'd say, 'No one, I'm inventing an irrigation system,' thinking constantly of Grace.

'Irrigation? How you entertain yourself with that is a mystery,' Napps said.

'Personally, I enjoy it,' Millet-Bass said. 'I enjoy anything which distracts me from remembering that we'll all die on Everland.' Smiling in the furiously merry way of the obstinate pessimist, he lay back for a session of daydreaming about Grace. With a shave and a smart set of clothes, he thought, and no chat about collectible guns or field-dressing carcasses. He was sure his nervousness around Grace could be overcome with practice, so he rehearsed various scenarios. He pictured them sitting together on a riverbank, or in some restaurant where the new Millet-Bass would be the embodiment of charm. He'd limit himself to one moderate swallow whenever he lifted his wineglass, and if Grace was interested in carpentry or horses the conversation would flow. Maybe if I told you about horses, thought Millet-Bass, but God help me I never will . . .

Napps said something unflattering about Millet-Bass's defeatism as Millet-Bass imagined the crustless sandwiches he'd offer to Grace. Napps said it took a certain kind of arrogance to be so deliberately negative, and Millet-Bass applauded himself for looking so spectacularly desirable on this riverbank in his new suit, with his hair combed and his shoes polished. But he did hear Napps say, 'Lawrence will wonder what happened to you, Millet-Bass.'

'Then that makes us even,' Millet-Bass said, opening an eye. 'Because I'm certainly wondering what happened to Lawrence. It's been weeks; where is he?'

Napps ploughed into an exasperated answer about the *Kismet* being *imminent*, which he'd said *hundreds of times*, which he was *saying again now*, which he was *tired of having to explain*.

'Another tiny sandwich?' Millet-Bass said to Grace, who was enthralled by his knowledge of beetle species, and keen to learn how to guddle fish. Millet-Bass held her hand and told her there was a decent, respectable man under the fur and filth. You could trust me if only you knew me. But God help me, I don't think you ever will . . .

Dinners hoped that Millet-Bass's shut eyes and restfully methodical breaths were not actually the signs of sleep they appeared to be. He became nervous around Napps without Millet-Bass to defend him. As Dinners couldn't will Millet-Bass into consciousness, he would compensate by willing himself into unconsciousness. 'I might have a short nap,' he said to Napps, 'if you'll be awake to guard us.'

'From what?' Napps had a habit of sighing to remind Dinners that pitying him was an arduous task. It wasn't the sigh of a man who placed any value on the idea of guarding them.

'Hmm, no,' Dinners said in mock-contemplation and then

instant resolve. 'I don't believe—no, I don't want a nap after all.'

The men did an incredible amount of sleeping. Millet-Bass and Napps lay at the sides with their heads at the top end of the tent, and Dinners, in the middle, found it less claustrophobic to lie the opposite way with his head near the tent entrance. Their debt of exhaustion found a release in the storm and often knocked them unconscious before they'd finished a sentence. Napps's experience of the blizzard was a journey through semi-coherence as he drifted out of conversations or emerged into them. He dozed and woke and floated from one extract to the next.

He'd once surfaced to find Dinners perched above him, saying, 'I wanted to come, but I need help getting my boots on.' In a blearily thick voice Napps said that he didn't understand. 'And then you were back,' Dinners said.

On several occasions, Napps felt his awakening had interrupted something. Hushed conversations would promptly become stilted and abnormally bland the moment he stirred. He'd lean up and Millet-Bass and Dinners would perhaps seem to have a voltage of guardedness running between them. Their smiles were perhaps unconvincingly enthusiastic, and their glances at him were perhaps a little too long and a little too intent. These anomalies either did or didn't really exist. Millet-Bass pulled a face of amused concern when Napps eventually chose to risk humiliation and ask if they'd been talking about him. He'd said, are you crazy now, Napps?

Another time Napps was roused by a hasty scribbling close to his ear. Dinners had crawled up the tent to rake through Napps's belongings for his diary and was putting something between the pages. He seemed entirely ignorant of the fact that Napps would dislike this violation of his privacy, and dislike being startled awake, and dislike uninvited things being hidden in his diary.

'It's my oath to you,' Dinners said, his voice quivering when Napps snatched the journal off him. 'I won't disappoint you, Napps, I swear. I'm giving you this photograph of Elizabeth to prove it. It's the most precious thing I have, and I want you to keep it until I've fulfilled my oath, so that you'll know I'll be good to my word. I've written a quote on the back.'

Napps neither wanted nor had any interest in Dinners's oath or his photograph. 'Go to bed,' he ordered.

The tentative noises Dinners made as he sat there clutching his own shoulders implied he was preparing a statement. He said, 'Died in the night,' and Napps half shoved him down the tent in his desire not to know the rest of the sentence.

'Wouldn't survive,' Dinners said, lumpishly resisting the efforts to propel him away. 'That's what you said to Lawrence.'

'*Bed*, Dinners.'

'Said I wouldn't survive the night. I know you don't want me here. And you're so angry with me.'

Itching with spite for this man and his sick-making neediness, it occurred to Napps that he could take Dinners by the neck and shake him. Just grab his arm and bite him. It also occurred to him that it wasn't actually Dinners he wanted to attack. It wasn't Dinners who'd insisted on his brilliance as a scientist, or slammed his fist on the table and enforced mindless decisions.

'Lawrence sent you to Everland,' Napps said, images of the Captain's reaction to a knee to the groin flashing through his head. 'You can't be blamed for his mistakes.'

'My mistakes, Napps,' Dinners said. 'And I'm so angry at myself.'

'Fine, good, I accept your oath,' Napps said. He had no idea what Dinners was babbling about, and he'd never cared less about anything in his life, but he saw that Dinners wasn't going to stop until his wish to coerce the First Mate into taking his stupid photograph and nonsense promises had been granted.

'Thank you, thank you, Napps,' Dinners said with gasps of relief. 'I won't disappoint you,' he pledged, finally shuffling off down the tent.

Hours had passed. Napps awoke to whispering in the dark.

'Don't ever mention it to him . . . '

In the long silence which followed, Napps thought they knew he was listening. Then muffled crying broke out again. The accompanying voice was so quiet it couldn't be traced to anyone.

'I didn't think, I never thought—'

'*Shhh*. For your own sake, don't say a word about it.'

There was a quick rustling when Napps seized the lamp. His match flared to illuminate Millet-Bass crouched by the tent entrance.

'Do we want to wake him?' Millet-Bass asked as the candlelight freshened and grew to a steady white flame.

'Careful, Millet-Bass,' Napps said. 'I heard you both talking.'

'But he's asleep.'

Napps looked at Dinners motionless inside his sleeping bag.

'You heard me, Napps. Not him,' Millet-Bass said, the two of them arguing back and forth in murmurs, like men quarrelling in a church, or beside a baby's cot.

'Talking to yourself. About what?'

'About nothing,' Millet-Bass said. 'It was a dream, I think. I didn't know I was talking, it happened before I came to my senses. That's why I sat up.'

Napps remained suspicious for a frostily tense minute. Then he relaxed, slapping a hand across his forehead. '*God*, Millet-Bass, don't go mad. Don't be another Dinners.'

'Ah, you're too rough on him,' Millet-Bass said with a good-natured type of disapproval. Although he was smiling at Napps, his focus kept twitching to the lamp.

'I admire your patience. It's more than I have,' Napps said. 'Whining on about ghosts and hallucinations, his utter—'

Millet-Bass cut him off with a flustered laugh. 'He's getting better.'

'You don't believe that,' Napps said. 'And there are other ways a man can be ill. Listen.' Whatever he was deliberating on was contentious enough to generate intense anticipation. He leant forwards. 'Have you considered what our—'

Millet-Bass sensed an awful confession. 'It's late—'

'Tell me you've never wished it was Castle here with us instead,' Napps said. 'Or Addison. Even bloody Coppers, I don't mind.' He stopped Millet-Bass from reaching for the lamp. 'Let's play a game. Imagine the ship didn't come for us, just say it didn't. And then tell me what you'd do. What you'd be willing to do.'

Millet-Bass corrected himself. For a second he'd glanced at the still shape of Dinners. Now he stared purposefully at Napps. 'I don't want to play these games.'

'Oh, save your puritanical act! We don't have an audience.' Napps raised his hands at the self-evidence of this, grinning. 'Tell me truthfully it wouldn't have been easier for us without him. Tell me that it wouldn't be easier—'

'*Napps*, don't say it.'

'If he'd died in the dinghy.'

Millet-Bass's expression was so painfully clenched, it struck Napps as insulting. It forced him to regret letting the private but abstract evils out of his mouth to become conscious and free. The sanctimonious Millet-Bass had put him in a morally disadvantaged position. More than annoying, Napps felt it was rude. He told Millet-Bass to extinguish the candle.

Millet-Bass spoke with a curious generality. 'No one meant what they said tonight, I'm certain of it.'

The second before the light died into blackness, Napps understood. His eyes flicked from Millet-Bass to look again at Dinners.

S orry for being such a jerk.' Decker shot Brix a remorse-
ful smile. 'Well, I say jerk. Jess used the word asshole,
which is perhaps a more fitting description.'

What mattered when living jammed together in a tent was
harmony, and that quality had been noticeably absent as they
returned to the camp. The seal tag incident at the cove had left
Decker sheepish, and Brix feeling awkward. For the past half-
hour, they'd addressed each other with overly polite tentative-
ness, mostly avoiding eye contact. Although this was their
problem to resolve and Jess had decided to stay out of it, she'd
eventually lost patience. Announcing that the volcano drama
was an excellent reason to treat themselves to the tub of frozen
sausages and bacon, she'd tramped off with a shovel to dig
them up, leaving Decker and Brix alone in the tent.

Brix had to repeat Decker's last sentence in her head a couple of times. The idea of Jess defending her was unexpected,
but also evidence that her theory was correct. She and Jess
were undergoing a transition. Brix's opinions about Jess's surli-
ness and irritability, her rudeness, her general awfulness, had
been replaced with more benign feelings. And Jess's views on
Brix also seemed to have become more forgiving. Learning to
like each other was a project they were both working on in
secret, and similar to unstable chemicals or light-sensitive
paper, it was a very delicate project which would be ruined if
handled carelessly. For example, by mentioning anything, or
displaying overt friendliness.

What Brix hated nearly as much as tension was lengthy apologetic discussion.

'Well, here's the good news,' she said, hoping they could let the topic of the seal tags be forgotten. 'We've only got three weeks left on Everland.'

'Three weeks,' Decker said with obvious longing. 'You won't believe how good that first hot shower is, or that first night in your own bed.'

However much he enjoyed his job, the centenary expedition didn't have any particular significance to Decker. Unlike Brix, to whom everything about Antarctica was exotic and strange, it was all familiar to him. Everything was commonplace in its own habitat, and after twenty years of Antarctic research, penguins and glaciers were no more astounding for him to witness than cows or trees. Which left him plenty of time to think about other things, such as roast chicken, king prawn jalfrezi, his local pub, the Sunday papers. He stopped himself. Brix clearly didn't find thoughts of beds and showers as transporting as he did. Still, he had a good idea what she would be pleased about.

'Three weeks, and then no more field assistants,' he said. 'Got to be good news, eh?'

To his surprise, Brix made a small ambiguous noise and shrugged. 'I don't know, Jess isn't so bad,' she said. 'I occasionally think she might be okay underneath that attitude.'

They heard footsteps outside and Brix fell silent. Jess was back with upsetting information. The meat wasn't frozen. It was black and wet, and oh my God, the smell.

'The hole can't have been deep enough,' Decker said, rolling his head away as she showed them the rank tarry substance on her gloves. 'Or the covering of snow was too thin . . .'

No, Jess swore that she'd done everything perfectly. It was hardly the first time she'd buried fresh produce on an expedition, she said, growing more defensive, and she'd never had an issue with it before. Sensing an air of unfinished business underneath the new affability between Brix and Decker, she asked, 'Did I interrupt something?'

'Nope,' Brix said in the carefree tone specific to lying. 'We were talking about the dead bulls. Remember you wanted to know why we only collected teeth from the female seals?'

If Jess did remember, she didn't answer. Decker's suggestion that she was so talentless with a spade she couldn't even manage to bury a little plastic tub of meat correctly had wounded her. Jess's attention returned to her disgusting gloves.

Brix continued, explaining that, scientifically, it made no difference whether teeth were retrieved from a living or dead animal. A tooth was a tooth. But as female seals almost always died at sea where they couldn't be found, their teeth had to be extracted while they were alive. Whereas the bulls conveniently tended to die on land, so their teeth could be removed when dead.

The notion of harvesting teeth animated Decker. 'That convenience does come with a price, though.' He shook his head, recalling a historic trauma. 'Wear clothes you'll never want to use again.'

They returned to the cove the next morning to see the fur seals lazing around, untroubled by the previous day's volcanic activity. Now the cows' fertile period was over, the bulls had reverted to their former slothful ways.

The stench billowing from the seal corpses had a thickness and throat-coating acridity which seemed capable of leaving a visible residue. It was hard to believe a bare hand held directly above a reeking carcass wouldn't be painted with a brown nicotine film. Decker, Jess and Brix roved about with pliers, disturbing the scavenging gulls which lifted in shrill, flapping unison. By mid-afternoon the beach was at its fullest clamour and pitch, the snow flats dazzled to chrome under a sky as hard and scouring as pumice.

Jess had failed to master the technique to yanking out teeth. The tooth either rocked in its socket with a noise of rasping bone, or didn't move at all. Pulling harder caused the tooth to splinter, pulling from a different angle caused the pliers to slip. 'Gross,' she said in frustration as another tooth snapped into pieces.

'What? It's amazing,' Decker said, holding up a fang. 'See this? It makes me wish I wrote poetry, it really does. Our guy here has archived everything, not only his age. Each tooth is a prism reflecting entire chains of events.'

It was beautiful to him, he said, describing the isotopes of carbon in each tooth. Comparable to the rings in a tree trunk, the isotopes created a record of growth and age. The tooth was a transcript of a conversation between the seal and his environment which had run for his whole life. It told you, year by year, whether food was plentiful or scarce. It told you how competitive or productive those years had been. And comparing the health and lifespan of one generation to the previous generations of fur seals produced a larger narration of every flux and consequence in the wider ecosystem. What appeared was a history which lived through the death of its speakers. What appeared, ultimately, was the story of Antarctica.

Jess was only partly listening. If the skull didn't want to surrender its stupid transcript isotopes, then Jess didn't see why she shouldn't just kick the skull down the beach. She was considering this when she heard Brix's voice directly behind her.

'It's easier if you twist the pliers while you pull. Let me show you.'

Jess's red, frustrated face turned to stare at her. That she was actually being given advice by Brix took her a moment to adjust to. Watching Brix then achieve effortlessly what Jess, who understood herself to be infinitely more capable, had found impossible was no less discomforting.

Jess expressed her gratitude with a nod instead of words. It was a type of thanks. Appreciating help wasn't the same thing as liking it.

'We're finished here anyway,' Brix said, rattling her full Kilner jar of teeth.

'Well, then I should probably. . .' Jess let the sentence trail off. She glanced around for something important and preferably impressive to do.

Childish or not, Jess felt easier about being outdone by Brix when she recalled that the next task once the teeth were collected was to investigate the cave. What she wanted to do was listen to angry music in a room by herself, but since she couldn't, she reasoned a cave was a decent enough substitute. Brix followed after her a couple of minutes later, once she and Decker had packed up the Kilner jars.

The cave walls were glazed with layers of rime and the viscous sheen of algae, acid orange stains revealing where iron oxide deposits had seeped from the rock. Water bled through seams in the roof with the steady patter of trees dripping after heavy rain. It made clear notes as it fell into shallow water, deeper notes in deeper water, and ticked dryly against sand. Visibility inside the cave started as smoky outlines and gradually improved as Brix's eyes became accustomed to the light. The ground ahead sloped down in a two-and-a-half-metre shelf, and beyond the slope, at the rear of the cave, were two small alcoves.

Jess was standing at the edge of the shelf, peering over at the base. When she saw Brix, she started to descend, saying, 'I just want to check something.'

Decker traipsed into view as the sound of coursing gravel became louder.

'Check what, Jess?' Brix said.

As Jess's feet skidded and sank beneath her, she considered what had inspired her to start sliding down a loose gravel slope in the first place. Confidence perhaps, or intrepidness. It was more likely that pride was the main factor. She'd wanted to prove her competence to someone, herself maybe, or the world in general. And she now thought that she could have done it differently. Her boots were driving deep troughs into the surface and she was moving too fast.

'Check what?' Brix said again.

There was an abrupt intake of breath. Scrambling down the slope to reach Jess, Decker and Brix found her clasping her ankle, her leg bent at an uncomfortable angle. She answered in a tight, breathy voice when they asked her if it hurt to move.

'Yes, hurts,' Jess said, leaning against them heavily as they laboured out to the beach. 'I thought I saw—' Whenever the ankle made contact with the ground it activated a megavoltage of pain. 'Wait, wait, wait,' she said, her eyes screwed shut, needing to stand still for a few seconds or possibly a year.

'Frightening to realize how dependent we are on each other,' Jess said when she opened her eyes. 'Not so different to Napps and his men.'

'Except that we've got better food, better equipment,' Decker said. 'We've got better clothing, better season, better everything.' He sighed about the impracticality of being hurt in a cave and turned to Jess. 'Okay, this is taking for ever.'

'You're not going to give me a piggyback.' Jess considered him. 'Or are you?' The embarrassment and gratitude were about equal. Riding around on someone's back was fine for a child, less so at the age of twenty-nine. Also, Jess wasn't a little pixieish woman.

'We've also got a better attitude to team members,' Decker said, carrying Jess to the quads. 'Way better. Are we abandoning you? No, we're a team, which means your problems are my problems, your injuries are my injuries. *Mi casa es su casa*, and vice versa. I don't know the Spanish word for body. You get the idea.'

'But pull another stunt like that again,' he said, his smile a bit too strained to be humorous, 'and I might decide we're better off without you.'

The Officers' Mess had the doggish smell of damp wool as jumpers steamed in the warmth. Lawrence was playing cards with Coppers and McValley when he saw Addison enter to find him. Standing quickly, he and the doctor had a low-voiced discussion.

'Look, I don't see that we can delay telling the crew any longer,' Lawrence said. 'They have a right to clarification.'

Addison felt Lawrence's idea of what constituted discretion could be refined. That every pair of ears in the room was straining to listen to their conversation appeared to concern him far more than it did the Captain, and he stared pointedly at Lawrence to remind him of their audience as he spoke.

'Please be careful, I'm asking you to bear in mind that—'

'You think rumours haven't been seething through this ship from the moment we found Dinners?' Lawrence replied, loudly enough to provoke McValley into glancing over his hand of cards at Coppers, who raised his eyebrows. 'What do you think, Addison, that the men haven't discussed it? I'm confirming what they already know.'

Addison leant closer to Lawrence. 'Napps has a family who'll never see him again, as does Millet-Bass. I'm asking you not to ruin these men for the people who love them.'

'They ruined themselves,' Lawrence said at a volume everyone could hear as he turned to address the crew.

'We're all aware of the terrible blow our expedition has suffered with the loss of Napps and Millet-Bass,' he said. 'So I ask myself, what possible solace can be found in such a tragic situation? And then the answer comes to me: it's you men, my crew. I'm heartened by the bravery of your efforts to find those missing men; I'm heartened by your resilience and spirit . . . '

Addison crept down the side of the room to one of the empty chairs next to Castle. Unpopularity was a terrifying illness, and the doctor was now the only person who chose to sit beside Castle. Even Smith, who'd spent years following Castle about like a devoted pet, avoided all contact with him, scuttling away with a smirk of apology.

'You're all right?' Addison said, noticing the red mark on Castle's face.

Castle cocked his head once. 'Been worse,' he said.

The injury was the result of a bizarre spat the night before over a song called 'Boiled Beef and Carrots'. Don't live like vegetarians on the food they give to sparrows, McValley had sung as Castle laughed and said, 'Parrots! The food they give to *parrots*. Which rhymes with carrots.'

'No, sparrows,' McValley said with an ominous smile.

'Boiled beef and carrows?' Castle nudged the man closest. 'He's having us on, isn't he, lads? Making fools of us.' McValley had jumped to his feet.

The hot sting of the slap faded into nervous, complicit sniggering as Castle put a hand to his cheek.

McValley had sighed in disappointment. 'You see, that's the *third* time you've called me a liar.'

'I'll be sure to mention the "carrows" assault in my book and give you justice,' Addison said to cheer him up.

'You're writing a book?' Castle said. 'Good.'

'I've been considering it,' Addison said. 'After all, Lawrence isn't the only one on this expedition with a diary. He's also not the only one with an opinion.'

'Then make sure you destroy McValley,' Castle said, despite knowing the doctor was incapable of vindictiveness. 'I'm serious;

don't be decent about this, Adds. I want you to tear him apart, line by line. My reputation is at stake here.'

Castle himself wasn't immune from the appeals of malice. There were pages in his journal entirely devoted to listing the faults of others, and vengefully loathing them for whatever crimes they'd committed against him. A few of those pages concerned Napps, who for one reason or another had infuriated Castle, perhaps by being dismissive of some idea, or for a terse remark, or for a woundingly sarcastic correction of a wrongly stated fact. After spending years cramped together, even the best of friends were occasionally ready to kill each other. So Castle would brood, rant his way through ten thousand words, and then feel restored. The difference between McValley and Napps was that Castle loved Napps like a brother, rowed with him like a brother, forgave him like a brother, but hated McValley exactly like he deserved.

'. . . Which makes me truly honoured to call myself your Captain,' Lawrence finished. The crew accepted his praise, not that interested. Their minds were bent on the real issue.

Lawrence finally gave them what they wanted. 'And I'm afraid the only logical assumption is that Napps and Millet-Bass have perished.'

'What do you suppose happened?' Smith asked.

'Haven't you figured it out?' Coppers tapped a finger against his skull. 'Anything in there, Smith? The *Joseph Evelyn* leaves with a mountain of gear, yet we find Dinners in an empty camp without so much as a pair of extra socks. Why's that?'

Smith crossed his arms, his eyes starting to brim.

'It disgusts me, both as a Captain and as a Christian man, but I believe Dinners was abandoned by Napps and Millet-Bass,' Lawrence said, his eyes downcast in sorrow. 'The two men stripped the camp and left Everland to trek over the sea ice. I can only presume the Mate believed they'd reach Cape Athena.'

And here, Lawrence explained, were the things Napps must have assumed.

The first was that rescue was far off, since Napps couldn't know the ship was trying to reach them, but had been trapped across the bay at Cape Athena. Napps had also assumed the early-season sea ice would hold out. And considering the extraordinarily low temperatures, who hadn't thought the same? The ice which had locked around the *Kismet* during the frightening temperature drop at the Cape had seemed thick enough to last through winter. Not a man aboard had ever expected such leaden, deeply established pack could get swept away overnight, yet that's what had occurred. The bay waters were entirely clear of ice by morning. It had astonished them, and they'd been studying freeze cycles for years. They were virtually ice savants.

'Napps's final assumption,' Lawrence said, 'was that Dinners would never be found alive.'

Someone said, 'Cautious enough to take his diary though, weren't they.'

'Well, you can probably guess the reason,' Lawrence answered. 'They didn't want Dinners to write an account of what they'd done and consequently leave behind a journal full of evidence waiting to be discovered with his body inside the dinghy. I suppose if Napps and Millet-Bass had made it to Cape Athena, they would have said that Dinners had died on Everland weeks earlier. And no one returning then or later would have ever known the difference.'

Fists hammered in delighted outrage. Almost all the men had volunteered for the Everland expedition and now they couldn't believe their lucky escape. Any one of them could have been cursed to go ashore with Napps, to get served with Dinners's barbaric terms if they'd crocked, or die on the ice as the worst kind of traitor. The Officers' Mess filled with bragging self-righteousness and moral horror, as if none of them secretly wondered, couldn't I? To save myself, couldn't I do just about anything? And the answer for some, without hesitation, was *yes*.

Napps and Millet-Bass were now human in name only. Their characters had been refined and refined again until the proportions were grotesque. Millet-Bass was a violent apelike thing with mad unspeakable lusts and a history of being unable to control himself. He couldn't be blamed for his actions, though, because he was incapable of logical thought. It was accepted as common knowledge that Millet-Bass couldn't read or spell and thought the moon was magic. He ate bones; they'd seen him do it. Napps was a schemer and a spy who lurked in the dark devising ways to hate a man. They'd all sensed his ear pressed to the door, his fingers rifling through their private letters. McValley's bout of scurvy was one of a dozen incidents when Napps had verbally wished someone dead. It was amazing they hadn't been murdered in their sleep. Smith heard his name called and readied himself for more unpleasantness.

Instead the man joked, 'Hey, Smith, maybe Napps was looking to snuff you on Christmas Day instead of your little cat?'

Smith's slavish hunger for approval immediately overwhelmed any sense of loyalty. He pretended to reflect and then said, *Definitely*.

'Oh, this story? Great, I love it,' Castle said with bitter enthusiasm. 'My memory of that night never seems to correspond, but we'd all had a lot to drink, so.'

Smith shifted in his chair to block Castle from his eyeline. 'Yes, I've no doubt Napps believed it was my throat he was wringing between his hands,' he said, rewarded with the laughter he craved.

Smith's tolerance to alcohol extended to two smallish drinks. After a third drink, and a fourth drink, and another drink which turned out not to be the water he'd asked for,

Smith had thought it wise to start the semi-crawled journey to his bed. The *Kismet*'s Christmas Day celebrations always started early and went on until dawn. Lurching around in their paper hats, Napps and Castle had spotted Smith as he banged from wall to wall and fell headfirst into his room. Then he'd screamed.

Forcing the door open, they'd found Smith howling over his cat as it writhed and flapped in agonized circles. He'd snapped the cat's back when he'd tripped, and he begged them not to tell anyone and begged Napps to help. He wept as he answered Napps's questions, saying yes, he did understand that there was no other way to stop the cat suffering. Yes, he did, he did understand, he'd sobbed, becoming hysterical. So Napps had done it. And moments later, Coppers had walked into a chaotic scene. Smith was inconsolable, cradling his dead cat and wailing, '*On Christmas Day! On Christmas Day as well!*' while a white-faced and shaken Napps instructed him to quieten down. But Coppers knew exactly what he'd witnessed. That no one involved would ever explain the situation to him merely confirmed it.

'Well, at least the Dinners family will have good news,' McValley said. 'We'll be bringing their boy home alive.'

'Their boy, yes,' Lawrence said. 'Right, Addison?' When the doctor didn't respond, he said it again, louder. 'Isn't that right, Addison?'

Addison's nod affirmed nothing beyond that he had heard the question.

32
April 1913

Napps remembered the October sky. It wasn't the plush blue of summer, but thin and distilled with an early-morning moon. Rosie had caught him looking at her and he'd kept on looking. Whenever he went to sea, that last awful day before he left was always met by a bravely cheerful Rosie and an uncharacteristically demonstrative Napps. He needed to make sure that she understood he loved her. Because he did, and had done from the moment he met her at a Christmas party hosted by her father, which the surly fifteen-year-old Napps had been forced into attending with his parents. That was the evening a dark-haired girl came over to Napps and asked him why he was so boring. She'd been observing him, she said, and he'd spent the whole night staring at the floor. Napps knew nothing about women or how to talk to them. Having a mother was the limit of his experience. But he'd instinctively understood that the way to impress attractive girls was to ignore them. About twenty minutes later, Napps had become aware of three life-changing facts: the first was that a certain type of person just won't be ignored; the second was that drinking a tumbler of rum on an empty stomach would produce strong feelings of both sickness and elation. The third fact was that whoever this girl was who'd stolen the rum and made him hide with her at the end of the garden, she now somehow owned him.

'Listen!' Dinners cried, accidentally kicking Napps as he scrambled to open the tent.

The storm had died overnight to leave a gentle, ruffling breeze, and the men emerged from their long bedridden period. On stiff legs, they hobbled around the tent to inspect it for damage and found nothing more serious than a few small tears in the outer lining. Dinners said it was miraculous. Not only had they survived the blizzard unscathed, he thought they'd actually benefited from it. He wanted to know if they agreed that a few warm days of enforced sloth had done them good. Didn't they also feel better? His hands and feet were healing and he personally felt a great deal better. So well, in fact, that he said he would now accompany them to the cove to check on the supplies.

While the other two walked in front discussing some ludicrous theory of Millet-Bass's, Napps fell behind. He didn't believe Millet-Bass had been dreaming that night in the tent, or that Dinners had been asleep during his badly judged confession. The proof was in Millet-Bass's watchful awkwardness and Dinners's grovelling enthusiasm. His face brightened hopefully whenever Napps looked at him. Whatever Napps wanted, Dinners would offer immediately. And his constant efforts to please only succeeded in making Napps angrier with both men, since his bullying of Dinners forced Millet-Bass to intervene. Napps's temper might possibly have improved if he'd been able to rage at them for betraying him as he wanted, but the situation was complex. Napps was as guilty as they were. He'd also behaved shamefully that night when he admitted he resented Dinners to Millet-Bass. So their pride relied on a pact of mutual ignorance. No one could mention the incident without disgracing himself in the process.

'It's certainly an unusual theory,' Dinners said when Millet-Bass claimed that it was possible to smell shattered ice on the breeze when enough of it was broken. Learning to detect its faint, cleansing smell was just one of the skills he had honed over his years of sailing. And honestly, he could smell broken ice.

'Don't believe me? What will you stake on it?' Millet-Bass said.

'The sugar I put in my evening drink,' Dinners answered, which was a bold wager for him. Their one mug of sweet tea was a luxury he obsessed about from the second he opened his eyes.

'And what else?' Millet-Bass said.

Immersed in his daydream, the volume of their voices was almost inaudible to Napps. He was with Rosie on the October morning before he left.

Although he'd never spoken these words to Rosie, he recited them to her now. No man or deed or sin or obstacle, he said, even as he heard his name being shouted. The midday sun was a frayed stain on the horizon, and its light cast everything in the same dusky shade of blue. It was the colour of wistfulness, Napps thought, as he pictured the translucent October moon. Millet-Bass suddenly broke into a full sprint, and Dinners faltered, clasping his head, and then chased after him. *No man or deed*, Napps promised Rosie, distracted by his name still echoing along the beach. *Or sin*, he said, and broke off to look in the direction of the interruption.

'*Napps!*' Dinners was stepping erratically from one foot to the other. '*Napps!*'

Beyond Dinners was an indecipherable scene. The cove had been transformed by the blizzard, the cliffs partially buried under an avalanche of rubble. Taurus had ruptured to flood the bay with tons of ice and its horns lay in fractured segments. Of the colossal-sized chunks which had smashed down into the cove, one had fallen on to the tethered supplies and caused rations to explode from the flattened crates. The stylized emblems of familiar brands, with trademarked illustrations of happy animals, or ripe harvests, or picturesque farmhouses, were strewn among shattered wooden slats. Crushed tins had leached their contents, marking the snow with red and orange splashes of soup, pulpy brown streaks of stewed beef, the black charred-looking patches of spilt tea-leaves. Out of the twenty crates, only half had survived intact. Six were in motion, sliding loosely towards the sea before tumbling up the shore on the next wave. The other four undestroyed crates remained on land, their saltwater-drenched webbing of snapped and knotted ropes iced solid to the beach.

'Rescue whatever you can,' Napps said when he reached Dinners, who stood alone amid the wreckage. 'Anything you can lift. Get the supplies to higher ground. Where's Millet-Bass?'

'The crates won't move,' Dinners said, doing his terrified dance from foot to foot. 'The ropes are frozen to the beach.'

Napps held Dinners by the arms to make him concentrate. 'Cut the ropes.'

'But Millet-Bass has both the knives.'

'Then get them,' Napps said, shaking Dinners harder than he meant to. 'Where is he? Get the knives.'

'I tried to stop him. Napps, he's in the sea.'

Every wave sent a flotilla of supplies and ice crashing against the rocks. Heinz and Colman's and Tate & Lyle were churning through the surf, and another box splintered to release a shoal of canned herrings into the water. Standing waist-deep in the ocean, Millet-Bass made no effort to avoid the debris floating around him. He didn't seem aware of the cold, or the spray flung across his back with each swell, or the danger of being hit by one of the crates and knocked down. When Napps shouted that the cold would kill him, he didn't even turn his head.

'Leave what's in the sea, we can't save it,' Napps ordered.

To leave it would be to leave everything they had. It was distressingly clear to Millet-Bass that Napps hadn't understood the situation. He might have explained it to him, but Millet-Bass found that parts of the explanation were in another language he'd lost the ability to translate. He wanted to tell Napps about his plan to resolve the crisis, except the details of his plan were difficult to recall. He'd stormed into the sea, he remembered doing that, yet what he'd actually intended to do once semi-immersed in icy water was now a mystery. Because it seemed like it might be the answer, Millet-Bass grabbed a can of pears and absently threw it towards the beach. He went for a pouch of tobacco suspended below the surface with tobacco flecks wafting from the ripped lid. He caught a bag of flour and it disintegrated, a thick paste of soaked flour covering his glove.

The task of surviving Everland took the combined effort of Napps and Millet-Bass. It was so beyond the capability of one man, that unless they were both well, they were all finished. Therefore in order to save himself, Napps had to save Millet-Bass, which meant he had to endanger himself by wading into the sea. He was dependent on a man whose reckless contempt of his own life was killing them together, and the torment of his powerlessness, his reliance on someone who was now destroying him, manifested in Napps as a violent nihilism. He would die if he couldn't stop Millet-Bass from dying, and if Millet-Bass couldn't be stopped from wanting to die, then Napps would give him what he wanted. He'd take Millet-Bass round the neck and squeeze the life out of him, he'd happily stamp the life out of him. Using his own two fists, he'd beat the life out of him.

'Our fortunes can't be separated, yet you choose to act as if any loss is yours alone,' he said, plunging across to Millet-Bass.

Millet-Bass stared at Napps as though surprised to see him. 'How many days is this?' he said, gesturing at the cans bobbing nearby. 'Four days? Five days lost?'

A crate rode over the wave and Napps didn't have time to

answer. He twisted to stave off the collision with his shoulder and the force of the impact rolled him underwater. He felt a pain score along his side from the hip. When he choked back up to his feet, Millet-Bass didn't seem to have noticed the incident. He continued to talk to Napps in the same vague, reminiscing tone.

'So what have we lost in total, Napps?'

Hearing Millet-Bass's voice as a remote and dispossessed static buzz, Napps banged his ear with one hand, the other hand grasping his waist.

Millet-Bass pointed at the wider slick of tins and packets which drifted around them. 'How many weeks?'

'Stay in the water and you'll ruin us,' Napps said. At a certain temperature the freezing becomes indistinguishable from burning, and his chest was searing hot. His legs and arms were in flames. 'But what do you care. You don't have a wife worrying, children you haven't seen for years. You wouldn't understand what I have to lose.'

Millet-Bass regarded him with an impassive expression. 'You think I've got less to go home for.' Then his eyes focused. 'You genuinely think that.'

'Say another word and I'll drown you,' Napps said.

'You *bastard*.'

Napps burst towards him.

The sky was darkening. Dinners watched from the shoreline as Napps struck at Millet-Bass, causing the bigger man to overbalance. With Millet-Bass tripping and fumbling on his knees, Napps dragged him to the beach by his collar and flung him down on to the snow.

'Get him up,' he said to Dinners, and would have said more. A rush of nausea stopped him. He turned his head to better concentrate on swallowing it back.

Dinners cringed towards Millet-Bass and took him under the arms, hauling him to his feet. 'Napps, are you injured?'

Napps needed to put pressure on his side. Without pressure, the pain spread into other areas of his body and his mouth filled with gastric-tasting fluid. 'Get the knives,' he said, pressing his side so hard he felt his ribs flex.

The tremor of mortification which passed through Millet-Bass was more chilling than his soaked clothes. He glimpsed the madness of his lunging into the sea from the perspective of the near future. In about an hour, he would be engulfed in a cyclone of self-hatred and shame. Hoping to make amends for his unforgivable behaviour by being useful, he tore off his gloves and ransacked his jacket pockets for the clasp-knives. His clumsily moving numb fingers wouldn't grip and the knives dropped, clattering to the ground.

Dinners bent to snatch the knives as a huge wave with ragged foam on the crest came gliding towards the beach.

'Dinners, quickly. Give me my knife,' Millet-Bass said.

Unlike the handle of Millet-Bass's knife, the handle of Napps's wasn't bound with a thick truss of string. The wood had been polished smooth by years of use. Dinners didn't think when he passed one of the knives to Millet-Bass. He was frightened his frostbite wounds would deteriorate if he got wet in the wave which had broken and was surging towards them. He thrust a knife towards Millet-Bass, saying, *here, take it, take it.* Millet-Bass accepted the handle in his bare hand and raised his arm to slash at the ropes.

The blade had largely severed the rope and for a moment there was no sensation. Once the water receded, Dinners began ferrying the loose crates to safety as Napps limped after him in the hunched posture that his pain would allow.

Millet-Bass opened his hand, looked at it, then closed it and rinsed it in the water. He put his gloves on and stood with his eyes shut as the blood in the water bloomed red, then pink, and then dispersed.

33

June 1913

Castle was perched on the slim shelf inside the crow's nest, embellishing the carving of his wife's name as he did every shift. It was one of the few distractions available to a man trapped in a barrel one hundred and ten feet up a mast. He chipped at the oak with his penknife and refined his many homecoming lists. Some of the lists were very chaste, and concerned things he would eat and drink, or things he would buy, such as a motorbike. Other lists were naughtier.

'Castle, I said all well?'

The barrel had small holes drilled through the sides so that its occupant could avoid exposing his head to the raw wind. Castle pressed a cold watering eye to one of the holes and spotted Lawrence and Smith down below on the lamp-lit deck.

He appeared above the rim. 'Having the time of my life, sir.'

'Castle! You ass, stop hanging over the side of the barrel,' Lawrence said. 'I've got enough to worry about.'

The sky was clear, the flat black ocean illuminated by a full moon. Although it was one of the nicer evenings for a shift on watch, no one was ever that happy to stand alone on deck at night, policing the sea for hazards. Smith, however, seemed oddly giddy about the prospect. He waved at Castle with both arms until Lawrence restrained him by an elbow, telling him to sober up.

Castle tried not to sound resentful. 'You've been drinking.'

'Yes! All of us!' With only Lawrence around to witness it, Smith allowed himself to be friendlier to Castle. He shouted up that Jennet had delighted everyone by trolling out of his lair with brandy in order to commemorate his wedding anniversary.

Jennet's surprise toast had come as a relief to Lawrence. The atmosphere on the ship was restless and he was happy to have any excuse to lighten the mood. There was some diabolical connection between their proximity to home and the escalating pressure of the voyage. Each new day punished Lawrence for his success in navigating them closer to safety by presenting him with an ever wilder crew. He was increasingly forced to deal with gnashing bolts of craziness and conversations which escalated into violence. He'd begun to carry a bullwhip around as a menacing prop to jab at people while he demanded obedience. The situation had confirmed his very worst fears. He was the Captain, he had the title of 'Captain', but he didn't have the authority of a Captain. That talent belonged to another man, and that man wasn't here any more. That man had died on Everland. And without Napps, Lawrence's shortcomings were reflected back at him in the faces of every one of his untameable sailors.

Smith's brandy-silliness influenced him to say that it was probably better that Castle had been stuck in the crow's nest for Jennet's anniversary drink. What with the jokes Coppers was telling. What with the subject of those jokes. Smith very much doubted that Castle would have enjoyed the jokes.

Castle's smile had the rigid interest of someone absorbing offence. He said, 'Why don't you let me decide for myself?'

'Get back in the *barrel*, Castle,' Lawrence ordered. Shoving Smith further along the deck where he couldn't cause trouble, Lawrence strode off, thumping down the stairs to his cabin.

Castle spent another fifteen minutes carving his wife's name before the task struck him as infinitely sad and purposeless and he had to stop. He was whittling a tribute for a fondly forgotten stranger whose face he could barely picture. All that was left of his wife was a string of letters which spelt *Margaret* and a ring on his finger symbolizing an oath hollowed of its meaning. His marriage, which had once seemed so mountain-like and warmly encompassing, no longer provided him with anything more substantial to cling to than a few grams of gold.

Castle thought of himself in two ways. There was the nomadic, risk-loving self, which had drawn him into his career as a sailor, and there was the real self, the man he was at home. Castle was anchored in being a husband and father, and in being both a brother and a son who would follow into the family business. For sensible reasons, he'd separated that man and the man on the *Kismet*. Yearning caused heartache and a listless inability to do anything constructive. Self-pity was a paralytic disease. So Castle had trained himself to think of home as a heavenly entity. He believed in it and knew it existed somewhere, yet its distance was magical and beyond comprehension. Home was real in the same way a thousand years in the past was real. It was a strategy which freed Castle to enjoy his work. But since they were now returning to Britain, Castle changed his tactics. After three years of refusal, he allowed himself to pine, only to find it wasn't the bittersweet pleasure he'd expected. Instead it made him feel unbearably lonely.

When Castle thought of his children, he thought of babies, yet these babies would have vanished. They'd have grown absurdly tall and be speaking, reading, running, and they wouldn't know their father. And when Castle thought of his friends and family, he thought of himself in a central role. Except he'd become peripheral. Their news would define a togetherness which didn't include him, whilst his own news only defined his absence.

Other, more malignant concerns festered underneath. Although three years wasn't so inconceivably long to be separated from everyone, Castle wondered if the important factor wasn't the duration of time but the nature of that time. He worried about this when he remembered walking the same little routes around the same little town. He worried about repacking himself into the man who'd admired the furniture business established by his grandfather. He remembered his previous ability to be satisfied in the tight confines of domesticity. Those miniature clockwork weeks. He'd been strutting about in his chicken-run kingdom with each tiny day ticking neatly to the next. When he wondered whether the man he'd taken from his family was now as vanished as those babies, he worried he knew the answer.

There was a sharp snap. Castle saw the feathery spray as a bullet smacked into the water. A gust of suction and large wet plume came from the diving whale.

'Smith? What are you doing?'

Hearing his name, Smith acknowledged Castle with a nod. He was standing against the lee rail, the barrel of his rifle slowly patrolling the waves for a dorsal fin. Minkes were a smaller species of whale which regularly lolled alongside the ship. This one was swimming close enough for some of its spray to rain across the deck.

'Smith, don't.'

Smith couldn't concentrate with Castle yelling at him. He aimed and pretended to shoot at the crow's nest, *bang, dead*, and then said petulantly, 'What do you care?'

The normal Castle might have been able to restrain his temper, but an hour of devastating introspection inside a barrel had left him in a volatile mood. The cowardly way Smith ignored him in public suddenly made him angry. Smith's toadyism made him furious, and Smith's disloyalty to Napps made him incandescent with rage. To needlessly hurt a minke was one more reason for Castle to go down there and give him a beating. He was already out of the crow's nest and descending the ropes.

Another couple of rifle volleys mixed with the slack spout

of the whale's exhalation. The shots broke off while Smith reloaded. He didn't notice Castle jump the last rungs.

'Steady, girl . . . steady,' Smith said with one eye shut, pressing lightly against the trigger as he aimed for the fin. 'I'm going straight through the centre.'

Castle's first strike knocked the rifle stock into Smith's jaw. The second caused Smith to stumble backwards, the rifle clattering across the deck. Castle had grabbed him by the collar before he could regain his balance.

'The last minke we might ever see and you want to bleed it to death,' Castle said, inches from Smith's face. He roughly threw him loose. 'What's happened to you, Smith?'

'Why don't we ask what's happened to you?' Smith said, pulling his twisted coat into shape. He picked up the rifle and hugged it to his chest. 'What's this about? A whale? Well, how strange. I've watched you with a hook, dragging them aboard with everybody else.' Then Smith understood. 'No, this is about Napps. It's the *cat*—' He almost laughed. His bloody cat. Again, the cat!

'Napps helped you, he protected you. But you're a small man, Smith, and you'll hurt a better man if it flatters you to do so.'

'A better man?' Smith looked like a pink-faced, indignant young boy. 'We found evidence to the contrary lying abandoned under a dinghy.'

'That you can stand there and say that to me,' Castle said scornfully, hating him. 'How do you live with yourself? And how can you go along with them?' He angrily lifted an arm in the direction of the stairs which led below deck to the Mess. 'How do you sit listening as they eviscerate him when you know none of it is true?'

'As you and Addison keep saying. On and on you go, despite everything. Except I think your memory may be hazy when it comes to Napps,' Smith said. 'It certainly is when comes to the story you have about the cat. Because what I remember is him killing it for no reason.'

'You deceitful little—' Castle lunged at him.

'What's the matter with you?' Lawrence cried, pushing in between them. Uneasy about the prospect of stormy weather, he'd stomped back up from his quarters to walk another lap of the deck.

'It's just as Coppers joked earlier, sir. Castle's head is wrong,' Smith said to Lawrence. 'He objected to me shooting at a whale. It was only sport, but I'll apologize regardless if you want.'

Lawrence released an epically bored sigh. Of all the countless seals and birds and dogs and ponies and marine beasts they'd shot, snared, cleaved or bludgeoned, Castle wanted to detonate now about a whale which was where? Bobbing in the dark, perfectly alive.

'I objected to the context, sir,' Castle said. 'I don't believe it's honourable to injure a creature when you don't have to, especially when the harm done has no motive and comes at great expense to another being's dignity.'

What an odd statement, thought Lawrence. A whale's dignity?

'You seem so determined to make things harder for yourself, Castle,' he said. 'You cast your judgement on others very freely, but don't seem to realize that you're also being judged, perhaps more harshly than you suspect.'

Comprehension of where this was leading started as a tightness in Castle's throat as he thought of Lawrence, sitting at his desk every night. Just chatty bits to show the reality of life on board, he always said when asked about his journal. And he remembered Addison's concern about the power the Captain wielded over another man's reputation. The tightness spread to Castle's chest as Lawrence continued.

'I hear nothing but complaints about you. Aggressive,

uncouth . . . woefully antagonistic.' Lawrence's head tilted in a way which could be either patience or condescension. 'Can this really be the legacy you want to leave behind? Because you're building a certain picture of yourself, Castle, which you are running out of time to amend. You see, once the expedition is over, that picture is set. Both in memory and in anecdote, all those stories people tell, and possibly write.'

34
April 1913

Millet-Bass felt as though he was being observed by a giant lidless eye. Napps was watching him with an intent which far surpassed Millet-Bass's determination to ignore him. Millet-Bass tried to look unconcerned. If anything, he hoped his expression suggested boredom as Dinners jabbered about his favourite walks in Cornwall, and his boyhood toys, and other pointless things.

The hostile atmosphere in the tent resisted Dinners's attempts to neutralize it. None of the subjects he broached received any interest, even when he mentioned his latest flights of imagination. In an act of provocation, he said he thought he'd seen a buffalo or something at the cove, like an ox but partly human. Isn't that funny, he said to his stony-faced audience. Then he talked about the merits of a professional shave.

Millet-Bass wanted to be left alone to shiver through the indignity of his sea-wading, can-throwing shame until he could bear to speak. There was also another problem of a gigantic scale which demanded his full concentration to avoid. He couldn't bear to think about it, except the pain kept reminding him. His stomach would send up a mouthful of acid, and Millet-Bass wasn't always able to stop his lips bunching or his throat chugging slightly. The diabolical eye registered these actions.

' . . . Wrapped in a hot towel, your whole face swaddled in a warm turban.' A covetous shudder ran through Dinners as he relived the experience.

Dogfights often flared up on board the *Kismet*. Men raced each other to the borders of civil disagreement as opinions turned from criticism to abuse and then to the brink of violence. Happily, the ship had a culture which allowed brawlers to navigate back from a dispute without humiliation. Instead of chewing through an apology, the code for amnesty was a moderately restrained punch at the kidneys and a few obscene riffs about mothers and wives. It was possible to inform a man of your intention to slit his throat and then have harmony restored minutes later. Which was why Napps was graciously prepared to wheeze over to Millet-Bass and put him in a headlock. This tradition meant they could skip the tedious reconciliation and have the situation fixed.

But some puzzling obstacle had trapped them in stalemate. Napps noticed Millet-Bass was still wearing his gloves.

'What's wrong?' he asked sharply.

What? Nothing. Millet-Bass shook his head.

Dinners glanced nervously at him. 'Is something the matter, Millet-Bass?'

The three men had trudged back from the disastrous cove without saying a word. They'd sat silently in the tent, brewing tea which they drank in the same complicated silence. Then Napps had lifted his jumper to inspect where he'd smashed with the crate.

'Oosh, Jesus *Christ*,' he said.

'Is it bad, Napps?' Dinners thought it looked pretty bad.

A huge bruise was developing in various shades of ugly. It ran from his shoulder to his hip and seemed to radiate evil. Napps dabbed pressure on it and whistled out a low note. 'Is it really bad, do you think?' Almost as upsetting as the bruise for Dinners was the spectacle of Napps's semi-nakedness. It felt exploitative to see these foreign, vulnerably soft places. There was an odd disenchantment to seeing Napps's belly button and realizing he hadn't just sprung out of nowhere as a fully formed man, but had once been a baby like any other person, with all the fallibility that implied. Dinners averted his gaze, because he was tactful. Then he stared again, because any nudity, even a man's battered rib cage, demanded to be seen. For months, the human body, including Dinners's own body, had been reduced to hands, feet and head. The rest was a formless mystery hidden under a woollen rind of never-removed clothing. So to have other bits jump out for examination was thrillingly unpleasant.

'Take off your gloves,' Napps said to Millet-Bass. 'That one.'

Dinners began chewing his lip. The way Millet-Bass had protectively shielded his right hand made him very anxious.

Millet-Bass started to remove the glove. He exposed a portion of wrist and then hesitated. 'I'm not sure—'

'You'll do it now,' Napps said, fighting against a strong instinct to turn his face away when Millet-Bass did exactly what he ordered, and he caught sight of interior crimsons and a wet meatiness, and an arterial-coloured slash which carved open the palm and the base of two fingers.

'Can you move the fingers?' Napps said, as if asking the question would enable some universal force to grant him the gift of being wrong about the severed tendons.

Millet-Bass answered with a contemptuous smile. 'No.'

Napps remembered Dinners grabbing the dropped clasp-knives and passing one to Millet-Bass. And he remembered how carefully Millet-Bass had trussed the handle of his knife during the tent-bound storm days.

'I—Millet-Bass, it was an accident,' Dinners said with a tremor in his voice. 'I was trying to help.'

'Easy does it,' Napps said. 'It's nobody's fault.'

Dinners's anguish had a bolstering effect on Napps. Help *me*, he said to Dinners, help *me* by finding some bandages; help by holding the lamp closer so I can see what I'm doing. Panicking doesn't help anyone, Napps said while he treated

Millet-Bass's hand, thoughts of suppuration and infection flashing through his head, blood immediately drenching every cotton pad he wadded on to the cut. We'll be all right, he said, suffocating with secret panic because he wasn't a doctor and didn't know how to sterilize the wound or prevent grime from his own fingers contaminating it.

'Dinners, stop flinching from his hand like he's going to throw it at you,' Napps said while he pinned the bandage, wishing Addison was there with him more than he'd ever wished for anything in his life. 'He's not so crocked up. Eh, Millet-Bass? Not so crocked, are you?'

'I'm sorry, Millet-Bass,' Dinners said. 'You have to forgive me.'

'And why's that?' Millet-Bass replied with startling bitterness.

Dinners's eyes widened. 'It was a mistake.'

'Well, don't make another!' Napps said cheerily to alleviate the tension. 'And if you do another thing wro—!' He resisted the urge to gag at the blood on his hands and sleeves. There was blood on the groundsheet, blood on his trousers. 'Just one more thing wrong, Dinners! And we might decide we're better off without you.'

35
December 2012

'A re you all well?'

Decker glanced at Jess. 'We're slightly out of action.'

'How?' David's voice grew serious. An Aegeus interrogation began.

The radio phone was passed to Jess.

'I hurt my ankle,' she mumbled self-consciously into the receiver, saying she thought it was the Achilles heel sort of area. ' . . . David, honestly, it's nothing.'

David didn't sound convinced. He offered to get the doctor Canadian Sam for an impromptu phone consultancy. 'Because what are you doing to it?' he wanted to know. 'Don't guess at the treatment and then make it worse.'

Jess rolled her eyes for the benefit of anyone watching. This David! He'd have Sam hauled to the phone for a sprained ankle! It was embarrassing! She'd made a big deal of laughing about her fall in the cave. She'd laughed even louder when Decker and Brix asked if she was okay, like it was the most ridiculous question.

Jess wasn't going to let a dumb mistake jeopardize her Everland trip. She knew how quickly these situations escalated. Reservation became alarm, then panic, and then game over: you were hauled straight back to Aegeus. So once they'd returned to the tent, she had bandaged the ankle herself with the speed and blitheness of someone tasked with a trivial chore. She'd positioned her bag to hide the offending foot from sight as she treated it, cheerfully repeating how perfectly all right she was, and how unremarkable the incident was, and how they should just put it behind them. Then she'd made coffee and tidied the mounds of discarded clothing, working with the efficiency of someone who considered the matter resolved and really didn't have time to waste on further discussion. In unobserved moments, using great stealth, Jess allowed one of her hands to creep into her sleeping bag and gingerly touch the ankle as if she was examining stolen property. It felt several degrees hotter than normal and had an unhealthy watery balloon-ish roundedness. 'I was in the cave and thought I saw—David! I'm fine,' Jess said, aware that Brix had looked at her with interest.

David's lecturing continued. Any further stiffness, or anything unusual, and she must let them know immediately. He was absolutely not joking about this, he said, and then launched into a needlessly terrifying speech about their distance from help. Two and a half hours by Twin Otter in *good* weather.

In their haste to get Jess to the quads, Brix had forgotten about one detail. She reached over for her journal, flipped to a clean page, and wrote a giant-lettered note. She held it up to Jess. *What did you see?*

Still fending off David, Jess read the note and shrugged at Brix. I don't know. Something?

The stuffily warm tent smelt of dead seals and unwashed people. Decker was lying flat on his back, his hands meshed behind his head as he thought of the bathtub in his house, the towels, a bed which wasn't an insulated sack on the floor. He propped himself up on an elbow. 'If we did want to leave,' he said conspiratorially to Brix, 'you realize the whole ankle thing is a valid reason to go home.'

It was a ridiculous reason to go home, as Brix's confused smile informed him. Decker flopped down again. 'You'd understand if you had a Viv worrying, Brix. Or a flock of chickens you haven't seen for months,' he said, and then put on a faux-solemn voice. 'There is nothing I wouldn't do to return, nothing I can't live with if it gets me home.'

'Quoting Napps,' Brix said warily. 'A superfun sign for the rest of us.'

'It's because I'm extremely tired,' he answered, placing a sock over his eyes. 'The Napps attitude starts to make a lot of sense.'

'Yeah, yeah, yeah. Bye, David, yeah,' Jess said, ending the call in order to discuss her cave theory. 'It looked like material. Green cloth.'

Decker grunted, amused. 'Come on, Jess. That's extremely doubtful.'

'I saw green cloth,' Jess insisted. Taking advantage of his blindfolded eyes, she permitted herself to clutch her ankle. For one careless second, she gave in to the instinct which made her want to take the beef-hot ankle in both hands and just squeeze it. The pain was exquisite and must have shown on her face. Because then Brix was studying her with exactly the kind of concern she'd wanted to avoid.

Jess appeared to deflate. Her shoulders dropped, her eyes lowered. The aura of confidence was replaced with something more lifeless. That she didn't for one minute expect Brix to do her a favour was conveyed in the despondent way she shook her head: please don't say anything.

Fieldwork protocol, or the fact it was irresponsible to withhold information from Decker, meant Brix should have discounted Jess's request. She couldn't do it, though, as it seemed so unfair. Everland had represented Brix's opportunity to redefine herself as a courageous, resilient person instead of a dejected wreck, and she knew Jess would have come here with her own hopeful agenda. While the inexperienced, initially clueless Brix had semi-swindled her place using Angie and Decker's influence, Jess deserved her place, and her work had been faultless. And Brix remembered what Decker had said about the centenary trip being sentimentalized, with no real need for it to last for two months. An ill-judged comment regarding Jess might be enough to convince him to abort it. There was always a self-serving element to any expedition, whether that was a desire for achievement, or adventure, or fulfilment. So considering the extra pressure Brix's numberless mistakes had put on the team as she sought to satisfy her personal ambitions, compared to whatever Jess's ambitions were, which hadn't impacted negatively at all, Brix thought it would be an act of supreme hypocrisy if she used this, Jess's one single setback, as an excuse to nuke her.

'Green cloth?' Brix asked. 'You're sure?'

Jess didn't seem to hear her correctly. She stayed braced for disappointment. Then, as if she'd been slapped awake, her voice resounded with its typical cockiness as she answered that, er, *yes*, she was sure. Decker lifted the sock, examining Jess with one eye.

'A million pounds says you're wrong.' He put the sock back down.

There was a warmth to Jess's expression, a sweetness and earnestness which Brix had never seen from her before. Thank you, she mouthed. Thank you.

36
April 1913

I 've got some news,' Napps said agitatedly as he came into the tent.

He had been to dig up the seal meat and transfer it to their ice locker, and Dinners's initial thoughts were a crazy notion that the meat would be gone, or somehow lost in the storm. But that wasn't the problem. Napps had located it quickly enough. The problem was worse.

These were the last smog-coloured days before four months of night fell across Antarctica. Beyond a distance of a hundred feet, the sky and the landscape merged together in an unfocused mass. Napps had felt troubled when he reached the seal meat and saw the snow covering the catch was tainted with odd liquorice-brown discolorations. And he'd felt ill when he discovered the stains were caused by blood seeping from meat which was wet, not frozen.

'It resists description,' Napps said, trying to explain what he'd hacked out of the ground. Instead of being red and firm, the meat was black and waxy and he could press his fingers through it. The tissues smeared into a coarse pulp when he rubbed it. And the smell, God. He couldn't even begin to describe the smell. He showed them the thick treacle residue on his gloves—*look at this*.

'More than decayed,' Napps said. 'Digested is a better word.'

'Both carcasses?' Millet-Bass said.

This was the first time he'd spoken in over an hour, since

Dinners had unwittingly poisoned the mood by enquiring if his hand hurt, which he was gruffly informed it did. When Dinners asked if he could do anything to help, Millet-Bass's expression had an inward-looking conclusiveness which suggested the question of 'what Dinners could do' was a subject he'd discussed many times with himself.

'Your "help" is the reason I'm in this state,' Millet-Bass said. 'So how will you help me next? Spinal damage, perhaps? Cut off a leg?'

Cringing through his apologies again, Dinners said he was sorry he'd offered the wrong knife, and sorry for Millet-Bass's injured hand, and sorry for the tendons, and sorry for everything. Yet he did think this stubborn refusal to forgive him was a bit unfair. It was an accident, after all, he hadn't planned it.

'You're right,' Millet-Bass said with biting irony, the five-fingered source of their misery papoosed inside his woollen top. 'You are very sorry, and maybe I am being unfair. It's just one of the many outcomes you didn't anticipate. Because how could you?'

Not wanting Millet-Bass to see how thoroughly ashamed he was, Dinners lay down and turned his face away.

'I expect you're starting to regret your little confession to me that night during the storm, aren't you?' were the last words Millet-Bass said until Napps returned to the tent with his bad news and his wicked-smelling gloves.

Napps told them that every piece of meat was in the same state of decomposition.

'What could have happened?' Dinners asked, the numbers three and four eclipsing any other thought in his head.

'The holes might have been too shallow,' Napps replied. 'Or the snow covering wasn't thick enough.'

Dinners knew the human body could go *three or four* weeks without food, *three or four* days without water.

'No, it's nothing to do with the cache,' Millet-Bass said

defensively. 'I've built them countless times before, and never once had a problem.'

'Well, precisely. It could be any number of reasons,' was Napps's diplomatic answer. He wasn't about to admit to the shameful scene at the cove where he'd flung his axe and sworn in a voice so violently angry he didn't recognize it as his own, kicking chunks of ice around in a fit of rage over Millet-Bass's inability to correctly *bury chunks of meat*. But he'd gradually thundered himself into resignation. Whether it was human error or not, Napps had accepted that staving in Millet-Bass's head with a rock would not ultimately improve the situation.

Thinking *three or four, three or four,* Dinners asked, 'So how long do we have with the remaining supplies?'

'It's this place,' Millet-Bass said. First the crates had been ravaged, and now the meat they'd been counting on to bolster their depleted rations was wrecked and inedible. With complete predictability, Millet-Bass blamed the island.

'We've got just less than three weeks at full rations and possibly one month of fuel,' Napps said to Dinners.

The heartbreak of knowing proved to be slightly less painful than the raw anguish of hoping. It was a different kind of pain which entranced the sufferer. Dinners closed his eyes and thought of jellyfish.

In Dinners's mind, the men and their provisions had assumed the form of a single and elegantly simple jellyfish-like organism. If the organism remained connected, the men were able to survive Everland's barrenness. Any severance to the connection, however, resulted in terminal breakdown. Without those supplies, they were as helpless as the transparent, immobilized domes of beached jellyfish.

'But the *Kismet* will arrive soon, though,' Dinners said, opening his eyes. He looked expectantly at Napps, as if the Mate's agreement would cast a spell on the future and convert this wish into reality.

'Of course, I'm expecting the ship any day now,' Napps said, although his reassurance didn't have the comforting depth of faith Dinners had hoped for. What he heard instead was a man distracted by his own misgivings.

'Any day now? Well, that's news,' Millet-Bass said. 'Although I'm sure Dinners will believe you. After all, this is the man who also believes that horned things are lurking in the shadows.'

The way Millet-Bass treated whatever Dinners said as an act of unendurable provocation had become tedious, even for the Dinners-intolerant Napps. He advised Millet-Bass to keep his mouth shut, preferably for the rest of the afternoon, and then he smiled. 'Oh, I'm Dinners's guardian in this party, am I?' he said. 'God help us if that's true.'

Napps laughed at how unbelievable he found the situation, either oblivious or crushingly indifferent to the bleak expression on Dinners's face.

'It seems your motto's right, Dinners,' he said. 'The times are changing and we with them.'

37
December 2012

Over there somewhere?' Jess said once they'd descended to the base of the cave's slope in search of her wacky hallucinated cloth.

'Zillion pounds,' Decker said. 'Not going to find it, because it doesn't exist.'

This was one of his two recurrent subjects of conversation. If he wasn't commenting on the pointlessness of searching for an imagined flag, he was grilling Jess. It had been less than twenty-four hours since her accident and he wanted to know if she was all right. Because he thought she looked ill and kind of weak. Sickly. Could she manage okay? Because, seriously, not wanting to make a big deal about it or anything, she didn't look great.

'Right, because we all look so great,' Jess answered as they searched around in the bluish gloom.

With their blisters and scaly skin, and sun-bleached unwashed hair like tufts of coconut matting, it was true that they weren't overly attractive. Jess's face did seem pinched, though, with a tightness around her mouth. There was a cautiousness to her steps, as if the ground was an uncertain surface which couldn't be trusted. She was, however, as she kept repeating, fine. That something grated against something else when she walked wasn't a detail she wanted to think about.

Brix, who knew more than Jess would have chosen, had shown herself to be admirably discreet. It was interesting and kind of embarrassing to Jess how profoundly this one small act of kindness had changed her outlook. Whereas she'd previously categorized Brix as an insipid person, a boring one, devoid of any of the qualities Jess respected, she was discovering that Brix wasn't such a pointless nonentity. There was actually quite lot to like about Brix.

'Here!' Brix said, kneeling to scrape at the gravel. Frozen into a creased tangle beneath a crust of dirt and frost was half of a torn green sledging flag. What remained had a scalloped rim, a wreath of embroidered oak leaves and a faded Latin inscription.

'What do you think Aegeus will make of it?' Jess asked, crowding in next to Brix. 'It must have belonged to one of Napps's team. Has to, doesn't it?'

Brix had turned to look at the two alcoves behind them. They were stunted, low-roofed little dens with a depth of around five metres. She was thinking about the flag's location. 'Won't be a minute,' she said, handing the flag to Jess.

'Well, hah . . . ' Decker's face lit with boyish excitement as he inspected the flag. 'Seems I owe you an apology, Jess,' he said, unable to stop smiling.

After decades in the ice, the cloth had become a type of pottery fabric which could snap or shatter. Jess stood at his shoulder as he turned the brittle flag to examine the inscription again. She slowly mangled out the Latin text. *'Tempora mutantur, nos et mutamur in illis.'* She shrugged at Decker. 'Did you understand any of that?'

He laughed. 'No.'

'Hey, Brix,' Jess called. 'You learn any Latin?'

Brix didn't answer. She'd stooped to walk the length of one alcove, then come back and gone to explore the other. She was crouched at the far end of the alcove next to a cluster of pebbles in the black volcanic sand when Jess found her.

'This is weird,' Brix said, holding one pebble up to catch the light. 'There's six of them gathered together. I think it's amethyst.'

Jess saw the stone glint purple. 'There might be tons of the stuff scattered around.'

'I'm not a geologist,' Brix said, 'but I don't believe amethyst is found in Antarctica.'

'Amethyst?' Decker said. 'No, you're talking Brazil, Zambia, areas of North America, some parts of—Brix, are you digging?'

Having piled the stones to one side, Brix was burrowing at the ground with her hands. 'Don't you wonder what the flag is doing here?' she said. 'Because I've got this hunch—*wow*.' She reared her head back, blinking. 'Can you smell that?'

'Petrol,' Decker said as he and Jess followed Brix into the alcove.

They all started to dig, shovelling out handfuls of sand, and the acoustics changed as the hole got deeper. Listen, Brix said, and banged her fist against the bottom of the cavity. It had a hollow, metallic pitch. Wiping off the film of grit revealed a flat surface. Working faster, they levered their fingers under the corners and heaved it free. The oilcan came up with a scattering of sand, a peal of viscous liquid swilling inside.

The can's seams were stained brown with corrosion, its paint eaten into blistered patches. The cap was crusted shut with a thick batter of oxidation. The sides of two other cans were dimly perceptible in the empty crater.

The fun had drained out of the situation for Jess. Whatever odd and inexplicable event had happened here, it seemed to her that the cave was now a sinister place which possessed the ability to absorb old misfortune and then to reflect it back on to them. The ghosts of Napps and his men were suddenly very present. She asked in a volume which betrayed her irrational sense of having three dead men as an audience, 'Does anyone else feel a bit uneasy about this?'

'Ah, yep,' Decker said, trying to twist open the rusted cap. 'I feel uneasy pretty much every second of the day.' He shook the can and estimated it contained half a gallon of fuel.

'It doesn't make sense,' Brix said as they prised up the two other cans and then unearthed a fourth, a fifth. These last four cans were entirely full. 'When Napps and Millet-Bass left Dinners, why did they also leave their fuel?'

'Perhaps they intended to return?' Jess said.

'So why bury it?' Brix answered.

'Well, they marked the site,' said Decker. 'You found it yourself.'

'But it's their most precious resource, why leave it at all?'

38
April 1913

Birth and Death, an infinite ocean; A seizing and giving, the fire of living.

The Adélie hadn't been dead long: it was still warm beneath the chilled feathers, and Napps was now in serious danger of crying. It was the first time in twenty years he'd remembered reading Goethe's *Faust*, and it certainly hadn't made him cry then. The situation was so critical he had to keep his head turned away from Millet-Bass. Trusting himself to speak or even make a friendly conversational noise was out of the question.

'Because, Napps? There's a good chance it's diseased.' Millet-Bass felt he'd been talking to the back of Napps's head for far longer than seemed normal. He assumed the Mate's silent fixation on the dead bird was the result of a debate over harvesting meat from its corpse, which was a bad idea, as he'd already explained several times.

Napps had done nothing more than touch the penguin. That was all he'd done. He'd innocently reached down and something very simple and astonishingly powerful had blasted him to pieces. In feeling the heat of a life just departed, Dinners's awe at the orange lichen suddenly made perfect sense. It was like hearing the voice of God.

'I don't trust meat that can't keep itself alive. I mean, you might, but . . . '

Napps was ready to slap himself in the face. A gusting sigh restored enough emotional balance for him to stand up, mostly dry-eyed. 'You're right, let's go.'

It was the end of a dispiriting hunt. Carrying oil lamps, the men had traipsed the full five-mile route around the dark island without encountering a single living thing. Old animal tracks were erased by new snowfall which lay undisturbed, and there were no bird or seal calls in the low soft notes of the wind. A summer's worth of roosting and breeding and basking had been entirely swept clear in preparation for next year's migration. The beaches were fallow.

In Napps's single hopeful moment, he'd heard Millet-Bass yell about a catch and blundered across to him.

'The only one left on Everland and the task's been done,' Millet-Bass had said, prodding the Adélie with his boot. It was supposed to be a joke. The bird had cunningly avoided having the men kill it by dying slightly before they arrived.

'Are you all right? You look cold,' Napps said while they returned to the camp. His tone was suspiciously carefree. 'How's the hand?'

Millet-Bass unclenched his arms and straightened his posture. Famously immune to temperature, with a reputation for happily wading around in appalling conditions, he didn't want to admit he was so profoundly frozen it was making his stomach cramp. He didn't want to admit, to himself or anyone, the severity of his condition. He didn't want to think about what his increasing susceptibility to the cold might mean.

'And I'm still waiting for an answer. How's the hand?'

A minute stubbornly passed with no reply. Fine. Perhaps Millet-Bass would rather discuss their hike. Napps had been the quicker of the two men for the first time in history, with Millet-Bass dithering behind when previously he'd have left Napps trotting to catch up as he marched off into the distance.

'Can't I be sensible without you finding fault?' Millet-Bass replied. 'You complain that I walk too fast, and when I walk slower, you complain.'

'I genuinely fail to—'

'Complain, complain!' Millet-Bass said.

Back inside their tent, the industrious Dinners had already got the tea boiled and pemmican simmering on the stove. Even better than both of these luxuries was his surprise of five muscatel raisins each.

'Where did you have these hoarded?' Napps asked gratefully.

Well, it was a funny story. They'd been in a rag wedged at the bottom of Dinners's pocket and he'd completely forgotten about them. Dinners then made the mistake of describing the rag's condition. He was going to use it to scrape some of the muck off his trousers when the raisins fell out.

Napps pretended Dinners wasn't talking. Instead he sucked an ancient dirt-covered raisin and imagined it getting plumper and returning to a grape, then spiriting him to the gnarled vine where he would bake in the heat, shirtless. But he wasn't so occupied with his daydreamed vineyard that he didn't study the way Millet-Bass ate, particularly which hand he used and which he didn't.

Millet-Bass could feel Napps's eyes drilling into him. He'd prefer to let the raisins sit untouched in his dished palm and rot to dust than give Napps the satisfaction of seeing that he could only use his left hand, as it was no longer possible to form a workable pincer with the bad hand or move those fingers in any useful way.

This obsession with Millet-Bass's well-being was a game they played every waking minute of the day. If Millet-Bass looked up he saw he was being watched with unblinking reptilian interest. If Millet-Bass mentioned the hand, he was trapped into another inquisition. If Millet-Bass didn't mention the hand, he was scrutinized distrustfully. If Millet-Bass ever snapped that it was *his fucking hand* he got the same lecture about the fact that, no. No, it wasn't actually his hand. On Everland, his health was their health, his wound a problem for everyone, and therefore a democratic forum. Millet-Bass didn't get to decide how well or ill he was. It was decided collectively. Rather, it was decided by Napps.

So Millet-Bass did his reckless best to treat the wound as an ugly accessory. It was unsightly, yes, but of no consequence. What he couldn't hide was the wound itself. The cut hadn't sealed. It was discoloured and the edges gaped. It wept a foul-looking liquid which soaked the bandages. Each evening Millet-Bass was forced to submit his hand to its nightly inspection, where it was pored over like a holy text, undressed and re-dressed, inspected and re-inspected. And each evening Millet-Bass's confidence was splintered a little further.

In contrast to Millet-Bass, Dinners's physical heath had vastly improved. The new energy this gave him was largely wasted on trying to bond with Napps, who remained resistant to bonding, and endearing himself to Millet-Bass, whose behaviour since the accident was increasingly cruel.

Napps interrupted him in the middle of a dull story about picking berries. Something about Dinners's rambling chatter suggested critical fatigue.

'Dinners, when did you last sleep?'

'Oh, well, recently.' He smiled tightly at Napps. 'It doesn't matter.'

Taking advantage of Napps's redirected attention, Millet-Bass was clumsily scooping raisins to his mouth.

'You need to get more rest.'

Dinners dismissed the problem with a fussy gesture. 'I sleep whenever I get the chance, Napps, honestly. Any time I can.'

By making the mistake of dropping a raisin, Millet-Bass was instantly aligned in the centre of Napps's crosshairs. It was enough to drive anyone crazy.

'I'll help,' Dinners said. 'It'll be easier if I give them to you one at a time.'

He remembered Millet-Bass's kindness to him when his

own fingers were deadened and blister-swollen from frostbite. He'd fed Dinners and dressed him and held a cup for him to drink from.

Millet-Bass looked at Dinners. 'Don't you come anywhere near me.'

'Less of that, Millet-Bass,' Napps said.

'Then tell him to keep the hell away from me.'

'I said enough, Millet-Bass.' Napps was becoming accustomed to his unnatural new role as Dinners's protector. He noticed Dinners's quivering chin. 'What were you talking about?' he said, changing the subject. 'Foraging berries or something?'

Ha, Millet-Bass interrupted, telling them they'd come to the right person if they wanted to talk about scavenging food. He'd got a lifetime's worth of stories.

'The mushrooms on my grandmother's grave were so abundant they were almost too much for one man to finish on his own,' he said. 'I managed it though.'

Dinners's spoon clattered into his pannikin. 'Really.' The idea of grandmotherly fungus had destroyed his appetite. He put down his meal.

What? Millet-Bass didn't understand the reaction. 'Fried them and ate them with toast. They were delicious. Cheered me right up on a lonely Valentine's Day.'

'That's the most Gothic thing I've ever heard,' Napps said.

'Oh, you think that's morbid?' Millet-Bass had no tolerance for such finicky attitudes. 'A few mushrooms? Tell it to the creatures, to the whatever they are. The whatever it is,' he said, amused at how ludicrous he found himself. 'Actually, no, tell it to me. My head needs a bit of sense banged into it.'

Napps ordered him to explain and he became flustered. 'I expect the dark's getting to me. Or it's your fault, Dinners, constantly peddling your mad visions.'

'Such as,' Napps said.

'Such as funny things with the light. Such as perhaps on occasion I've seen things, and attributed sounds with false meaning.'

Dinners's eyes widened. 'I think I know what you mean.'

Napps asked about the sounds and Millet-Bass became defensively self-conscious. No, he didn't want to say. It was too stupid.

'But it's not voices, Millet-Bass. It's not men,' Dinners said, happy to finally know something useful, although no one paid him any attention. 'It's only the wind. I'm always having to remind myself of that.'

39

December 2012

The windows were always open and it was a spring morning for ever when Decker transported himself to Viv. He only had to close his eyes and he was home. Less of a man than a vapour, a spectral presence, Decker floated along past the turmeric-yellow walls and clustered picture frames, the Balinese lion sculpture. He wafted into their bedroom. Without doing anything, without even thinking, he found he could just materialize under the covers with his head beside Viv's head on the pillow. *I miss you,* he said to her. *I made a mistake, I want to come home.*

The tent was as muggy as a hot car. With a temperature of five degrees outside, the once thick snow covering the beach had virtually disappeared, and the sky was now a neon white twenty-four hours a day. Bird and seal calls could be heard constantly, from everywhere. Gulls and skuas collected near the refuse sacks, attracted by the smell of decaying food. The camp was overrun by the noise and reek which covered Everland.

'Kimiko, hi,' Brix said, checking in with Aegeus. She relayed the usual details. Yes, they were fine, life on the island was fine. The next day's schedule involved weighing Adélie chicks and surveying the glacier. 'Weather forecasted to remain stable,' Brix said, passing on Kimiko's information to Decker.

Eyes still shut, he replied with a nod so as not to break his trance. He was in the garden with some friends, drinking cider. The group were laughing at some incredible speech he'd just made, which wasn't only hilarious, but deeply moving. Having no talent for speeches in reality, Decker skipped straight to the applause. Please raise your glasses, he said. Here's to being back with you fuckers, and most of all, here's to Viv. I promised I'd come home, and I have. So, bad luck, you're stuck with me now. Cheers as he kissed her.

Blah, blah, blah, Andre. Trapped on the phone to the effusive and uninterruptable Kimiko, Brix tried to catch Jess's attention to exchange some eye-rolling.

Jess kept her head firmly turned away as she cleared up after their meal of soupy, baby-food beige chicken korma. From the second Kimiko answered the call, everything had become too difficult and claustrophobic and frustrating. The tent was shrinking to strangle her and there wasn't room to unbend a leg or move without crawling into the piles of stuff thrown across the floor. But Jess had a talent for enduring discomfort in any of its forms, whether that was a Kimiko-shaped catastrophe, or the hot, sharp pain in her ankle which grew hotter and sharper each day.

Unlike many other things in Jess's life, work never disappointed her. The formula was simple and perfect: she had a purpose, she accomplished it, she felt good; and repeat. Work wasn't just a job but a form of self-expression to Jess. It was the best friend she'd ever had. There were no inconsistencies in this relationship: it didn't sideline her, or suddenly favour someone else, or draw her attention to qualities she lacked in comparison to, say, a Japanese meteorologist. Instead it could be relied upon to deliver exactly what she hoped it would, which was the sense of being valued. She invested her time and was rewarded with a sense of fulfilment. She strived wholeheartedly and was allowed to excel. She wanted to be the best and she was the best, she wanted to feel proud of herself and she was. Whereas outside of her job, Jess was subject to forces of doubt and dismay and envy, she was always protected from those horrors within work's cosy confines. So the idea of going back to Aegeus early as a figure of sympathy and failure, unsuccessful at the very thing she depended on for self-esteem, was more heartbreak than she could bear.

Which is why Jess had resolved to ignore whatever was wrong with her ankle. The solution was simple. All she had to do was carry on crunching down the painkillers. The problem was that the box of codeine was in her yellow medical kit, which was on the other side of the tent, and getting it would involve crawling over Decker, the sleeping kraken.

Once the call to Kimiko had finally ended, Brix began the gruesomely satisfying task of unpeeling the grubby collage of Band-Aids from her fingers to replace them with fresh plasters. Wound inspection was part of the nightly regimen of preparing for bed. They all sported various nicks and lesions, and the small but disproportionately painful splits caused when skin cracked in the cold. Each injury required care in order to prevent it from becoming septic, as the Antarctic climate had suspended the healing process, and even the tiniest cut would remain open for months.

A balled-up mitten bounced off her foot and Brix raised her head. Jess signalled at the drift of clothes and equipment heaped along Brix's side of the tent, wanting her to throw over the medical kit.

Brix's first thought was: okay. Her next thought was: no. Jess's covert gesturing and edgy, addict-like staring didn't exactly comply with Jess's assertions that her ankle was improving and had probably only been bruised. In the spirit of her newfound cordiality with Jess, Brix had agreed not to disclose the injury to Decker. She had, however, added a caveat. If it got worse, then maybe keeping it hidden wasn't such a great idea. A better idea might be to do the sensible thing and get some proper medical care. She had definitely not agreed to get involved in a silent pact which enabled Jess's health to secretly deteriorate. She picked up a snack-sized carton of Sun-Maid raisins instead and chucked it to land next to Jess's knee. The packet showed a woman with a red bonnet and enviously fresh complexion smiling youthfully as she carried a tray of grapes.

Jess suppressed a grin. 'Brix!' she mouthed. 'Please!'

'This feels wrong,' Brix mouthed back.

Jess's signalling became more insistent. Her finger stabbed towards the little yellow kit. She put her hands together in a prayer for Brix to stop being such an idiot.

Giving her a look which implied that she was a generous, forgiving person who didn't approve, but was willing to trust Jess, Brix passed her the medical kit.

Jess had taken one pill and was gulping back a second as Decker hauled himself upright. He blinked, half asleep. 'Did Aegeus have anything else to say about the cave petrol?'

'No, nothing,' Brix said.

In a seamless move, Jess had buried the codeine under a discarded jumper and extracted a pocket mirror. Holding the little mirror very close to her face, as if the task required total concentration, she began rubbing E45 cream on to her sunburnt forehead. 'What is there to say about the petrol?' she said. 'We've discussed it a trillion times.'

Decker had informed the base during a scheduled call and then listened as Aegeus made surprised, interested noises at the discovery of a sledging flag and the exhumed petrol. Toshi had googled the Latin inscription.

'*Tempora mutantur, nos et mutamur in illis,*' he'd told them with the measured, deferential tone of someone reciting a sacred text. 'Huh, it means get on with your scientific work, which you are being paid to do, you should be collecting data, not tattered old flags.' He'd laughed as Decker replied with a damning critique of his talents as a comedian. 'Yeah, okay, whatever. It means, "The times are changing and we with them."'

'Do I look like the raisin woman?' Jess asked, finished with the E45 cream.

Decker assessed the Sun-Maid carton. 'You would if her face was more barbecued-looking. And if her hair hung in matted ropes. And if she was covered in dirt and wounds.'

'I wish you had Temazepam in your medical kit, Jess,' Brix said, lying down. 'Or any kind of drug to knock me out so I could get an uninterrupted night's sleep.'

Decker thumped his pillow into shape. 'What's interrupting it?'

'Oh, just noises.' Becoming shy, Brix rolled over towards the tent lining in order to avoid seeing their reactions. 'The constant light is messing with my head, I think. Sounds become distorted and start to sound like other things.'

'Monsters, Brix?' Decker said. 'Aren't we a bit old for ghost stories?'

Jess was watching her intently. 'No, I know what you mean, Brix,' she said.

It was a scream or a yell, loud enough to shock her. Brix wrestled one arm from the sleeping bag to check her wristwatch. It was nearly 4 A.M. The sulphurous orange tent gave everything inside a soft over-saturated focus. Jess was there next to her, faced the other way. Decker was in his bag on the opposite side. Brix thought, go to sleep, you know what it is. It's just the seals.

Nearly formed words filled the glistening white night. Voices were carried across the dunes, first nearer, then further, and then within metres of the tent. A low, agitated moan came from directly outside.

In a whisper which was barely more than her breathing the word, Brix said, 'Jess?'

The whispered reply was instant. 'I'm so glad you're awake.'

40

June 1913

H e heard them talking outside the room, a brief muted dispute. Using pure dumb hope, Addison willed the door to remain shut. He didn't want them in here. He fiercely didn't want to talk to anybody.

Addison required isolation in order to concentrate on his recovery, in his bed, in his own room for the first time in weeks. He wasn't able to bear the men's sympathy because he couldn't trust his response. There was no way of controlling it. One moment he'd be fine and the next he'd be wretched as composure switched to devastation with no warning. In deciding that it was undignified and needed to be dealt with privately, Addison hadn't left his quarters in three days.

Lawrence was the only person who couldn't be turned away. To his credit, he knew better than to address the issue which simmered contentiously between them. It would come out later, probably in a horrible manner, but for now he perched on the bed, smiling uncomfortably and saying the same things whenever he visited.

He'd say: just a candle? Let me get a lamp. Addison, don't lie here in the dark. He'd say: can I persuade you to eat? Tell me what you want and I'll have Jennet send it. He'd pat Addison's arm and say, what are you scribbling in that diary of yours? Confide in *me*. What do you write about that we can't discuss together? He'd say, Adds! Come on, Adds! Have a drink with me, please. He'd keep trying until Addison thanked him in a tone which was a request to be left alone.

'So there's nothing I can do. So you want to suffer by yourself and make me ill with worry, as if I'm not sick enough with it already.' Lawrence wearily lifted himself off the bed. 'Because, God help me, Addison. If there was a way of sparing us both from such misery you must believe I would have done it.'

'Then why didn't you?' The flickering candle stub on the desk filled the room with elongated shadows, and Addison's silhouette towered over the wall as he sat up. 'Dinners was an impressionable young man and I asked you not to send him. I told you my concerns and you chose to disregard them.'

Addison said he was aware of the private conversation that had happened between Lawrence and Dinners before the Everland selection. And, yes, he could well imagine the enthusiastic case Dinners had put forward, the keen promises of biological and geological discovery, his starry ambitions of a place in the scientific canon.

'I'm sure it sounded very inviting, very prestigious for the expedition,' Addison said. 'But I wish you'd thought more of your captaincy and less of prestige.'

'Ah, you see, there you're wrong, although I sincerely wish you weren't,' Lawrence said, his hand on the door handle. 'I was thinking only of my captaincy.'

'You could have prevented him from going, Lawrence.'

'Not really, as it turned out,' he said with a hard, embittered smile as he left the room. 'No more than you could have prevented him from dying.'

On that awful night and for those hours after it was over Addison had been hit by a supreme and instantaneous tiredness. He'd have gladly stooped forward in the chair, put his head on the bed and slept. He remembered going to the Mess, chairs scraping as he stood there and everyone went quiet, anticipating what he was about to say. He remembered Lawrence's ashen face. Addison had broken the news with a short, respectful announcement, and then returned alone to the infirmary, his mind blank of much sentiment. It was a pity and he was sorry. He'd washed his hands in the sink and changed his shirt and thought, I'm deeply sorry. He'd tidied his hair in the mirror and said aloud, I did what I could and I am so sorry. Something had gone wrong at that point. Grief had overpowered him. And when a man knocked to bring in a bowl of soup, Addison was so unable to cope with seeing anyone he'd behaved disgracefully.

I will apologize, Addison promised. I will speak to the sailor and explain. Because it's not my fault. It's not my fault because I was half out of my mind.

Not every death is peaceful, and not every death is clean. Some of the worst can be savage as the body lingers in the final stages of illness. Although Addison had witnessed cases like this before, nothing in his experience had ever been as cruel as the last days of Dinners's life.

Both Addison and Dinners had exhausted themselves in the battle to find a route through the havoc of his agony. Since the job of tending to Dinners required every single minute of his time, Addison's own health suffered as he neglected himself. There were moments when Addison dozed, perhaps for as long as half an hour, or managed to eat some of a meal, but mostly he worked without respite, because the work never stopped. He changed soiled sheets and clothing, and treated Dinners's fever with cold compresses and spoonfuls of chipped ice. He did his best to bathe Dinners, and feed him, and make it less lonely by holding his hand. He soothed him, singing the songs he'd sung to his children when they were very young. And throughout those eight sleepless, famished days of Dinners's end, two oppositional arguments concerning morality and humanity had raged inside the doctor. One of the arguments was lawful, and the other was inborn and merciful to the detriment of his professional sanctions. Each had a consequence, but when Dinners asked for something which contravened Addison's religious and medical ethics, he could no longer see how those laws made any sense. He couldn't see the God he believed in, all he saw was the man in front of him.

'Explain it to me again. What did you do?' Lawrence had said with an impenetrable expression as Addison stood with his shakily written letter in the Captain's quarters, past midnight, on the night that Dinners died.

'To refuse Dinners's request was to engage in torture,' Addison said, watching Lawrence read and then re-read the letter.

The line about dispensing a fatal dose of morphine wouldn't remain clearly in Lawrence's mind unless he stared at it. The moment he stopped, it became dreamlike and muddied and made him search through the page to find it again. He'd slammed the letter down on to his desk. 'I want to hear you say it.'

'I freed him.'

'*Lies.* You freed yourself.'

'Lawrence—'

'What happened to the Hippocratic oath? Do no fucking harm?' He'd clutched his head in the manner of someone condemned. 'Have you any idea what you've done?'

In those very last hours Addison's sequence of duties had diminished until every one was hopeless and all he could do was talk. So he talked as Dinners strained to cling to the safety of his voice. He talked while Dinners was overtaken by enormous sensations which lifted his eyes back, or rose through him and made his body arch. Addison said, I'm here with you, when Dinners saw things standing at the room's edges which came and went silently, or were beside the bed or were hovering above it. Addison tried to soothe him as a flush of lucidity gripped Dinners and he spoke for the first time in weeks.

'I want to go, I want to go, I want to go.'

'Shhh, it's all right,' Addison had said, putting his hand on Dinners's burning forehead. 'You're all right, I'm still here.'

'Help me, will you help me. I can't.' He'd grasped Addison's sleeve.

Addison had bowed his head. 'Do you know what you're asking me?'

'*Let me, let me. Let me go,*' Dinners had cried, rattling on the bed in seizures. '*Please, I want to go.*'

Addison's memory became hazy at this point. He'd wept, he'd pleaded with Dinners. He'd made promises and begged. And, then, unable to deny Dinners any longer, Addison recalled the frantic search. He'd emptied the medicine case on to the floor, scattering glass tubes and bottles in his urgency to find the morphine.

Now Addison lay alone under his blankets, remembering how he'd knelt beside Dinners and administered the injection. Then I'll let you go, he'd said, and was still saying even when Dinners was no longer there to hear it. But Addison felt there was a moment of suspension after the transition from dying to deceased. Like the delay between lightning and a thunderclap, the sentience of life took a few seconds to dissipate. So he'd spoken to Dinners anyway, and said goodbye to him, and he'd thought that the sense of peace which came over him might be Dinners's response.

Addison stilled himself. He leant up on one elbow to drink a glass of water. The emptiness in his wrinkled, intolerant stomach was salving. The comfort he wanted was found in abstinence, and an instinctive desire to reject the contentment and warmth of eating meant he'd been fasting for two days. Addison rested, cooling and slowly deactivated; a lizard at dusk in the dark of his room. He heard footsteps and waited. They passed and he lay welcoming the dull steep of inertia.

41

December 2012

The Adélie bay was an industrious arena of commotion and squalor. It became louder and livelier and filthier as the temperature rose. Everything was stained pink with bird dung, and the smell had intensified until it was no easier to breathe than chlorine. The chunks of stranded ice along the shoreline had now melted completely, leaving deep indented pits. Tiny flowers bloomed in the plush green fur of moss and lichen that covered the scree slopes beneath the cliffs.

Death was just as endemic as life in the colony. Dead chicks lay on the stones with the breeze through their marabou fluff, trampled by penguins and the pursuing horde of frantic chicks. Every passing adult bird was bombarded by these gangs of juveniles, who were also under continual bombardment themselves from the gulls which loitered around, prospecting for opportunities. There wasn't an inch of beach which didn't heave with movement. The noise was unbelievable.

'Does anything here ever shut up?' Jess said, taking her hat off and using it to fan her hot face. The sun which scorched their skin to leather, and plagued them with a nagging, unquenchable thirst, had also faded their red jackets to a peach colour. Having started as blonde, Jess's ponytail was now a white woolly tassel. She yawned in a way which Decker thought suggested the beginning of another discussion on the topic of 'unexplained night sounds' and 'sleepless fear'.

Decker didn't want to talk about it. The sounds Brix and Jess had heard were absolutely not odd, as he'd already explained several times. There was nothing spooky or ominous about it. It was a fur seal, or some sort of bird. Some sort of whatever, it didn't matter. The empty canvas sling he was holding was rigged to a spring balance. It was a device used for weighing small animals. 'Next,' he said.

They were at the colony to weigh chicks. The morning's target was to collect the data from forty chicks, then go to the northern end of the island to survey the glacier. In the fifty days it took for a hatchling to grow into a self-sufficient Adélie, a chick needed to bulk up by around a hundred grams every twenty-four hours if it was to grow large enough to fledge. The rapid transformation from tiny scrap to sleek adult was ungainly, and the chicks had reached the gawky adolescent stage. Their flippers were too big for them and dragged on the ground like long sleeves. They had little heads, fat bodies, and a scruffy coat of down.

Brix put the thirty-fifth chick in the sling, where it sat with stately patience until its weight was recorded. Once freed from the sling, it squealed off to rejoin the chase of parent Adélies ferrying through the turmoil.

Brix looked at the sky as if it was sending her cryptic messages. Despite the weather forecast of normal conditions, there was a charge to the atmosphere which had amassed as a migrainous static behind her eyes. She was unable to work out whether her increased awareness of the static was due to preoccupation on her part, or because the atmospheric heaviness was becoming more distinct. 'Low pressure,' she said, clapping a hand to her forehead. 'Can you feel it?'

Decker could definitely feel it. He'd woken up with a headache of crushing proportions and the stench of infinite penguin turds was doing nothing to improve it. What he wanted to do was to leave the bay as quickly as possible and go to the glacier. Then, once they'd finished there, they could go to the tent, then they could sleep. Then the next day would be closer, and so would the day of the Twin Otter's arrival, and therefore their departure from Everland. 'Next,' he said.

'Jess, do you want to get the next chick?' Brix said, since Jess hadn't handled any birds or really done much of anything. She'd made no attempt to get involved beyond standing there, watching.

A couple of Adélies were within easy catching range to one side of her. Jess didn't move. 'Nah, I'll let you do it.'

She was trying to avoid all but the most necessary of physical actions for secret reasons related to acute leg pain. This ruled out the chasing of penguins, even though a young, baffled Adélie required no more skill to trap than a potato. But leaning down hurt, standing up again hurt. Twisting hurt, lifting hurt. Grappling with a bird might cause her to tread clumsily, and that would hurt. It was just better if Brix was the one who lugged reluctant sack-shaped creatures in and out of slings.

It was a suspiciously non-Jess-like response. 'Are you okay?' Brix asked.

Jess's expression implied this was the craziest question. 'Of course.'

'Because you're not usually much of a spectator when it comes to work,' Brix said.

'Then I guess the flag was right,' Jess said. 'The times are changing and we with them.' She smiled as though this was a brilliant comeback.

Decker rattled the sling to get the attention of either Jess or Brix, he didn't care who. 'Come on, guys,' he said. 'Keep the momentum going.'

Instead of reaching for another Adélie, Brix studied Jess. After a pause, she said, 'I was thinking that maybe we should wait and go to the glacier tomorrow.'

Decker made a point of checking his watch. Eleven fifteen. Ten hours before bed, minimum. Fourteen days before home. He was impossibly tired. 'Why?'

'Toshi won't appreciate us going to the glacier when there's fifty billion Adélies to chase around,' Brix said.

It was a weird and feeble excuse. Jess shot Brix a cautionary glance. Her reason for wanting to postpone the scheduled glacier trip could only be bad. A problem with equipment, Jess concluded, self-deludingly. She'll have forgotten something. Then she thought, no. It was pointless to kid herself. The answer was in Brix's forcibly carefree tone. And this was the trouble with befriending women, Jess decided. This was the trouble with Brix. First, she paid way too much attention to what you said. Second, she became extremely invested in concerns you might have divulged, even if you hadn't really meant to. Perhaps, in a moment of weakness, you'd wanted a bit of reassurance about a matter that was beginning to frighten you. An expanding, purple swollenness which caused a foot to look misshapen, for example.

'Our job is to survey the island,' Decker said. 'That's why we're here. Toshi would agree. So, Brix. Just tell me. What's the problem?'

When she said there was no problem, Decker nodded as though he'd received welcome yet completely predictable news. 'Then, good. Perhaps we can stick to the work schedule.' He wondered if a few minutes at the tideline, taking in air which wasn't ninety per cent penguin vapours, might help his headache. 'If you finish the weighing,' he said, already departing, 'I'll do a round of the colony to check there's no damage to the fencing.'

Jess had only shown Brix the ankle because it was so sensationally freaky. All she'd wanted was a bit of sympathy, ideally a dismissive shrug. Clearly, on reflection, it had been a terrible error to allow Brix to view it, as it then forced Jess to see the injury through Brix's eyes and accept that, no, it didn't look normal. No, words such as 'ordinary' and 'minor' probably didn't apply. And no, if she was honest, she wasn't feeling great. There was actually quite a lot wrong with her. In the instant it took for Brix to react with a sober frown, Jess had already regretted her mistake. Her leg was now like a bone child they both shared custody over, with Brix in the role of world's most neurotic parent. It was boring. It was also hazardous, as Brix's worrying posed a direct threat to Jess's determination not to worry.

Using eye contact alone, Jess made it clear to Brix that her health was a vetoed subject.

'Scrabbling around in a gorge at the other end of the island isn't a sensible plan for someone who's not well, Jess,' Brix said, immune to the commands Jess's eyes were transmitting.

'I know you think you're being helpful,' Jess said, 'but you're going to get me shipped straight to Aegeus. Which does not qualify as help.'

Decker was starting to tramp back to them. 'It seems like a risk, Jess.'

Although Jess wanted to explain that fieldwork was a splint which supported the other problematic areas of her life, her ability to confide in Brix was constrained by the few seconds she had before Decker's return and her own natural reticence when it came to personal admissions. 'There is no risk,' she said. 'Nothing's going to happen.'

'Spider farms,' Brix said inexplicably. 'Locust forecasting is a genuine job. Blizzards can happen; it doesn't have to be your birthday. Have you guessed who I'm quoting? And accidents can definitely happen.'

Jess countered Brix's pessimistic quote with a gutsy quote. 'Hard pounding this, gentlemen,' she said. 'Let's see who will pound longest.'

'Two Everland quotes in one day,' Brix said.

Jess saw she should have thought it through more. Citing Napps and his men wasn't the best method of filling Brix with optimism. Still, Jess knew enough about Brix to know that despite her fretting, despite her indecision, she was as invested in the trip as Jess was, and didn't want to terminate the expedition by having her recalled to the base. In some ways they weren't that dissimilar, Jess thought, which was a bizarre notion, but not necessarily unpleasant.

'We've got what, just over two weeks left on Everland?' Jess said with her most persuasive smile. It was deliciously easy to convince someone who wanted to be convinced. 'Why leave before the end?'

42
April 1913

illet-Bass's hand was almost a fourth man in their group. It dominated their thoughts, their days and practically all of their conversations. Millet-Bass treated his hand as an intolerable object. He couldn't bear talking about it, so Napps and Dinners avoided the subject. He couldn't bear their fussing, so they never fussed. He rejected the notion of Napps going anywhere without him so furiously that Napps was left with no option but to consent.

Millet-Bass and Napps were toiling along the beach on another of their ship-scouting patrols. At minus twenty-five degrees the human body's capacity for producing and expelling moisture becomes diabolically apparent. Whatever wasn't being breathed out to freeze around blistered nostrils and mouths, or evaporating from pores to freeze on to clothes, seemed to be freezing internally. But regardless of the cold, watching for the *Kismet* outside was better than idly fretting inside the tent. Marching created enough heat to make it bearable, and a job of any kind, doing anything, at least burnt off some of the dread which otherwise gathered in the abdomen as a lump of cement.

Although every hour of the day was now the same bottomless black, the full moon and greenish luminance of Aurora Australis were so bright they almost negated the need for oil lamps. In admiring the vivid constellations of zodiac symbols and mythical creatures shining above them, Napps had unintentionally overtaken Millet-Bass. When he looked back he saw Millet-Bass stumbling with his injured fist crushed to his chest. They hadn't been out long, perhaps a couple of hours, yet Millet-Bass was already flagging. It was a tricky subject to broach, and Napps knew better than to mention his concern. Millet-Bass's ego was as damaged as his hand, but twice as sensitive.

Napps stopped and hunted through his knapsack. He'd brought some biscuits each and a can of pineapple in syrup to share. 'You have your spoon?' he shouted.

They passed the can of pineapple between them and Napps took the smaller chunks. He manipulated it so that the last bite and the privilege of drinking the sugary juice ended with Millet-Bass.

'Sure you don't want some?' Millet-Bass asked. Napps told him to finish the juice and then stared at the horizon. He said he was concerned about a storm.

There was no storm, it was a perfectly clear and cloudless sky, but Napps sighed and tapped a finger on his chin, deliberating. 'Should we turn back, that's what I'm wondering. Umm. I'd say, yes, it's probably best we return to the tent.'

Millet-Bass looked at him, then got to his feet and pitched the empty can down the beach. 'You're a poor actor, Napps.'

The wound had deteriorated to a stage where it now frightened them all. An infection was spreading. Despite Millet-Bass's pig-headed efforts to trivialize it, he got colder, he got tired. He got weaker. His other hand became badly frostbitten, and Millet-Bass could have bitten it himself for its treachery.

Once, mistakenly, Dinners had joked that his title as chief patient was being usurped. A two-man race and, oh, he'd been edged into second place!

'Say that to me again,' Millet-Bass threatened, 'and I'm coming over there with a sledging pencil to give you back the advantage.'

Dinners's reply was a very mild and pacifying smile.

'You did this,' Millet-Bass said. 'This hand is your doing. So crack another joke like that to me and I'll take your eyes out.'

'Not another word,' Napps said, glaring at him. 'That's an order.'

The weeks had tracked his angry defeat. Millet-Bass, unquestionably the strongest man among them, found himself reduced to the mortal limitations of Napps, and then, worse, of *Dinners*. His plunge into feebleness was marked by the rising number of tasks he was forced to delegate. It was little things initially. The more fiddly jobs around camp became unsolvable puzzles. Millet-Bass couldn't lash the tent or assemble the primus or strike a match. It gradually became the bigger humiliation of needing assistance with his clothing and food. As much as he despised his injury, he loathed his dependence on Napps and Dinners even more.

Let us, they said sympathetically while Millet-Bass burned with shame and rapped, 'What next? Being fed like a fucking baby?'

'You certainly behave like one at times,' Napps would answer, lighting Millet-Bass's pipe for him.

Millet-Bass reacted with fury in order to stave off despair. He raged when his attempts to manoeuvre a button or operate a buckle failed.

'This was you not long ago,' Millet-Bass sneered as Dinners dealt with the impossible jacket. Dinners said meekly that he knew.

'I'll remind you that we coped with Dinners, and together we'll cope with you,' Napps said, annoyed into twisting round in his bag. 'Your health is my health, remember? Your worries are mine. And if that's galling for you, Millet-Bass, just think how I feel. Dinners, give him some chocolate, it might cheer him up. And have some yourself. You look terribly pale. You aren't sick, are you?'

'Not when you're here,' Dinners said. 'But I don't feel well when I'm alone.'

'Dinners, you're either ill or you're not, which is it?' Napps said.

'I get muddled if I'm on my own. I worry I trust the wrong things.'

Napps's tolerance for this type of conversation was spent before Dinners could finish the sentence. 'Listen, can we please try and cling to sanity. Yes? Shall we make staying sane a priority?'

Millet-Bass talked about Everland as though it had a vendetta against him. If they wanted proof, they only had to look at his undignified transformation. He had wild theories about the island having malign powers. He could sense some sort of evilness, he said again and again until Napps finally snapped in exasperation, 'Can't you sense it quietly? We didn't have this racket from Dinners. Say what you like about Everland, at least it's deathly silent.'

Despite his temper and foul-mouthed rants, there'd only been one night when Millet-Bass allowed himself any self-pity. 'I'm not winning here,' he'd said desperately. 'You are watching me lose. What am I to do?'

Dinners had become uselessly upset but Napps had become terrifying.

'What are you to do?' he'd said. 'How about apologize. You can start with your parents, for allowing the boy they raised to become such a weak-willed disappointment. You can also apologize to the British Navy, since your cowardice is an affront to the intrepid spirit it's founded on. And then you can apologize to me, because this obsession with your own misery is turning my stomach.'

The method succeeded. Millet-Bass was so murderously offended it stunned him into regaining his head.

'Right,' he'd threatened. 'I'll be using that sledging pencil on you, too.'

'Good,' Napps had answered, smiling.

The two men trudged back to the camp in silence. Millet-Bass hated that he was the reason they couldn't continue scouting for the ship, and he hated that Napps tried to blame it on other factors.

'I'm about done in. The cold's knocked the strength out of me,' Napps said.

Millet-Bass didn't answer. The visible portion of his face was indignant. He knew Napps was fine. And before his injury, Millet-Bass would have also been fine. They'd both worked in lower temperatures than this before, and for hours longer without being anywhere near 'done in'.

'And Dinners! We've been gone so long he'll think we've abandoned him.'

Dinners. Millet-Bass pursed his lips.

Getting within earshot of the tent, they started yelling their traditionally crass greetings to Dinners. Getting no response, Napps shouted that he honestly wasn't above slighting Elizabeth Dinners to provoke an answer.

'So you'd best reply before I lose my sense of humour,' Napps said. '*Dinners?*'

The entrance to the tent was untied and flapping open. Dinners had cast off his sleeping bag and blankets, leaving them half strewn around the tent. A trail of clothing led towards the cliffside as Dinners had thrown down one glove, then his jumper; the other glove lay discarded further along, and then his hat.

He was crawling on his knees in a gully when they found him. He said he didn't feel well and looked at Napps with the drugged vacancy of hypothermia.

Napps skidded as he lifted the deadweight man. 'God, what happened?'

Dinners wasn't sure. He said he couldn't describe it. From the moment they'd left him, he said he'd heard his name being called. It sounded like Castle, or sometimes Lawrence, or other men he didn't know, and they kept telling him to leave the tent. So he'd done it, and something awful had come towards him.

'I don't understand what you're talking about,' Napps said as they dragged him inside the tent and put him in his sleeping bag. 'How could Lawrence have called you? He isn't here, Dinners. No one is but us, you know this.'

Dinners responded in semi-conscious mumblings, already half asleep.

'Dinners? Who would have called you?' Napps said, and then turned to Millet-Bass. 'Can you make sense of it?'

Millet-Bass's answer was so unexpected Napps had to repeat it. '. . . You could hit him?'

'Weeks of tending him, and for what? To have it wasted. I could kill him.'

Napps stared at him. 'I'm ashamed on your behalf.'

'I'd save your disapproval for our little friend here.'

'And I'd be careful before I said anything else,' Napps said. 'I'd think hard before I said another word.'

'Imagine the many benefits of being Joseph Evelyn's nephew,' Millet-Bass said with curious intent. 'All that money, all that influence. Say you were hungry for adventure, well, what's stopping you? It's simple, you just buy your way on to an expedition.'

Napps face showed the start of several reactions.

'As being rich negates the need for qualification, you can buy yourself a place on any voyage you choose,' Millet-Bass continued. 'You could go to Everland, for example. You don't care about legitimate concerns; you want to go to Everland. You're a reasonable enough scientist and Everland has scientific promise. The Captain is powerless to stop you, since Uncle Joe is the Captain's great benefactor. And the First Mate is powerless to stop you, since the Captain has authority over him.'

Napps finally trusted himself to speak. 'How do you know this?'

' . . . Except there's one problem to which you can't buy a solution,' Millet-Bass said. 'Because although ambition is free, experience has a cost. Ability has a cost. Talent has a cost. But they don't have a price.'

'Answer me. How do you know?'

Millet-Bass looked at him guiltily. 'The way you very nearly knew yourself that night during the blizzard. You just didn't know what you'd overheard. And then I lied and said I'd been speaking to myself.'

'And why didn't you tell me before?'

'For the same reason I'm admitting it to you now. I thought it was in everyone's interest to keep quiet. Except I've learnt that it wasn't in my interest, and it wasn't in your interest, Napps. We've been sold as part of one man's trophy hunt.'

Millet-Bass remembered Napps saying, *the weak aren't buoyed by the strong, the weak sink them.* He remembered Napps leaning forward, saying, *tell me that it wouldn't be easier if he'd died in the dinghy.*

'So ask me to imagine that the *Kismet* didn't come,' Millet-Bass said. 'Ask me again what I'd be willing to do.'

43

December 2012

T he intensity of the low atmospheric pressure now felt at once nosebleed-inducing and strangely dreamlike to Brix as they drove to the glacier. Everland's cyber-white sunshine added to the sense of unreality, causing the landscape to simmer with refraction and the *Joseph Evelyn* to appear in the distance as a hovering black scorch mark.

The cove's accumulation of flotsam had thawed into view as the snow dissolved. Brittle strings of seaweed and old animal bones had emerged, along with an assortment of nightmarishly decrepit toys. These, Brix discovered, were the remains of mummified seal pups, their bodies so desiccated they sounded hollow when tapped. Lengths of ancient rope still holding their complicated sailors' knots lay tangled among the stones, beside fragmented wooden slats that had once boxed food. Brix turned one of the slats over with her boot. Some were emblazoned with incomplete words, such as 'Huntley & P', 'Bov', 'Kidney S'.

Wandering about in the distracted manner of someone whose thoughts are engaged elsewhere, Decker had said it was interesting and then continued on, either unaware or untroubled that Brix and Jess weren't following.

'Forgot to give me your keys,' Jess said to Brix.

Although Brix and Decker were only carrying what they could fit in their pockets, the limping Jess was stuck with her cumbersome blue field assistant's rucksack. It was an idiocy which overshadowed even the ridiculous keys ceremony. A better idea, Brix suggested, would be for her to take this burden off Jess, or at least help out.

Jess's response was a predictable grimace of refusal.

Brix passed over the keys. 'For a little while. Just until we reach the glacier.'

Jess zipped them into the front pocket of her rucksack. She was partly thinking that this proposal was beyond ironic, since the only purpose of her storing the keys was to prevent Brix from losing them, a meaningless exercise if she then gave her the bag. She was also thinking that Decker wasn't around to disapprove, which allowed her to relax the boundaries of her own disapproval, and consider Brix's offer seriously. Perhaps even accept it.

'You could almost be a field assistant,' Jess said finally, handing her the rucksack.

'That could almost be flattering,' Brix said.

'Well, maybe Aegeus didn't make such a bad choice when they selected you,' Jess said. 'Maybe I'm quite glad you're here.'

Jess wasn't around to hear if Brix answered. Her pace had rapidly accelerated.

She'd been complimenting Brix, and complimenting people wasn't something Jess could do without embarrassment. More painful to her than the impact of fast walking on an injury was the black hole of vulnerability which followed an expression of gratitude. There was always the chance her appreciation wouldn't be welcomed in the right way, or that she'd see it returned to her as pity. The cure was to put some physical space between herself and Brix.

If Decker's headache was a poison, then idle thoughts of home were an antidote. Because he knew Viv as well as he knew himself, he could hold entire conversations with her in his head. He'd say something to her, and without him consciously trying he could generate such a spontaneous reply. His imagined Viv was so fluent and responsive it occasionally surprised him. Checking on the whereabouts of Brix and Jess, he saw they were only three or four minutes behind him, so he went on, his daydream carrying him another quarter of a mile further along the beach and into the glacial bay.

The plastic process of deformation and shift which drove a glacier forward also churned clay and grit into its layers. Newly forged glacial ice started as an ectoplasmic blue at the summit and became dirtier as it progressed to the base, eventually arriving at the shoreline as stained as an underpass blackened by decades of traffic fumes. The recent volcanic activity had sped up the process of crumbling and advancement, causing huge sootily marbled chunks of ice to collapse down over the narrow beach at the foot of Everland's glacier. In sizes comparable to shipping containers and meteorites, pieces balanced at slanting, improbable degrees, or had collided together and split. Sections with vehicle-like dimensions were smashed in a colossal pile-up, as furrowed and dented as crushed cars. To cross the beach meant navigating a path past megaliths the colour of smoke damage and wreckage which lay piled in dumper truck quantities.

'All right over there?' Decker called.

'Fine.' Jess waved him on with both hands, the briskness of her gesture interpretable as either assurance or impatience. Whichever it was, she seemed keen he keep going. 'We'll follow,' she said, her voice travelling faintly.

Good. It was an answer which enabled Decker to continue his discussion with Viv. She'd mentioned that as this was his final expedition, this might also be the final time he saw an Antarctic glacier. Quite a momentous event, after having seen them every few months for the last twenty years. It was an interesting point he hadn't considered before.

Everland's glacier had bulldozed a deep, highway-wide gorge through the island. As the weight of countless tons of compacted snow chewed into the bedrock, the loose debris which piled at its edges had amassed into thirty-metre-high moraine walls. These moraines acted as a benchmark, showing how much the glacier had receded in modern times. The ice that would have once filled the gorge was now a thinner, lower flow which had shrunk back from its former margins, like a drought-stricken river. And as the ice's edges retreated, borders of dry ground between the moraine and each side of the glacier were exposed, inviting the curious to enter.

Decker stood at the entrance to the moraine and considered his options. He'd first seen a glacier at the age of twenty-five, when he signed up for a tour of the Franz Josef glacier during a holiday in New Zealand. Visitors queued to join guided ice treks at tourism bureaus which were styled as Swiss-style wooden chalets, and helicopters flew above it hourly, carrying the wealthier sightseers. Hundreds of people were visible on the surface, following rope-fenced trails. The Franz Josef glacier was somewhere between a celebrity and a zoo exhibit, with its own merchandise of printed mugs and tea towels, postcards and calendars. It was tame and primped, unlike the glacier on Everland, which Decker classified as wild, and therefore more authentic. And if this really was to be his final encounter with a proper glacier, then he felt the moment deserved some respect, some solitary contemplation. Which he could afford to give it, since Brix and Jess were lagging behind. Just five minutes, he said to himself, starting into the dry channel which ran alongside the moraine.

'Jess? Hello, Decker?' Brix said, splashing through streams of silt. Shallow rapids of melted glacial ice had flooded over the beach, and the sound of rushing water was everywhere. She'd been no more than twenty seconds behind Jess, but in the time it took her to round the same corner, past the same five-ton glacial block to the moraine, Jess had managed to vanish. 'Hello?' Brix said again, her calls rebounding from the ice.

'Yeah?' Jess said absently from somewhere hidden. Although the puddled recess she'd found in the cliff face was only ten metres away from Brix, the oblique angle of its entrance meant it was partially concealed. And obviously, once Jess spotted it, she was compelled to investigate, which led to further investigations once she saw the tapering, three-metre-wide fissure inside the recess. Its person-accommodating dimensions and mysteriousness, along with the thrilling promise of menace inherent to any cave, was enough to coax Jess into side-stepping her way up the gravel bank to take a look.

'I lost you there for a second,' Brix said from directly behind her.

In turning at Brix's unexpected closeness, Jess's centre of gravity shifted, which led to a grinding and sudden resettling of loose pebbles, a scattering and sinking, followed by an almost slow-motion buckling.

Brix heard a pop, or a crack. The sound of a rope snapping. And then Jess was sitting in several inches of grey, sediment-filled water, unable to register anything except the compulsive need to sway. Her wet, silt-plastered hands relayed from clutching at her ankle to clutching at her head, her face streaked with handprints of dirt.

Jess was conscious of being sick, which happened quickly, and then kept happening. Although Brix filled her field of vision, Jess was unable to see her, and the high, insistent pitch of Brix's voice tuned in and out of audibility. She deciphered the application of upward pressure around her waist as Brix's attempts to lift her. The heavy thud beside the fissure was her field assistant's rucksack landing as Brix took it off and threw it. Jess wanted to keep the rucksack with her, but not enough to say the words. Similarly, she wanted to be on drier ground, but not enough to move from the muddy pool. She would have stayed in the water, in her private realm of agony, except Brix pulled her, and wouldn't leave her alone, repeating that she needed to stand, and finally succeeded in dragging her to her feet.

With Jess propped at a tilt to transfer as much of her weight as possible on to Brix, they travelled in centimetres at a time the sixty metres to a less sodden patch of beach to the right of the moraine. Brix strained and encouraged, trying to find strength she didn't possess in order to support Jess, who slumped and cramped, tortured by every minuscule hop.

'You'll be fine,' Brix told her, visions of a ripped belt-like tendon flashing through her mind as she set Jess down beside a large boulder of ice. 'Jess? You're okay,' she said, thinking of a slack rudderless foot, the plaster casts and surgery, the months of rehabilitation. 'It's all okay, all okay,' she said over and over again, before shouting for Decker, who seemed to have disappeared, and never replied.

44

April 1913

Think about it, Millet-Bass,' Napps said as they slogged along the beach on another *Kismet*-scouting trek. 'If I'd genuinely wanted him dead, why wouldn't I have just kicked him to death? What logic is there in risking my own life to save the man I want to kill?'

'I'm only telling you what Matthews told me,' Millet-Bass replied. 'You apparently said it would have been better if McValley had died.'

'Well.' In his annoyance, Napps directed his comments up at the universe. '*Matthews* should learn to differentiate between what's said in sincerity and what's said when mad with exhaustion.'

Since Millet-Bass's hands had degraded to the stage where it was now difficult for him to grip anything, Napps was in ownership of the one oil lamp they had between them. His angry marching made it swing on its handle, spokes of light veering across the snow in an erratic pattern.

It was Millet-Bass who'd instigated the conversation about the infamous trip where McValley nearly died of scurvy, unaware or seemingly unaware that a tactless comparison could be made between McValley and their situation with Dinners. He said there was one aspect of the Ross Barrier journey he'd never understood.

Millet-Bass remembered the yells of surprise as two haggard men were spotted approaching the Cape Athena hut. Despite Addison's arguments that the battered and frostbitten

Napps remain behind and rest, Napps had stubbornly insisted on accompanying the rescue party. Matthews had done the opposite. He'd complied with Addison's demands entirely, letting himself get put to bed where he lay in a state of deathly hibernation for a week.

'Which is my question,' Millet-Bass said. 'Why did you go back with Addison?'

Suspecting an underlying reason to Millet-Bass's interest, Napps raised the oil lamp to study his hairy, blackened face.

'Why are you so curious about the incident?'

'*Why?*' Millet-Bass's eyes were strikingly white and expressive in the mask of his soot-grimed skin. 'Because it means nothing to McValley. He isn't grateful to you, he's as derisive as ever. Makes me wonder if another man's life is always worth endangering yourself for.' Attempting to sound indifferent, he added, 'It could be claimed there are times when it isn't.'

'It was my duty to go back for McValley,' Napps said. Millet-Bass had a habit of leading a conversation into dangerous territory with his insinuations. The subject of Dinners would often infiltrate into non-related matters to tempt Napps towards dishonourable thoughts. He needed to crush this line of conversation before either of them had the chance to pursue it further. 'As leader of the expedition, I was obliged to go with Addison. You don't have to like a man in order to honour your obligation to him.'

'Very noble,' Millet-Bass said with a trace of mockery.

'I'm not sure about that. I do know that our decisions eventually come to define us.'

'I've an idea of how McValley defines you.'

Napps directed his attention to more important matters than the idiotic McValley. In the dark, he sensed the depth of the landscape rather than saw it, and was aware of a vast space surrounding them. They were at the northern end of the island, which meant the *Joseph Evelyn* was nearby, but Napps felt the beach was much wider than normal in some perplexing way. Although he judged they must be close to the shoreline, there was no sound of breaking waves. Napps walked a few paces and then walked back. 'Why can't we hear it?' he asked. He opened his arms in a gesture of exasperation and said, 'Where's the sea?'

Millet-Bass stood in silence, his head turned. He remained quiet for so long that Napps was about to interrupt whatever reverie he'd fallen into when Millet-Bass let out a long, whistling breath. 'The sea?' he said, chipping at the ground with his heel. 'Napps, we're on it. This isn't the beach, it's sea ice.'

Napps envisaged the glass-like splintering, the sudden capsize. He got control of himself. 'It's too early in the season.'

'Nothing else about Everland seems to abide by the ordinary rules,' Millet-Bass said. 'Check for yourself.'

Napps put an ear against the ground and detected the muffled swirl of water. He ground the blade of his knife down through the ice and it resisted solidly to the handle. Retracting the knife, he bent to listen again, then gouged up a chunk and skimmed it into the blackness. They heard it whir and blip out over the floe.

'A foot thick at least,' Millet-Bass said.

'No matter, the *Kismet* can force a path through,' Napps said. 'She's equipped for heavy floes, her bow is practically solid wood.'

Millet-Bass wasn't thinking of the ship. 'My guess is that it stretches all the way across to Cape Athena.'

During that first summer, as part of a twelve-man group assigned the task of constructing the hut, Millet-Bass had stayed at the Cape for a full six weeks. He'd been wild and optimistic and invincible, and he'd not known those sun-filled, white-skied days nailing matchboard to the roof and building a porch and cobbling together a ventilation system for the blubber stove would be some of the happiest of his life. He hadn't assigned value to them. There were other days to come, many thousands. He hadn't known that there was always a value to anything which could be taken or spent, such as his strength, such as the promise of time. Staring in the direction of the Cape, he said, 'Napps, I think I've had about enough.'

Napps told him they'd go back to the tent.

'That's not what I mean,' Millet-Bass said. 'We can't stay here and hope any more. If you need me to be useful, you'll have to make a choice. And you don't have long.'

A longish pause followed before Napps spoke. 'My choice being to leave Everland and march to Cape Athena.' His expression conveyed the battle he was having to subjugate his true, heartfelt wants. 'How would Dinners fare? He couldn't travel in his present condition. I must take account of the cost to him.'

'I'd suggest the cost of delaying is harsher,' Millet-Bass said. 'It takes two good men to haul the larger sledge, and I'm getting worse, Napps. The question is how we'll fare when this option is gone, as it will be if you wait.'

'You don't believe we can expect rescue any more.'

'I never did,' Millet-Bass said. 'And I don't think you do either.'

It was in answering that Napps realized just how long he'd known this. 'No.'

45
August 1913

N ot too long now,' Lawrence said, taking his customary place on Addison's bed. He watched the doctor snap shut his diary and put it on the desk.

Looking fixedly at the diary, Lawrence said, 'Just imagine that view of Oamaru harbour.' There was a rehearsed quality to his chat as he summoned the shoreline of the New Zealand port. Trees, Addison! Can you picture it! Grass! Lawrence said he'd be unable to stop himself diving overboard at the first sight of a house and then laughed at his own joke. Addison recognized these signs. They meant Lawrence was about to start an awkwardly confessional discussion. He'd always prelude the fact he needed to talk about something important by saying, shall we have a drink?

Addison said it for him. 'Shall we have a drink?'

'*Please.*' Lawrence rubbed his face with both hands. He hadn't slept a full night in months. He toasted their health when Addison gave him a tumbler of whisky. 'I'm surprised we haven't all dropped dead, Adds. I certainly don't know how I'm alive. It's not like I eat anything. And the others just get crazier by the day.'

The last few weeks had tested even the most resilient of spirits. There'd been tempests with all their mess and fury, the continual hazard of thick pack ice. Waves had thundered across the lee rail, men thrown down the deck as the *Kismet*'s bow lurched from the sea. Crisis had struck in the form of a flooded engine room, a near-fatal concussion, the endless repair emergencies. The crisis of the rudder struck eternally as it froze and jammed and needed incessant care like a troubled iron baby. And the strain had weathered Lawrence. His old self-assurance, which implied that destiny could be trusted to favour the handsome and charismatic, was now marred with frustration. The voyage was problematic, Everland was a catastrophe, and handsomeness hadn't protected him from any of it. Lawrence felt the injustice deeply.

'Well, there are a couple of matters I want to discuss,' he said to the doctor.

Yes, of course. Addison was ready to help.

'I think I'll start with my eyes.'

'Your eyes.'

Like all the officers' quarters, Addison's room had a small mirror cabinet and a porcelain washbasin on a wooden dresser. He invited Lawrence to take a seat in front of the mirror where the lamplight was best.

'I doubt you'll see it, no one else has,' Lawrence said as he was examined, his head gently angled and re-angled. Addison asked him to look left, and he gazed at the coat hook. Requested to look right, he examined the doctor's scrubbing brushes. His blue eyes were so pale they were silvery.

'What do you feel is wrong with them?'

'There's nothing wrong as such,' Lawrence said. 'It's more that I started with brown eyes.'

Addison's response to this disclosure was to sit in silence for what felt like a year. Then he leant and stared into Lawrence's eyes with such precision Lawrence found it difficult to keep a straight face.

'Your vision is normal?' Addison asked. Yes, he had normal vision. 'You don't have any pain from them?' No. No pain at all. 'And you're sure they were brown,' Addison said, and immediately withdrew it; of course he was sure. 'Well, that's certainly unusual. I have to admit I can't find an obvious reason.'

'I only noticed myself this morning while shaving,' Lawrence said. 'I thought it might possibly connect to your bizarre white hair, a similar process.'

Possibly, yes. Addison was as mystified as everyone by his piebald scalp and beard. The patches were pure white and randomly placed. It had happened to a few of the sailors over the course of the expedition, one in his very early twenties.

With unconvincing nonchalance, Lawrence said, 'Oh, and yes, there was also this other tiny thing I wanted to talk about.' He retrieved an envelope from his inside pocket. 'Napps handed it to me to add to the ship's mail collection before he boarded the *Joseph Evelyn*. What with all the drama of leaving for Everland, I think he'd forgotten about his letter. And unfortunately, once I'd put it in my pocket, so did I.'

Addison had volunteered to look after the crew's mail and would gladly put Napps's letter in the box for post he kept under his bed. A weaselly hesitation sparked through Lawrence's newly blue eyes as the doctor took the envelope.

'You read it,' Addison said.

'If I answer no, that's not entirely correct. Enough to gain a sense of enlightenment, let's say.'

'Meaning you read most of it.'

'Most of it? No. Enough to explain the consequent disaster, which—'

'Lawrence, he gave it to you in good faith.'

'Adds.' Lawrence let out an affectionate little sigh. 'Although touching, I should tell you that your loyalty to Napps is a waste of time.' He pattered his fingers suggestively against the letter. 'His loyalty was to himself alone. There was nothing so callous or base your champion wouldn't have done to ensure his own safety.'

Addison had a particular expression that managed both to be impassive and also to convey great regret. It was a talent which meant the source of his disappointment grasped exactly how disappointing they were without the doctor needing to say a word. For a second Lawrence was sidetracked by the ancient need not to displease Addison. Then he recovered. A larger, more important principle was at stake.

'But,' Lawrence said, the sly humour in his tone indicating he was about to ask a favour he knew was unreasonable. 'But it does, whatever your objections, conveniently lead me on to the subject of letters. Your letters, Addison. Specifically in that journal. Because I suspect you're writing more than letters.'

Addison seemed prepared to grab the diary if the Captain moved to touch it.

'Now, Adds,' he said, affably offended. 'Now hold on a minute. I'm not going to steal it.' He smiled. This was so horribly difficult. 'What I'm going to do is worse. I'm going to request that you stop, since I believe you're writing a book about the expedition which will contradict mine. And that puts me in a very tight situation.' Before Addison could speak, he made a conciliatory gesture. '*Ah, ah, ah*, let me finish.'

Lawrence said there were three things the doctor needed to understand, and the first was that explorations took a lot of funding. An enormous amount of funding. It was important Addison grasped how difficult it was to secure that funding. Addison wasn't a lump of gristle or some insentient amoeba-type creature. He wasn't ignorant, he knew about funding. But Lawrence had to beat this point into obscene clarity before he felt able to continue to Sir Joseph Evelyn, his second point.

The steel-manufacturing magnate Evelyn was a huge supporter of polar exploration. He'd been the major benefactor of most of Lawrence's voyages. So when his academic nephew Dinners expressed an interest in Antarctica, Uncle Joe obviously approached Lawrence, who was obviously unable to refuse him anything. A meeting had been arranged between Lawrence and this scrawny nephew. Dinners wanted to join the *Kismet* crew because he believed it gave him the chance to prove himself on his own terms, as his own man. Whilst he loved Evelyn, being the old man's nephew was clearly suffocating as his uncle's achievements overshadowed everything he did. Dinners said he'd spent his life feeling like a useless, spoiled pet. Therefore, in order to be recognized for his scientific work rather than for his relatives, Dinners was adamant that his identity be concealed on board the ship. Being patient, yet extremely sceptical, Lawrence questioned if he was serious about the whole anonymity thing. Dinners replied that yes, he was serious, very much so. It seemed extraordinary that Dinners would want to be subjected to the same muck and privation as the rest of the men, but yes, he did, absolutely. Telling Dinners to think carefully before replying, because sailors were a rough bunch and his connection to Evelyn would buy him immunity, Lawrence asked for a final time if he genuinely didn't want the crew to know who his uncle was. And the answer was no. No, never. Not anyone. Dinners made Lawrence swear that he'd be treated exactly the same as everyone else.

Except, of course, he wasn't the same. Dinners was the only son of the only sibling of the unmarried, childless multi-millionaire Joseph Evelyn, and therefore breathtakingly wealthy in his own right. At best, Dinners was a king-like figure masquerading as a lowly serf. And at worst, such as during the Everland selection dispute, Lawrence felt like a castrated little plaything. Because how could a Captain have any real authority over a man when beholden to him? The power bestowed by money unbalanced everything. It made the frailest man a giant, while a thousand stronger, poorer men were born with their hands tied. And the financial incentives Dinners had offered were enough to tie the hands of any ambitious Captain. He'd pledged to influence dazzlingly large sums of money from Evelyn, and also offered Lawrence thirty thousand pounds from his own private funds for the next expedition. So show me whose hands wouldn't be bound?

'And here's where it becomes upsettingly problematic for us,' Lawrence said.

The third point in his argument was ambition, because Lawrence was insatiably ambitious. He'd envisaged a brilliant legacy for himself which stretched across every ocean, across every continent, and covered an entire career of voyages. And that legacy required funding. And that funding would evaporate if Evelyn believed the long-standing recipient of his generosity was feckless, unsound, or in any way responsible for his nephew's tragic end.

'You see what I'm getting at, Adds?' Lawrence said. 'I'm asking you not to endanger me by mounting a heartfelt yet misplaced campaign to defend Napps. I'm asking you not to deflect the severity of his wrongdoing, as you will inevitably do if you write your book. Whether Dinners should have been prevented from going to Everland is an unnecessary debate. I'm saying don't dilute the issue by implying fault lies anywhere else except with Napps. I'm saying let the culpability remain with the culprit. I respect that he was your friend, but I'm also your friend. And I'm asking you to respect me.'

'Lawrence.' Addison lifted his hands helplessly. 'You're asking me to help you bury him.'

'Do you want to put it like that?' Lawrence cocked his head, disappointed. 'I'd put it another way. I'd say you were helping someone capable of appreciating your help. As I'm alive, I'm here, and I'll suffer in a very real way if you choose to make me suffer. Which is of course disastrous for you, Adds, because you'll suffer if I do.'

He paused for Addison to appreciate the dilemma. 'I wonder if you understand what I mean.'

Addison replied with an air of battered dignity, 'You're referring to my assistance to Dinners.'

What an awful pity, Lawrence's expression said, that life forces these unpleasantnesses. 'I think it would be better, would it not, if that extra help remained confidential? You're an excellent doctor, you were doing your best for your patient. But it's a clouded issue, isn't it? And it will harm you if it comes out. So maybe we should agree to keep it in. You dispose of your book, drop any sentiments about Napps and Everland, and I'll never say a word about Dinners's final moments. Except . . . ' Lawrence sucked air through his teeth. 'Oh dear, I can't guarantee my own discretion if I'm not fully persuaded of yours.' He stood up. 'So shake my hand and let's have the matter done with.'

For a moment Addison saw a future where he resisted blackmail. He remembered the letter he'd scribbled in the delirium of grief. He remembered Lawrence shouting, *have you any idea what you've done*, as he studied the lines about morphine. But he hadn't been so furious he didn't recognize the intrinsic value of the letter. And now Addison understood what Lawrence had seen. His letter was a noose. He'd undermined a career he'd spent a lifetime building. With inexpressible self-loathing, Addison accepted the Captain's outstretched hand.

'There, that wasn't so bad, was it,' Lawrence said. 'No thunderbolts. No devastating consequences. You didn't go up in flames.'

Addison looked at him with something close to pity. 'There's a consequence,' he said. 'Of course there is. Every single day you've ever lived has a consequence, although you can't often see it.'

'Not that I'm aware of.'

'But there are moments, like this one, when you can. The possibilities speak to you. And you listen.'

The disagreeable task was over and the world was beautiful again. Lawrence radiated cheer. 'Oh, that's good, that's very good,' he said as he left the room. 'And you listen? That's going in the book, Adds.'

After twenty minutes of contemplating the envelope on his desk, Addison found himself succumbing to curiosity. Lawrence had scrambled the letter's order and what Addison opened first was the last page.

To Rosie, how much Napps missed her. The Captain had requested that he volunteer to take a run ashore with two other men, a sailor and a scientist, to scout out an uncharted and unknown island.

Addison read the next paragraph and then refolded the letter. Lawrence's trace of enlightenment was there, as his pattering fingers had indicated.

Dearest Rosie, as Napps was sure she'd imagined: 'Pitiful defeatist that I am, I've had to battle my apprehensions. Although the sailor is highly competent, the scientist doesn't seem at all suitable. I had a decent old row with the Captain about it. However, as always, I'm reassured by the sheer force of my will to return to you. No man or deed or sin or obstacle could stop me. There is nothing I wouldn't do to return, nothing I can't live with if it gets me home. And what courage it gives me! Your devoted pessimist is transformed into a bigger man who embraces adventure and even pursues it. How time tricks us into seeing who we really are, and what choices we make.'

46

April 1913

S*peed*, Napps,' Millet-Bass said. 'It's mid-morning already.'
The moon seemed disproportionately large. It cast a hal-
lucinatory light which made ice crystals reflect, covering
the snow with diamond dust. The glow of the oil lamps looked
jaundiced and vulgar in the sparkling indigo dreamscape.

Millet-Bass told Napps there was an atmospheric heaviness
he didn't like. He could feel some sort of blizzard-bringing
pressure, he said, his breath steaming to linger around his head
as a raggedly empty speech bubble. 'There's no time for second
thoughts.'

'I know, but we can't rush Dinners. Show some patience.'

'Rush him?' Millet-Bass said. 'Your lenience with him is
crippling us. You do nothing but indulge him. In fact you're so
busy being Dinners's nursemaid you've never mentioned you
know he's Evelyn's nephew.'

'You want me to confront Dinners about Evelyn?' Napps
said in a low voice. 'What, to punish him for it? What good do
you imagine that would do? Something's wrong with him,
Millet-Bass. He's barely holding himself together.'

Two days had passed since Millet-Bass's ultimatum on the
sea ice about either leaving for Cape Athena or losing their
chance to leave. The first day was spent in a tent-bound con-
ference. Dinners remained watchful and mute as Napps and
Millet-Bass had the same fraught, looping conversations about
the same unanswerable questions. When Millet-Bass argued
for going to the Cape, Napps countered that they might die on

the journey, which caused Millet-Bass to rage that not going meant they'd die on the island instead. It was Millet-Bass who eventually won the battle. One factor was his steeply declining health, which forced Napps into action. Another factor was Millet-Bass's horrifyingly true assertion that dying whilst attempting to escape was still preferable to sitting in the tent, waiting for death, without the decency to act as though your life was even worth trying to save. The decision was made.

Having spent the second day devising a route, the three men had risen early to pack up the camp. Napps couldn't stop his mind circling down to the same ugly conclusion as they prepared for the march. The truth was that they needed a fourth well man, or they needed one less ill man. Because to haul the food and fuel required for three when only one of the team wasn't badly crocked amounted to an equation which wouldn't ever balance.

Dinners stood trembling in his harness. 'We shouldn't go,' he whined to Napps. He'd come up with countless reasons to abort the march. He said he wasn't strong enough today. His feet hurt. His legs hurt very badly. And for every problem Napps dismissed, Dinners created a hundred more.

'Just try a few steps,' Napps said.

Dinners tottered unsteadily with his sledge. Since it was impossible for the large sledge to transport all their supplies, he was charged with drawing five of the six cans of oil and his sleeping bag on the smaller sledge. Yet even this minimal load seemed unworkable.

'You know what to do, though, Dinners,' Napps said brightly to mask the worry in his voice. 'You'll follow us, won't you? It's easy, isn't it, Millet-Bass?'

'Faster,' Millet-Bass said. 'Get him going or let him stay behind.'

The larger sledge was packed with an enormous weight of food and equipment, including the leaden frost-rimed tent.

Despite the burden he'd given himself, Napps had still wasted hours trying to pare Dinners's load down further. He'd experimented to see if he could add Dinners's sleeping bag to their cargo, which he couldn't, no matter how he tied it on. He'd managed to transfer one single can of oil to his own load, despite a long, frustrating battle to take more, or at least two. He'd ferried oilcans away from Dinners's sledge and then put them back in a combination of different failures. He'd agonized over the knapsacks, emptying and refilling them, before finally deciding to shoulder Dinners's knapsack himself. To free all available room, he removed the non-essential items from the bags and filled Dinners's coat pockets.

'Twenty feet of visibility,' Napps said as he stuffed their three diaries and a box of matches into one of Dinners's pockets. 'Understand me? You'll lose sight of us if you allow the distance to lapse.' He put some chocolate and Dinners's crumpled sledging flag in the other pocket. 'For luck,' he said, hanging Dinners's small drawstring pouch of rocks around Dinners's neck.

'It's getting late,' Millet-Bass said. 'We planned to be gone by noon.'

'Hard pounding this, gentlemen,' Napps said quietly to Dinners. 'Let's see who will pound longest.'

Dinners thought of the photograph of Elizabeth he'd given to Napps, and the quote he'd written. 'You read it.'

'It's in my knapsack,' Napps said. 'It's your oath to me, remember? You promised you wouldn't let me down. So trust that I won't let you down in return. We'll both be brave, won't we?'

The men established a rhythm once marching. Millet-Bass and Napps maintained a solid plod at the front, Napps carrying an oil lamp, while Dinners trailed behind them, chanting to himself in a high, strained whine. Their pace held until the optical illusions surrounding Dinners grew too vivid for him to ignore. His path was obstructed by phantom boot prints which elevated off the snow to disrupt him. The lines of writhing black ribbons left by the runners of Napps's sledge wanted to knot around his legs. Dinners needed to be prudent and dodge these impediments and also march quickly, except striving to do both jobs cancelled either. He tried and failed and tried and couldn't do it, and gradually dropped thirty feet from sight range, now forty. Now fifty feet from sight, now sixty.

'Wait for me, will you wait,' he'd bleat, forcing Napps and Millet-Bass to stop until he stumbled up out of the blackness.

He'd pant his apologies, receive harried instructions, and then the tedious process would repeat.

When the ground began to revolve under Dinners, he smiled conspiratorially. This was another ploy to sabotage him. It meant his efforts to walk at a good pace as Napps wanted him to were useless. He was walking to remain at the same point, and if he didn't walk he'd reel backwards. Then it became obvious that the speed was wrong. The ground was moving too fast. With epiphany-like clarity, Dinners understood that the sense of accelerated motion was a trick caused by all these things fleeing in the opposite direction.

'Napps?' he said very cautiously in case Millet-Bass overheard.

Fissures in the ice were twisting past him, as mobile as swimming snakes. Armies of stones were evacuating across the beach, whole embankments contracting and expanding in propulsion. Even the cliffs were in retreat with a folding concertinaed gait. And what Dinners should do was report it to Napps immediately. He should call to Napps and ask why inanimate objects were roused and running. Hadn't he noticed? Everything was in migration, and it was of crucial importance that Napps consider what the objects were migrating from. Dinners couldn't say anything though, because he was scared of Millet-Bass. If he mentioned it Millet-Bass would yell again about atmospheric pressure and threaten him.

Napps stared back. 'Where is he?'

'He was there a moment ago,' Millet-Bass replied, sick beyond endurance of fucking Dinners. 'Napps, just because we can't hear him doesn't mean he's not close. Maybe he's stopped chanting.'

'He never stops chanting,' Napps said, unbuckling his sledging harness.

The real dilemma, Dinners now saw clearly, was that they were being watched by something devious. It lurked outside the boundary of his limited vision, but it was certainly near enough to sense. And he'd caught glimpses of movement, yes he had. There'd been definite sightings he could not in any way convince himself were imagined. So whenever Millet-Bass was out of earshot, Dinners would veer towards Napps and hiss snippets of information. Baffled at Napps's lack of response, he'd swerve closer and mutter his updates in louder, more agitated tones. Occasionally, if he wasn't mindful, Dinners would accidentally overtake Napps. When that happened, he'd have to loiter on his own until Napps caught up.

Dinners nodded craftily. 'I thought it was upon us then.'

Napps was hurting him. He'd gripped Dinners by the arm to make him trot alongside. And he didn't sound particularly interested as he said, 'What was?'

Dinners tutted at Napps's coyness. 'I keep telling you and you don't answer.'

Napps slowed to a halt. 'Dinners, how could I? You were nowhere near us.'

'I was beside you and you didn't answer!'

'Beside?' Napps's expression confused Dinners. He seemed dismayed. 'Look, it doesn't matter. You're doing well. But we'll hurry now, won't we?'

The cove's huge columnar stones were haloed with moonlight. Its unusual lustre removed sharpness and altered texture. The granular surface of rock looked like bark, as though the men had entered a petrified forest. Boulders appeared quilted, almost spongy. Whilst areas of shadow were so black as to appear void, large expanses of snow were an unearthly chemical blue. Further down towards the shoreline, the dinghy was identifiable by its smooth shape among the angular debris. Napps spotted the dinghy and then forgot it, sloughing on. Although this was the last time he'd see the *Joseph Evelyn*, it produced nothing beyond a twitch of recognition. No sadness, no regret, no sentiment whatsoever. To feel any way about the dinghy would require Napps to emote with that distant moment when they first arrived on Everland, which was impossible, because it concerned three other men, and some other life, and no longer applied to him. If Millet-Bass was aware they were passing the dinghy, he didn't even turn his head.

A rubble slope at the northernmost edge of the cove led down on to the sea ice, the hiss and crash of spray replaced by a flat, deadened tundra. Millet-Bass objected when Napps interrupted their march to rally Dinners, who lagged behind. They needed to set up the tent, he said to Napps, sleet beginning to speckle against them as a thunderhead rolled across the sky. Anxious about the loose, pulpy shoreline floes, Millet-Bass implored they get further out on to the more solid ice.

'Head down the slope, Dinners. Do you see it?' Napps said.

No answer. 'We don't have time for this,' Millet-Bass said. 'Where is he?'

'Dinners?' Napps shouted into the dark. 'Answer me, Dinners.'

Once, faintly, the wind carried the sound of a shrill, wraith-like voice incanting, '*Yes I will, yes I will, yes I will.*'

47

December 2012

As if tolerating the scrape of cutlery against porcelain, or the grating of metal chair legs across concrete, Decker locked his head at an angle. His migraines had various triggers. Red wine was one of them, so was caffeine. Low atmospheric pressure was another. Too much salt caused lightning to spark behind his eyes. Whatever acid saturated his brain during these attacks also caused multi-coloured shapes to float around in his vision. It meant he couldn't be absolutely sure whether the blue thing on the ground in the distance ahead of him was imagined or a real three-dimensional object.

Snow had begun to fall for the first time in days, the powdery flakes sticking like wet ash to clothing and skin. Decker ambled along the empty channel between the glacier and the moraine ridge. He could have clambered up on to the glacier's mounded surface if he'd wanted. It wasn't much above two metres high, and the glacier's edges were a smashed, easily climbable incline of debris. But his headache had developed a metallic frequency, and the length of his five-minute jaunt was now closer to fifteen.

The blue object hadn't moved from its position. It was still at the end of the channel where the moraine ridge opened out on to the beach. As he approached, Decker identified it as Jess's rucksack. Neither she nor Brix were anywhere in sight. The bag had seemingly been dumped by its owner, and this kind of negligence would have usually bothered Decker. Except he wasn't thinking about Jess's irresponsibility in leaving her bag, he was thinking instead of the medicines she always carried. A few sweetened glucose tablets and a rehydration sachet mixed with water might help him. Aspirin would definitely work. Decker picked up the bag, unzipped the main compartment, and thought he heard his name being called as he poked through the bag's contents. There, buried among the usual junk she lugged around with her, shining at him like a little yellow plastic sunrise, was Jess's first-aid kit.

A grittier sleet had replaced the fine snow. Once outside the shelter of the gorge, the wind was noticeably stronger and several degrees colder. With an arm looped through one of the rucksack's shoulder straps, Decker opened the first-aid kit and pressed a couple of aspirins out of the blister pack, swallowing them dry. Hearing his name again, he stopped and listened. The rattling sleet confused the direction of her voice.

Her next call was more insistent. 'Brix?' he said.

The glacial rubble obstructed Decker's view of the beach. It sounded as though she was shouting from somewhere to the left. Stuffing Jess's medical kit into his pocket, he broke into a jog, wet silt flecking his trousers as he splashed through ankle-deep streams.

The fractionally more distant volume of Brix's next shout revealed his error a minute later. In turning left, he'd just gone fifty metres the wrong way. He'd started to jog back when he caught sight of something which brought him to an abrupt halt. Framed between two huge segments of ice was a panorama of the ocean. What he'd diagnosed as a pressure headache had manifested into a billowing white mass which obscured the horizon. With the slow, automatic movements of a man transfixed, Decker let the rucksack drop beside his feet, and stood watching the storm move towards Everland at such a speed the advance was visible.

48
April 1913

H ead down the slope, Dinners. You see it?' Napps
shouted from the sea ice.
Yes I will, yes I will, yes I will!
Dinners would not disappoint Napps. No, he'd ignore any
distractions.

Except the distractions were invidious and plentiful. Despite
his efforts, he kept hearing things. Such as the wet, pulmonary
grunts of a monster. And he kept seeing things. He saw something larger than a man come loping behind him, its heavy head
sawing from side to side. He ran and steps came hammering after
him. When he ran faster, his pace was matched. So he broke into
a wild gallop and the runners of his sledge skewed wildly and
shovelled under the snow. With an abrupt wrenching halt, the
sledge jammed and Dinners was thrown over on to his side.

'Stay away,' he shrieked, crawling around to untangle the harness and shove free his sledge. 'Don't come near me,' he said,
fists raised to defend himself from an empty windswept beach.

Dinners sobbed and beat his hands against his skull, terrified of being mad.

The distant voice of Millet-Bass said, *'We don't have time
for this.'*

Listening to Millet-Bass and Napps talk gave Dinners the
courage to make his way across the cove. The shadows were
insulating and safe, and he skulked from one boulder to the
next. He pressed into the dark, embracing its natural protec-
tiveness as he neared the island's border.

Dinners could see the amber disc of lamplight, and was less than thirty yards away from Napps, when he stopped. Another few steps would have taken him on to the slope which led down to the sea ice, but he stood perfectly still. Some things are just known. It was a physical certainty rather than a conscious one, and Dinners understood that he was not to let himself be seen. An instinctive apprehension demanded that he stay concealed and silent.

'Dinners? Answer me, Dinners.'

Dinners pushed himself further back into shadows. He wasn't able to answer Napps until he'd completed his surveys. He didn't trust the jagged banks of rock which edged the shoreline. They were blackly stencilled against the plutonium blue of the sea ice, and Dinners wasn't fooled into considering them harmless. A danger resided there, a cunning but nonspecific thing, which had underestimated its opponent. Because Dinners would outmanoeuvre the threat, he was vigilant. He remained in the shadows as one minute became three minutes and Napps shouted that they didn't have long. He said they needed to put up the tent.

Dinners cupped his gloves over his mouth and whispered into them to contain the sound. 'It's a *trap*,' he warned Napps. Four minutes became six.

'Dinners, please answer me,' Napps said.

Because it was not possible for him to reply, Dinners put his face against the stone and wept for Napps. The situation was reaching a climactic point and Napps hadn't understood any of the signals. Unlike Dinners, he didn't have an innate precautionary system to inform him of hazards which eyes and ears weren't sensitive enough to perceive. In order to survive the suspense, Dinners swayed from one foot to the other as he watched the rocks. Seven minutes became ten and he began to make a low keening noise.

None of his preparations readied him. The oilcans clanged

together as Dinners yanked at his sledge, stumbling in his haste to reverse away from the sea ice. He ran, fleeing back into Everland with Napps's defeated voice still calling for him.

'Dinners? Please don't do this.'

But too late, it was done. Dinners had seen it hidden among the rocks. It had waited for him. A creature with a huge, misshapen body. And then, unable to wait, it had turned its head.

J ess, can you walk?'
She didn't need to reply. Decker could see the answer in
her face. Despite his efforts to remain unaware, and therefore keep alive the dream of being wrong, there was nothing
about the situation Decker hadn't known immediately from
the moment he saw Jess on the snow, Brix kneeling beside her.

'Jess, can you even stand?' Decker asked anyway, because
he couldn't stop hoping that his rational mind was deceiving
him. Jess obviously couldn't stand, there was no possibility of
her being able to walk. She'd have to be carried, he'd have to
carry her, and this meant recalculating the situation to include
the additional weight and time and risk. But to accept those
truths meant accepting that their predicament was more disastrous than he could bear to consider.

Decker estimated they had less than half an hour before the
storm hit. He said he didn't have to tell them what would happen if they were caught in it. To outrun the blizzard they'd
have to get to the quads, get to the camp, and then get inside
the tent.

So all they had to do was follow this straightforward plan,
Decker said, thinking it sounded as naïve and neglectful as a
lecture on how best to survive a head-on car crash. He listened
to himself say, 'Very clear strategy, very easy,' and heard the
evangelical pitch of the hopelessly self-deluded. Brix was making him frantic. She wouldn't maintain eye contact or concentrate in the way he wanted her to.

'Get ready. This is going to hurt,' Decker said, hoisting Jess up off the ground.

Brix didn't know what she was trying to find. She looked searchingly across the beach, agitated by the sense that something was missing which disconnected their plan. Not just compromised it, but derailed it terminally. From a soft powder, falling vertically, the snow had changed to a thicker slush which blew at fiercer, more horizontal angles. When Decker set off to the cove, hoisting Jess along with him, Brix was unable to surrender her search. She stayed there and kept looking as Decker and Jess got forty metres ahead, then fifty, then sixty metres, and she was finally forced to run after them. They were midway to the cove when she remembered what they'd left behind.

There were three sets of keys to the quads and two of them were in Jess's rucksack.

It was Jess who spoke first. 'Then we'll manage on one bike.'

Brix's voice was shaking. 'I put the rucksack near the moraine. I can get it.'

'Brix.' Jess inclined her head, her eyes wide in dismay. 'We might manage on one bike.'

And they might not, thought Decker. Three bodies on one quad would result in a slow, unstable journey. It would be challenging, the drive would take longer, and what he needed was speed. Things needed to happen *fast*. He felt their options shrinking with the visibility.

The situation required Decker to either return to the glacier himself, or allow Brix to return. He decided the answer to this quandary lay in deciding which of them was responsible for going to get the bag. If he admitted the rucksack wasn't where Brix claimed it was, then that responsibility would be his. Which was a problem, because he had virtually no idea where he'd put the bag. In his distraction, he hadn't noticed he'd dropped it. But since he'd not said a word about moving the rucksack, or even seeing it, while Brix kept repeating that she had done both, Decker found his memory to be a willingly malleable tool. The more Brix insisted, the simpler she made it for him to doubt what he recalled. She was so adamant that she could find the bag, and he was so sure that he couldn't, he decided to assume his memory had betrayed him and elect to believe her instead.

'You can't go.' Jess was leaning against Decker, one arm clinging round his shoulders. Using her free arm, she snatched at Brix's jacket, grasping her sleeve. 'Decker, tell her to stay.'

'I'll be back in three minutes,' Brix said. 'Will you wait?'

'*Decker*,' Jess said, fighting to hold on to Brix. '*Tell her.*'

Decker thought the distance between himself and safety had either doubled or tripled with the addition of Jess's weight. Everything had deconstructed into a series of numbers. He was fifty-four. There was a seven degree internal temperature difference between a functioning body and a fatally malfunctioning body. The quads were approximately four hundred metres away. He had one life. He had around fifteen or sixteen minutes.

'Will you wait?' Brix asked again. 'I'll be three minutes. Can you wait for me?'

Make sure you come home, Viv had said, to which Decker promised that he'd always come home. 'You'll have to catch us,' he said, staring towards the cove so he wouldn't have to see Brix leave.

50
April 1913

illet-Bass was the one who said it. 'We do have a can of oil.'

Napps looked at him. Yes, they did. They had that single can; the product of Napps's futile efforts to minimize Dinners's load. He would have taken all six cans on to his own sledge if there'd been any way of doing so. He should have kept trying.

'That's enough to heat a little water, if we're sparing,' Millet-Bass said. 'We might manage on cold food.'

Here, if Napps wanted it, was his excuse. It was being laid before him. He thought about the fact he had seventy miles of sea ice to cross, in winter, with the sick Millet-Bass. Despite aiming to cover ten miles a day, Napps suspected they'd be lucky to achieve six. There was also another ugly, bestial thought. Although the lack of oil was a disastrous problem, both Napps and Millet-Bass knew that Dinners himself was no less of a problem. He'd be slow and incapable, weighing them down with his helplessness. Napps remembered what he'd written to Rosie. *There is nothing I wouldn't do to return.*

He said, 'Can you climb back up?'

Millet-Bass couldn't. Even with Napps's assistance, he'd struggled to climb down the borders on to the sea ice. It wasn't possible for him to scale the slope again.

No man or deed or sin or obstacle. 'Not even try?'

'If the weather breaks before we've set up the tent— Napps, we've got twenty minutes at most.'

Napps considered the situation. No heat, no hot meals, but further each day, and faster. They might be able to manage on cold food, as Millet-Bass had said. All he had to do was choose to believe this decision was not only forgivable, but necessary and right. With enough determination you could perhaps convince yourself of anything. *There is nothing I can't live with if it gets me home.*

Napps unbuckled his harness. 'We can't leave him.'

Because if he left Dinners he would never be without him. He'd be a bitter taste at mealtimes, a weariness at midday, a chill at night, and an insomnia which started in the hour before dawn for the rest of Napps's life. Dinners would be present at every Christmas and holiday, every weekend and birthday to remind Napps of the joy he'd stolen from him, just as every animal Napps killed was witnessed by the spectre of the pony Nelson. To abandon Dinners meant abandoning any hope of peace. Napps couldn't go home, he couldn't expect to ever find contentment, if he had to sacrifice another man to do so. How time tricks us into seeing who we really are, and what choices we make.

'Don't,' was all Millet-Bass could bring himself to say.

Napps gripped him by the shoulders. 'I'm sorry.'

Millet-Bass's voice cracked. 'Please, Napps.'

'We're all right,' Napps said. 'We're all right.'

With that, Napps started back into the dark towards Everland. Three steps, four steps, and he was gone.

ecker and Jess reached the cove as the storm was breaking. The wind drove against them, Decker's steps weaving as he went to his bike and placed Jess on the saddle. He climbed on in front and they watched as the snow blew harder, in increasing volumes, until its density acted as a wild, airborne corrosive, dissolving the beach into opacity.

Jess willed Brix to appear. As a spell to protect Brix from danger, she devised hazards and then neutralized them with the corresponding solutions. The fear of not having much time was offset by the fact they didn't need much time. That Brix had returned alone to the glacier, in a burgeoning storm, wasn't going to alter the island's geography in some menacing way. The distance between the glacier and the cove was non-variable, regardless of blizzards, and so remained short and easily negotiable. Similarly, the anxiety of the left rucksack was defused by the confidence that Brix knew where to find it. The difference between a setback and a disaster, Jess assured herself, was the ability to control unregulated factors and therefore determine the outcome. Which meant there was nothing to worry about. But as five minutes ticked into seven, and Brix still hadn't returned, the protective force field of Jess's spell began to wane. Something had clearly gone wrong and was becoming more wrong by the second.

'We could return to the glacier and search for her,' Jess said.

Decker refused outright. He was terrified that his hands would freeze into incapacitation, leaving him unable to drive the quad. As the nature of sensation loss made it impossible to gauge the percentage of numbness in his feet, he decided it was as bad as he imagined. Decker thought he noticed the sallow mark of frostbite on Jess's cheeks, which indicated that he was getting frostbitten, which led him straight back to agonizing about his hands. Every additional moment of exposure widened the gap between what might be physically recoverable and what would become unsalvageable. He knew that to stay much longer would mean losing fingers to the first knuckle, then the second, and then losing the fingers entirely. The same with toes, the same with ears and noses and parts of the face, as ice scorched flesh into blackened deadness. Shortly after that, their brains would begin to slow and they'd lose cognitive function. And then they'd lose everything. So when Jess said that they could wait, Decker knew he wasn't going to wait. He wasn't going to stay here. He wouldn't just patiently let himself die.

Jess cried and argued against it when he told her there was no alternative.

'I'm sorry,' Decker said. 'Jess, I'm sorry.'

'Hold on to me. Tighter,' he said, starting the ignition.

April 1913

E very mistake was costing Napps time. He'd see Dinners and go to him, only to have Dinners morph into the wrong shape as he approached. The convincingly human outline would become stumpier and oddly proportioned, with no discernible head, and then reveal itself as a rock formation. But no matter how many plausibly Dinners-shaped silhouettes disappointed Napps, he'd spot another and his optimism would renew. He'd let this maddening cycle of hope and frustration steer him in one direction and then another until he was no longer sure if this was the route they'd used.

At some point he remembered the ground had caved beneath him and he'd fallen into a thigh-deep, slushily iced pool. He'd plunged forward, his sodden clothing stuck to his body, the leather knapsack bleeding water from its seams as water gushed to fill the pits left by his boots. The wind-chill against his drenched clothes induced a type of recklessness in Napps. He either felt cold or very hot, it didn't interest him enough to resolve. No, I won't be long, he said to Millet-Bass. When he didn't reply, Napps turned to admonish him and was bewildered by his absence. Then he nodded at his foolishness. Being wet is making me illogical, he told Millet-Bass with a self-congratulating kind of laugh. I've got to get less wet.

You're helping the wrong man, Millet-Bass said to him telepathically.

Napps held up one finger to silence him. I'm coming back

for you soon, he answered. Taking off the waterlogged bag, he dug through it, rummaging past the photograph of Elizabeth Dinners to get a few biscuits to put in his pocket.

'There you are, Dinners,' he said to a manlike object in the distance. He pushed the bag against a rock shelf and set off after him.

The snow whipped into Napps's face and made his eyes sting, which bothered him intensely. With an enraged tooth-bared grimace, he scrubbed at his eyes, wiping them and blinking, grinding them with his sleeve, until it stopped being important. With all efforts to shield his face suspended, he waded along, nearly blind as the moon dimmed into nothing behind the clouds. He arrived at the place he thought he'd seen Dinners, but Dinners had either left or never been there, and frankly Napps didn't have the time to stand around thinking about it. His father was waiting for him, so was his mother. They wanted him to hurry because otherwise they'd be late. Napps whispered to Dinners anyway in an act of hushed rebellion, telling him to stop playing these stupid games. It was already twenty past six and the invitation said it started at seven.

What Dinners needed to understand was that there was some party Napps's parents were forcing him to attend. And although he didn't want to go, his opinion had been overruled because he was fifteen years old and therefore powerless.

Napps's hands paddled at the dark and hit against a solid thing, which he spent a while tapping at and patting before he established that it was a cliff face. Since he was having trouble coordinating his legs, he used the cliff as an assistive device and slid himself along it. When the cliff unexpectedly vanished, and he lurched sidelong into a nothingness of some sort, Napps systematically decrypted this new mystery with more patting, and quizzical nudges, and a sustained period of investigatory tapping. He was, he finally concluded, in a fissure. He hadn't intended to stay there, but it offered shelter from the blizzard and he needed a minute to think. Some brown-haired girl had appeared in front of him, and she wanted to know why he was being so boring. What a question. The answer, he thought, was probably to ignore her. Also, she was making him very shy.

Then Napps found he'd crouched down or overbalanced. Whatever he'd done, he was now on the ground and she was sitting so closely beside him their knees were almost touching. He didn't mind, though, to the point where he thought he might even like it. That he felt light-headed was almost certainly because he'd tried to impress this brown-haired whoever-she-was by drinking a tumbler of rum on an empty stomach. He was hiding with her in the garden, and despite the fact he'd never met her before, they were already talking as if they knew each other. Like this could be the start of something. And although it was bitterly cold, he didn't want to go inside just yet.

53
April 1913

M illet-Bass sat on the sledge and said, 'What a fix.' It didn't matter what the words were, he wanted to hear his own voice.

He'd watched Napps go, and then kept watching in the hope that he might come back. But after counting to a hundred very slowly, three times, he'd understood what the situation was and begun the process of trying to put his affairs in order. There was a list he needed to tick off. It involved rolling through Christmases and holidays and birthdays and long gauzy summers. The time was a metronome tilting left with one age and tilting right with the next as the boy stretched out of the infant and the man hulked out of the boy.

He thought of the family planets which had orbited his fast, furious sun. His four sisters had been enemies, become friends, become mothers, and Millet-Bass was a good uncle. His parents had been tyrants, become confidants, become equals, and Millet-Bass was a good son. And no matter what he did to reassure them, they worried constantly when he was away. They saved every single one of his short, infrequent letters. He docked and they sent packages containing exhaustively detailed letters and thoughtful presents. He left and they missed him. He returned and they made transparent, wishful jokes about him settling down. And three years ago, had he said enough?

He'd bid goodbye to everyone in his traditional emotionally cool style in order to repel the sensational crescendo of wailing love. *Yes, yes*, he'd say as arms were flung around his neck. He'd escape from one rib-splintering embrace only to be crushed in another. The same ludicrous promises would be wrung out of him as he was forbidden to smoke his pipe in bed, or socialize with atheists, or carry a knife, or forget to wash, all of which he did as a matter of principle. He was absolutely never treated as an experienced man who'd been sailing for more than two decades and always come home fine. Instead he had to tolerate being sobbed over like an ailing baby or talked to like an idiot pet. He had to duck a thousand more attempts to cling on to him. He had to listen as weepy women tortured him with sentimentality.

But perhaps once he could have put aside his awkwardness and invested some energy into the departure. For your mother, you brute. Except he'd had this idea that he could afford to say everything of importance at some other distant point. He wouldn't be an absent son and brother for ever. He'd tell them he loved them later. How differently he'd do it now.

Millet-Bass smiled, mystified by his behaviour. It made no sense to him when he thought of these things he valued so highly, yet treated with careless abandon and ran into the ground. He was mostly useless with people, pretty much all people, especially himself. He was famously useless with himself. For his whole life he'd considered his body with a curious detachment, viewing it as a big biddable horse which had been unluckily loaned to him, the world's cruellest owner. He'd done such ruinous things to his miraculous body. He'd starved it and gorged it and mistreated it and driven it headlong towards annihilation. Millet-Bass would always gladly volunteer to labour under the harshest extremes while Captain and crew looked on, stunned. When younger, before learning any respect for his limits, he'd work at slavishly gruelling speeds until ordered to stop. And each crime was forgiven. His poor exploited horse of a body would absorb the punishment without exception. He'd collapse down, destroyed, and then bounce up half an hour later, ready to wreck himself again. So the knowledge that in any other situation he could have salvaged his health triggered a particularly crucifying depth of sorrow. Anywhere but here, he knew he could have been saved and maybe grown old and done more with himself yet. Millet-Bass said quickly, 'Ah, don't break your own heart.'

Sitting on the sledge, he hummed whatever tune he could find and said, 'Come on now. It's all right.'

There were the inevitable mistakes. Millet-Bass examined the ones at the front of the queue. The majority of them were foolishly avoidable. It was too mortifying to remember the occasions when the alcohol had turned to gunpowder and he'd sought out and compulsively scratched at a tension. His beery face would leer to within inches of the chosen target as he deliberately misunderstood the conversation until the whole room just exploded into a brawl. He generally regretted and pleaded guilty to those times. Yet there were also times when he'd done a kindness which cost him dearly. There were many times when he'd acted selflessly. He had an almost simplistic honesty and a gentle side which he did what he could to hide. He wasn't a hard man to decipher, and he knew he drank too much, but he was sorry. He knew he might have done better, but he'd tried his best. He was loyal except in his head, and that was only sometimes.

As the worst mistake, Grace was harder to conciliate. What would it have been like? Millet-Bass had spent about five years wondering, because he was a man with a baffling quirk. His natural boisterousness meant he was one of the louder people and could easily be too loud, apart from when Grace was anywhere near him. When she was close he reacted very mildly, if at all. With her he preferred to stand there as dumb as a pile of sand. He remembered with acute frustration the single instance he'd gathered the nerve to take action. It had been midnight and the party was dying at a mutual acquaintance's wedding.

'Hey-hey-hey, hold on,' Millet-Bass had said quietly as they passed each other. They'd both been alone and she'd stopped to talk to him, perhaps noticing how gawkily embarrassed Millet-Bass's pose was as he leant on the bar. The chemistry between them had built to such intense levels it was almost scorching before he was finally emboldened to say, 'Grace, if I told you—'

A pack of cackling friends appeared. Draping themselves over Millet-Bass, they'd demanded with the fun-hunting belligerence of the very drunk that he come with them now and do something somewhere. And without knowing what he'd wasted, Millet-Bass had shrugged good-naturedly and let himself get towed away.

At that point he'd still believed he could afford to bank his hopes entirely in the future. It was just one of the things he'd do later. As always, he'd tell them he loved them later.

'I think I should . . . ' he said, lying back on the sledge. 'Grace, I wish—' But he couldn't finish the sentence and decided not to try again.

What a life you've made for yourself, he thought, unsure whether his accomplishments tallied to anything much. The seafaring paradox of freedom and regimentation was so claustrophobic it would be intolerable to most people. There was never a second unobserved or an action done in independence, and he'd spent years as celibate as a monk in an environment of suffocating intimacy. And although he obviously corrected this once he was on land, he could never stay ashore for long.

'There's nothing to worry about,' Millet-Bass said, because Napps was perhaps returning with Dinners this very second. He only had to remember all those times he'd been proved wrong when absolutely sure of the outcome.

'You never know,' he said encouragingly to his boots. Except he did know.

Millet-Bass had a knack with nature and knew how to make a home anywhere. He had a knack with ships and understood them with a rough, intuitive rhythm which came effortlessly to him and went beyond expertise. He listened to the ship and the waves, and he grasped the elegance of their exchange as the sea spoke its fierce language and the ship responded in sweet agreement. And whatever else he had or hadn't done, he could at least be proud of his expeditions.

'Judge me by my own standards,' Millet-Bass said to the night sky, 'and I think I can live with it.'

T he rucksack wasn't there.

Because this was impossible, Brix continued to stare at the place where it had been as if disbelief would force the bag to materialize. When this didn't work, she turned to survey the area behind her in case miracles only happened when you weren't watching.

Thoughts of Decker and Jess waiting, thoughts of diminishing time, of the seconds counting down to nothing, were manageable to Brix as long as each stage of her journey complied with her expectations. For a while they had. The trek down the beach had segued faultlessly into the arrival at the glacial bay and the relocation of the moraine, and now everything was in chaos. The rucksack was gone, she was alone in a blizzard with no idea what to do, and her awareness of the passing seconds had become a distinct and more physical sensation. Every sixtieth of a minute developed the ability to inflict its own individual misery as it went by, wasted.

Less of a fluid gaseous substance, the blizzard wind was a resistant material composed of flying glass filings. Hoping that something might change if she kept reordering the same actions, Brix paced up the moraine, paced back, searched the same area, felt the same despair, and paced back up the moraine. It was the first of several theories which proved to be useless. That the rucksack might have been buried under the snow in such a way that it was somehow invisible, instead of being a bulky rucksack shape, was disproved as Brix scratched about with the gloved hoof-things she had for hands. The erratic notion that the heavy rucksack had lifted into the air and blown directly into the cliffside fissure was equally hopeless, but also needed to be disproved.

Whatever monumental force of pressure had split the cliff, the resulting hall-width fissure seemed designed to evoke human contemplation. Removed from the noise and turmoil of the blizzard, it was a vacuum of serenity, with an enchanted and chapel-like stillness. The fissure's roof peaked three metres above Brix, rubble and atrophied seaweed littering the ground. She went inside and saw no bag. Despite knowing that the likelihood of the rucksack being thrown the length of a train carriage to the back of the fissure was zero per cent, a misplaced sense of either conscientiousness or desperation had compelled her to walk the full distance.

Brix was already halfway out of the fissure again when she registered him. At first he was a darker object in her peripheral vision. Something lying contorted and wrought like an iron girder. Then came the hot, sickish shock of recognition. Once she'd regained enough self-possession to consider the situation with a clearer mind, Brix wondered if there was a memento of his she should take for posterity. Perhaps rescue his wedding ring from under the dog fur gauntlet. But she couldn't bear to touch him, didn't have time to think, and moments later she left.

Exempt from decay and degeneration, Napps's skin glowed greenish, and his eyes were closed, his head slightly crushed to set his mouth in a palsied, down-turned smile. His clothes had distorted into hardened pleats along the contours of his warped torso. One side of his body was embedded in the ice-lined wall, his left arm bent rigidly across his chest, both legs disjointed at the hip and melded together in a grotesque, balletic curve. Napps would remain here and drift through the centuries, preserved at the age of forty-three for eternity. Everland had defined his life and historicized his death. It had rendered him immortal. And now it would keep him.

Dinners had run. There was no other thought in his head except the impulse to flee.

Then he'd talked to himself. Frowning at how serious his predicament was, he'd slowly gained enough restraint to start making a plan. His main objective, he saw now, was to get back to Napps and Millet-Bass. So Dinners decided to retrace his steps back to the cove and out on to the sea ice. Fixing a map in his mind, he started confidently.

But the landmarks he anticipated didn't come, or came in the wrong arrangement, or were new, unknown landmarks. Each surprise caused a different response in Dinners. He sometimes dismissed it and stuck to the original plan, and sometimes he modified his route with hasty deviations. He corrected and redrew his plan so often that before long the map was in unsolvable chaos and had to be abandoned.

Dinners raged and stamped his feet. Calming down, he took solace in his internal compass and made a new, better plan. To his left was the seaward side, the island's borders. If he went right, he'd veer to the cliffs. So he put the sea to his left and couldn't understand it when neither the sea nor the border appeared. He tried with the sea on his right, and turned again to retry having the sea on his left. Then, dismayed by his stuttering and numb compass needle, Dinners sat on the sledge to regroup.

These regrouping sessions increased. It seemed to Dinners that sequences of time had started to dissolve and he needed to address the problem. He diagnosed it as either a conspiracy against him, or a type of collapse in the fabric which linked one minute to the next. He wasn't yet clear on the issue. What he did know was that events hadn't always got an order, and parts were missing or didn't exist. Dinners would march and he'd suddenly be on the ground. He'd set off, determined, and then something would happen. He'd find his face in the snow and leap up, yelling with anger. He strode forward energetically, reciting the Lord's Prayer, and awoke to find he was curled tightly, his arms shielding his head.

The cycle was endless. He'd become a man of vapours who dissolved without warning and then reappeared lying back across the floor. When he materialized he'd jump to his feet and lunge along, incanting so he didn't forget, 'The sea is on your left, on your left.'

It had been hours since his last meal. Remembering the bar of chocolate in his pocket, Dinners unwrapped it and went to take a bite, only to find the same evil magic had snatched it from him. Astonished to discover his hand empty, he was reduced to tasting around in his mouth for clues as to whether he might have eaten some of the chocolate. Then he was inexplicably down on the ground again.

In his dream, Dinners saw a half-man beast standing above him, a chimera. Squealing with horror, he thrashed away on his hands and knees as it walked behind him, trailing a mace. With an abdominal grunt, the chimera swung the mace high across its shoulders. And Dinners surrendered. Kneeling in the snow, he looked up and opened his arms. Then he reappeared, running with his sledge, the sea to his left.

How long had he been searching for Napps? It might be years and years and years. Even the vaguest summary of time was now utterly beyond him. The concept of one moment directly relating to successive moments had been erased to leave a vacuum of lawless independence. Nothing connected to anything any more, not that it mattered. As Dinners grew colder, helpful people came to gather nearby and offer advice. He laughed and slurred questions to Captain Lawrence, Dr. Addison and Uncle Joe, and nodded at their wisdom as they all agreed that his strategy should be to keep going. Yes, he said to them. Good, good, good.

The only things on earth for Dinners were the tug of his harness and the rhythm of his feet. He had embers of conscious thought which frayed from his mind and wasted to drifts of ash. Once, briefly, he'd become aware of the pull of his sledge and considered unfastening it, but then that idea was gone and didn't occur to him again. He knew he'd lost Napps and Millet-Bass, although the significance of this fact was obscured, the consequences skimmed off before he could decode them. Dinners turned into one single mechanical action. He was a marching husk.

At some point later, a minute maybe, or another year, Dinners grew conscious of a hole in his body where his stomach had been. A look of devious intrigue sneaked over his face. He could sense the wind sculpting the hole wider as it flowed through, and the aerodynamics produced a low resonant note which he tried to harmonize with, singing and humming. It was obvious to him that he'd begun to transform into his black surroundings, a change he both approved of and accepted. Clouds of particles were billowing from his limbs with every step, his whole body streaming with smoke as he abraded to non-existence. Feeling serene, Dinners noticed a large object looming out of the dark and tottered towards it.

The thing refused to be identified, even though Dinners knocked gently at the curved sides and clopped around it, and then kicked and pounded his fists against it. When he eventually recognized the *Joseph Evelyn*, he spoke in an excited, unintelligible language and banged his hands together. The dinghy was somehow hollow and somehow safe, he remembered that.

All he had to do was find a way to get inside, which he did by pawing tentatively at the snow. He burrowed about for the dinghy's edge, the sledge toying along in his wake, until he finally uncovered the entrance and pushed himself through.

Dinners made long toneless groaning sounds and blew his breath down the neck of his coat. He rubbed his legs and squeezed his fingers until he'd thawed enough to writhe out of his harness. Unfastening the ropes which bound his sleeping bag to the sledge, Dinners began the exhausting process of pulling the bag into the dinghy, and then levering and prising at the frozen reindeer hide until it opened enough for him to force himself inside.

The cold had left Dinners mercifully ignorant of any description of pain or anguish while his body died around him. But as his brain started to defrost in the shelter of the boat, he wept and howled with grief. Because what he'd done, he understood now, was leave Napps and Millet-Bass. He'd lost them. He wouldn't ever find them. And now he himself was lost.

56
December 2012

Listen to me. Stay where you are, we will take it from here. Do you understand?'

'We're in serious trouble,' Decker said to Aegeus.

'I need to hear you say you understand.'

'There was nothing else we could have done,' he said. 'Nothing.'

He'd informed them of the situation. The keys, Brix's promise that she knew where to find the rucksack. Her inexplicable failure to reappear, their lack of any other choice. He didn't want to let Brix go, he said, but he was carrying Jess. And they'd waited, the storm breaking.

Aegeus was beginning to mobilize. The person at the other end of the radio line started a rapid, heated discussion with someone else at the base.

'Hey, Jess?' Trapping the phone against his shoulder with his chin, Decker reached across to touch her arm. ' . . . Jess?'

It looked like she might cry and Decker intensely did not want that. There'd be a descent into havoc if she cried, a catastrophic explosion of feelings he was working hard to contain.

He'd driven to the camp at reckless speeds, the quad hitting snow gradients to lurch upwards and swerve through various potentially toppling degrees as it hurtled over uneven plateaus. Decker had thought fleetingly and remotely of Brix, yet concluded that Jess's injury more than justified his decision. No, there was nothing else he could have done, he kept saying to himself. During those first few minutes in the tent, breathless with pain as blood started to circulate back into frozen extremities, Decker was not only convinced of his blamelessness, he was almost angry about it. For a short while, he'd been a beautifully free man.

Proof of his rightness was in the wind battering against the tent, and his frostbite, and his will not to die in a blizzard. Undeniable proof of his rightness came with the agony he inflicted while easing off Jess's boot. Decker's apologies had taken on a new enthusiasm as he pulled the sock from her monstrously swollen foot and saw how much it hurt her. Drink something, please, he'd begged with euphoric concern. Jess, eat something, *please*, he'd said, getting happier by the second. As long as Decker kept his mind occupied with their own immediate suffering, he could forget about the rucksack, forget about leaving Brix, forget about the consequences of his actions, forget about guilt.

'Jess? What do you need?' he asked. 'What can I do to help?'

Nothing. Jess didn't want to be helped. She didn't care about herself.

His insistence eventually forced her to answer. 'Codeine,' she said. 'But it's outside. In the medical crate.'

'There's got to be some in the tent,' Decker said. If codeine would prevent her from crying, he'd find it, or something like it. The amount of plasters and antiseptic, bandages and crumpled blister packets of tablets strewn about everywhere, there was surely a variety of painkilling drug buried among them. He continued talking to Aegeus as he hunted through miscellaneous drifts of clothing and equipment.

'We aren't sure. The Achilles tendon, we think. Yes, she's managing. She's okay.'

Jess was not okay and doubted she'd ever be okay again. If the storm hadn't come, wished Jess, unable to stop replaying the same anguished scenarios. If I hadn't fallen, if the bag hadn't been left. If we hadn't gone to the glacier. If only Brix had come back. This last wish kept devising new ways to torment her. When she wasn't remembering grasping Brix's coat to stop her going, or those final hopeless minutes on the quad bike, Jess was imagining the cause of Brix's delay. Except there were no good reasons. The rucksack had been a short distance away, Brix knew where it was, and whatever Jess thought of to explain the crisis she then overruled. The more she tried to make sense of it, the more incomprehensible it became. Jess watched Decker throw stuff around, his frostbitten hands delving into pockets and bags. He searched fleece jackets, trousers, sweaters, the drifts of clutter on the floor. Then he grabbed his coat, distracted by the information Aegeus was firing at him as he fumbled with an object in the side pocket. It was a small yellow first-aid kit, 'Jess' scrawled across the lid in big black capitals.

With a tone of subdued finality, Decker relayed the conversation to Jess while he pried open the lid and retrieved a box of codeine: they should expect hourly updates, a Twin Otter would leave at the first opportunity. The weather was under constant surveillance. And yes, when it came to Brix, all anybody could do was try to remain positive.

'Could you get a message to Viv? Tell her I'm all right,' Decker asked Aegeus as he held out two pills for Jess. When she sat motionless he said, confused, 'Take them.'

'Why have you got that?'

Decker frowned at her. 'Take them, Jess.'

'It's my medical kit. From my rucksack.'

'Just a minute,' he said to Aegeus, covering the receiver with his palm. Now he smiled in bafflement. 'You've lost me. Do you want the codeine or not?'

'Brix knew where the rucksack was, you didn't.'

He made an exasperated sound. 'I've no idea what you're getting at.'

'But you must have known where it was, Decker, because that first-aid kit was inside. Did you move the bag?' Jess stared at him intently. 'When Brix went back to get the rucksack, was it there?'

Decker might have responded differently had he been less exhausted. He could have concocted an excuse, a plausible defence of some sort. Instead he shrugged with disappointment.

'Then give me the phone. We need to tell Aegeus,' Jess said, looking at him with disgust. 'If we both made mistakes then we're accountable.'

A long pause followed before he answered. 'Do you want to do this? If you're sure then I'll let you have the phone, and you can give them the whole story. Begin with the injury you concealed, then work your way up to this second now.'

The idea of allowing Brix to take sole responsibility for what had happened made Jess blaze with shame. 'We don't have a choice,' she said.

Decker tilted his head in an attitude of both sympathy and assessment. 'I want you to think hard about what you stand to lose, Jess. It's only, what, the past ten years of your life. The past thirty for me, twenty of them in the field.'

'You said it yourself, I hid my injury,' Jess answered. 'So I deserve to lose my job. And if you're complicit in the situation, then you should admit it.'

He nodded patiently, as if humouring a recklessly contentious stance. 'Let's be honest. Brix compromised us many times, and errors can have deeply tragic outcomes. After all, it was Brix you saw leaving the rucksack behind. You never saw me anywhere near it. And as far as I'm aware, your ankle was fine until you fell. You never told me you were hurt, so who's really to know what state it was in before the accident. I'm not a doctor, neither is Brix. Maybe it was just bruised.'

Jess was thinking of the polar coordinates tattoo she'd got

at eighteen, and how long she'd striven for a career in Antarctic research. She thought of how good she was at her work, and how devastating it would be to waste those skills. And she thought, at first in a distant way, and then more intensely, that harming herself and Decker professionally wouldn't benefit anyone. Brix would still be lost, the accident would still have happened. Time wouldn't reverse and magically amend everything. Her indignation turned into something else more engaged and increasingly willing.

'I know how much your job means to you, Jess, because I feel the same about mine. I've spent a lifetime building my career,' Decker said, speaking in the persuasively compassionate tone of someone who sees their arguments are gaining traction. 'And I'm saying, why complicate matters with accusations? I'm saying, why put either of us through it?'

'Are you there?' the tinny voice of someone from Aegeus said. 'Decker?'

There was a complex silence as Decker held the receiver to his ear again. 'So what do you want me to say?' he asked softly.

She didn't do much. She perhaps shook her head.

'No, we're fine,' he said, continuing to look at her as he spoke. 'Jess didn't feel well for a minute there, but she's doing much better now.'

Brix couldn't recall the moment when she'd truly understood the situation. Returning to find two quads, not three, should have explained it, except the thought that she'd been abandoned was too enormous to consider and therefore resisted being processed. Because she could neither ignore nor resolve the fact that she didn't know what to do, and the superhuman resolution and tenacity she'd always thought would be activated in times of crisis didn't appear, Brix had opted to just stand beside her quad for a while, as if patience might be a substitute for decisiveness. She'd watched as the blizzard threshed nearer, obliterating the horizon into whiteness, then the outline of the cove, and then drew close enough to obliterate the *Joseph Evelyn*. It was when Brix realized she couldn't even see something as large as a dinghy six metres away from her that she grasped exactly how little her patience was going to achieve.

They'd left her and she was stranded. Brix accepted this and felt she ought to react. The problem was that she was very tired and very cold, which made it difficult to judge what an appropriate reaction might be. Her thoughts were disordered and wouldn't focus on the subjects. So Brix rocked on the spot as she imagined a despairing person would, and made promises to herself. She cried a bit, out of a sense of obligation more than anything. None of it was particularly authentic-feeling or satisfying.

'Formulate a plan,' Brix said, and trawled the lumpen

impenetrable things her mind offered in response. It occurred to her that one possibility was to shelter inside the cave on the bull seal beach, and she broke into a lumbering run.

The fact that she might die, and maybe was dying, was an issue she decided would be better reflected upon while sitting on the ground, or perhaps lying on the ground. When Brix opened her eyes again, she reconsidered. She felt strongly that she should keep moving. The instincts which translated the frozen wind as a harmless pressure and drugged her with sensations of false warmth were not to be believed. The blizzard would kill her, and Brix fully appreciated the seriousness of the matter. She devoted her full attention to it whenever she wasn't busy with other important things. Such as sleeping for brief periods in the snow. Such as trying to solve the problem of her laces, which couldn't be solved, and frustrated her efforts to remove her boots. Brix wanted to take off her coat as well, but whatever mechanism fastened her into the jacket, her cautious pinching and pulling at the fabric didn't reveal how to unfasten it, and then she had no more time to devote to the issue because she was trundling along on her forearms.

The distance to the cave was approximately forty-five metres, but that journey had now taken over thirty minutes and Brix was trapped in a mystifying pattern. Whichever direction she headed in, she always found her path had circled back to the quads. She'd wobble up to her feet, aim north, or east, and then collide with the shin-skinning obstacle of a bike tyre. The curved shape of a leather seat would come out of nowhere to catch her in the stomach. If any of this hurt, Brix only registered it with mild interest. The sense of being rooted in her own body had gone, replaced by a pleasant abstractness. She was a kindly yet uninvolved witness to her own efforts as she floundered along. Colliding with an embankment of rock, Brix's hand met an unspecified object.

She stopped to feel out a name for it. With the impotent

tone of someone talking in their sleep, she said that the object in her hand was *a rope*.

Tied here by another lost person a century ago, the rope led Brix to the *Joseph Evelyn*. She remembered that it was somehow hollow. That there was a way inside. That she should dig at the snow to uncover the boat's entrance.

Once Brix finally tunnelled her way inside the *Joseph Evelyn*, she brought her knees up to her chest. Sleep had been a gift she'd wanted for reasons which were now unimportant. Still, she accepted her gift with a sense of polite gratitude, and lay there, sometimes drifting, sometimes moored.

58
September 1913

Everyone was gathered on deck. The air smelt of woodsmoke and rain-logged soil. A dense pine forest was visible through the evening mist, and no one could absorb how beautiful the colour green was, or stop talking about it. Once, more exotic than any noise they'd heard for years, a dog had barked.

This was New Zealand, where the sun rose and set tamely every single day of the year. It was the kingdom of dry land, an incomprehensible place after such a long time away. The men began to remember the pleasures of civilization. It yielded fresh fruit and vegetables and agreeably normal meat. It offered safety, leisure and choice. It contained other people, including the euphoric addition of *women*. To think that they'd just lived among this extravagance and found it mundane. The men were baffled at themselves.

Unpacking their civilian clothes caused more puzzled amusement. Inside the cases were a heap of foreign objects. Compared to their bulky Antarctic gear, the tailored jackets and trousers seemed tiny to the point of ridiculousness. The men examined improbably flimsy leather shoes. Cotton shirts were held up at arm's length and assessed primly, like they were lacy girlish underwear. The modern world not only demanded they wear these fancy-dress costumes, but also that they repair three years' worth of personal neglect. Straggling holy-man beards were razored away and their mad woolly hair was chopped into tidy styles. The pinkly bald faces which emerged were startled and naked-looking. Snorting with laughter, they all waited for their turn at the full-length mirror.

Each man's smile hardened into an introspective grimace as he confronted his reflection. The differences between the person who'd first boarded the ship and this person newly rehabilitated from his dirt and fur caused quite seismic shock-waves. It wasn't simply about appearing older and weather-beaten. Staring back from the mirror was an impostor. He was a high-quality facsimile, but there were imperfections. He was shorter than the original man and not as handsome. There was something weird about his mouth. His eyes were smaller and his shoulders were less impressive. He couldn't do a signature eyebrow raise with the same panache.

'Not a word, tell them nothing,' Lawrence ordered the crew as two men steered a rowboat towards the *Kismet*, swinging a lamp and hallooing.

As Captain, Lawrence's first mission on reaching Oamaru harbour was to send an official telegraph message to England without saying anything about the voyage to anyone. His various press contracts embargoed him from discussing any ele-ment of the expedition. It was also a matter of decency that the Everland men's families were contacted before the news became public. To help project an attitude which discouraged friendliness or curiosity, he'd chosen two thuggish and patho-logically untalkative sailors to go ashore with him.

'Welcome back, sir,' the rowboat men shouted. They looked edible. Both were robust and red-cheeked piglet-men whose coats strained over porky stomachs. A low-voiced dis-cussion estimated that they'd feed between ten and fifteen sailors.

'Fifteen?' Lawrence said under his breath. 'More like twenty. Tell them *nothing*, understand me?'

The piglet oarsmen gawped up at the three intimidating creatures which came down the rope ladder to join them.

'What stories you must have, Captain,' the slimmer oarsman said.

Lawrence didn't answer. He smiled cryptically.

'We probably wouldn't believe it even if you did tell us,' the oarsman said, trying to goad out some information.

Lawrence sighed. 'Maybe I was wrong about twenty,' he said to the sailors.

'I bet you could shock us with the things you've seen!' the oarsman persisted.

'What do you think, boys? Could we manage one between three?'

'I'm not sure I understand,' the fatter oarsman said warily to Lawrence.

Lawrence stared at the shore. 'You will if you keep asking questions.'

The newly groomed Addison was a quaint and slightly heart-rending figure. Whilst his shapeless polar gear had disguised his weight loss, his tailored clothes emphasized it in pitiless detail. His jacket sagged and his trousers hung baggily. The collar gaped around his thin neck. His strangely white-patched hair seemed odder and somehow uglier now he'd done his best to comb it neatly. He was immune to the singing and rowdiness happening around him.

Since no outside contact was permitted before the cablegram's dispatch, the *Kismet* would spend the next twenty-four hours loitering evasively in the harbour. They had one last infernal day to go before docking, a fact which was both joyous and a form of torture. Being so close to land, yet still trapped on the ship, gave the men's celebratory mood a frenzied edge. They became even wilder after Jennet appeared on deck with a cauldron of punch. Standing alone with his glass, Addison didn't seem to notice Castle sidle across.

'They're obviously happy. Are you?'

'I think I am, yes.' Addison glanced at Castle. 'Why, you're not?'

'There he goes,' Castle said, with a nod at Lawrence in the rowboat. 'What's your guess . . . will his diary cover this chapter, or did it end when we left the Pole?'

He tried to hide his impatience when Addison replied with characteristic neutrality that they'd just have to wait for the book to be published.

'Here's a riddle for you to solve while we wait,' Castle said. 'This is the last day of Napps's life, although he's been dead for months. Isn't that a funny conundrum?'

Castle set himself his own dilemma and then resolved it for Addison's benefit. Yesterday Napps was alive on the *Kismet* as far as anyone outside knew. He was just plain old Napps, a respectable First Mate with other titles of father and husband, son, brother and friend. He was destined to finish his days in anonymity to those who'd never met him, be fondly forgotten by those who had, and leave behind a solid, if unexceptional, legacy.

'But tomorrow, well. That's when Napps becomes a brand-new man,' Castle said. 'The second Lawrence delivers his cable, Napps's forty-three years will condense into a few weeks. He'll live on Everland, he'll die on Everland, and that's all he'll have ever done. Same for Millet-Bass and for Dinners, more or less.'

'Castle, shall we be straight with one another? I suspect you don't need to enquire whether I'm aware of what will happen to Napps.'

Castle kept talking. 'It's not only Lawrence's cable, though, is it? It's Lawrence's book. And it's not only Lawrence's book, it's the queues of books behind it.'

'Shall we speak openly, Castle?'

What Castle wanted to say wasn't easy. He needed to get to the point before his nerve failed. 'I mean, you've had your conflicts with Lawrence, haven't you? What's to stop him reworking events which concern you? There's a chance you won't recognize yourself either.'

'I'm sure I will.'

'You can't be certain!'

'I believe I can,' Addison replied.

'You say that, but you can't censor what Lawrence puts in his book.'

Except that Addison and Lawrence had an agreement which guaranteed Lawrence would censor events. In Lawrence's version of history, Addison had never upturned a medical case over the floor and never filled a syringe. He'd never come to the Captain's quarters with a letter. As long as Addison kept his vow not to write his own account of the expedition, these career-destroying events simply didn't exist.

'Makes me wish you'd publish a book, Adds. You were considering it.' With a terrible joviality, Castle added, 'And then I wouldn't be in this predicament!'

Castle's worries about Lawrence's poor opinion of him and its outcomes had deepened as they approached New Zealand. He'd thought about how Lawrence's paper version of him would tower over the flesh-and-blood version. The real Castle was known by so few and was so logistically restricted, and the paper Castle would be known by countless people and travel everywhere. The idea of the book reaching strangers was painful yet endurable, but the idea of it accessing familiar and cherished people was intolerable. The paper Castle would threaten him directly as it came into his town to be read by his friends, and came into his street to be read by his neighbours. It would come into his house, into his marital bed, as it was read by his wife. It would gradually pierce into his family as it was read by his children, and their children to follow.

While Castle was alive the book would always contest him. It would undermine his word with contradictions and dilute goodwill towards him, perhaps making it hard for the people he loved to love him in return. And the paper Castle would live on after he'd perished to replace him and then finally eclipse him. So he'd made a decision. He'd intercepted the paper threat.

'Castle, listen to me,' Addison said, 'Lawrence doesn't have the last word on your life. Unlike Napps, you get to have your own last word.'

'That's not quite true, though, is it,' Castle answered. 'Which is why I gave Lawrence my diary and said he could use what he wanted.'

Castle looked somewhere off to one side in order not to see Addison's reaction. 'I told him what I'd written about Napps. His antagonism, his tempers, the occasional rows we'd had. I could see it pleased Lawrence when I said the arguments against Napps were valid.'

Addison smiled bitterly. 'Oh, I'm sure it did.'

'He shook my hand and called my honesty brave,' Castle said with hatred. 'Addison, look, you and I know there's no truth in all this. Napps was one of my greatest friends. But the Captain can't touch him, can he? And I can't be in opposition to Lawrence. I've got to think of my family and how it will affect them. This isn't just about Napps any more, Adds. There are consequences for other people as well.'

'There always are.'

'You'd do the same,' Castle said, unable to interpret whether Addison was being ironic or sincere.

Addison's expression was unreadable as he stood watching the waves. 'I wish I could tell you differently.'

Evening became late, became later, and slowly became dawn. Everyone was out on deck long before the sky softened into the early pinks of daybreak. No one said much. From Antarctica, a place they'd once dreamt of, they were finally going home, the place they'd dreamt of every single night they'd been gone. And neither felt real today.

I t doesn't matter about me,' Decker said to Canadian Sam. 'As a doctor, I'm saying that it really does matter.' Sam was an attractive, serious woman in her mid-forties, who had a talent for remaining composed in any situation. But this was not the time for heroics, she'd told Decker. Finding Brix wasn't his job. He'd been through enough. 'You've got deep-tissue freeze injuries to your face and hands which require clinical attention. You need to let me help you.'

Behind them, teams with survival and rescue gear were assembled around a man outlining a strategy to find Brix in clear, methodical tones. The word *casualty* was used. The word *fatality*.

The blizzard had lasted for five hours, and the silence left in the aftermath was so perfect it had a tinnitus resonance. Two more desperate hours had passed before Decker and Jess finally heard the faint whine of a Twin Otter's engines.

No one at Aegeus had slept. No one could get over the horror. Despite endlessly repeating that they had to stay positive, it was an empty slogan which no one believed. Coffee was percolated in giant amounts throughout the night and taken to the harried staff manning the weather systems and the radios until every desk was stacked with dirty cups. Dishevelled, sallow-faced people dissected the tragedy in rapid over-caffeinated debates, trying to find some grounds to explain it. Everybody at Aegeus was suddenly a psychologist.

Being friends with, or even an acquaintance of, one of the

Everland team wasn't deemed necessary in order to provide a detailed character analysis of them. Jess, Decker and Brix's personalities were examined from a hundred different angles. The radio conversations were a point of intense scrutiny and certain details had emerged. For example, Decker had implied to Toshi that one of the team members wasn't coping as well as the others. Andre had a similar story. He'd spoken to Decker and got the impression that things were difficult. Extracting information from Canadian Sam wasn't easy because she was irritatingly discreet, but, yes, she eventually concurred with Andre and Toshi. It did perhaps seem that Brix was having a tough time. No, it didn't appear likely that she'd manage well in an emergency.

Beyond their heartbreak over Brix, people felt deep sympathy for Decker. Almost everyone at Aegeus had applied for the centenary expedition, and the fact they hadn't been selected was now an immense relief. Any one of them could have joined the Everland team and then been forced to make that terrible decision. But what choice did Decker have, they asked, fretting that he'd blame himself as he was leader of the trip. They were adamant about his guiltlessness in such a situation. The general, yet unspoken, consensus was that Brix should never have gone to Everland. It didn't need to be said. People looked at each other with troubled expressions and saw the same opinion mirrored back at them.

Sam was holding an aerial plan of Everland and wanted Decker to concentrate. It was essential that he shows them where Brix was last located so they could begin the search.

'I'll show you in person,' he said.

'Decker.' Sam shook her head. 'Just show us on the map.'

'I'm going with you.'

'Look, Deck, I'm not sure that's a good idea,' one of the rescue team replied.

Decker tried to speak and choked on his answer.

'It's not your fault,' Sam said. 'None of this is your fault. You did everything you could.'

He nodded, his head lowered. He covered his face with a hand. 'Yes, I did.'

'Decker, we know,' Sam said gently. 'Everybody knows that.'

Dinners woke in his tomb and started again with his cat-alogues. Anchor knot, bait loop, dogshank, monkey's fist, sailor's knot . . .

If he recited his lists, he could keep himself present enough to think. If he didn't then he crumbled into absence. And there was another state between the two where he drifted through a purgatory of horror. So he went through the names of animals and countries, like beads on a rosary. He bit the inside of his mouth and sometimes tasted blood, and chanted the alphabet.

Dinners lay in his reindeer-hide coffin without any sem-blance of peace. He didn't believe he ever slept, although he often discovered himself gobbling peaches and buttered toast and custard tart. Or he'd be sitting with his little daughter, reading to her. Or he'd be cycling around a sunny June park. He was at a restaurant telling the waiter, no, he didn't want the steak rare since he could taste blood already and didn't care for it. He was in his childhood home as a very young boy until he was here in the dinghy, with only his wife's name for company. Elizabeth, Elizabeth, Elizabeth.

Because he thought incessantly of Napps and Millet-Bass, and because he was haunted by their voices pleading for him as he hid and then ran away, Dinners chose to believe they'd escaped over the bay and reached the hut at Cape Athena. He designed a victorious journey which saw them finish with hot meals and clean beds, surrounded by the jubilant *Kismet* crew. He imagined the heavenly moment when Napps, thrilled with shock, told his audience that he hadn't expected to survive. Each scenario was brighter and more rapturous than the last. Dinners added champagne and woollen slippers. It was so easy to conjure these things that he added a gramophone playing dance-hall records. He could add anything he liked, yet the trouble came when he tried to hold the pictures together. They were too thin and kept tearing. He was never able to stop his happy ending of a safe hut from rotting back into a blizzard. The beds and meals and jubilance always decayed to leave Napps there on the sea ice begging, 'Please answer me, Dinners.'

You can still hope, Dinners would instruct himself. Except he feared he'd ruined hope when he took his sledge with the oilcans. Napps and Millet-Bass had one can, but that was such a tiny amount. By separating the sledges he worried he'd made both loads useless. He had access to heat but no way to use it, and they had access to food with no way to eat it. Without oil to cook it the pemmican was indigestible, and without oil to melt it water was impossible to retrieve from the ice. Then, in a flare of confidence, Dinners remembered the cans of fruit and stew. Fruit can be eaten uncooked, thought Dinners. The stew doesn't need cooking, and neither do tinned sardines. Neither do biscuits.

The problem was that the food would be iced into a frozen slush, and eating it would chill the last vestiges of internal warmth. Even if they could manage on cold food, Dinners knew he'd halved their chances, or quartered them. And the need to make atonement for his crime was something he fretted and writhed with. He was scared he'd die before he could honour it and fought in panic to the surface of his bag, snatching at the diaries.

Dinners found his pencil. He was unable to see the marks it left in the pitch black as he wrote a statement of apology. To whomever this concerns, he scrawled on a page at the end of his diary. To whomever locates this book, let it be known the loss of the Everland expedition group is my fault. Let it be known that I am a coward. The events are as follows. I record below an accurate and honest account. Dinners spared himself no blame. He was so merciless with himself it made him weep with sorrow for the poor, lonely corpse waiting to be uncovered beneath the boat. He visualized the diary balanced on his dead chest, his face yellow and parched, his eye sockets empty as the summers rose and set through long, forsaken years. Dinners cried and wrote, to you, to whomever this concerns, will you take my remains from Everland if possible? Please don't leave me here. He shakily spelt out these words in capitals and immediately felt better. Comforted by the idea of leaving the island, he put his signature underneath and the atonement was complete.

Although was it complete? After he'd finished his letter, Dinners wished he could read it since he wasn't certain what he'd written. He might have used a match, he had a box of them in his pocket, but he'd wastefully burnt most of the matches to stave off strange terrors and now there were only six left. It seemed sensible to just draft a second letter in a different diary. At this point he'd still been brimming with contrition.

Once the new letter was finished, Dinners practised lying straight on his back with the diaries balanced in a pile on his stomach, ready for his tragic discovery. Then inspiration for a third letter struck him with such urgency he leapt up and knocked the diaries everywhere. Dinners wrote to Elizabeth, explaining that he did not expect her to forgive him, but it was important she knew how much he loved her. And he was sorry. He wrote several times that he was deeply, deeply sorry. Dear Elizabeth, it's my fault. Dear Elizabeth, I would *never*—

Never what? Limestone, quartz, diorite, pegmatite. Dinners recited a list and didn't know what he'd been so desperate to inform her of. He went through his purgatory horror world, and perhaps lost consciousness, and recovered again questioning how he could begin to tolerate burdening his family with such dishonour. What about baby Madeline, he thought. She didn't deserve to be tarnished as the daughter of a shameful man. Since he was not the one who'd be affected, Dinners wondered if it was an act of selfishness for him to leave these letters. It also occurred to him that the contrition he'd felt wasn't as strong. The guilt had been distorted by a thousand retellings until it was at the very edge of meaninglessness. And from then everything gradually became less clear.

There were two incidents Dinners could identify as positively real during the confusion which followed. He'd stuffed all three diaries into his pocket and untied a coil of rope from the sledge, lashing one end to the dinghy's gunwale and the other end around his waist. Dinners had groped along to the full extent of his leash beneath a feeble pattern of stars. When the rope snagged he was at an embankment of rock. Undoing the rope from his waist, he knotted it around a rock to create a shuttle-line, and retrieved the diaries from his coat.

He'd written: I am a coward. I don't expect you to forgive me. These declarations now seemed abhorrent. And Dinners suspected Napps and Millet-Bass had written worse things about him. Who knew what slurs and damning accusations were lurking inside their two journals, hidden by the dark. So Dinners ripped apart every single page. Some fragments he ate, some he threw into the wind. He tore it all to shreds, even the thick covers, even the leathery spines. He redrew a sterile record where his crimes didn't exist. He cut out their tongues. Still chewing a wad of paper, he crabbed back along his rope to the dinghy.

At some indefinable time later, Dinners was only partially inside the dinghy because a percentage of him had been siphoned off to flow back through his entire life. While the present was cold and dying and infinitely black, the past arrived in orange and lilac hues, and a spectrum of beautiful pinks. Although he was in no state to receive guests, Dinners heard people come to talk to him. He was almost tearfully apologetic about his dishevelled condition, and confessed that he'd vomited an evil-tasting fluid over his clothes and made a mess in his trousers. He didn't even have the energy to pull himself off the ground into a respectful upright position. But he hoped they might excuse him. The snow crunched under his head as he moved it to look at each visitor in turn and notify them of his intentions. He had some good news, he told Lawrence, then the cousin who'd died when he was eight, then the King, and finally a collection of faceless, nameless entities. Dinners would see to it that Napps and Millet-Bass got a funeral.

With the sledge clanking behind him, Dinners tottered to a cave and felt his way along towards a steep scree slope. With no ability to plan a safe descent, he just walked over the side. Rolling to the bottom with the sledge upturned beside him, Dinners made agonized noises. He'd gashed his leg open above the knee, and he took the sledging flag from his pocket and split it in half to tourniquet the wound. He listed knots and countries and bird species as he worked, until he suddenly couldn't understand why he was sitting there, motionlessly gripping his leg. He righted the sledge. Forgive me, he said to Elizabeth, I think I was resting.

Dinners began his funeral service in a small alcove to the rear of the cave. He dug a trench in the sand to lay the five oil-cans alongside each other. 'I wish you well, Napps,' he said as he raked the sand. 'I wish you well, Millet-Bass. I wish that you both find peace,' he said, burying the men's oilcan bodies.

The closest thing he had to a memorial ornament was inside the drawstring pouch of stones worn around his neck. Dinners balanced on his heels and emptied his treasures on to the ground. It took two of the six matches for him to sieve out the amethysts, their purple edges winking against the lava-grey sand. Replacing the other specimens back in the pouch used the third match. Decorating the grave with a neat circle of amethysts used the fourth match, and most of the fifth match.

'Will you be my witness?' Dinners said, talking to his shadow.

It hunched deformed across the uneven surface of the opposite wall like a man deboned. This solitary black creature turned when he turned, and aped his movements with huge misshapen arms. Whenever Dinners spoke it wagged its jaws in mimicry of speech. Dinners waited and the shadow waited, and then it disappeared into the rock.

'Have you left me?' Dinners struck the sixth match and the creature returned, wiping at eyes it didn't have in sympathy with him.

'I want you to witness that I said I'm sorry,' Dinners said before it could abandon him again. 'I'll say it now in case I don't ever say it again. I am sorry. Will you remember?'

The shadow leant forward on its knees, straining to hear him.

'Will you remember?' Dinners said as the tiny white light cooled into darkness.

Back underneath the *Joseph Evelyn*, Dinners wanted to forget the lists and the expedition, and England, and the *Kismet*. He wanted to forget everything which stopped him flowing off into the brightly coloured past. Dinners wanted to forget all the people, and at last he had.

Running on the beach. Chaotic noises, busy. A call; a male voice shouting in the wind. The sound of something happening.

A dream perhaps . . . or perhaps a memory leaching out. Such a sweet dream though. 'Brix? Are you here?'

A glimmer of consciousness brought her back into the overturned dinghy. She remembered Everland as a colour, a white immensity, where the cycle of time had dilated to a single endless day.

She heard digging. Snow was being shovelled away from the dinghy's buried sides, and calls began to echo from every direction.

'We have her! She's here.'

A burst of activity surrounded her as people crawled into the dinghy, others gathering outside. Her arms were clenched around her head, covering her face, and they talked in low whispers, afraid to touch her.

Someone said tentatively, 'Is she alive?'

'I don't know, I can't tell. Where's Sam? Get her, *hurry*.'

Boots pelted off across the beach.

People were talking to her, but only some things still made sense, such as her name. Such as one voice she recognized above the indistinct noise.

'Can she hear me?' Decker asked anyone.

'Give Sam some room,' Oar said. 'Decker, move.'

Sam arrived and knelt close. 'Everything's okay, Brix.' She

leant down to speak to her directly. 'Brix? We're here and we've found you now.'

Then she requested assistance from those nearby. 'Really careful, this will hurt her. So take it slowly. All ready?'

There was the clatter of equipment, the weight of blankets. Brix felt herself being lifted on to a stretcher. Before the dinghy, she remembered standing beside the quads. Before that, she remembered arriving to find Decker and Jess had gone. And before that, she'd been searching for something lost. But the significance of these events had gone. They no longer meant anything.

Brix half opened her eyes and saw Decker was beside her. He seemed afraid to speak and looked at Brix as though waiting for clarification. As if she was the answer to a question he couldn't bring himself to ask.

It seemed so unimportant now that she herself had been found. Brix shook her head to tell him not to be sorry.

There were things that would leave Everland, and there were things that would remain behind, waiting to be discovered. A rucksack dropped among the ice, or a cluster of six amethysts. The history of these items and their placements might one day be understood, or not. If what actually happened and the perceived truth were contradictory, it was irrelevant. Because no one would ever know the difference.

'Better than it could have been. All's well that ends well, I guess. I don't know, hopefully,' someone said, talking on a satellite phone to relay the news to Aegeus as the rescue team prepared to leave the cove.

Decker was still looking at Brix. 'Yes, I think so,' he said. 'As long as it ends well, that's all that matters.'

Oh, that's good, that's very good, Lawrence once remarked when Addison told him that every day had a consequence although you can't often see it. But there are moments, he'd said, like this one, when you can. The possibilities speak to you. And you listen.